Born and raised o⋯
England, **Charlot**⋯
intrepid boys who⋯
games with them, and object loudly ⋯ ⋯
of time she spends on the computer. When she
isn't writing—or building with blocks—she
is company director for a small Anglo/French
construction firm. Charlotte loves to hear from
readers, and you can contact her at her website:
charlotte-hawkes.com.

Hopelessly addicted to espresso and HEAs,
Kristine Lynn pens high-stakes romances in
the wee morning hours before teaching writing
at an Oregon college. Luckily, the stakes there
aren't as dire. When she's not grading, writing, or
searching for the perfect vanilla latte, she can be
found on the hiking trails behind her home with
her daughter and puppy. She'd love to connect on
Twitter, Facebook, or Instagram.

TRAUMA DOC TO REDEEM THE REBEL

CHARLOTTE HAWKES

THEIR SIX-MONTH MARRIAGE RUSE

KRISTINE LYNN

MILLS & BOON

First published in Great Britain 2024
by Mills & Boon, an imprint of HarperCollins*Publishers* Ltd,
1 London Bridge Street, London, SE1 9GF

www.harpercollins.co.uk

HarperCollins*Publishers* Macken House, 39/40 Mayor Street Upper,
Dublin 1, D01 C9W8, Ireland

Trauma Doc to Redeem the Rebel © 2024 Charlotte Hawkes

Their Six-Month Marriage Ruse © 2024 Kristine Lynn

ISBN: 978-0-263-32169-2

08/24

This book contains FSC™ certified paper
and other controlled sources to ensure responsible forest management.

For more information visit www.harpercollins.co.uk/green.

Printed and Bound in the UK using 100% Renewable Electricity
at CPI Group (UK) Ltd, Croydon, CR0 4YY

TRAUMA DOC TO REDEEM THE REBEL

CHARLOTTE HAWKES

MILLS & BOON

To my boys,

12 years and 10 years *already*—
where have those years gone?

Congratulations on the M-thing, so incredibly proud
of you both—make the most of it!

Mont, thanks for reading the first couple of chapters
and enjoying them so much!

Means more than you can know.

$(xxx)^{n+1}$

CHAPTER ONE

CONNOR MASON SLID his motorbike—an Italian super-sport racing motorcycle that was equal parts impressive and aggressive—to a razor-sharp halt in the layby and glowered down the valley to the chocolate-box-quaint houses below as they basked in summer's evening glow. This was the place at its best, the bucolic-looking villages of Upper Meadwood and Little Meadwood, and Connor's glower deepened.

He'd never really had much of an appetite for either place.

Gripping the handlebars of his bike white-knuckle-tight, he allowed his gaze to sweep from one side of the valley to the other. Rolling meadows swept down the south-west side, all dotted with cows and sheep, whilst a vast woodland still blanketed the north and east sides. Meadwood, where the meadow and woods met, and all held within the gentle embrace of two remaining arms of a freshwater river, which was the destination of eager fishermen all year round. Those picture-postcard houses with their pretty thatched roofs, hewn from local stone, all circled a village green that hosted everything from farmers' markets to national cross-country events, and from summer fetes to Christmas fairs.

And Connor loathed it all.

In the city you could slip by unnoticed. Anonymous. In a place like this, where everyone knew everyone else's business, it was impossible to do anything without the entire village having an opinion on the matter and voicing it. Loudly.

Not least the disdain many of them had felt at having the roustabout spawn of a drug-addled mother foisted on their peaceful little haven. He hadn't been that welcome the first time, and he'd been positively loathed the second time. Little wonder that he'd made his final escape a couple of months before his sixteenth birthday. If he could have left earlier, then he would have.

But he wasn't that angry, poverty-stricken, good-for-nothing kid any more. He didn't have to be here.

With a sharp kick, his obscenely expensive and even more obscenely well-tuned motorbike rumbled comfortingly into life as Connor held it motionless in the layby. Quietly reassuring him that with one acceleration, one spin, it could take him back away from this damned place with little more than a cloud of dust and a deep-throated roar and no one would ever know that he had come back.

But then…that would mean *Vivian* would never know that he had come back.

Vivian.

The foster mum who had been the closest person he'd ever had to a proper maternal figure—the only person. His biological mother wouldn't have even noticed whether he was there or not, had it not been for the fact that she could put her toddler son to work as a useful distraction whilst she stole more from whichever unsuspecting target had fallen into her path on any given day. Actually being loved, or cared about, had never factored into Connor's early life—until Vivian.

From the day he'd first been brought to her as a scrappy, dirty, malnourished six-year-old to the day his wicked excuse for a biological mother had tracked him down and snatched him back—and then again from the day he'd made Vivian his one phone call from that police station to the day he'd left her for that army assessment centre at fifteen years and ten months.

No matter what, Vivian had been the one person to always have his back. Unequivocally and vociferously. Taking no nonsense from anyone who had tried to say that she was wasting her time on a down-and-out kid like him.

Connor grinned suddenly—unexpectedly—at the memory of his foster mother. He remembered her as characteristically calm, caring and gentle, but when someone mistreated one of her foster kids...woe betide them!

As for her fierce independence...

Well! If that was why she hadn't told him about her declining health months ago—*years*, even—then he was only grateful for the message that had reached him via his former army commander's widow, whose husband had once been one of Vivian's contacts for her fostering.

He owed her everything, and now she needed him. Which meant that turning around and leaving simply wasn't an option.

Dammit.

With that grim curse, Connor straightened up and rotated his hand inward to give the bike some throttle, and then began to pull out of the layby just as a loud rattling broke the silence, and a rusty pick-up truck appeared out of a hidden dip in front of him.

Hurtling up the narrow, winding country lane from the village, clearly on the wrong side of the road, the vehicle rattled worryingly as it lurched and bumped on the gravelly surface, bearing down on Connor far too fast. It was all he could do to throw all his body weight on one side in order to skid himself and his pride-and-joy motorbike into the safety of the ditch on the opposite side of the road as the truck flew by.

A few heart-stopping seconds later, the old truck careened off into the ditch on what would have been Connor's side of the road.

But there wasn't time to lie there. There wasn't even time for him to catch his breath. Scrambling to his feet, adrenalin still pumping through his veins, Connor threw off his crash helmet and vaulted out of the narrow channel, ignoring the screams of protest from his right thigh and arm. In the split second before the crash, he had caught sight of the elderly driver and now, with his surgeon instincts prickling the back of his neck, he couldn't shake the notion that something had been...*off*.

Connor raced back up the road and to the crashed pick-up truck, ignoring the way his stomach churned in horror.

The rear end was up out of the ditch with one wheel barely skimming the road, and the other clearly in the air, with most of the weight resting on the crumpled tin can of a bonnet. However, it was the stench of burning oil that assailed Connor's senses the most, clinging in the air and warning of a potential explosion.

Half jumping, half sliding into the ditch, he made for the driver's door and peered through the mud-caked window. It wasn't entirely a shock to see the grey-and-white-haired driver slumped unconscious against the steering wheel—if Connor's fleeting pre-crash memory was accurate, then the man had already been slumped over the wheel at the time of the accident—a heart attack, perhaps? Either way, the blood seeping out of a wound on his forehead and down to his equally grey beard was a concerning sight. Grasping the rusted handle of the pick-up's door, Connor yanked with all of his considerable might.

The metal creaked worryingly, but it refused to open, no match for the buckled vehicle's frame. A second heft yielded no better a result. Connor released the door for a moment to regroup. He could smash the glass, but that would mean raining shards down on his impromptu patient. Hardly ideal.

With a low curse, Connor launched himself over the bonnet and to the other side.

The angle of the car into the ditch meant that any effort to open this door was going to be just as futile, but at least smashing this window wouldn't risk harming the unconscious driver. Taking a deep breath and turning his head over one shoulder, Connor lifted his elbow and showered glass over the grass below him and the dirty, ripped passenger seat. A few seconds later, he was through the window and into the compact cab where a melee of aromas seemed to attack his olfactory senses.

First was the smell of alcohol that was somehow both fruity sweet and gut-wrenchingly sour, but, more concerningly, there was the pungent smell of leaking fuel.

He needed to get the old man out of there. Fast.

'Hey. *Hey!*' Connor shouted, hoping to rouse the man even as he lifted his fingers to check for a pulse, the adrenalin kicking harder at the incredibly weak beat. 'You awake?'

It wasn't a good sign that the man didn't even stir. From alcohol? Or from some medical emergency?

The lack of a seat belt certainly couldn't have helped the old man's chances, either. Though it might make it easier for Connor to move him now—if he could figure out how to get his patient out of the vehicle.

Leaning back on the filthy seats, Connor carefully extended his good leg across the man's chest and kicked hard at the driver's door, shocked when it groaned but then gave way.

Crawling quickly back out of the passenger window, he raced around the truck and heaved the damaged door open the rest of the way before hauling the old guy out a foot. Then, keeping the old man's back to his own chest, and slipping his arms under his patient's armpits, Connor prepared to haul him all the way out.

'Wait. *Stop!*'

Connor lifted his head at the shout, just as a woman ran down the hill towards him.

And for a moment, he forgot where he was.

Dressed in running kit, with a longish, blondish ponytail swinging over her shoulders, she was certainly pretty, yet there should have been nothing so strikingly arresting about the woman to cause such an uncharacteristic, uninvited response. An instant attraction, but unlike any he'd experienced before. In Meadwood, of all places.

Well, there was no way he was letting *that* happen.

Irritated, Connor thrust the unwanted sensation out of the way, and instead turned his attention back to getting his patient away from the vehicle.

'Stay back,' he instructed, gritting his teeth as he moved the deadweight of the old man a little further out of the seat. 'You need to call for an ambulance. Fire service, too.'

'Stop!' the woman shouted, a little louder this time as she waggled a phone before thrusting it in her back pocket. 'I already called them. Air ambulance is on its way. In the meantime, don't move him. He could have neck or back injuries.'

'I'm aware of that.'

'Then you shouldn't move him until I've assessed him.' She hurried over to within feet of him and he was abruptly struck by stunning blue eyes.

As vivid as the blue of the morpho butterfly that he'd seen on his travels through South America.

Where the heck had that thought come from?

He dragged himself back to the moment to find the woman had inserted herself into his rescue, her head bent to the old man.

'Excuse me...'

'Lester?' she said, ignoring him, concentrating instead on the patient. 'Lester, it's Nell, can you hear me?'

Lester?

The name scratched at something deep inside Connor's chest. In that black place where other, normal people had a heart.

Lester Jones? Old Farmer Jones? One of the villagers who had made Connor's childhood at Meadwood even harder than it had needed to be? The man who had spent the better part of a decade helping to spread one malicious rumour after another about the feral kid who Vivian Macey had had the poor sense to foster.

Connor had lost count of how many enemy combatants he'd saved over the past decade but he'd take any one of them over Lester-ruddy-Jones right now. Lucky for the farmer that the Hippocratic oath meant so much to him.

Gritting his teeth, Connor secured his grip even tighter on the old man.

'Stop!' The woman—Nell—glowered up at him. 'Can you just set him down for a moment?'

'Not really.' Connor didn't know why it took him such an effort to keep his voice even—he was usually renowned for his cool head under fire. 'Smell anything?'

'It isn't about whether Lester has been drinking or—'

'Not that; smell again,' he commanded quietly, even as he hauled Lester out a little further.

The woman—Nell—took a reluctant sniff before her eyes widened slightly.

'Diesel?'

'It's coming from the truck.' Connor nodded. 'With the damage to the engine, it could go up at any time. Hence why you should stay back.'

It would be bad enough for him or Lester to get caught in a fireball, he didn't need this innocent bystander getting injured too.

'Good call,' she muttered instead, paling slightly even as she held her ground.

Connor didn't know why that impressed him as much as it did.

'Just stay clear.'

'No.' She shook her head, moving to the truck door. 'You keep lifting and I'll grab Lester's legs as soon as his torso is free.'

His chest pulled tight.

'You need to get out of harm's way…'

'Not happening.'

The woman was positively infuriating.

'The truck could go up any moment.'

'Then the sooner you pull Lester free, the sooner we can get him secured and both get out of harm's way.'

And as much as he didn't like it, there was a steely quality to her tone that warned him that she was serious. But the quicker they achieved their objective, the better. His brain whirred.

'Fine. I think there was a tattered blanket in the footwell. If you can grab that, then perhaps we could use it as a bit of a makeshift stretcher.'

Nodding briskly, Nell obeyed. Moments later, she was back out with the ragged material spread out on the gravel above the ditch.

'Ready?' she asked.

'Lift on three,' he confirmed. 'One, two, lift.'

The pair worked together quickly and efficiently to free the unconscious man, moving him as far away from the truck as possible before assessing his injuries. The breathing wasn't as shallow as he might have feared, and his pulse was surprisingly strong.

Mean drunk or not, looking down at the unconscious man, Connor was glad that he nonetheless felt a sense of duty and responsibility. As a doctor he'd pledged an oath to help people—*all* people—including those who had made his already miserable childhood even more unpleasant. As a human being, it meant that the lessons Vivian had taught him hadn't been wasted.

He didn't care to imagine the hardened, cold human he would surely have become without the intervention of his foster mother. A brief moment of relief stabbed through him.

Returning to Meadwood might have been the last thing he'd ever wanted to do, but if Vivian had died before he'd had a chance to see her again, then he wasn't sure he'd have been able to live with himself.

'Breathing and pulse seem good, no broken bones or obvious injuries, and no indication of internal bleeding at this stage. Though I'd have preferred to stabilise him better before moving him to assess any further.'

'The air ambulance shouldn't be too long; the base is only about thirty miles away as the crow flies.'

And there was no reason for that to make him feel suddenly oddly nostalgic for the army life he'd only recently left behind, and the fellow soldiers he'd actually thought of as friends.

Then the moment passed as two deep blue pools turned to him and he told himself his insides couldn't possibly have just flip-flopped in some ridiculous way.

'Okay.' His gaze flickered between the old man and the wreck of the pick-up truck. The stench of fuel was now almost overpowering, and Connor felt an odd sense of foreboding. 'Maybe we should risk moving him a little further away.'

She followed his gaze, her lip caught in her teeth in a way he was sure he had no business noticing.

'You could be right.'

Taking each end of the blanket and trying to keep it as taut as they could, the pair moved their patient another twenty metres or so down the road, closer to where Connor's bike was still lodged in its own ditch. They had barely set Lester back down when there was a loud explosion, and a burst of flames shot up from the wrecked pick-up.

'Your second good call in the space of ten minutes,' Nell muttered calmly, though her white face betrayed her shock.

'We need to keep Lester stable until the helicopter arrives.' He dismissed the compliment. 'There's an emergency medical bag in my motorbike top box. Can you grab it?'

Nell nodded, and as he tossed her the keys he got the impression that she was glad of the distraction.

'I can't believe he isn't worse than he is,' she called over her shoulder. 'I'd thought maybe a broken rib, maybe even a pneumothorax, given the size of that old steering wheel, but you didn't find anything?'

'Nothing apparent,' Connor confirmed.

Then again, if he was right that the old man had already been half passed-out before the accident—arguably due to alcohol—then his body might not have been braced for impact and so he might have managed to avoid the usual type of RTC injuries.

Not that he was about to say any of that to Nell. She clearly knew and seemed to like Lester, so he wasn't about to set her against him before he'd had a chance to tell the police his side of events. It was almost a relief when she returned with the medical bag.

'Thanks. Okay, we should start by stabilising his head and neck,' Connor determined, delving into the bag. 'Then we can do a more thorough check-over. Can you hold his head steady whilst I put this on?'

For the next twenty minutes or so, they worked together surprisingly seamlessly as they attended to Lester's injuries, using the equipment from Connor's emergency medical kit. Connor found himself uncharacteristically stealing glances at Nell as he admired her calm, collected demeanour, which matched his own so well. By the time the air ambulance touched down in the field next to them he was confident that their patient was as comfortable as he could be.

'Connor Mason, trauma surgeon,' Connor introduced himself briefly to the paramedic who reached him first. 'Patient is a male, late sixties, approximately half an hour ago he drove off the road at around thirty miles per hour, and crashed into the ditch over there but he was already unconscious moments before the accident.'

'How can you be sure?'

It wasn't a challenge, merely fact-checking.

'He nearly collided with me,' Connor explained. 'I just about managed to get my motorbike out of his path but he was no more than two metres away when I saw him through the windscreen.'

'Right.' The paramedic nodded, clearly taking in all the information.

'I managed to reach him within a minute after the crash, and he was still totally unresponsive. He hasn't regained consciousness since, but BP is a little elevated. However, there's a strong smell of alcohol both on his breath and in the vehicle, so you might want to include that in your initial assessment since heavy alcohol consumption is known to diminish baroreceptor sensitivity.'

'He has a laceration to his right temple, and a possible head injury hasn't been ruled out,' Nell added.

'I take it that he wasn't thrown from the vehicle, then?' the paramedic asked, kneeling down beside the older man to begin a preliminary assessment of his own. 'You moved him here?'

Connor sensed, rather than saw, Nell nod and open her mouth to speak but he wasn't about to let her take any blame for moving the patient.

'That was my call,' he interjected. 'I could smell diesel leaking from the vehicle and I felt it safer to move the patient rather than risk him being inside when the explosion happened.'

'We both deemed it safer to do so,' Nell added firmly, evidently not wanting him to protect her.

The paramedic nodded, taking in all the information, and beginning to relay it to the doctor who was already hurrying over. Still, Connor held his position until a hand touched his arm gently.

'Let them take over,' Nell murmured. 'You're clearly a great doctor but he's their patient now.'

'Yeah, but—'

'They have all the equipment, too,' she cut him off softly.

Reluctantly, Connor bit back any further objection. Whether he liked it or not, she had a point. Forcing himself to take a step back, he watched the crew complete the same assessment that he had, and then be able to check further. Ultimately, however, they confirmed Lester was stable enough to move and began loading him onto a stretcher and into the helicopter.

'Not accustomed to being on the sidelines, are you?' that voice asked quietly. Almost empathetically.

'I prefer being busy,' he heard himself admit, wondering what it had been that had made him answer this relative stranger, when he usually didn't reveal much about himself, even to colleagues.

Finally, Connor watched as the bird lifted off, its rotors thrumming powerfully, and felt a strange wave of disappointment that—aside from the less-than-desirable circumstances—his time with the unexpectedly captivating Nell was at an end.

Though perhaps that was a good thing, since he was all too aware of her beside him, brushing against his arm as she turned, and exhaling a long, deep breath.

'Well, that wasn't exactly the Saturday afternoon that I'd anticipated. Doubt it was yours either.'

That might have been the understatement of the century.

'Not exactly,' he agreed grimly, and then before he could stop the words from tumbling unbidden from his mouth, he heard himself ask, 'Can I buy you a drink?'

He wasn't sure which of them was more surprised.

CHARLOTTE HAWKES   19

'I…can't,' she answered regretfully after a moment. 'I was supposed to be somewhere about half an hour ago. I have to go.'

'I understand.' He forced a bright smile though he couldn't explain what it was that made him wish she would delay her plans a little longer. 'Well, I should see if my ride has fared any better than Lester's pick-up truck.'

Still he didn't move.

Why was he wishing he could find a reason to stay and talk to her some more? Properly.

Whatever that meant.

He was hardly known for his love of conversation. After all, why use fifty words when a handful would suffice? Yet in this instant, he would happily have spent the evening sitting across a table from her, in some quiet country pub, learning all about this one particular woman.

Ridiculous.

He stuffed the curious notion back down and resolutely made his way back up the road to where his prized machine was still languishing in the ditch, trying not to notice how fluid it seemed when Nell fell silently into step beside him. This…*peculiarity* he felt had to just be about the strangeness of being back in this place, after all these years.

They walked together in companionable silence until they reached his crash site. Surprisingly, aside from a few dings to the usually polished paintwork, it looked as though it had come through the ordeal relatively unscathed.

Which was more than could be said for himself.

And he didn't just mean the burning sensation in his right arm and down the side of his torso.

'Right,' Connor announced, manoeuvring the heavy motorcycle upright and out of the ditch before retrieving his crash helmet. 'I'd offer you a lift but… I don't have a second crash helmet on me.'

Plus, he'd never offered anyone a ride on his motorbike. *Never.* The bike had always been his, and his alone.

'It's fine,' Nell confirmed, shifting her weight from one foot to the other without leaving.

He wondered if perhaps she was reconsidering the idea of getting a drink.

Wondered, or hoped?

'Well, thanks again for your help with Lester,' he told her, hoping to break the awkwardness. 'And for letting me use your medical kit.'

'Of course.' She nodded, still hesitating. As though there was something else she wanted to say but was holding back. 'And now you're heading…?'

He could feel the shutters coming down inside him. Familiar. And usually welcome.

But now…? He couldn't quite explain this odd sensation firing him up inside. As if *she* was the one causing the blood in his veins to effervesce.

But an attraction was the last thing he needed. This visit was about paying his respects to Vivian; it wasn't about getting to know some stranger.

'I'll just stay here a while,' he told her. Coldly.

'Right. Well… I'll leave you to it.'

One last pause and then she was gone, jogging down the hill in the same direction as the one Connor was headed. Hardly surprising, of course, since the road only led into the Meadwood valley or out of it. Still, Connor found himself pretending that he didn't lament the loss of her company.

At all.

Nor the evaporation of that inexplicable…*something* that appeared to have set all sorts of thoughts tumbling through his head—none of which he was ready to identify yet.

And still, as he faltered there on his bike and glowered

accusingly down the valley, he couldn't seem to stop the thoughts altogether.

Like the fact that he couldn't remember a time he had felt such a strong spark of attraction, but that it should happen here, of all places, was particularly galling.

Another reason to hate this place.

He could pretend that it was because he'd never been built to appreciate the countryside—it was too dull, too uneventful, the exact opposite of the life he'd ultimately craved for himself.

He was a thrill-seeker, a risk-taker, and, more than that, he was a man who had always loved a challenge.

But it was more than just the location.

As pretty as it was, as far as Connor was concerned the quaint, chocolate-box Little Meadwood was all a façade. A mere veil shrouding people who had never really made him feel as if he was one of them. Take an old soak whose own sins were carefully overlooked simply because he'd been born and bred in the village, whilst newcomers like him—even an innocent six-year-old who had simply had a shamefully bad start to life—would always be viewed with suspicion, and distrust.

And Upper Meadwood—lorded over by Lord Percival and his family—was even worse.

Without warning, something flickered deep, deep within him, and Connor was startled to realise that the hurt and resentment that he'd thought he'd long since buried were still simmering somewhere inside.

Or maybe it's more like fear.

The voice whispered in his head—almost startling him.

Maybe you're just afraid that coming back here is too much a reminder of the angry, lost kid that you once were?

Swiftly, Connor slammed the uninvited thoughts away—but it was too late. Like it or not, that voice held more than a grain of truth. When he'd turned his back on the village almost twenty years ago to join the army, he'd sworn to himself that he would never, *never* return.

And by God, he'd remained true to his word.

He'd toured the world, from Cyprus to Belize, and from Iraq to the USA—relishing the fact that he never stayed in the same place for too long. He'd lived the life of ten other men. Maybe a hundred. And he'd put his bitter, grimy childhood firmly in the past where it belonged.

Until now.

And until the unexpected phone call that had him feeling adrift. Lost. Struggling to come to terms with the idea that this unparalleled woman might not be for this world much longer.

It seemed so…*wrong*.

So now, here he was. Back in Little Meadwood after all.

Something bowled around in his chest, though he pretended he didn't notice. He'd get in, get out, and be back to his proper life.

Connor revved his engine, the sound echoing through the valley as he skidded out some shale, taking off down the hill towards the village. Adrenalin pumped as he inhaled the mixture of hot, oily engine, tyres burning on the asphalt, and the freshly mown grass of a nearby field, and then he hurtled skilfully through the narrow, winding roads.

And hoped that he wasn't racing back into the hellfire that was his past.

CHAPTER TWO

AROUND VIVIAN'S LITTLE COTTAGE, Nell was faffing.

There was no getting away from it.

She'd been edgy ever since her encounter with the deliciously sinful Connor Mason on the road into the village, and no amount of heroic stories on Vivian's part—or their foster mother's proudly shared blurry photos—could possibly have prepared Nell for the impact of meeting the man in the flesh.

The man defied all belief, and surely no picture could have adequately captured how impossibly broad-shouldered, how ridiculously chisel-featured, how outrageously masculine he was. Enough to make her blush just thinking about him.

Stop it!

Setting down one of the few knick-knacks Vivian had, Nell forced herself to back away from the side table as she pressed her free hand to her chest. As though that might somehow rein in her racing heart.

What on earth was the matter with her? She never acted like this—as if there was something wholly carnal lurking inside her that had never once shown itself to her before, in all her thirty-three years.

Yet how else was she supposed to justify her body's almost visceral reaction to Connor Mason, out there at the crash site? How else could she explain why—as dedicated to her career as she usually prided herself on being—despite the circumstances of their encounter when she should surely have been solely focused on the injured Lester, she'd found herself noticing all kinds of things about the man whose very presence seemed to make the air around him crackle with thrilling electricity?

And Lord—what about that understated strength and power he'd exuded? More potent than any cologne.

Her heart gave another crazy lurch in her chest as another delicious image bounced around her head.

It certainly hadn't hurt that his motorbike leathers had hugged his powerful thighs like a second skin. Or that his short hair had been slightly tousled from his crash helmet.

And it didn't matter how fiercely she chided herself for such wayward thoughts, nor how carefully she pointed out to herself that the last thing she should want was to be attracted to some hot, biker bad-boy who—once he'd done his duty seeing Vivian—would likely roar out of their village as quickly as he'd roared into it.

Yet, she couldn't seem to shake the effects of their chance encounter.

Despite her having been back home for over an hour now, her nerves were even more frayed than before. It didn't help that every time she could have sworn that she heard a growling engine she found herself peeking out of the living room window and half expecting to see him race past, revving the kind of motorbike that she usually hated, but that seemed to match him so seamlessly.

There was something about the man that had seemed to draw her in, and so now here she was—*faffing*.

Aside from the knick-knacks, she'd fussed with the cushions on Vivian's armchairs, straightening them for the hundredth time that hour. She'd clicked on the kettle on the worktop at least five times yet each time she'd forgotten to actually make a drink. She'd even adjusted the picture frames on the wall, making sure that they hung straight and true.

Nell sighed heavily. Clearly, she was being ridiculous, but she couldn't seem to stop. She'd felt…odd. Unsettled. So unlike herself.

And it hadn't been because of the circumstances of Lester's accident—although treating a patient right there in the field, rather than having them brought into her in A & E was certainly a very different experience—it had been about Connor himself.

Was it the way he looked, with sharp jawline, smoky-grey eyes, and to-die-for body? Or perhaps the way he carried himself, with an air of both danger and confidence woven so tightly together? Maybe it was the stories she'd heard about him over the past twenty years—almost folklore around Little Meadwood—combined with the shock of actually meeting him for the first time ever?

Whatever it was, the effect had been so much, and so fast, that even now it was almost dizzying. A rush that went straight through her body and right up to her head. Like a large hit of ristretto after a year-long abstinence from coffee. But she was being utterly ridiculous if she actually believed a man like Connor would ever look at someone like her—even if she had wanted him to, which she certainly did *not*—since the man was clearly everything she wasn't: confident, daring, and unapologetically sexy.

Pacing the living room, she stopped by the bureau to straighten the photos on there, her hands automatically reaching for the one of a sixteen-year-old Connor in his military uniform, taken the last time he'd ever been back to Little Meadwood—months before she herself had arrived at Vivian's as a recently orphaned thirteen-year-old.

But, even if she'd never met him, Connor had never been a

complete stranger to her given how she'd followed his progress over the past twenty years through Vivian.

The older woman's love and pride was evident for all of her many charges, but perhaps few more so than the boy who had essentially been like a son to her for nine years. Photos were proudly hung all over the tiny cottage of all Vivian's longer-term charges over the decades—including one of herself when she'd graduated as a doctor—and it was good for a foster child to see just how much they meant to the endlessly caring and patient Vivian.

Everyone in Meadwood—and no doubt several villages beyond—had been proudly told how well her former charges were doing, and Connor Mason was no exception. A career-driven, dedicated trauma surgeon who had travelled the world and learned his craft within various theatres of war. Nell knew the stories almost off by heart.

Even so, seeing him in action today—seeing the way he moved with purpose and precision whilst saving mean old Lester Jones's life—made something in her shift, in a way that she couldn't explain.

There was something magnetic about him. Maybe it was his broad shoulders, or his piercing grey eyes that seemed to stop her heart from beating in her very chest. Or maybe it was the way he had rushed into that life-threatening emergency, completely fearless and focused, taking charge of the situation without hesitation.

Or perhaps it was the way he had looked at her, with a hint of curiosity and something else that she couldn't quite identify in those gunmetal depths, that made her feel fluttery and a little light-headed. Like a swooning schoolkid rather than a grown woman.

She should hate herself for it. Instead, she found it strangely thrilling.

Boy, was she in trouble.

Nell shook her head, trying to clear her thoughts. She needed to focus on Vivian, not on some mysterious and attractive stranger. She took a deep breath, reminding herself of the reason she was here—to take care of Vivian, just as Vivian had taken care of her all those years ago.

But as she went to the kitchen to finally make herself and her foster mum a cup of tea, she couldn't help but feel a sense of anticipation that stubbornly remained even when she chided herself that Connor was clearly back for Vivian, not to meet or spend time with herself or any other of his fellow foster kids.

So why, when she carried the steaming mugs of tea into the living room and called Vivian down from upstairs, did she sneak a glance in the hallway mirror to take in the flushed cheeks and the strange excitement in the eyes of the woman in her reflection?

As though there was something about her encounter with Connor today that had her feeling alive in a way she hadn't felt for a long time.

Maybe ever.

It made no sense, yet by the time the doorbell rang for the other visitors she knew Vivian was expecting that evening, it was all Nell could do not to leap out of her chair like the proverbially scalded cat.

Her heart hammered so loudly as she moved down the hallway to open the door that she was shocked her eagle-eyed and bat-eared foster mother couldn't hear it—that the entire village couldn't hear it. And when she opened the door to find Ruby and Ivan, two of Vivian's other former long-term charges, standing on the doorstep, Nell tried to tell herself that any sense of disappointment she felt that they weren't Connor was purely on Vivian's behalf. Certainly not because she herself was eager to see him again.

And then she hastily set down the already spotless photo

of a teenage Connor in military uniform, which she didn't realise she'd picked up to dust.

Connor hadn't been able to stop the sense of unease that had washed over him even as his motorbike had crossed the single-lane humpback bridge into Little Meadwood. So much so that he'd carried on straight through the village to the old toll bridge on the other side, and back out of the valley and into the next county. Then, when he'd forced himself to turn around again, he'd driven straight through it and back to the city. Third time was—as the saying went—a charm.

Not that it felt much like a charm.

He might want to see Vivian but still couldn't reconcile being back in this place.

Not even if it gives you another chance to talk to the woman from earlier?

Too late, he silenced the needling voice in his head.

He was just here to see his foster mother. In. Out. No harm, no foul. Easy.

But as he pulled up to the small cottage on the outskirts of Little Meadwood, he felt a surge of memories flood back.

The home looked just as he remembered it. Small and quaint with the ubiquitous thatched roof and painted timber window frames.

Vivian's beautiful garden was as awash with colourful flowers as it had ever been and it was like stepping back in time. For a moment, Connor forgot why he was there, then he took a deep breath and got off his bike and removed his helmet and gloves, his boots crunching on the gravel path as he made his way towards the front door, a painted stone winking up at him from the side of the path, making him stop abruptly.

How had he forgotten about the tiny stone frog family? Vivian had encouraged each foster child to choose and paint their own stone—a green frog, a yellow frog, a blue-and-red frog, it didn't matter—and then they added it somewhere in the front garden. Her idea had been that every one of her foster kids would know that they were remembered by her; but also that kids who really needed it—kids like him—could hold onto the idea that they were a part of some kind of family, somewhere.

Of course he'd resisted at first, choosing to paint a black-and-orange poison dart frog—his way of warning others to stay away. In response, Vivian had painted a bromeliad on another stone and set it down next to his, and then she'd taught him about the symbiotic relationship between the two. It was the first time he'd actually felt *heard*. By anybody.

It was strange to be back here, in this place that was the closest thing to a home that he'd ever known. Pausing for a moment by the alliums as the scent unexpectedly assailed his brain as much as his nostrils, Connor was unprepared for the memories that suddenly dislodged themselves and dropped into the periphery of his mind. Memories that he hadn't even known he'd made, and which he couldn't quite grasp even now. But far from the hollower echoes that he'd replayed all these years, these new, hazy recollections gave the impression they were of happier moments. Or, if not actually *happier*, then at least snatched moments that had been less miserable.

He paused a moment longer, waiting to see if they would become any clearer, but instead they remained stubbornly out of view.

Perhaps he'd imagined it.

Shaking his head as if to dislodge the nonsensical ideas, Connor took another couple of steps forward towards the house but then another scent hit him. Harder this time. And, as if on autopilot, Connor reached over the wall and selected a few plump, juicy blackberries from the neighbour's tempting blackberry bush that had always been there. How many times had he been yelled at by Old Man Luddlington for stealing his blackberries, or his apples?

Strange to realise the old man would be long gone by now. Almost…sad?

Popping the blackberries in his mouth—as mouth-watering as they'd always been—Connor took a moment to savour the taste, shocked when another memory crept inside his head. Again of Vivian, and the first time she had taken him blackberry picking in the hedges by the farmers' fields, and then showed him how she made her famous blackberry jam. The wave of nostalgia slammed into him hard, almost knocking him over.

It was one thing knowing logically all that his foster mother had done for him. But it was quite another reliving it in such vivid detail after all this time.

She'd taught him more about nature in that one afternoon than anyone else had ever taught him in his life until that moment. It was the afternoon he'd discovered his love for foraging and wilderness training that had led him to take survival courses, and ultimately realise that the military was where his path lay.

She'd probably saved his life that day. Without her, his free time would doubtless have been spent in increasingly more criminal pursuits rather than building dens and wild food harvesting.

Maybe if she wasn't too sick yet he could talk her into joining him in the kitchen so that the two of them could whip up a batch of that special jam together? It might be the better part of two decades since he'd last made it, but he figured he could still remember how.

Strangely buoyed, Connor strode down the remainder of the garden path and knocked confidently on the front door. But when the door swung open seconds later only for a familiar face to stare back at him, it felt as if he'd just been punched squarely in the chest.

It took him a moment to realise that the blow that seemed

to have knocked every last bit of air from his lungs wasn't physical. Then another moment to try to regain enough of that air to breathe.

'You?' He barely recognised his own voice.

But it was too late to walk away now.

'Nell,' she prompted tightly. As though she thought he'd already forgotten her name.

He hadn't.

He couldn't have even if he'd wanted to. Though the effect she had on him made no sense.

Connor tried to give himself another mental shake. It wasn't as though he hadn't experienced instant attraction before—he might have spent his adult life avoiding romantic entanglements but he wasn't exactly a monk—yet this was more than just lust. More than mere chemistry.

Now that the emergency with Lester was no longer taking his focus, there was nothing to distract him from experiencing the full pull of this woman. And the sensations she sent coursing through him were far more volatile; explosive, even. So irrational that he couldn't even think straight, let alone speak straight.

And he hated himself for his lack of control.

'I'm here,' he managed to grit out, 'to see Vivian.'

Because—as if he needed to remind himself again—his foster mother was who he'd come back to Little Meadwood for. Not to go off indulging in some unwanted enthralment with her carer—or whoever Nell was.

Of all the times to be attracted to someone, this had to be the most inappropriate.

And the most unacceptable.

He commanded himself to pull his head together.

Yet still that peculiar punch of enthralment vibrated painfully somewhere inside his chest as his gaze drank in the woman in front of him.

Now out of her running gear, she wore an electric-blue V-neck T-shirt that clung to feminine curves—no less mouth-watering for their subtlety—and only intensified the hue of her expressive eyes that right now were less morpho-butterfly-blue and more the same forget-me-not-blue as some of the flowers he'd just been admiring. Even so, they were as captivating and vibrant as a few hours earlier.

More so, perhaps.

Out of the brighter daylight, her hair seemed more hon-eyed, but her skin was every bit as silky smooth as before. If he reached out, would it feel just as soft? His palms actually itched at the thought of finding out.

At his sides, Connor balled them into fists and shoved them into the pockets of his leather jacket, trying valiantly to keep his eyes from wandering to Nell's sinfully inviting mouth with the pale pink lips that had seemed bare this afternoon, but now had a hint of a sheen, making his mouth water every bit as much as the berries had done only seconds before.

He suspected that if he kissed her, she would taste even better than they had.

What the heck was wrong with him?

Connor dragged his head back to reality. Or tried to. But how was it that he was suddenly so much more aware of the evening breeze as it moved around him? Licking at his skin.

Making him feel…

Suddenly, a couple of kids shrieked from the playground down on the green and both he and Nell jerked their heads to watch.

Something and nothing— but at least now it gave him a beat to regroup.

Whatever his attraction to this woman, it was wholly inap-propriate. And he refused to allow it to take root.

The woman must be here to care for his foster mother, and therefore he needed her focus to be entirely on her patient—

with no distractions. Although, to be fair, from her actions with their impromptu patient earlier, he was already under the impression that her patients were always her primary focus regardless of a situation. Just as his were.

Which, unfortunately, only made him all the more attracted to her.

Still, stuffing down the unsolicited thoughts, Connor pasted a polite smile on his lips and thrust out his hand to Nell.

'It seems we meet again. Perhaps I should introduce myself properly this time. I'm Connor Mason, one of Vivian's former foster kids, and I'm guessing you, Nell, are Vivian's doctor?'

'I know who you are.'

Nell stared up at the newcomer, fighting to keep the dismay from showing on her face. At least, she told herself that it was *dismay* that she was feeling in that moment.

Certainly nothing else.

It definitely wasn't *awareness* sizzling through her at being confronted by all that startling...*maleness*...all over again— and this time right on her doorstep. Well... Vivian's doorstep.

It had been one thing working alongside the guy when she'd had the distraction of Lester and the accident, but now there was nothing else to focus her attention on besides the man standing right in front of her. Almost too close for comfort. His six-foot-two frame—or six-foot-three, maybe—filled up the narrow doorway of the cottage, with shoulders so deliciously broad and strong that they blocked out the rest of the warm, summer light. In all the years she'd spent with this cottage being her home, she couldn't recall it ever having been graced in such a way. As if it had shrunk a couple of sizes in the rain and was now too compact for a man like this. As though it might burst at the seams just from trying to contain him.

She couldn't even imagine him having grown up here—

having actually lived here, in this cottage, in the same place that she had—all those decades ago.

He just seemed so...*out of place* for a village like Little Meadwood. A sleek, jagged, thrilling shape that was too restless to slot into such a soft, sleepy, laid-back jigsaw like this.

And yet she knew he had spent years as one of Vivian's first foster kids. For something like a decade?

How many times had she stared at the photos in Vivian's album, or listened to his name included in the 'absent friends' toast at the village Christmas Fair, and wondered what this man—this war hero—might actually be like in person?

Now, however, she found herself thinking that it was just as well that Connor hadn't returned before now. And not because she was finding it so disconcerting the way her very core seemed to crackle with sheer chemistry at the feel of all that heat emanating from his body; nor because the vague scent of his leathers was making her nerves jangle with all that *maleness*.

It shouldn't be such a struggle to get control of herself.

'I'm not Vivian's doctor,' she answered at length, somehow—*somehow*—managing to step aside far enough to allow him entry, though he had to duck under the cottage's low doorframe.

'Oh?'

With such a dark look he didn't need words to ask her what she was doing here.

Bizarrely, despite her reputation for being calm and unflappable whether she was facing a yelling patient or a terrified relative, Nell found herself reacting. Bristling. Allowing this man—this relative stranger—to get under her skin.

'Given that you've been away for the better part of two decades—' she tried to keep her voice even, nonetheless '—I'm not sure you have the right to waltz in here and demand to know precisely who everyone is and what they're doing here.'

His dark look turned to one of amusement.

'I didn't ask who everyone is,' he pointed out. 'I merely asked who *you* are.'

It was hardly an unreasonable question. So why was she reacting as she was? So out of character.

'For your information—' Nell fought to regroup '—I was also one of Vivian's foster kids.'

'Is that so?'

His voice was level but she knew she hadn't imagined the look of surprise flashing across his features.

'From when I was thirteen to when I turned eighteen,' she heard herself continuing. As if she owed him an explanation. 'I arrived a few months after you'd left, though Vivian used to mention you regularly.'

His look darkened again.

'So you knew who I was on the road, earlier?'

'Not immediately.' She hesitated. Apparently she'd said something wrong, though she wasn't quite sure what that had been. 'I was more preoccupied with Lester.' Which wasn't exactly a lie. Just perhaps not the whole truth. 'I realised who you were afterwards.'

He grunted, but didn't answer. She drew in a breath, trying to reset her professional head.

'Look, Vivian took a late nap but she'll be down any moment. Do you want to just go through to the living room?'

She gestured down the narrow hallway, grateful that he went without argument. For a moment a part of her had feared he might turn around, fling one of those muscled legs over that powerful machine on the road, and roar off again.

Then she closed the door with deliberate care before taking a deep breath and following him down the narrow hallway.

'I should introduce Ruby,' she began, just before he turned into the room. 'And Ivan. Both were also former charges of Vivian.'

He stopped so abruptly that Nell almost ran into the back of him. She opened her mouth to speak, then stopped, noting the odd expressions on the two men's faces. Her heart hammered for a split second as she realised that it might have been a mistake to have two Alpha males in such a cramped space. But then they each gave a gruff, almost incredulous laugh.

'Ivan?'

'Connor?'

As the men stepped towards each other as though to shake hands, only to instantly turn it into a wide bear hug, Nell glanced at Ruby. Her friend looked even more shocked than she herself felt.

'How long has it been?' Ivan growled, with an unexpected crack of emotion.

'Too long,' Connor's voice rumbled, and Nell wished she knew him well enough to understand what he was thinking in that moment. 'Decades.'

And then they lapsed into a silence that somehow seemed to make the air crackle.

'I'd forgotten that you two had known each other,' Nell confessed, when she couldn't stand the tension any longer. 'But I'd never realised that you'd been so close.'

The two men eyed each other somewhat wryly. A whole shared history passing between them in that one look.

'You could call it that,' Connor confirmed gruffly.

'What does that mean?' Nell and Ruby chorused. It seemed they were both as curious as each other, but the beat of silence didn't help.

'It means that if any of the local kids started beating on one of us then the other would have his back...' Connor offered simply in the end.

'And that was good enough,' Ivan finished just as simply.

Clearly that was all either of them was going to say.

'Right,' Nell offered flatly, trying not to let her mind race.

'Okay.' Ruby nodded, sounding equally bemused.

But they both knew only too well how fragile things were when you were a foster kid. And how hard it could be to feel truly at ease around others. It seemed they weren't about to press either of the men now. Even so, Nell found it harder to bite her tongue than it should have been—certainly harder than it had ever been with anyone else. She suddenly found that she wanted to know more about Connor. Wanted to know everything.

She was more than a little relieved when she heard Vivian begin to make her way downstairs, and all four of them leapt instinctively to help her. Ultimately, as the one closest to the door, it was Nell who won the honour.

'You've got a full house tonight,' she murmured quietly to her old foster mum, who squeezed her arm tightly as they made their way slowly down the hall.

'Is that so?' Vivian wheezed cheerfully. 'What did I do to deserve such wonderful kids like you lot?'

'Everything.' Nell made herself chuckle, but it was harder than it should be to speak past the lump in her throat.

Her foster mother had always been so strong, so full of life, and even fuller with love. To see her so frail now was like a kick in the teeth. And Nell knew the others felt exactly the same.

A moment later and the two of them were making their way through the door and to Vivian's chair. But she might have known the determined woman wouldn't allow herself to be settled down so easily.

'Well, if it isn't my favourite foster kids,' she rasped in delight, stepping forward to hug Ruby, then Ivan.

'You always say that to all of us,' Ivan rumbled in amusement as he enveloped her in his arms.

Nell's chest pulled tight at the way his powerful figure only highlighted Vivian's diminishing form. Not that Vivian would let that easily daunt her.

'Doesn't make it any less true,' she told him firmly. 'Just means I am truly blessed.'

Finally, she turned to the figure behind the door—the one she must have clocked out of the corner of her eye, but hadn't quite appreciated his identity until that moment.

'Connor,' she breathed, her voice rattling with emotion.

'Hey, Vivian.' Connor seemed to hesitate only for a moment before leaning down to wrap his muscled arms around her. Making her seem even more fragile than ever.

Nell couldn't help wondering how strange it might feel for him, being back in this place after all these years. Their foster mum had never said as much, yet Nell had always got the sense that Vivian had felt as though joining the army had been Connor's way of running away. From Meadwood, but also perhaps from his life.

Nell had always felt as though his departure had made Vivian sad, and a little disappointed—as though she'd felt she'd somehow failed him. But now, watching him hug the older woman, it appeared to Nell as though a sense of peace had begun to wash over both of them.

And she could certainly understand how that might be true.

For all that all of their circumstances might have been different—hers, Connor's, even Ivan's and Ruby's—the troubles and hardships any foster kids experienced could be similar. And through all the upheavals and changes, Vivian had always been there for them. Even if they'd had nothing else, she had been the one constant in their lives, a source of light.

Nell watched as Connor slowly—and, it seemed, reluctantly—pulled back as he scanned Vivian's face. What did he make of the lines etched into her once smooth skin—those telltale signs of the illness that was slowly taking her away?

Nell's chest tightened painfully at the thought and she

fought to swallow the beastly lump in her throat. She was grateful when Vivian finally broke the thick silence.

'You look good, kid.' Her voice was still raspy but filled with her characteristic love.

'You look like you're holding up pretty well too,' Connor replied with a smile that Nell just knew was his attempt to mask his sadness at the sight of her fading away.

She wasn't surprised when Vivian gave a weak snort of laughter.

'You never were a good liar—at least, not to me. Well, I might be stuck in this chair most of the time, but there's still a little life left in the old dog.'

Again, Nell found herself drawn to the way Connor's throat constricted, as well as the little tic in his tightening jaw that betrayed the fact that he was fighting to keep his emotions in check.

The way they all were right now. None of them could bear losing Vivian.

It was heartening, in a way, how many visitors she had enjoyed these past few months. Mostly former foster kids—and all of them demonstrating just what an incredible impact this one woman had had on so many lives.

Vivian Macey—foster mother and superwoman. Vivian was the reason why she and Ruby had never really left Meadwood. And why Ivan and a few others had each returned this week and declared their individual intentions to stick around, or at least visit more, for however long they were needed.

Did Connor intend to stay indefinitely, too? Or would he leave as abruptly as he had arrived? She couldn't answer that, yet she couldn't help hoping he would stay.

For Vivian, of course. She had no vested interest in what he did.

None at all.

Still, as the group settled down to chat, Nell found her

gaze seeking him out despite herself. Assessing him. Trying to read his thoughts. And, inexplicably, trying not to let her mind wander into less acceptable territory.

Connor Mason was clearly a man accustomed to commanding attention and respect—that much had been clear from their encounter on the road with Lester—yet there was also something far more primal about him.

Something that made her mind keep wondering what it might be like to run her hands through his thick dark hair, to feel the strength of his broad shoulders against her fingertips.

She shook her head as though that might dispel both the heat from her cheeks and the unsolicited thoughts from her head, but even if that scattered the images for a moment, they crept back in all too quickly.

Since when did she indulge in such hormonal fantasies?

Jerking abruptly to her feet, she muttered some excuse about making tea and lurched around the crowded furniture, almost relieved that everyone else seemed too caught up in their conversations to hear her. Vivian was catching up on Connor's past few years, whilst Ruby and Ivan seemed to be having their own quiet, oddly intense conversation. There was no reason for her to feel this strange, pushed-out feeling. It made no sense.

Maybe she needed a bit of air.

Her head buzzing, Nell padded through to the kitchen and busied herself tidying up plates that were already neat, and wiping down counters that were already clean. And still, her thoughts crept off on a journey of their own.

In the other room, she could hear the sound of their laughter, and the occasional catch in Vivian's voice, and Connor's kindness and compassion with their foster mother was evident. Nell stared out of the window thoughtfully. Of course, she and Ruby had never really left Little Meadwood, and Ivan—despite being a busy surgeon—had always visited at least once a year. But in twenty years, Connor had never returned—although Nell was aware that, every few years, he had flown Vivian out to wherever he was working around the world, just for a break and so the two of them could catch up.

It had never made her feel quite so...envious before.

Filling the kettle, she absently set out the mugs and Vivian's favourite cup and saucer.

What was it about Connor Mason that was so unsettling? Was it really because a part of her feared that he was trying to swoop in and take control?

Or was there another reason why this one particular man affected her so strangely? Like it or not—and she did *not* like it, she told herself firmly—he seemed to have a crazy way of getting under her skin as no one else ever had before. Not even Jonathon.

Which is all the more reason for you to get a grip.

Nell began to pour the boiling water over the teabags, still schooling herself, when she heard the sound of footsteps behind her. The finest hairs prickled on her neck even before she turned to see Connor standing in the doorway, his watchful grey eyes raking over her and making her skin physically tingle.

And despite her stern warnings to herself it made it impossible to suppress the frisson of excitement that shot through her at such a gaze, pinning her to the spot and stealing every last bit of air from her lungs.

CHAPTER THREE

'CAN I HELP?'

Nell jerked her head up. It was such a mundane question yet it caused such a visceral reaction in her that it was almost laughable. And she probably *would* have laughed if only she'd been able to breathe. Instead, she simply stared back at him, hoping she didn't look as foolish or as jacked-up as she felt.

'Everything okay?' Connor's impossibly handsome frown skewered her all the more.

'Everything's great,' she answered, perhaps a little too quickly as her breath came back to her in a rush. 'No problems here. You get back to Vivian.'

'Actually, that's partly why I came in. I wanted to ask about how she's really doing.'

'You mean when she isn't pretending she's completely fine?' A wry smile tugged at the corners of Nell's mouth, the tea-making momentarily forgotten.

'Clearly I believed her these past few years when she told me it wasn't that bad,' he admitted. 'I should have returned earlier.'

Though Nell got the sense that he would rather have pulled out his own fingernails.

'She has been pretty sick. But you know Vivian, she'll fight to the last.'

The rush of love for her foster mother momentarily overcame the inexplicable...*oddness* she felt around this man.

The way he made her body feel suddenly unfamiliar to her—as though it were not quite her own.

Desperately trying to shake off the crazy notion, she forced another bright smile.

'And she's had Ruby and me, so she hasn't had to do it alone. But don't let her catch you talking about her behind her back. Grown adult or not, she'll give you *what for* and ground you for a week.'

'I don't doubt it.' Connor laughed, a deep sound that seemed to fill up the tiny kitchen, and seemed to somehow set Nell's skin alive with a delicious energy. 'Fortunately, right now Vivian's instructing Ivan and Ruby on some stall she wants them to build for the upcoming village fete.'

'Yup.' Nell nodded with a grin of her own. 'She wants them to do a photobooth, with pictures of the locals as well as Little Meadwood. I think I'm supposed to be doing a vintage clothing booth or something. I'm surprised she hasn't found something for you, too.'

'Oh, she's trying,' he confirmed.

'Ah well, since you live and work so far away with the army, you get to dodge that bullet.' Nell, laughing, was pretending she didn't feel the slightest bit disappointed at the idea that when he walked out of the door later, that would likely be the last time she'd see him.

He hadn't returned to Little Meadwood in decades, so he was hardly going to start visiting regularly now.

'Actually, I left the army.'

'Oh?' That shocked her. 'Does Vivian know?'

He gave a wry chuckle, causing a warmth to emanate from the tips of her fingers to the very soles of her feet. Like every time he smiled at her, or crinkled his eyes with laughter, it made her wonder if there was someone out there who got to see and experience that every day.

Which was even more ridiculous.

'No, I haven't mentioned it to Vivian yet.' His voice dragged her back to the present. 'I only left a few months ago.'

'Why?' The question was out before she'd even thought about it. 'Vivian always said the army was your life.'

The expression on his face turned instantly shuttered. Stark, even. His leaving didn't appear to have been his choice. Or, at least, not entirely.

'Life moves on,' he clipped out, clearly shutting her down. 'I work as a locum surgeon in a civilian hospital now.'

'Nearby?'

His jaw pulled tighter. She could see it.

'Other side of the country,' he gritted out.

Clearly that was deliberate. A host of additional questions swirled around her head but Nell bit her tongue. It was apparent this wasn't a subject that Connor wanted to discuss.

Nell searched for something else to say instead.

'I still can't believe you and Ivan were so close. He was quite closed off when I first arrived here. I thought it was just the way he was. Now I suspect it was because he was missing his mate.'

For a moment, she thought Connor wasn't going to answer. Then, slowly, he dipped his head in confirmation.

'Maybe, we came from similar circumstances that we bonded, I guess. I might have been the same way if the situation had been reversed.' His voice was tight, as though he wasn't accustomed to talking about his past. 'Anyway, I gather that all three of you spent time here together?'

'Yeah, Ivan and I were long-term foster kids.' Remembering the tea, Nell busied herself around the kitchen as she spoke. 'When I arrived he was fifteen and I was thirteen. My parents had just died in a car accident.'

'Sorry for your loss,' Connor acknowledged simply. Sincerely.

Sadness clenched at her stomach as it always did when

someone mentioned her parents. No longer raw, as it had been for years after their deaths, but there all the same, especially since she hadn't been ready for the memory.

Everyone in Little Meadwood knew her history, they never really mentioned her parents any more—it was one of the comforts of staying in this small community. Although Jonathon had never understood that—he'd always accused her of using the village to *hide* away from facing the real world.

Nell thrust the unwanted thought from her head, and concentrated on pouring milk into the tea mugs.

'Thanks,' she managed instead, using banal facts to push through her tight cheerfulness. 'Anyway, Ruby arrived for the first time a few months later and she and I grew close instantly. Ivan left a year or so later, but Ruby was backwards and forwards for years. Her mum was ill, so whenever she needed to go into hospital for treatment, or an operation, Ruby would be fostered here. Sometimes it was just for a few nights, other times it could be weeks or a couple of months.'

'I see. I just thought that he and Ruby seem to know each other more recently, that was all.'

Nell jerked her head up. So he'd noticed that, too? She shouldn't be surprised: Connor Mason gave the impression that he spotted everything and missed nothing. Perhaps she ought to ask Ruby about it tonight when they were on their own and back in the cottage next door that they had shared ever since they'd officially left Vivian's care.

But for now, Nell lapsed into a thoughtful silence amidst the electric atmosphere that could only be Connor's presence. She tried to rally herself as she finished stirring the tea before setting the mugs on a tray to take through.

'To answer your earlier question about how Vivian really is, when she isn't pretending nothing is wrong at all, let me just say that Vivian is just being *Vivian*.'

'Understood.' His grin returned unexpectedly, and Nell

wished her chest didn't thud so hard at the pleasure of it. 'In other words, if her arm was cut off, she'd claim it was just a scratch.'

'She would.' Nell laughed.

And this time it was a brilliant smile that was so genuine and unrestrained, and filled with such affection that it made Nell's chest pull tight. Tight enough that, just for a moment, tiny stars flashed in her head.

She scrambled to pull herself together.

'Anyway, it sounded as though you and Vivian were having a good chat.'

'We were,' he agreed, reaching to the tray to take a drink for her, and one for himself. 'It was…nice.'

'Right. Good.' They lapsed into another silence, with only the sound of the clinking porcelain to break the tension. And she took the opportunity to try to get a handle on her crazy reactions to him. 'Are you intending to stay long?'

'Here, you mean? Tonight?'

'In Little Meadwood in general,' she clarified.

His expression closed down abruptly, and he didn't answer straight away. Instead, he seemed to take a moment to organise his thoughts.

'I hadn't planned to.'

'Initially the plan had been to call in and see her tonight and then…that was it?' she supplied evenly, but he still cast her a sharp gaze.

'My life is hectic,' he bit out sharply. 'I'm usually travelling.'

'I wasn't judging.' She held up her hands quickly.

Had she been? She hoped not. She'd learned long ago not to judge people. You never knew what another person might be dealing with.

'Right.' He blew out a breath and at least he had the grace to look a little rueful. 'The point is, that was the plan. But now…'

Nell waited for him to continue, telling herself it was of no matter to her what he chose to do; that her heart hadn't picked up a beat. Again.

He didn't answer, but instead raked a hand through his hair whilst the muscles in his jaw clenched. It was a trait that was already becoming familiar to her.

'But now that you've seen her, you don't want to leave?' she suggested at last.

'Pretty much,' he agreed tightly.

'She has that effect.' Nell smiled fondly.

'But I can't stay. I have a job across the country, and I have to be there for it. I just…don't like the idea of her being here alone and going through everything.'

'She isn't alone, though. I'm here,' Nell pointed out gently, 'as is Ruby. And now Ivan has arrived.'

Connor dipped his head in assent, but didn't look wholly convinced.

'I understand, but… I thought I might rent a house, or something. Pay for a full-time carer to be on hand. And it could be somewhere I can stay when I come back to visit.'

And she told herself there was no reason for this revelation to send a flurry of sensations skittering inside her.

'There's nothing in the village to rent,' Nell pointed out, hoping her tone was even. Level.

Connor frowned.

'Nothing? There were always cottages to rent here. In fact, you couldn't give them away.'

'Things have changed over the last twenty years.' Nell shrugged lightly. 'Both Upper and Little Meadwood are now part of the commuter belt and loads of people live here but work in the city. They even built a housing estate of about two thousand houses just outside over to the east.'

'I know, I saw it earlier,' he acknowledged grimly. 'Looks a monstrosity.'

'Then you should see what they charge for them.' She

snorted. 'And they still elicit bidding wars every time one goes onto the market.'

'I can't have Vivian here alone. And whilst you all might be here in the area, you aren't *here*.'

'Not in this cottage, no,' Nell agreed. 'But Ruby and I do live in the village. In fact, we live in the cottage next door.'

'Next door?'

And there was no reason for his voice to rumble through her the way that it did.

Instead, she forced a proud nod.

'I bought it ten years ago, luckily enough—for a reasonable price, since the new A road hadn't been built then.'

'You stayed in Little Meadwood?' Connor's frown deepened. 'After coming to Vivian?'

'I left when I was eighteen to do my training, but as soon as I could get a job at City Hospital, I came back.'

'Why?'

She paused, not quite understanding his question.

'I don't follow.'

He raked his hand through his hair again.

'Why on earth would you want to stay somewhere as small, as parochial, as Little Meadwood?'

'Maybe because I don't find it parochial,' she pointed out gently, refusing to take offence.

'It's small, and insular, and petty,' he ground out, before clamping his jaw closed as though he hadn't intended her to hear any of that.

She filed it away.

'Despite the circumstances of being a foster kid, I loved it here,' she offered carefully. 'Though I get that some foster kids couldn't wait to get away.'

'Not from Vivian,' he growled. 'Just this place.'

'Again, not judging.'

'So why did you stay?'

'I guess I found it friendly. Safe. *Home.*' The word thick in her throat. It meant more than she could express. 'Ruby felt the same. As did another foster girl around at the same time as us, Steph.'

Nell stopped abruptly, wondering what had made her mention this to a perfect stranger like Connor.

Perhaps because he didn't feel like a perfect stranger—the false lull of having both been Vivian's foster kids, no doubt.

Or maybe something else?

'Want to talk?'

The question was a gentle invitation but not pushy. And even though she suspected she should deflect, she found herself meeting his gaze.

'Steph was our friend,' Nell began slowly. 'Mine and Ruby's. She arrived after Ivan had left so we were here at the same time, though, as I said, Ruby was in and out of here, and home, depending on when her mum needed support during her chemo.'

His expression changed instantly to empathy.

'This must be particularly hard for Ruby, watching Vivian, then.'

'I think so,' Nell agreed. 'But she hides it well. She always says we all have unenviable pasts or we wouldn't have ended up foster kids.'

Connor inclined his head a fraction.

'Anyway, the three of us became inseparable. The Three Macesketeers.'

'Ah, *Mace*sketeers, as in Vivian *Macey.*' He understood at once.

Something rippled through her, but she chose not to examine it too closely. As it was, she didn't care to properly examine why she was still spilling personal details to this newcomer.

'So even after we'd transitioned out of the system, we all wanted to stay close. When I bought the cottage and moved back, they moved in with me.'

'Until Steph suddenly left.' He dipped his head, putting it together quickly.

A sharp pain stabbed at her.

'Three years ago. Abruptly, and with no explanation.'

Yet even though she didn't add how much that hurt, Connor somehow seemed to pick up on it.

'Sometimes people just need to move on. It doesn't mean there was something you did or didn't do.'

She blinked at him, startled.

'I know, but I can't help feeling there was something I could have done. Said.'

'Maybe.' He inclined his head. 'But maybe not. You've reached out to her, I take it?'

'Several times,' Nell confirmed sadly. 'Both of us. But we only ever get superficial replies. That she's fine. That one day we'll meet and catch up.'

'But even though she has been to visit Vivian, you haven't seen her?'

'Not once.'

And it hurt, even though she and Ruby both pretended it was fine.

'So a part of you is hoping that maybe Vivian's illness might finally bring you all back together.'

Nell blinked, staring at him.

How could he possibly know that? She hadn't even confided it to Ruby, as though doing so would somehow make it seem as though a horrible part of her welcomed Vivian's illness.

'You don't need to feel guilty.' Connor narrowed his eyes thoughtfully at her. 'You're not wishing anything on Vivian. Her illness is there—it has already happened. You're just looking for those tiny silver linings in life that we all hope for. It's part of what makes us human.'

'Well…' she shrugged, as if she could also shrug off any residual lapse in judgement '…anyway, the point is that I like living here. It's a bit of a commute to the hospital, but not too bad. Certainly worth it.'

Without warning, the silence dropped again; though she wasn't sure what she had said to cause it.

She took a sip of tea in the hope of steadying the nerves that had once again started jangling. Then, after what felt like an age, Connor spoke.

'That's what Vivian just said.'

'Ah.' Nell took another careful sip of tea and pretended her stomach didn't flip-flop.

So, Vivian had already tried to put ideas in Connor's head. The question was, would he be interested enough to listen?

A part of her couldn't help hoping so, although Nell couldn't explain what it was—this pull that seemed to keep drawing her to the man.

She was determined not to ask any more. It wasn't any of her business.

'Are you thinking about staying, then?' The words slid out despite her efforts.

His gaze was trained out of the window for the longest time.

'She was ostensibly talking about Ivan—apparently he transferred to a temporary post at City Hospital last week?' He paused as if for confirmation, so Nell nodded.

She still didn't know exactly why Ivan had stayed, but she sensed it was what he and Ruby were so intent about. Not that she was about to confide that part to Connor on top of everything else.

'Vivian suggested I might consider a temporary post in their emergency trauma department, too.'

His eyes slid to hers all too tellingly, his expression so neutral that it was almost comical, and Nell felt a gurgle of laughter rumble up inside her.

'Vivian merely suggested it?' Her lips tugged up at the

corners. 'She hasn't already called them to demand they create a vacancy?'

'She suggested it,' he repeated dryly. 'Strongly. Like I said, I haven't yet had a chance to tell her that I've left the army.'

This time, they both chuckled. Vivian Macey had always been an infamous tour de force.

'Good luck with that.' Nell chuckled. 'She'll have you here even if it means you sleeping on that tiny couch in the living room.'

'I've endured worse.' He grinned and lifted one muscular shoulder. 'I've been locuming and couch or hotel surfing as it is.'

Her heart thumped loudly against her ribcage. Once. Twice. Her mouth felt inexplicably dry.

'So you're actually considering it?'

She didn't care either way.

Definitely not.

Her heart offered another thump of betrayal as Connor's eyes held hers, intense and unwavering, and Nell found herself holding her breath. She couldn't shake the impression that the room was suddenly closing in on her—on both of them—and yet it was far from an unpleasant sensation.

'The contract at the hospital I'm currently at is due to expire and I was planning on moving on anyway,' he said finally, breaking the silence.

'They don't want you to renew?' she managed to ask.

'Yes, but I have no intention of taking up their offer.'

'So you could move up this way?' She had no idea how she managed to keep her voice level. 'If you wanted to.'

There was a sudden shift in the air between them, a charged tension that Nell couldn't quite explain but couldn't ignore either.

'I'm…considering it.'

What was it that made a man like Connor tick? In the short

time she'd known him, she'd already felt ridiculously drawn to him—and she could tell herself that it was just their shared experience of being foster kids, and having Vivian as a foster parent, but deep down she felt it was more than that.

Ivan had the same experience, and she'd never felt drawn to him the way she did with this particular man.

Watching Connor over the rim of her mug, his expression as unreadable as ever, she couldn't help but wonder what was going through his mind. What had led him to leave Little Meadwood for the army when he hadn't even been sixteen, and what had spurred him to leave the forces now after Vivian had recently read that he'd just been honoured with some prestigious military commendation?

Connor Mason was a closely guarded mystery. And she had more than enough to occupy her time without taking on yet another puzzle to solve.

No matter how tempting this particular conundrum might be.

Forcing herself to look away, she set her mug down on the table between them. She should probably take the drinks through to the others before they got cold.

'Well.' She plastered a cheerful smile on her lips. 'I'm sure you're capable of making your own decisions.'

The expression on Connor's face was as indecipherable as ever.

'Indeed,' he told her, his voice neutral as he got smoothly to his feet. 'Thank you for the tea. It's time I got going.'

So soon?

'What about Vivian?' she asked quickly.

'I have a feeling she was beginning to get a little tired in there with all of us, which is another reason why I came in here—to give her some space. I feel she would benefit from some rest.'

It shouldn't have been such a battle to stuff down the sense of disappointment, and simply nod her agreement.

'But come back tomorrow.' The words spilled out before she could stop them. 'It was clear Vivian loved seeing you.'

'I'm back on duty tomorrow.' He shook his head.

'After duty, then?'

'One hundred and fifty miles away.'

'Of course.' And there was no reason for her insides to tumble like that—as though a part of her was disappointed. No reason at all. 'You did mention it was across the country.'

'Anyway, I should have twenty-four hours' downtime after my next shift, so I'll make another quick visit then. And another a couple of days after that.'

Nell's stomach flip-flopped. She pretended not to notice.

'That's quite a drive.'

He dipped his head, looking unconcerned.

'It's a couple of hours each way on the motorbike. The ride clears my head.'

Even so, after long shifts at the hospital he would soon be exhausted.

'Can't you stay in a hotel at least?' she asked. 'Ride back tomorrow?'

He shook his head tersely, though all he said was, 'Hate hotels.'

The clipped tightness warned her not to ask questions. Even so, his tone revealed more than she suspected he had intended. What must it be like to be one of the few that a man like Connor would trust enough to confide in?

She thrust the thought aside. She would never be one of those few—and she had no idea why she would even want to be.

Liar, a voice whispered in her head. So, she thrust that away, too.

She could always offer Connor use of the sofa at her and

Ruby's cottage next door—Ivan had slept there a couple of times the previous month, before he'd found his own lodgings in the city—but her throat suddenly turned dry and the words didn't come. As ridiculous as it might be, it somehow felt different offering this man a bed for the night than it had felt offering the same thing to Ivan. And she could tell herself that it was because she'd actually known Ivan when they'd both been Vivian's foster kids whilst, technically, she'd only just met Connor, but the truth was it was more than that. A different feeling in her gut. A draw that she didn't care to try to explain.

Nell was grateful when Connor abruptly broke the silence.

'Anyway, I really should get going.'

'Right,' she managed awkwardly. 'Well, safe ride. Take it easy.'

Take it easy?

But Connor was already crossing the small space, his hand on the door handle. For a brief moment he paused, as if he was going to say something else before he changed his mind. The next moment, he was gone—back into the living room.

And by the time Nell had loaded the mugs and Vivian's cup on a tray, adding a few of Vivian's favourite mini-cakes—even though her foster mother's illness meant that she couldn't really enjoy them any more—Connor was already out of the door and revving up his beloved motorbike.

Leaving Little Meadwood as quickly as he'd apparently entered it. And for the sake of her galloping heart, that was surely a good thing.

Wasn't it?

CHAPTER FOUR

TEN FORTY-EIGHT AND it had been a particularly hectic shift in Resus so far. No sooner had Nell and her team managed to clear one patient out of the bays, than another two arrived.

But at least she loved her work—and at least being slammed meant she didn't have time to dwell on things that she really shouldn't be dwelling on.

As if things were completely normal.

As if she hadn't spent the past two weeks fighting the odd notion that life at Little Meadwood had somehow been nudged out of kilter ever since Connor Mason's unexpected arrival.

As if she weren't still fighting her mind from wandering back to that distracting evening with him. The one and only time she had met the man who she had grown up thinking of as some kind of an unspoken legend around Vivian's home.

Was it really only a mere fortnight ago? It felt like a lifetime.

And if being in that kitchen with him had felt like sticking her hand into an electric socket, then the subsequent absence of contact had only amplified that thing she chose to call *nervousness*, which coursed through her veins.

It certainly didn't help that she'd visited Vivian several evenings after work, only to discover that Connor had already been there earlier in the day but left before she'd arrived. She'd spotted him once, from a distance. He'd looked a little more exhausted than that first time, though no less sexy for it. No less arresting.

It really shouldn't be allowed that his slightly tousled look only made him all the more attractive. Perhaps that was why it was proving impossible to get him out of her head. Memories lingered of that tall, broad, mouth-wateringly muscular physique, and that voice, which was as smooth and deep as molten chocolate—no matter how hard she tried to eject them.

Just as she was trying and failing to do right now. And she couldn't help wondering if Connor had been avoiding her.

Which has to make you the most ridiculously self-absorbed person in Little Meadwood, a scornful voice instantly piped up in her head. *Possibly the country.*

Shame flushed through Nell's body. Hot. Restless. It made her clench her hands in her lap and struggle to even out her shallow, rapid breaths.

She needed to get a grip; Connor was only here to visit their foster mother. To think anything different was pure self-centredness. And still, no matter how quickly she found herself racing home after work and into Vivian's, the man had always *just left*. Her heart picked up its pace inside her chest.

It was almost a relief when the shrill ring of the Resus emergency phone rent the air, and even as Nell snatched it up she could feel the department swinging to life behind her.

'City Hospital,' she clipped out efficiently, instantly tuning into the case that was being relayed to her.

A few pertinent questions later, confident she had all the information available at that moment, she quickly set about putting a call over the Tannoy system to call her team.

Ten fifty-nine. Nell noted the clock on the wall. *The heli would be here within the next sixteen minutes.*

'Okay, guys, listen in. Patient is a female in her forties; sudden-onset thunderclap headache and a GCS of three, now hypertensive. ETA is fifteen minutes. Allie, can you get a CT scanner put on standby? Kris, can you advise Neurology?'

The acknowledgements were instantaneous as the team bustled around preparing the bay for their patient.

Nell's heart kicked in her chest, keeping the adrenalin coursing around her body. This was the tensest part—the waiting. Only having the basic details for the patient, and waiting to see exactly what state they were going to be in. Waiting to do her job.

But at least this kept her mind busy…and away from certain grey-eyed individuals.

Her eyes flitted to the well-equipped tray that ensured the most likely tools would be to hand, the glistening mattress still fresh from the Steri-wipe but that would be dry in minutes, and the monitors with their lines just waiting to be hooked up to their patient.

Everything was ready.

'What have we got?'

The voice appeared around the curtain, fractions of a second before the material moved. But in those millionths of a second, a myriad emotions shot through Nell faster than any rush of adrenalin. Her heart kicked again—but this time for a very different reason. She turned carefully, fighting the urge to whip around. This had to be her imagination playing some nonsensical prank.

It wasn't.

Connor?

'Nell.'

She wasn't sure if she was gratified or not that he looked as surprised as she was.

'You're working here now?'

She didn't know why she should feel so surprised—*shocked*, even. He might have been adamant about not leaving his locum post part-way across the country, but she could well imagine the toll taken by those past couple of weeks of making that torturously long round trip. And at least he looked as caught off guard as she felt.

'I thought it better to be on hand for Vivian,' he rasped.

But then his expression shifted and smoothed, though not before she thought she glimpsed a flash of guilt.

Of course, he'd at least known that she worked at this hospital. And Ruby, and Ivan, she reminded herself hastily. He could have mentioned it to any one of them—not necessarily just her.

'A heads-up would have been nice,' she heard herself clip out, all the same.

'I didn't expect it to happen so fast,' he replied in what might have been an approximation of an apology. Or maybe not. 'My former boss was more understanding than I would have thought.'

She wanted to ask what else he had expected. It had only taken a few Internet searches—which she was telling herself were out of professional interest and nothing more—to reveal that Connor Mason was a decorated veteran whose innovation in the field had led to the army modifying at least two of its approaches to treating wounded soldiers. Any hospital chief would want a man like Connor Mason on their rotas, and if his foster mother was ill and needed him to move close by only a short-sighted boss would stand in his way.

Or perhaps that was just because Connor had spent so many years following orders. No doubt the chief of the hospital Connor had just left was banking on a show of compassion and support to lure Connor back after Vivian...well, after his presence in Little Meadwood was no longer necessary.

Nell's heart kicked for a third time as she thrust that unwanted thought from her head. She scrambled for something more banal to say instead.

'Well, you're here now so you might as well know that

patient is a female in her forties with sudden onset thunder-clap headache...'

And she gave a silent word of thanks for the distraction as she reeled off the remaining scant details to him, as well as letting him know she'd advised Neurology and CT.

'Understood.' He inclined his head in tacit approval.

But anything else she might have said was sucked from her head as the Resus doors opened and the Heli-med crew clattered in with their patient, and her team sprung to action taking the handover, changing beds, and setting up the monitoring equipment. It was several minutes before the verbal handover could take place. But at length, the Heli-doctor began.

'This is Annabel, forty-three, an estate agent. Around forty minutes ago she was working at her desk when she suffered a sudden onset thunderclap headache, quickly became unintelligible before sliding to the floor and becoming unresponsive. When we arrived she had a Glasgow Coma Scale of three, this increased to seven and she vomited several times in the air ambulance.'

The handover continued as the team carried out their own checks, hooking their patient up to their own monitors and trying to establish the situation.

'And her blood pressure now?' Nell verified, when it was complete, craning to see the readouts over the sea of heads.

One of the nurses closer to the monitor pushed the screen a little higher and a rush of adrenalin coursed through Nell.

'Right, let's get her to the scanner,' Connor cut in abruptly, causing Nell to turn to him.

'She seems quite restless and agitated.' She pursed her lips. 'Do you think we can risk it?'

'I think time isn't on our side,' he answered.

He had a point. If it was a ruptured brain aneurysm, then the sooner it was diagnosed, the better. The first few hours would be vital.

'Okay, let's get her to CT,' Nell concurred. 'Everybody ready to move her?'

Connor moved in beside her. 'Good. On three; one, two, go.'

The next half-hour was a race against time as Nell and her team hurried their patient to CT and got as clear images as they could. Despite their patient not being entirely still, the images were enough to confirm her and Connor's suspicion that she had a significant subarachnoid haemorrhage.

At least now they could begin to administer medication that would help lower the woman's blood pressure, ready for her transfer to the neurosurgical team who would carry out the aneurysm clipping.

Exhausted but relieved, Nell stripped her gown and gloves off, turning around to check the surprisingly quiet Resus ward…and slammed straight into Connor.

'Oof. Sorry.' Nell quashed the kick of traitorous flip-flopping in her chest.

'Not a problem. Good work there, by the way.'

And she told herself that she hated that *oh-so-casually-sexy* way about him he had that made her whole body sizzle. Yet she didn't make any attempt to carry on walking.

Then again, neither did he.

'I should have told you I was starting work here,' he acknowledged after a pause that might just as easily been a moment or a lifetime. 'Like I said, it really did all happen so quickly.'

'So today is your first day?'

'It is.'

'Oh.' She hadn't really expected him to agree.

At least it meant that he hadn't been here for a week or something without even thinking to mention it to any of the rest of them. And although the initial kicks had subsided, her heart was still beating out its humiliating tattoo.

It seemed too cruel that her stomach chose that moment to rumble again, then growl. Loudly.

This time there was no stopping her body's reactions as she felt the heat bloom across her cheeks. She quickly pressed her hand down harder in the vain hope that she could silence its embarrassing protestations.

'My shift started at seven and I missed my break because it's been mayhem down here,' she garbled even as she told herself that she didn't owe him any explanation.

Connor, however, simply offered a casual dip of a shoulder.

'Occupational hazard. You haven't eaten at all?'

'No, so I should probably grab a sandwich now that it's a little quieter again.'

He consulted his watch.

'You must be starving. I'll walk with you if you've got a moment.'

'Oh. No. I…'

But either he didn't hear her, or he chose to ignore her hesitation.

'Where's a good place to grab a bite? I seem to recall seeing various cafés in the atrium back there.'

And even though she opened her mouth to object—because getting lunch with Connor suddenly felt like a ridiculously dangerous idea—she heard herself telling him that they were all decent eateries.

'Although Re-Cup-Eration is my favourite.' Her mouth was still moving, despite her efforts to stop it. 'It's a great place, and they have a nice selection of good food. I…was just heading over there.'

'Great, lead on.'

Firmly telling herself that it meant nothing, Nell led the way out of Resus and down the corridor. Yet she was still acutely aware of Connor's presence beside her like a magnetic pull, tugging at her with every step they took. It was all she could do to stop herself from drifting closer, especially when she happened to glance over to him to find him looking at her with an intensity that made her already flushed cheeks feel even hotter.

Her brain scrabbled for a safer topic.

'Vivian must be really pleased you've taken up the post.'

'She doesn't know yet,' he confessed.

'So you aren't staying with her?'

Could he hear the thudding in her chest? Surely it was loud enough to drown out the entire hospital.

'No, I'm in hospital accommodation.'

'Really?' Nell pulled a face. 'It's okay, but wouldn't have thought you'd find it good enough.'

'I've lived in shelled-out ruins when in theatres of war.' He didn't appear to take offence. 'I can stay anywhere.'

A heat bloomed through her cheeks.

'Sorry, I forgot.'

'It isn't important.' He shrugged it off. 'But, as it is, the accommodation for senior staff is in some new apartment block across the fields at the back of the hospital.'

'Oh.' She just about restrained herself from smacking her forehead with her hand. 'I'd forgotten about that place. It's new. And swanky.'

Should she have said that?

To her surprise, Connor nodded his head.

'Like a five-star luxury hotel.' He laughed. 'Apparently, I have a third-floor suite.'

A deep, genuine sound that seemed to spark all her senses. The kind of laugh that she realised she wanted to hear again, and again, and again. It made her wonder what it must be like to make this man smile, and laugh, *and love*, on a daily basis.

Crazy.

Nell shoved the errant thought from her mind and fought to steady her nerves. A thought occurred to her.

'Wait, didn't they evacuate the third floor yesterday?'

'Sorry?'

'Yes, I'm sure they did.' Her brain spun trying to recall what she'd overheard that morning from a surgeon she recognised but didn't know well. 'Apparently there's a fault with the sensor system on the third floor and it keeps going off every hour or so. No one on the third floor got any sleep last night. They've had to clear the suites whilst they find the faulty sensor so everyone has either swapped to work tonight's night shift or booked a hotel. You ought to call now or they'll be booked out.'

It was too late for him to swap his current shift to tonight. But then Connor's jaw tightened.

'Do you want me to recommend which places to try first?'

'No.' He shook his head. 'I'll just see if I can find an on-call room.'

'I don't think that will work—' she began but he cut her off.

'It will be fine.'

Except that he sounded anything but fine.

'Are you okay?'

'Never better,' he ground out.

Now she thought about it, hadn't she thought he'd reacted a little oddly last time hotels had been mentioned? But then she'd put it down to her imagination.

Nell bit her bottom lip uncertainly.

'You could always crash on our sofa.' Her heart wasn't clattering against her ribcage. It wasn't. 'Ruby won't mind, since she's away at the moment.'

'I'll be fine,' he declined quickly, before adding a terse, 'thank you, though.'

Evidently that was him shutting the conversation down. Only she couldn't let it go that easily.

'It isn't an issue; Ivan crashed with us for a few nights a couple of months ago.'

'Nonetheless.'

A wiser person might have let it go. And she would…after one more comment.

'Okay, but if you change your mind, I have a spare key. So does Vivian.'

'I won't but, again, thanks.'

This time there was no doubt that the subject was definitely closed, and they descended into silence for the rest of the short walk to Re-Cup-Eration. But once they entered the soaring glass-and-metal atrium, Nell felt lifted again—just as the bright, plant-filled space had been designed to do. Leading the way across the polished stone floor, she skirted the smaller carts and stations, as well as the more than acceptable Tyler's Café, and to Re-Cup-Eration.

'I don't think I've sat down to eat in months,' Connor commented casually, picking up a laminated menu from one of the free tables and skimming it. 'The hospital I've come from only has one cafeteria, and it's always hectic.'

'No restaurants for dates in the evenings?'

Nell's stomach dropped even as the words left her lips. All the blood seemed to rush from her body and pool in her feet— what the heck was she doing asking him about *dates*?

But incredibly, Connor didn't seem to notice.

'No time recently.' He lifted one shoulder a fraction. 'It's been sandwich vans, salad bars and microwave meals all the way.'

'Right,' she managed.

'So, what's good?' He lifted his eyes from the menu to lock with hers.

Nell struggled to ignore the answering *zing* inside her. He was just making conversation; it didn't make this any kind of *date*.

What was wrong with her?

With a superhuman effort, she pulled herself together.

'Everything here is good,' she told him sincerely. 'But right now, they do an amazing ploughman's hot panini with mature cheddar, sun-ripened tomatoes, and a homemade chutney. And their Sweet, Sour 'n' Crispy Salad has pomegranate seeds and the most incredible balsamic vinegars. It's the perfect blend of sweet and sour and is to die for. That's what I'm getting anyway.'

Was she waffling? She felt as if she was waffling.

'Okay, two lots of ploughman's panini and Sweet, Sour, 'n' Crispy Salad it is, then,' he confirmed, selecting a tray and placing it down on the serving rail as Nell tried to stop herself from ridiculously reading too much into the fact that he'd followed her recommendations to the letter. 'What drink? And do you want to get a table for us?'

'You can't buy my lunch.' Nell just about managed not to squeak at the prospect of sitting down and eating lunch with the man.

As if she'd never eaten with any other man in her life.

As if it were some kind of date.

'Call it a thank you for being there for Vivian all these years,' he answered simply.

'But…'

'Nothing more than that,' he added, silencing her objection.

Of course not. Nell struggled to regulate her wayward thoughts.

'Right,' she managed. 'Well, then, thank you, I'll just have a bottle of water, please.'

And then, before she could let her thoughts scatter off again, she turned and headed for one of the quieter, out-of-the-way tables.

Not because she wanted to be alone with Connor, she told herself hastily, but because she didn't want all her colleagues seeing them together, and then making them a hot topic on the hospital grapevine.

Whatever it was about this man that had her acting so uncharacteristically, it needed to stop.

By the time Connor appeared with their lunch, Nell was confident she'd sorted her thoughts, and her head was back in order.

She thanked him again as he placed the tray down with their meals and slid into the seat opposite her, then busied herself with the plates.

A few moments later, she took a bite of her panini, and let the tangy deliciousness of the chutney and sharpness of the melted cheese transport her momentarily out of the hospital and to somewhere far more relaxing.

'So how long have you worked here?' Connor asked, drawing her back to the present.

'Almost eight years. I went to uni when I left Vivian's care at eighteen, though she always kept her littlest spare room for me to crash with her every other weekend, and in the holidays.' Nell smiled warmly.

'Really? I never realised she stopped fostering.'

'Vivian didn't stop fostering,' she admitted. 'Did you know she received an MBE for fostering one hundred and fifty kids?'

'I had no idea.'

It was his clear guilt at the idea that he hadn't kept in touch enough that caused something to shift inside Nell.

'Anyway, she kept my room for me, and in return I helped out with other foster kids every other weekend.'

'So you returned to help with the other foster kids.' He nodded in understanding. 'That was generous of you.'

'My ex-fiancé didn't think so.'

Nell clamped her mouth shut, shocked at her admission. Or at least, shocked that she'd voiced it to Connor, of all people.

'You were engaged?'

She wished she could understand that unreadable expression on his face.

'For a year,' she heard herself tell him. 'He was a surgeon at the hospital where I was training.'

'And he didn't like you helping Vivian with the fostering?'

She pulled a face.

'Not so much that…' She tailed off. 'It's complicated.'

Which was an excuse, and she knew Connor knew that. But she certainly wasn't going to tell him that the truth was that Jonathon had always felt she'd been doing it for the wrong reasons. He'd felt Little Meadwood was her safety net—a world she'd retreated into after her parents' deaths—and that fostering was her excuse to race back there and out of the 'real world', as he'd called it.

'Is that why he's your ex-fiancé?' Connor asked instead, after the silence had stretched that little bit longer between them.

Nell lifted her shoulders in feigned casualness.

'He was offered a promotion in a hospital across the country. It was too good an opportunity to pass up.'

No need to add that he'd found her a great opportunity too, she just hadn't wanted to be that far from Little Meadwood. That made it seem as though Jonathon had been right about the village being her 'crutch'.

And clearly that wasn't true.

'Sorry that happened to you,' Connor offered, evidently assuming her ex-fiancé had just upped and left her.

Nell cranked out a bright smile.

'Don't be. I had just been offered a job here, and I'd managed to buy the cottage next door to Vivian. So everything worked out well.'

'This place is lucky to have you. You're very good at what you do,' Connor told her in that low, gravelly voice that seemed to scrape deliciously somewhere deep inside her.

'Thank you.' She managed a rueful smile. 'Though I don't

feel good right now. I have a case that's bugging me for some reason, but I can't understand why.'

'Oh?' She wasn't surprised that he looked instantly intrigued. 'What's the case?'

She wrinkled her nose, trying to order her thoughts. She had nothing more than a gut feeling that something was *off* about the case, but none of the tests had supported her doubts and the rest of her team had let it go. Yet still, she couldn't seem to.

'In a way it isn't so much that it's just one case, but two. They aren't identical but I can't shake the feeling that they're just a bit too similar.'

'Go on,' he encouraged when she trailed off.

She drew in a deep breath.

'Two girls presented on different weekends. One last weekend, one this weekend. Both had been at a nightclub drinking when they fell unconscious. Each girl's friends report that neither had had much to drink but out of nowhere one of them stopped making sense when she talked, and the other simply lost the ability to stand. Both girls only had drinks from bottles and covered the tops, and there's no CCTV suggesting their drinks got spiked.'

'No memory?'

'One girl describes it like a black hole in her brain. But out of nowhere, you know? One minute she seemed fine and normal, dancing with her friends; the next moment everything is gone.'

'And toxicology?' Connor asked thoughtfully.

'Nothing indicative, but then given that some drugs are designed to leave the body in under twelve hours, it's possible that by the time we realised the circumstances and tested, we were already too late.'

'Unfortunately, that happens,' he acknowledged. 'Did you check for puncture marks? Needle marks.'

Nell stared at him for a moment.

'Needle marks?' She realised slowly. 'You think they might have been spiked by injection?'

'It's becoming a big problem in the hospital I've just left.'

'Now you mention it, I've heard of cases up and down the country.' She nodded. 'But we hadn't seen it here before. I didn't even think—it's just too awful.'

'It is,' he agreed grimly. 'So when you get the chance, see if your patient will let you check her over. Could be anywhere, and it will be tiny. But I've often found them on backs of legs, or backside. Fleshier areas that a patient wouldn't be able to see for themselves.'

'Right. Will do.' She fell into silence for a moment as she contemplated the ramifications of it.

How many more patients might begin to present themselves at City Hospital? What if those victims didn't have friends around looking out for them? She couldn't decide whether she wanted to find telltale needle marks or not.

Well, she would have to deal with that issue if and when it arose again. It wouldn't help anybody if she started to fall into that particular rabbit hole right now.

Pulling herself back to the present, Nell summoned a bright smile as she turned back to Connor.

'You should know that Vivian's never made any secret of how proud she is of the way you worked your way through the ranks to become a surgeon.'

As far as pivots went, that had hardly been graceful, but she refused to regret it. Even if Connor's expression turned distant for a moment.

'That isn't exactly how it works.'

'It's how Vivian tells it.' Nell lifted her hands in silent apology. 'I just know you signed up the very day of your sixteenth birthday.'

Connor cast another tight expression, then appeared to relent.

'True enough, I suppose. Strictly speaking, I started the

application process the moment I could a few months earlier and, because I was so adamant, Vivian used her contacts and convinced a colonel and his wife to take me in for those last few months to help me get ready for it.'

'I never knew any of that.' Nell shook her head.

Interestingly, she felt her response seemed to ease some of the tension in his body language.

'Oh. Well.' He took a bite of his food and she couldn't help wondering if he was buying some time to reorder his thoughts whilst he finished chewing. 'I was lucky that the colonel took me under his wing. He was tough, and keen on the kind of discipline that I really needed back then, but he also encouraged me to keep my studies going alongside the training, and he helped me to see that I had more options. Pretty much everything Vivian had tried to tell me, but I think I needed the army's *tough love* approach.'

Nell nodded. Somehow, she could see that about him.

'Actually, it was the colonel's widow who managed to track down the civvie hospital where I was working, to pass on the message that Vivian wasn't well.'

'Oh.' Nell blinked in surprise. She'd never thought to wonder how Connor had heard about their foster mother's situation.

'Anyway,' Connor brushed the topic aside, 'I ended up getting army sponsorship to study medicine at uni, and they took me to places like Canada, Cyprus and Belize to enhance my training.'

'According to Vivian, you were also in warzones.'

'I did several tours,' Connor confirmed, but there was a neutrality to his tone that warned her not to pry too deeply.

'Did you enjoy visiting places around the world?' She tried to keep her own tone light. 'I haven't visited Canada or Belize, although I've been on a bit of a girls' holiday to Cyprus, with Ruby and Steph.'

For a moment, Connor only eyed her intently. As though he

were searching right inside her, rooting her to the thin plastic bucket seat.

'Yeah, I loved my time with the army. Did you know that Belize has stunning butterfly farms? Or that their national butterfly is the blue morpho?'

And she didn't think it was his imagination that he looked furious with himself for asking such questions. Was that…? Did he…? Was that some kind of reference to her eyes? Her entire life people had remarked on their colour and vividness, but it had never made her heart pound the way it was pounding now.

'I…didn't know that,' she confessed after a moment.

Connor cleared his throat and took a sip of his drink, his eyes flickering away from hers for a moment. Nell took the opportunity to do the same, taking a bite of her salad to give her mouth something to do besides ask him inappropriate questions about his time in the army.

They fell into a silence, both lost in their own thoughts. Nell couldn't help but feel a sense of intrigue surrounding Connor, coupled with a growing attraction that she wasn't sure what to do with. Eventually, it was Nell who broke the quiet.

'So now you're out of the military, and able to visit Vivian,' she pivoted cheerfully, relieved when the slightly darker shadow in his eyes lifted.

'I am.'

'Can I ask how long you intend to stay here at City?' she asked, taking a forkful of food as she pretended her heart hadn't suddenly picked up a beat at the question.

Connor didn't so much as shrug, but instead lightly extended the fingers of one hand.

'As long as Vivian needs me to.'

'Well, don't be surprised if Vivian throws you some "welcome home party".'

Nell had intended it as a little bit of light humour; she hadn't intended the distinct shift in his expression.

'She'd be the only one to attend.'

His tension was so unexpected and odd that she stared at him for a moment.

'Why would you say that?'

Connor met her gaze, and she could tell he wasn't going to answer her question directly.

'It's…complicated,' he admitted gruffly. 'Little Meadwood and I were never a good fit.'

That part surprised her.

'Even though your photo is up in the Willow Tree pub? And you're part of the annual winter toast.'

'Say again?' he demanded sharply, his eyes blazing. 'For what reason? As some kind of cautionary tale?'

'What?' Nell was confused by his sudden change in demeanour, her heart racing as she tried to think of what she might have said wrong. 'No, as one of the absent friends.'

'I seriously doubt that,' he growled.

'Why?' Nell asked instinctively. She paused, licking her lips. 'The photo is of you in your uniform. There's a photo of Ivan in his uniform, too. And one of Alison Tanner's son—I don't know if you remember him.'

'I do. Though I still don't…'

'Because you're all local heroes that the village is proud to call their own.' She shrugged.

'Then it certainly won't be me.' His voice was too even, too tightly controlled.

It hinted at churning waters beneath the apparently smooth exterior. Dark waters that hid so much.

And the thought of it tugged at her.

'It's you,' she confirmed in a low voice. 'Your pictures have been up for years. Everyone in the village knows about them. It seems it is only you who has a strangely low opinion of yourself.'

His eyes flashed at that.

'On the contrary,' he gritted out. 'Vivian taught me many things, but the most important of all was the ability to believe in myself.'

'Because if we don't believe in ourselves then how can we expect others to?' Nell grinned as she quoted their foster mother perfectly.

It was a lesson she suspected Vivian had tried to instil in all her charges. But though he didn't answer, Connor's gaze flickered away from hers and his expression was oddly perturbed. A yawning ache opened up inside Nell's chest.

And even though she warned herself not to be so ridiculous, she couldn't help wishing she understood this enigmatic man better. At least she was no longer resenting him for the idea that he was swooping in to take control after all these years—or lying to herself that it was the reason Connor Mason got under her skin.

But was that better, or worse? Nell couldn't tell. And as the conversation shifted to work, their experiences in the medical field, and even a few shared stories, Nell found herself feeling more and more comfortable in his presence.

There was no squashing the sense of disappointment that jolted through her when they realised that they'd been there for over half an hour. Definitely time to get back to work.

As they stood to leave, Connor's hand accidentally brushed against her—a small, innocent gesture, yet it sent another jolt of electricity through her body, causing her to pull her hand quickly away. The abruptness of her reaction seemed to catch them both by surprise.

'Sorry.'

Was it her imagination or did his voice sound different? There was a rasp that she was sure hadn't been there before, as though he was just as affected by the contact as she was. Just as caught off guard.

'It's fine.' She forced a smile, trying to play it off, but his eyes held hers a fraction too long and she knew they were both struggling to rebalance themselves.

The realisation was...*thrilling*.

Then, trays cleared to the side, they fell into step with each other as they made their way back to A & E, the only sound being the soft *schlep* of their trainers against the polished hospital floors.

'Thank you again for lunch.' Nell finally broke the silence.

She wasn't surprised when he waved it away.

'Nice not to eat on the hoof for once.'

Reaching A & E, he stepped forward to open the door for her and as she stepped through and thanked him those piercing silver-grey eyes of his caught hers and held her. Something indefinable in his expression sending delicious shivers down her spine and making her heart beat faster against her ribcage, especially when neither of them moved.

It was amazing how just that look from this man caused some song to start up deep inside her very core. She could feel that tension between them start to build again, and she couldn't help but wonder where it might lead. Even now, his eyes were scanning her face slowly, seeming to take in every feature before eventually flicking down to her lips. It was all she could do not to lick them.

The air between them felt so charged, so electric, that her entire body began to hum with anticipation. She had never been this attracted to anyone before, and it both terrified and exhilarated her. What might it be like to be held by this man? To be kissed? To be touched?

What might it be like if she leaned forward, just a few inches, and kissed him?

Before she could act on the impulse, Connor stepped back abruptly, breaking the spell and dispersing the tension.

'Take care, Nell,' he said softly, his voice rough with emotion, before turning and leaving the hospital.

Nell stood there for a moment, feeling as if something had been lost. Had she really been about to lean forward and kiss Connor Mason?

What had she even been thinking?

She shook herself out of her daze and headed back to work, her thoughts consumed with what might have *nearly* just happened between them.

And how she needed to make damned sure it didn't happen again.

CHAPTER FIVE

'HAVE YOU TAKEN the surgical role at City Hospital yet?' his foster mother demanded the instant he stepped through the familiar cottage door.

Connor didn't answer, instead focusing on helping his foster mum back down into her chair after she'd clearly exhausted herself with the effort of walking to open the front door.

'Well?' she pressed, once she was finally settled.

'And if I say I haven't?' he answered wryly. 'Or suggest that I don't have any intention of taking it?'

'Then I'd say you're being so stubborn,' Vivian huffed, if a little wheezily.

'Not stubborn,' he told her lightly, teasing her just as they had both done decades earlier. 'I just already have a job.'

'A job that's so far away that you're spending almost twelve hours a week travelling back and forth to see me.' Her eyes were full of concern. 'I know how you feel about staying in hotels, Connor, and I understand why. Perhaps it would be better if you didn't visit me so often.'

'Out of the question.' His humour evaporated in an instant. Though it was gratifying to see the flash of pleasure in her gaze, even if it didn't erase the concerned expression. 'For the record, I contacted City Hospital last week. I started there today.'

'You've moved back here?' Vivian actually attempted to

shift herself into a more upright position, her shrewd gaze pinning him—just as it had once used to do. 'What precipitated that change of heart?'

'You did.' He grinned.

'And who else?' Vivian snorted and he revelled in the sound. It suddenly felt like...*home*.

Lunacy!

'No one else.' Connor cocked his eyebrows at her.

But oddly—though logic told him that was true—something shifted within him. As though Vivian wasn't entirely incorrect.

Swiftly, he shut down the image of Nell Parker that had popped inexplicably into his head.

'You still look tired, though.' Vivian's voice seeped back into his consciousness.

He turned to face his former foster mother, summoning another light-hearted grin.

'Thanks for that.'

A smile stole, unbidden, over his lips as another image popped back into his brain. He couldn't stop it; he'd enjoyed his lunch with Nell earlier. More than he'd expected to. And it kept replaying in his mind. Even now, he could picture her in surprising detail—like her eyes, which were as crystal-clear and sparklingly aquamarine as the waters around the Bahamas where he'd once snorkelled.

Would Nell enjoy snorkelling?

What was wrong with him?

It was as bad as his inadvertent butterfly comments. It should concern him more that he hadn't been able to help himself. As if she had woven some kind of bizarre spell over him ever since that first day when they'd met out on the road, and then right here in this very cottage only a matter of weeks ago. She'd haunted him ever since. And trying to avoid her every time he'd visited his foster mother hadn't helped the situation—it had only made it worse.

It had left him imagining he could almost catch the scent of Nell's subtly sexy perfume every time he'd visited. Until he'd found himself driving to City Hospital on the pretext of talking to her about Vivian.

Connor fought to shake off such uncharacteristic thoughts. But not before Vivian had noticed, her sharp gaze narrowing again.

'You seem preoccupied.'

'A case,' he answered smoothly, wiping the smile from his lips.

He might have known that she wouldn't fall for the lie.

'Is that so?' Her eyebrows shot up. 'And here I was thinking whoever she is might be why you were so reluctant to leave your current hospital.'

Vivian thought he'd been reluctant to leave his current post because of a woman? Connor sucked in an unimpressed breath even as a part of his brain argued that it was better for his foster mother to think that than have her realise that his unwelcome occupation lay much closer. Even so, he cast her a sharp glance.

'No one would come before you,' he told her gruffly. Hating the way her eyes looked so regretful.

'That isn't how it should be, Connor. If you truly believe that, then I failed in raising you.'

'You did not fail.' He couldn't accept that. 'You're the only reason I made it through. The only reason I didn't end up in some juvenile centre. Or worse, dead. I owe you everything, so trust me when I say that's exactly how it should be.'

'Why? Because you're afraid to ever open yourself up to anyone?'

'And offer them what?' He snorted scornfully. 'I'm damaged, Vivian. You know that better than most.'

'No.' Vivian refused to agree. 'I know your early childhood was hateful, Connor. One that no child should ever be subjected to. And I know you were wounded when you came to me—inside and out. But that never made you damaged beyond repair. You've worked so hard to heal yourself, and I'm so proud of everything you've achieved. But you deserve to sit back now and be loved, as well as to love in return.'

His chest tightened at her words, as though the weight of his past mistakes were sitting on his upper body, trying to suffocate him.

'I'm broken.' He gave a terse shake of his head. 'We both know it. I couldn't offer anyone anything but heartache.'

'Oh, Connor, I wish you could see the boy that I knew. I wish you realised the man you've become. You deserve to be happy and have everything that you want.'

'I do have everything I want,' he replied curtly. Automatically. Forcing a smile.

The saddest part was that a year ago he'd have said that was true—for the most part, at least. Though there was always that part of him that felt restless, always wanting to see what else was out there in the world. To experience something new. Something *more*.

It had been strange, coming in here the other night and seeing Ivan. He'd been steeling himself for seeing his foster mother, but he'd long since forgotten that there had been at least one other person who had made his time at Little Meadwood less…nightmarish.

It didn't matter, except that it had made him realise that amongst the hostility he remembered encountering in Little Meadwood as a kid, there had been at least one or two people besides his foster mother who had brought friendship and fun into his time here. He was beginning to realise he'd just buried those good moments along with all the bad ones.

And now, every time he tried to look at it, there was another piece of the jigsaw. A new piece that had no image yet, except its silhouette that looked suspiciously like a certain doctor.

It was nonsensical.

Vivian regarded him searchingly for a few moments.

'I want to see you happy before I die. I want to see all of you happy.'

A band pulled tight around his chest. How could he refuse to answer her now?

'What if I'm perfectly content with the way my life is?'

'You're not content.' Her voice was still soft, but firm. 'You're just afraid to take a chance. To risk getting hurt.'

'I'm not afraid of getting close to anyone. There has just never been anyone I would *want* to get close to in that way.'

Yet even as he spoke the words he knew they were a lie. Still, he pushed away the image of the blonde-haired doctor that had sprung straight into his mind.

Vivian's eyes raked sadly over his face.

'You don't have to live your life alone, Connor. You deserve love. Someone who loves you the way my Albert loved me.'

'That's easy for you to say.' He knew that she meant well, but he couldn't keep that tinge of bitterness and self-recrimination from creeping into his voice. 'You've always seen the best in people, including me—especially me.'

'And look at everything you've achieved for yourself. You're a surgeon, a war hero, and essentially a loving son.'

A son?

He wanted to speak but his throat felt suddenly thick. Tight.

'I know what your early childhood was like,' Vivian continued regardless. 'And I've seen the scars it has left on you—I've always known that they wouldn't disappear overnight. But that doesn't mean you have to let them define you. You seem different now from the last time I saw you, what was it…four years ago, now? Touring those pyramids at Giza that I'd never imagined I would ever see in person.'

She stopped, the warm memory lighting up her taut face, her watery eyes. He smiled in response.

'That was a good week,' he agreed.

'It was. And we had a blast. But you seem different even since then, Connor. Less…dissonant with yourself. Perhaps now is the time to create a new life for yourself? One that's filled with love and happiness.'

The silence swirled around them. Perhaps a minute passed, perhaps an hour. Connor opened his mouth to object, then closed it again, then opened it again.

Was Vivian right? He wanted to say not, but a year ago nothing—not even Vivian's illness—could have dragged him back to this place. *Meadwood*. Yet visiting these past couple of weeks hadn't quite been the unbearable hell he'd imagined it would be.

Because being back in Meadwood was having more of an impact on him than he had cared to admit?

Or because someone *was?*

'But you still haven't discovered what it is you've spent the past two decades looking for.'

Connor's smile faded, replaced by a furrow of consternation.

'What makes you think that?' he asked quietly.

Vivian's eyes seemed to bore into his very soul as she regarded him.

'You're a gifted surgeon, dear. But there's more to life than just your work.'

Connor shifted uneasily in his seat, feeling the weight of her words bearing down on him. It was true that he'd always been driven by the need to excel in his career, to push himself to the limits of his abilities. But recently he'd also found himself questioning whether there was more to life than the relentless pursuit of success.

Nothing to do with Nell Parker, of course. It was just that her obvious contentment in staying in Meadwood seemed to have got under his skin in a way that he couldn't explain. Which had to be why it was her silhouette he saw.

'What if I don't know what I'm looking for?' he admitted, his voice low and uncertain.

Vivian leaned forward, placing her hand on his in a comforting gesture despite her tiredness.

'That's okay, dear, we can change the subject if you prefer. Just remember that sometimes it's enough to be open to the possibilities that life presents to us.'

'I remember,' he managed, determinedly thrusting any further images of Nell out of his mind.

'Like I said, I just want you to be happy.'

'I *am* happy,' he echoed.

'I'm sure you are.' Her voice was even softer. Almost…sad. 'But I worry that you could be happier. If only you'd just… let yourself be.'

'Happier how?' Even as he answered, he tried to swallow the words back.

Engaging with Vivian would only convince her that she was right. He should have just brushed her words off.

So why hadn't he?

'You could try settling down. Maybe not here, as much as I'd love it if you wanted that.' Vivian gripped his hand tighter, her bony fingers surprisingly strong as they bit into his skin. 'But somewhere you could call home.'

Home? The very word nearly made him scoff aloud. He wasn't sure how he managed to contain it.

'You could have a family, Connor,' Vivian continued urgently when he didn't answer.

This time there was no biting back the scornful response.

'*A family?* You and I both know that's the last thing I should ever do.'

'Because you have some foolish notion that since the man who sired you was no kind of father, then you would be the same?' Vivian challenged evenly.

'That,' he agreed caustically, 'and the fact that my so-called mother left me half feral. Evidently, it's in my blood.'

'That's utter nonsense, Connor, my boy.' And he couldn't decide whether his foster mother was more sad or cross. 'You're nothing like her. You're nothing like either of them. But you can't keep running from your past for ever. That won't make that hollowness inside you go away. It's time for you to start building a future for yourself.'

He gritted his teeth, wanting to refute her words There was always that *thing* inside him pushing him on, as if he was constantly searching for something to fill that empty space inside him that he couldn't quite name.

'This isn't a conversation I want to have right now,' he managed instead.

'Perhaps not.' Vivian shook her head tiredly. 'But if not now, then when? My time is clearly running out.'

Connor fell silent, not wanting to argue with her—and, worse, fighting that sliver inside him that seemed to want so desperately to believe what she was saying.

He *had* changed. When he'd walked away from Little Meadwood twenty years ago, he'd sworn nothing would ever, ever bring him back. He'd still held onto that ten years ago. Even a year ago.

But these past twelve months…he'd felt something shifting in him, even if he'd refused to acknowledge it at the time. Ever since that UN peacekeeper deployment that had turned into such a nightmare.

Even now, some nights, in those hazy moments between wake and sleep he could still hear the laughter and life of that small village by the wadi. And then sleep would bring the horror. And the sheer sense of helplessness when his unit had returned to find the entire village razed to the ground. The thunderous silence of innocent villagers who had all paid the ultimate price simply for accepting much-needed medical aid from the so-called enemy.

His shift in mindset had begun after that. But was it possible he was really so different now? That maybe opening his life to someone wouldn't be such a terrible thing, after all. That maybe he could have something to offer…if it was the right woman. Though he resolutely refused to allow that image of a certain blonde-haired doctor to lurk around the edges of his brain. That was just an inconvenient attraction. Nothing more.

He eyed his foster mother, as if it were her fault he suddenly couldn't control his thoughts, even as the silence hung between them for several more long, telling moments.

'Cup of tea?' He finally changed the subject instead.

'If you'd prefer.' She inclined her head knowingly.

He would prefer. Because it didn't make sense to dwell on his new colleague. He was here for Vivian, not to indulge in some dalliance—and he got the impression that dalliances weren't Nell Parker's style.

Heading out to the compact kitchen, he busied himself with the drinks and by the time he returned to the living room, he was confident that his head was back where it should be.

'I hear you received an MBE for fostering. You never said.'

She didn't look the slightest bit chagrined. Instead, she eyed him shrewdly.

'Who told you that? Nell, or Ruby?'

Too late, he realised his mistake. Vivian was too sharp to miss a thing. He had no choice but to brazen it out.

'I wanted to know how you were really doing rather than the "nothing wrong with me" line that you keep giving me.'

'I'm going to guess Nell,' Vivian concluded, and he still couldn't lie.

Not to Vivian. She'd always been able to tell if he was lying, from when he was a mere kid.

'We ended up grabbing lunch,' he confessed as casually as

he could, but he knew Vivian saw straight through it. Straight to things he wasn't even sure he could see himself.

Such as why he was so drawn to Nell.

Sure, she was beautiful with her swinging blonde hair and bright blue eyes, but he'd dated other beautiful women. Nell had more about her than just that. It was the way she carried herself, the way she spoke with authority and confidence, and yet had a kindness in her that seemed rare in the medical field. He found himself wanting to get to know her better, to learn more about what made her tick.

'Nell is a sweet girl,' Vivian said, perhaps a little too carefully.

Connor nodded, but didn't respond.

'Intelligent, and ambitious, too,' his former foster mum continued at length. 'Like you.'

'Why do I feel you're not precisely complimenting me?' he offered dryly.

'Do you need me to compliment you?'

It was an honest question, despite the light-hearted tone. Vivian had always had a knack for offering advice and guidance when it seemed as though he needed it most. Even now he couldn't deny that her words had a certain resonance that spoke of her deep personal concern for him. He felt touched by the gesture.

'No,' he replied finally with a slight smile. 'I don't need compliments.'

A slight smile tugged at her lips as she reached up and patted his hand. 'I'm glad you're here, Connor. I've missed you.'

There was no swallowing the lump in his throat as Connor felt an inexplicable wave of…something he couldn't describe. Or didn't want to.

He turned his head as if that would help. Outside, the late evening light was finally beginning to dim, causing him to launch to his feet.

'I hadn't realised it was getting so late,' he rasped. 'You need to get your rest.'

'I was thinking the same about you,' Vivian noted, ever the maternal figure. 'Where are you staying? Not in a hotel?'

'No,' he answered quickly. Simply.

'Hospital accommodation, then?'

'A new on-site block,' Connor confirmed, deliberately declining to mention the sensor alarm issue.

He might have known he wouldn't get away with it.

'You're going to try to sleep through the intermittent alarm on some oversensitive sensor system?'

'How could you possibly have heard about that?' Connor rumbled, half amused, half incredulous. But Vivian's expression caused something to hitch in his chest. 'Ah. It was Nell, wasn't it? She shouldn't have worried you.'

'She didn't worry me,' Vivian denied firmly. 'It was just that she left me a garbled message earlier about some alarm fault at the hospital. I thought she'd misdialled but when I tried to call her back she was clearly tied up with patients. But she offered to let you stay at the cottage, didn't she?'

He should have taken a bet on Vivian being able to deduce that.

'How could you guess?'

'Because an hour or so later she sent me a text to say that she thought she would have to stay late to cover the next shift and to remind me where the spare key is *should I need it.*' Vivian shrugged lightly. 'I thought it was rather strange at the time. I worried she thought I was going a bit senile. Now I understand it.'

'She wouldn't dare think you're senile.' Connor couldn't help but laugh. 'None of us would.'

His foster mother chuckled.

'You better hadn't. Now, in the drawer of that white unit over there you'll find the keys to Nell's cottage.'

'Thanks—' he shook his head '—but I'm not staying there.'

Although the thought that Nell didn't expect to return tonight did cause him to waver.

Or he told himself that was what it was, anyway.

'You should reconsider.' Vivian seemed to read him too easily. 'If only for tonight. The sofa pulls out into a bed and the girls keep fresh sheets in the airing cupboard at the top of the stairs.'

'It's okay, the hospital admin have offered a hotel. I wouldn't want to inconvenience anyone. I'm fine.'

He'd had to stay awake for days in various theatres of war.

'I'm sure you think that's true, but there's no point martyring yourself if you can't get any sleep,' she clipped out briskly. 'I know how you feel about hotels, Connor, and if Nell's on duty then she won't be there anyway. Like I said—'

'*You're fine.* Yes, I heard. Shame those stifled yawns don't exactly instil confidence.'

As much as he didn't want to admit it, Vivian had a point. As had Nell. So why did the prospect of spending the night in the latter's cottage—even alone—leave his mouth feeling oddly dry?

As though there was something unsettling about the idea of staying in Nell's home. At least, he told himself that what he was feeling was *unsettled*. He refused to allow himself to think it was anything else. Certainly not something that would risk further complicating this strange, unexpected draw between him and Nell.

But the idea of staying close to his foster mother tonight was particularly reassuring. Especially since it appeared Nell, Ruby and Ivan were all out of the village. Plus, Nell *had* offered him her couch. And at least she wouldn't be there tonight.

'Fine.' He dipped his head. 'I'll stay. If only to be on hand should you need anyone.'

It was only when his foster mother offered a weary smile that he realised how exhausted she must be.

'I'd like that. Just take it easy and get some rest.'

'I could say the same.' He stepped forward to help her up out of her chair. 'Right, let me help you upstairs, and then I'll pop back down and clear up our things so you won't be waking up to a mess in the morning.'

Because it was better to keep busy than to dwell on thoughts of Nell Parker, instead.

CHAPTER SIX

As NELL PULLED her car into the driveway, she was surprised to see the light on in the front room. She had expected it to be in darkness when she returned home. Nell had barely got out of the car when she spotted something else out of place. A large motorbike leaning against the drystone wall, silhouetted against the soft glow coming from the street lamp nearby.

Connor!

Her heart thudded abruptly as wild thoughts tumbled through her head.

Had he actually taken her up on her offer of crashing on her couch?

She shook her head, trying to stop herself from reading too much into it—it was only that she'd been convinced that, even with the issue of the faulty smoke-detection sensors in the surgeons' accommodation, Connor had been too proud to accept her offer.

It felt significant that he was here now. As though he trusted her in a way he evidently usually found hard to do.

Nell shook off those thoughts too, and instead headed towards the house. She paused just before stepping over the threshold, uncertain of what might come next when she opened her front door and stepped into a world that seemed to be getting ever more unpredictable by the hour.

And then she chastised herself for being ridiculous before pushing open the door and edging inside. She was met by silence as she moved down the hallway and to her living room, which now felt oddly unfamiliar to her, but even so she smoothed her expression into a neutral one before she rounded the corner.

She needn't have worried. Connor had obviously fallen asleep where he sat, his head resting back against the arm of the sofa with his hands crossed together over his bare chest—a breath-stealing sight—and that was even before her eyes settled on that faint quirk of a smile playing across his lips, as if he knew some secret joke only he was aware of.

Nell couldn't quite explain why, but something about the scene in front of her commanded her attention. She found herself moving closer and closer to Connor's sleeping form until she was standing right beside him. Her hand reached hesitantly forward, as if it weren't even under her control, and brushed a stray lock away from his forehead.

The contact was gentle yet jolting; a strange mix of electricity and warmth that thrummed through Nell like a current. But then Connor stirred and it was all she could do to leap away, as if she'd just been shocked.

By the time he sat up, instantly alert, she was turning her back to him and hanging her coat over the chair. Then again, that chiselled chest wasn't exactly helping her to stay focused.

Her heart pounded louder. Her palms actually itching with the ridiculous desire to reach out to him again.

It really ought to be a crime for any one man to be so tempting.

'I didn't mean to disturb you.' She had no idea how she managed to keep her voice so even.

'What time is it?' He reached for his watch, his voice entirely too gravelly, and sexy. And *just woken up*. Even when he let out a low curse. 'Just after one-thirty. Sorry, I understood from Vivian that you would be working the night shift. I never would have presumed...'

'It's fine, really. You didn't presume.' She couldn't stop a smile from quirking up the corners of her mouth. This was probably the closest this man ever came to being flustered. 'It isn't a problem at all, or else I wouldn't have offered in the first instance. And I *was* staying to cover the night shift after a multi-vehicle RTA on the main city road, and due to roadworks between us and City General, all the casualties had to be brought to us. It was mayhem so about five of us stayed on.'

'I was on duty, too, but I wasn't paged.' He didn't look pleased, though his gruff tone vibrated deliciously through her all the same.

'No, I think they were trying to give the surgeons from the third floor the night to sleep in peace.' Nell lifted her shoulders slightly.

'Ah, that makes sense. You were right about the smoke-sensor issue,' he confirmed. 'The hospital admin chief contacted me about an hour after you'd told me and assured me she'd secured courtesy hotel rooms for all affected, but I was here visiting Vivian this evening, and I thought I'd stick around to take her to breakfast tomorrow.'

'She'll love that.' Nell fumbled in her bag, as much for something to occupy her shaking hands as anything else.

'Okay, then.'

'And, as I mentioned, Ruby won't mind you crashing here either.' As if mentioning her flatmate could somehow make this moment feel even marginally less intimate. She was sure she wasn't just imagining it. 'She has gone away for a few days.'

'Apparently so has Ivan.'

'Ivan has?' She jerked her head up, suddenly curious.

Why couldn't she shake the idea that there was something going on between Ivan and her friend? But surely Ruby would have mentioned it? They'd always told each other everything, ever since they were kids.

Connor didn't exactly shrug, but there was a slight hint of a broad, muscled shoulder.

'I get the impression that whatever is going on with Ruby includes him.'

'I thought I was imagining things.' Nell gave a half-embarrassed laugh, heat stealing into her cheeks.

Connor grinned, his eyes glinting with amusement.

'Believe me, you're not imagining anything. There's a definite attraction.'

He stopped abruptly, right at the moment Nell felt herself freeze. And though he didn't move even an inch, it felt as though he had as something had shifted right there in the room. It made the air heavier, closer...and infinitely more intimate. She was painfully aware of her breath coming out faster than it should. Her very skin vibrating with awareness of him. The scent of freshly showered skin that seemed to fill up the space between them. Were they still talking about Ruby and Ivan? She wasn't sure. When was the last time she'd ever felt so flustered around a man? Especially one who was currently occupying her living room.

And still they each stared at the other as the night silence suddenly seemed to weave itself around them. Nell, breath caught in her throat, was desperate to break the moment before its intensity became too much for either of them to bear. She opened her mouth with no idea what she might say, only for Connor to beat her to it, his voice low and husky again.

'Anyway, I should probably get a drink and let you get some sleep.'

Nell nodded, feeling a strange mix of disappointment and

relief. She was beginning not to trust herself to be alone with Connor for much longer without doing something she might regret. It was a novel notion for her. When had any man ever got under her skin quite like Connor? Even Jonathon?

She moved to leave the room, then paused at the door.

'Oh, just thought you might be interested to know that after our conversation today I asked my patient where she had been and discovered it had been on the same street as my first patient. Then I checked her for needle marks.'

'You found them,' he said flatly, reading her face.

'On her backside, just like you said,' Nell confirmed. 'Obviously, I can't check the girl from the weekend before, but I remember her thinking she had a bite in the same location, and the itch was driving her mad. I checked it and it was a little bit raised and red but I wasn't looking for a needle mark back then. Now I can't help wondering.'

'They aren't easy to spot, especially if you aren't expecting to see anything like that. Did you tell your current patient to contact the police?'

'I did,' she confirmed. 'They came and took a statement, and when I mentioned about the first girl they said they would contact her and ask if she would be happy to give her story to see if there were any similarities that could help.'

'Not an easy conversation—' he held her gaze '—but better than them wandering around in the dark.'

Nell nodded.

'Bizarrely, I think it helped, in a way. I know both girls felt under pressure from others—one from her sister, the other from her parents—to admit they'd had too much to drink, yet both girls were adamant that they hadn't. I guess this possibility allows them to trust their own convictions. Although now I guess they have a whole other set of issues to try to wrap their heads around.'

'The worst of it is that we're seeing more and more of these cases coming into hospitals.'

She shook her head trying to clear it of the shock of the evening.

'Anyway, thanks again for the pointer. I never would have thought to look for a needle mark, otherwise. Goodnight, Connor.'

'Goodnight, Nell.'

He stretched, and stood, causing his muscles to ripple. Nell swallowed hard, looking away. But it was too late, and the image was already burned wickedly into her mind. All she could do was attempt to ignore the way her body was reacting to him. At least he was wearing jogging bottoms. She wasn't sure she'd have coped if he'd just been in boxers. But as he made his way towards the kitchen door, Nell couldn't help but feel a sense of…loss? Longing? She wasn't sure what it was, but it was a feeling she hadn't experienced in a long time. Maybe it was just the fact that she was tired, and her emotions were all over the place. Or maybe it was something more.

As he disappeared into the kitchen, her shaky legs carried her upstairs and into her bedroom where she collapsed on her bed with a shaky breath.

Her mind raced with thoughts she had no chance of quelling—not the least of which was the fact that she'd fled upstairs so hastily that she hadn't even had the coffee she'd been longing for all evening.

Connor's presence in her small cottage was intoxicating. As much as she'd tried before, it was now impossible to deny just how much she wanted him. Like some hormonal adolescent. Laughable really, since she'd never been like that even when she *had* been that age. Yet here she was, barely able to think straight. Obsessing over the man downstairs, cloistered in her room as she listened out for his footfalls that would tell her when he left the kitchen and headed back to the couch.

Clearly having Connor in her house, even just for the night, was going to be a challenge—one that she wasn't sure she was ready for.

So would she have preferred he hadn't taken her up on her offer?

Nell eyed her reflection in the mirror, as if she could somehow be more honest with the person she saw there. The inconvenient truth was that there was something about Connor Mason that made her feel alive in a way that she hadn't felt for a very long time. Perhaps ever. Even Jonathon had never made her feel so…*electric*. He had never looked at her with eyes so piercing that it seemed as though they saw right into her soul. He had never made her feel as if she were the only woman in the room, even when it was crowded.

But Connor had—which made him dangerous and thrilling all at the same time.

What would it be like to be with a man like him? To feel his strong arms around her, kiss those sinful lips, and run her fingers through hair that looked as though it was artfully tousled even when he'd hauled off his motorbike helmet after a long ride? Lord, but he was all so tempting, so enticing. And yet also so terrifying.

The woman reflected in the mirror blew out an exasperated sigh and rolled her eyes. Then, with a deep breath, Nell crossed her room and yanked the door open with a decisiveness that she didn't entirely feel, and ultimately made her way back down the stairs. As she entered the kitchen, she found Connor pouring himself another glass of water. He looked up when he heard her footsteps, and their eyes met once again.

'I know it's late and I'll probably never sleep but I've spent the past few hours on shift just dreaming of a decent, non-vending-machine coffee.' She forced a light laugh as she busied herself with the kettle and mug, her hand hovering over a second cup. 'Would you like one?'

There was the briefest beat of hesitation before he nodded once.

'Sure, why not?' Stepping beside her, he took the mugs from her hand and reached for the labelled coffee jar on the shelf. 'I'll make it whilst you sit down—you're the one who has just come off shift.'

'Oh…right…' Surprised, and more than a little gratified, Nell allowed him to take over. 'Thanks.'

It was such a small gesture that nonetheless made her feel curiously valued. She couldn't help smiling inside as he moved around her kitchen, his movements purposeful and efficient, murmuring her thanks as he held out the hot mug for her to take. And there was no denying that frisson that shot up her arm and around her whole being when their fingers brushed for that fraction of a moment. An unintended slip that felt ridiculously intimate.

Focus on the coffee.

Lifting the steaming mug to her lips, Nell inhaled the rich aroma before taking a tentative but appreciate sip.

'So good,' she managed, before taking another.

'Long shift,' he empathised.

'Very.' She twisted her mouth up. 'And a difficult one.'

He leaned back on the kitchen counter, his eyes fixed on hers.

'The nightclub case still getting to you? Want to talk?' he asked simply. Quietly.

As if he could read her every thought, making her feel exposed. Vulnerable.

Still, she forced herself to meet his gaze.

'Actually, the case really getting to me was a pregnant woman in that RTA. Neither of them made it.'

'Ah.' Connor nodded. 'That must have been a hard case.'

'Yeah.' She squeezed her eyes closed for a second. 'I can usually switch off to the trauma of it, and just do the absolute best job I can for my patients.' She shrugged. 'But tonight just got to me. It felt like such a kick in the gut. The loss… I don't know.'

'You're carrying around the worry of Vivian right now.' He reached out and placed a comforting hand on her shoulder—a simple movement, but it sent delicious shivers down Nell's spine.

It was all she could do not to topple sideways off her stool.

'Shall we go through?' she managed, jerking her head to the living room instead.

It was only when she stepped through the doorway that she saw that he'd set up his bed on the couch. At least the room was bigger than the kitchen though; moving to the furthest corner, Nell sank down in the oversized tub chair and folded her legs up underneath her. She wasn't sure whether to feel gratified or disappointed when he reached down to snag a black T-shirt from his bag and haul it over his head.

'I'll be out of your way in a minute or two,' she promised, taking another sip of gloriously hot coffee.

'Take your time.' Connor's voice rasped through the air. 'I'm probably up for a couple of hours now anyway. If you're hungry I could make us something to eat. What have you got in?'

Nell pulled a sheepish face.

'Porridge oats, bread, and couple of chocolate snack bars if we're lucky.'

'That's it?' He looked incredulous.

'Well, there are probably a few other ingredients out there— every so often Ruby and I decide we'll make something exciting, but then work gets in the way and we usually grab something on the way home from the hospital.'

Glancing at his watch, Connor stood up abruptly.

'Where's the nearest supermarket? I can probably grab us something decent.'

She pulled another face—this time more apologetic, despite her amusement.

'This is Meadwood, not the city. We don't have twenty-four-seven supermarkets, just Sylvie's corner shop, which will have closed hours ago.'

She was sure she caught the hint of an odd expression ripple across his face.

'How do you survive out here?' he muttered, his eyes scanning the room as if searching for a stash of hidden food.

'We manage.' Nell laughed, her spirits lifting in spite of everything.

'Well, that's not going to work,' he grumbled, running a hand through his tousled hair. 'I guess we'll just have to make do with what we've got. I'll see what I can rustle up.'

Nell watched him move back to the kitchen, and found herself following. He rummaged through her cupboards and fridge with a practised ease and she couldn't help but feel a little envious of his confidence in the kitchen.

'Breakfast or supper?'

'Supper,' she confirmed definitively.

'Okay…hmm…peppers, rice, onions, tomatoes. Have you any chicken broth…? Yes. Great. How about spicy Mexican rice?'

Her stomach rumbled obligingly.

'Sounds good,' she admitted.

'Okay.' He picked up a pan from the rack and began to fill it. 'I'll get the rice on, the broth, and then chop the onions. You chop the peppers.'

'That I can manage,' she agreed, leaning over to tap the small speaker on the side. 'Might as well have a little background music whilst we work.'

'Even better.'

Whilst he quickly measured out the rice by eye, she set to work retrieving half-decent knives from the drawer for each of them, then chopping the pepper. But Nell still couldn't stop her eyes from wandering over to study this man of such contradictions.

Even dressed in just a black T-shirt and joggers, he really was devastatingly handsome. She tried to push the thought out of her mind. It was dangerous to think of him like that—just as it was hard to remember that, despite the fact that Vivian had mentioned Connor for as long as Nell had known her, she herself had met the man only recently.

It felt like longer—and in a good way.

So as she took in the way his muscles moved under his shirt and the way his hair fell across his forehead that low, familiar ache crept back into her belly. It had been so long since she had been with anyone, let alone someone like him.

As if sensing her gaze, he turned to her with a half-smile.

'You know, you're pretty good company for someone who's exhausted and just had a rough shift,' he said, handing her a couple of tomatoes.

Nell grinned despite herself, a warm flush spreading across her cheeks.

'You're not so bad yourself.'

They fell into a comfortable silence as they prepped, the only sounds coming from their rhythmic chopping, and the speaker playing in the background. Cutting and dicing, then sliding the ingredients into a bowl whilst Connor moved around her kitchen as though he were utterly familiar with the set-up—as though he *belonged*—and worked on everything else.

Before long, the mouth-watering smells of the rice dish filled the kitchen and Nell's stomach began to growl louder in appreciation.

Connor ladled out two generous helpings onto plates and they sat together at the counter, their conversation flowing easily as they ate. And even when they had finished, they chatted for a little longer before reluctantly beginning to clean up and load the mini-dishwasher. Taking more time than they needed. Finding extra little tasks. It seemed that neither of them felt any desire to break the spell that had been cast over them.

And then the song on the speaker changed to something slow, and soft, and the atmosphere in the room shifted again. Nell couldn't stop her gaze from being drawn once more to Connor's, only to find him looking back intently.

'Wait, you have…' He reached out and brushed a stray pepper seed off her cheek, his mouth curved into a soft smile. His eyes lingering on hers for a moment too long.

Without thinking, Nell took a step closer until she was standing mere inches from him, revelling in the way his eyes dropped to her mouth when she flicked a nervous tongue over her suddenly dry lips. A thousand thoughts spun wildly through her head.

Did she say something? Move away?

Her heart fluttered even as her lungs appeared to momentarily forget what they had been doing—without issue—for over three decades. And then, almost without warning, Connor bent his head down and lightly brushed his lips against hers.

And it was as though the spark it ignited in Nell somehow both silenced those tumbling thoughts and sent them crazy all at the same time. She melted into the kiss, basking in the rush of exhilaration that cascaded through her body. And when his arms came around her waist to pull her closer, Nell was helpless to do anything but slide her hands up that gloriously solid chest of his to loop her arms around his neck.

It was everything she had been pretending not to dream about—and so, so much more.

He deepened the kiss, his hands moving to cup her face as though she were infinitely precious. Undisguised hunger. Demanding…*taking*. Every delicious sweep of his tongue against her lips made Nell shiver with delight. Every new sensation that he created sent electricity coursing through her veins. It was as if time had paused, leaving nothing else but the two of them and the heat between them. Every fresh touch sent a wave of heat through her body, igniting a fire that had been dormant for far too long.

Nell's hands roamed eagerly over Connor's body, savouring every detail as she mapped out the hardness of his muscles beneath his shirt. Down further, to where his shirt ended and his skin began. He had ignited a veritable fire in her belly just as he had infused molten lava into her very veins. It grew hotter and brighter with each movement of his hands, and still she couldn't get enough. She was addicted to his touch.

Could he feel the shake of barely controlled desire in her hands as she traced the delicious contours of his chest? Mapping them. Committing them to memory. And still his mouth demanded from hers—*took* from hers—whilst his hands sought out her waist, slipping underneath her shirt to tease her flesh into writhing pleasure. A strangled moan escaped Nell's throat as he explored further, a maddening desire filling her from the tips of her toes, right up. And when he finally dragged his mouth from hers, he lifted her off the ground and placed her onto the counter but still didn't release her. Not that she wanted him to release her.

Ever.

She pushed that thought away, instead concentrating on tracing the contours of his abs, feeling the hardness of his muscles and the warmth of his skin. The next kiss that was every bit as hot and intense as the last. His tongue exploring her mouth with just the right amount of pressure, her head cradled in his hand. Pleasure and need consumed Nell; a need that was as vital as breathing, too strong to contain. Her heart was beating so fast in her chest, she wondered if he could feel it. If this was what it felt like to be in a bubble suspended in time, and in the perfect moment, then she wanted it never to burst.

Connor broke the kiss to bury his face in her neck, his breath hot against her skin as he nipped at the sensitive flesh.

Dimly, she heard a soft moan that surely wasn't her. It was as if her mind were hazy and yet flawlessly clear all at once. His hands roamed beneath her shirt to caress her breasts. She gasped at the sensation, arching into his touch.

He looked up at her through eyes so dark. As if he was as lost as she was. Like nothing she'd ever quite experienced before.

Did she drive him as crazy as he drove her? Dimly, Nell could only hope so, if this desperate, primal kiss was anything to go by. A promise of what was to come. And it set every nerve-ending firing inside her.

The shrill sound of a mobile phone caught them both off guard, ripping through the air. Making them pull apart.

She couldn't help wondering if he was being battered by the same storm of stupefaction, and frustration, and regret, that was battering through her.

'It's Vivian's ringtone,' he rasped sharply, spinning from her and striding back into the living room.

Leaving her to slide down from the counter herself, her arms wrapped around her chest, heart still hammering, though for a different reason now.

'Is she okay?' Nell asked, though she knew he couldn't possibly know.

Her teeth worried at her lower lip as Connor slid his finger over the screen to accept the call.

'Vivian? What's wrong?'

Unable to hear the other side of the conversation, Nell hovered anxiously by the door, her arms still hugging herself protectively. She didn't want to just burst in next door if it wasn't serious, so all she could do was watch Connor's face carefully as she fought to control her lurching heart.

And then he looked up at her, meeting her gaze for a long moment.

'I'm fine, Vivian. I'm next door…at Nell and Ruby's. You gave me your spare key, do you remember?'

The tension in Nell's chest dropped instantly to the ground as her knees threatened to buckle.

Her foster mum was okay.

Another few reassuring words from Connor, and then he was ending the call, apologising again. He tossed the phone down to the sofa bed, his arms folding across his chest as he faced her.

But he didn't close the gap, and his expression was frustratingly impossible to read.

'She was calling to make sure I was safely back home. I usually call her to say I've arrived safely.'

'She hadn't realised you were here, then?' Nell asked, redundantly.

'I did tell her that I would be but I'm guessing that the meds she's on have disorientated her, especially as she had just woken.' He stopped, fixing Nell with a piercing gaze. 'She told me you had called her to remind her where the spare key was, right before she persuaded me that crashing here would be the wisest option.'

His considered tone didn't stop her heart from skipping a beat or two.

'Well…yes, I did do that.' Nell's mouth was dry and it was all she could do not to lick her lips. 'Was she alright when you reminded her? Did she remember?'

'She did,' Connor confirmed. 'She was a little cross with herself for forgetting but I think I reassured her that it didn't matter.'

'Okay, good. Then I'm just thankful she's well and there isn't an issue.'

'Right,' he agreed, his voice sounding as stilted as hers.

'I should…that is… I'd better head to bed,' she managed to stutter out.

As if her head and heart weren't still reeling. Still wanting more.

'Probably for the best,' he concurred, his voice taut. 'Good-night, Nell.'

'Night,' she managed before fleeing upstairs to bed.

Not that she stood a hope in hell of getting a wink of sleep.

CHAPTER SEVEN

'HEY, CONNOR, any update yet?'

Connor barely lifted his head as the surgical head of trauma ducked into his operating room, instead keeping his attention on the patient in front of him.

'Just getting into the wound now,' he confirmed. 'Give me a moment.'

He worked quickly but carefully, grateful as ever for the surgical work to keep his mind busy and off a certain blonde-haired temptress.

It had been three days since that night at Nell's cottage in Meadwood. Four nights since he'd almost forgotten himself completely.

He knew he owed her an apology but he hadn't been able to trust himself enough to return to her home once he'd left the following morning. He was only grateful the contractors had remedied the smoke-sensor system so quickly, but he would have taken a night of intermittent alarm calls over returning to Nell's cottage.

As it was, it had taken all he had not to stop her from leaving the kitchen that night. To stop her from racing upstairs—away from him. As if distancing themselves from each other could extinguish the spark of attraction he felt to her.

Not that it had worked.

Thoughts of Nell kept flooding his brain every time he left

it unoccupied—it didn't matter how strenuously he tried to deny replaying that night over in his head, or how vehemently he told himself that he didn't remember how it felt to kiss her, or even how staunchly he pretended not to recall the way her hands had so willingly explored his body in a way that still sent lingering waves of heat through him.

No matter what he told himself, Connor couldn't pretend that he'd imagined that pull between them—even from the first moment they'd met at the site of Lester's car crash—or tell himself over and over that it was simply a connection due to the fact that they'd both been foster kids under Vivian's care. Deep down Connor knew there was more than that.

But he couldn't allow himself to give into it. A woman like Nell deserved better than a man like him. Better than a meaningless one-night stand—because that was all he could offer her.

And no matter that a part of him imagined what it might be like if he had more to give.

He shoved the uninvited thought from his mind and focused back in on his patient.

'The pole ultimately created a seven-inch slash across the abdomen,' Connor confirmed to his colleague, carefully walking his fingers around the inside of the cavity. Feeling his way and checking. Then checking again. 'But the good news is that the wound doesn't appear to penetrate beyond the anterior wall.'

'That is good,' his chief agreed, peering over the table from as far back as he could. 'So no damage to either the spleen or liver after all?'

'No.' Connor continued probing, concentrating on anything that might get his attention. The spleen and liver were the organs most often damaged in these types of injuries, followed by the retroperitoneum, small bowel and kidneys. Nothing here looked out of place. 'Plus the patient doesn't appear to have unexplained bleeding, vitals have been relatively stable, and there's no evidence of peritonitis. He had a FAST scan to assess for hemoperitoneum, and hemopericardium.'

'Good.'

The operating room fell into silence as Connor made another sweep of the wound before satisfying himself that nothing had been missed, then set to work as diligently and efficiently as ever. Because no matter the circumstances here, it was always better than the conditions he'd had to work in whilst on tours of duty. And he still missed that time of his life.

'Haemostasis?' the consultant asked, when Connor confirmed he was happy.

Connor nodded.

'Haemostasis also seems normal.'

'Lucky boy, then.'

'Very,' Connor confirmed.

The boy had been thrown through the windscreen of his car when he'd lost control on a tight bend and contact with a jagged metal pole had left him with a seven-inch long, somewhat deep slash across the left side of his abdomen. The fact that it hadn't penetrated into the body cavity and damaged the internal organs had been little short of a miracle.

The last similar case Connor had worked on back at his previous hospital, the man in question had ended up with a torn smaller intestine, which had resulted in significant resection. This boy by contrast had been very fortunate.

'We're going to start closing up now,' he updated the consultant, as he directed his fellow surgeon to where he wanted to start.

'Actually, if you can hand off for closing up, there's an emergency case downstairs right now that could really do with someone of your experience,' the chief told him.

'Of course.' Connor ignored the jolt that charged through

him, like a thump from touching a live cable. 'I'll be right behind you.'

Was Nell on duty today?

He couldn't imagine she'd be delighted at being thrown together on a case—not after how they'd left things. But what choice was there? Besides, even if she was on shift, there were plenty of other doctors—and patients—who might need him. He was here for his patients—no one else.

Certainly not soft-lipped, hot-bodied Nell Parker.

And if he believed that, he'd believe anything.

Handing off to his colleague before stepping away from the table, Connor began stripping his gown and gloves and moving towards the sink area to scrub out.

Maybe moving to City Hospital hadn't been the wisest decision, after all—even if it did mean being closer to Vivian. Not to mention the fact that being so close to Little Meadwood was a little like taking twenty steps backwards into a past that hadn't exactly been fun the first time around.

He hadn't even begun to unpack that particular hang-up yet.

He hurried down the polished, pristine corridors around City Hospital's operating rooms—another reason to appreciate his new position at his new place of employment.

The recently refitted City Hospital was high-tech and bang up to date, with particularly forward-thinking surgeons. Despite his concerns about taking a job so close to Little Meadwood, Connor had to admit he was enjoying working in such an innovative environment.

Even the stairs were in a striking glass block that offered stunning views of the public park opposite, Connor thought as he raced down them three at a time, hurrying through the wide, quiet staff corridor and into the Resus department at the far end where his new boss was just concluding a conversation with another colleague.

'Connor.' His colleague peered around him. 'You're on your own?'

'Yes, where do you want me?'

With an appreciative nod, the consultant glanced at the digital board.

'Three cases but only two of us. The others must be on their way.' He grimaced. 'I'm about to take Bay Ten to emergency surgery, Bay Five is a blood clot on the chest, and Bay Eight is a fall due in. You'll need to assess both and identify priority.'

'Sure.' Connor dipped his head, sweeping the department quickly before heading over to Bay Eight.

'I'm Connor, the trauma surgeon you requested,' he announced as he stepped around the curtain. 'What have we got?'

And then he experienced the hardest wallop to his gut as Nell Parker spun around to meet his gaze, her familiar blue eyes stealing the breath from his lungs.

'Connor.'

Her sharp intake of breath told him everything he didn't want to admit he was thinking. He fought to regain control of his rattling senses.

'Nell,' he acknowledged briefly.

'I just didn't expect…' She faltered.

'Neither did I.' He cut her off, though not unkindly. 'How about you tell me about the case?'

She hesitated for another moment before bobbing her head quickly as he watched her professional side kick in.

Like him.

He pushed the comparison away—he didn't need another reason to suggest they were well matched.

'Patient is a twenty-six-year-old male who fell from an office roof and is complaining of lower back and pelvic pain,' Nell stated. 'He's with Heli-med, already landed and arriving any moment now and the only other information we have so far is that he had a GCS of fourteen when they arrived on scene, but there's been a period of hypotension.'

'Right.' Connor nodded grimly. 'After a fall like that, any hypotension would be consistent with pelvic injury and blood loss; possible spinal fractures; potential head injury...'

'Leading to something more serious,' Nell confirmed.

'Did you call anyone from Neurology?'

'I've alerted them.' She nodded.

'Good, I need to check on Bay Five, but I'll be back.'

Hurrying across the floor, he checked in on the other patient mentioned—a blood clot on the chest, which warranted surgery as advised, including deflating the lung to carry out the procedure. But he would need to wait for Nell's patient before determining which of them should take priority. He strode back to her bay just as the doors at the far end burst open and a Heli-med uniformed doctor hurried in with the gurney and she leapt into action.

'Bay Eight, please.'

Connor scanned everything at once as Nell began the primary survey with her team—smooth and skilled. He found he expected nothing less from her, which helped him shove his own jumbled thoughts out of his head.

'Okay, IV in?' He checked with his team. 'Good. Can we get oxygen, please? And suction? Great.'

The process continued quickly and calmly with the team responding until they finally confirmed they were ready for the handover from the HEMS doctor, and Connor gave the man a nod.

'This is James, a twenty-six-year-old male who, approximately thirty minutes ago, fell around twenty-five feet off the roof of a small office block. He landed on his back and when we arrived, he had a GCS of fourteen and has been complaining of lumbar pain and pelvic pain. Top down, he has a laceration to the right frontal region of his head, lumbar pain and posterior pelvic pain, but was able to move his legs normally on scene. We've administered one hundred and fifty mil of ketamine to help control the pain.'

'Okay, thanks.' Connor took over from the Heli-med team smoothly. 'Nell?'

He waited for her to confirm the checks with her team.

'Sounds equal airway bilaterally.' She nodded after a moment. 'No visible bruising to the chest. SATS ninety-eight. Good volume central pulse. Diminished volume peripheral pulse.'

Good. At least that could buy them a little time.

'Response?' he asked, but she was already on it.

'Hi, James, I'm Nell.' She kept her voice perfectly light and bright for the patient. 'Can you open your eyes for me? Great. And can you squeeze my hand? Good man.'

Connor dipped his head in confirmation when she glanced his way, before summoning her to one side.

'Can we get X-rays, please? Chest and pelvis,' Connor instructed. 'Can I leave this with you? I have to head to surgery with a patient with a blood clot on his chest. I'm going to have to collapse the lung and remove the clot via keyhole surgery.'

'Of course,' Nell confirmed. 'With any luck we'll have the results by the time you return.'

'Great.' He nodded.

Or else one of his colleagues should be arriving any moment.

And with that he was gone, leaving Nell to organise her team and get James the X-rays they needed—and leaving them both time to regroup.

'I've missed this,' Nell admitted as she and Ruby linked arms together and strolled through the park opposite the hospital. 'This morning was mayhem.'

For as long as she could recall, it had been their weekly

ritual to take a walk around Little Meadwood and share any worries or concerns—or just fun stories—at least one day each week when they both had a day off.

How long had it been since they'd managed that?

Certainly not in the past few months—which only made Nell all the more grateful that her friend had found her on shift and asked if she'd like to meet up for a lunchbreak in the nearby park. Exactly what Nell had felt she needed after her morning with Connor—even if working alongside him kept proving surprisingly easy.

Given the tension between them after that night at her cottage, Nell certainly hadn't expected to share such a professional harmony and synchronicity with the man.

It made her wonder...

No! She slammed the thought away before it could take root inside her head.

But the fact was that by the time Connor had returned from his blood-clot surgery, they'd had the X-rays back on their patient, James, which had confirmed a pelvic fracture as well as indicating a strong possibility of spinal damage. Then together, they'd worked seamlessly to prep their patient for surgery, anticipating each other's needs as they'd stabilised his condition enough to get him to the OR. As though they'd been working together for years. She couldn't help feeling a sense of pride in their joint efforts.

But now...?

'Tell me about it.' Ruby rubbed one hand over her eyes, pulling Nell back to the present. 'I'm used to Resus being slammed but that was insane. I think there are still roadworks in the city so it has been quicker and easier to get all the emergencies here. And, for the record, I've missed this too.' Ruby squeezed Nell's arm in a show of affection. 'I'm sorry if I've been a bit distant recently.'

Nell bobbed her head. She couldn't pretend she hadn't noticed, especially with the jumble of Connor-related thoughts tumbling around her brain right now. But more than that, she and Ruby had been close for so many years that the sudden disconnect had worried her.

It had made her feel oddly isolated. Which had set other, unexpected questions firing off around her brain—such as what Little Meadwood would be like without either Vivian or Ruby around? It was something she'd never considered before.

Or never allowed herself to consider.

But that wasn't a scenario she was ready to dig into right now. She turned her attention back to her friend.

'Want to share?' she asked gently.

Ruby opened her mouth, then closed it before rubbing her hand over her eyes again.

'It's crazy. And complicated.'

'You don't have to feel obligated.' Nell stopped her friend instantly, but Ruby shook her head.

'I know. But… I want to. I just don't know where to start.'

Nell knew how her friend felt.

'Start wherever feels comfortable,' she suggested.

Perhaps she ought to take her own advice.

'It's just I've been…wondering about what it would be like to live somewhere else.'

'Oh.'

Was this something to do with Ivan? If so, why hadn't Ruby said something, anything, before now?

'Haven't you ever thought about leaving Meadwood?' Ruby asked as Nell pressed her lips together.

The question was all too close to the bone.

So much for not digging into that scenario.

'Not really,' she lied evenly.

As if the worry hadn't been there festering in the back of her mind.

'Never?' Ruby sounded sceptical and confused all at once, only adding to Nell's sense of guilt. 'What about with Jonathon?'

The feeling of guilt intensified. It occurred to her that she had never really explained to Ruby exactly why her engagement to him had unravelled. In fact, hadn't she revealed more to Connor than she ever had to her friend? So much for her telling herself that she and Ruby always told each other everything.

So what did that say about her?

'I don't really like thinking about what it might be like to stay here if Vivian...wasn't next door any more,' Nell finally offered as a compromise.

They both knew what she was trying not to say.

'Everywhere we went there would be memories,' Ruby conceded. 'Good ones but still...how could we walk past Vivian's house knowing that she wasn't there any longer?'

'Are you thinking about leaving?' Nell asked directly.

Ruby hesitated.

'Not now. Not unless...like I said, it's complicated.'

Their arms still linked, Nell led her friend to a wooden bench and they sank down next to each other.

'What's going on, Rubes? Only, you're right, you've been so preoccupied lately.' And the worst of it was that she herself had been so caught up with thoughts of Connor recently that it had taken her until now to notice that Ruby hadn't been herself for weeks. 'You know I'm always here for you to talk to.'

Ruby bobbed her head, leaning back. She was ostensibly taking in the warm rays of sunshine that filtered through the trees, but Nell suspected her friend was trying to work out what to say. It was so unlike Ruby that it caught in Nell's chest. They'd always told each other everything, right from being foster kids together. She hated that there were now secrets, that Ruby had things she couldn't share. But wasn't she just as bad?

Nell sucked in a deep breath.

'Okay, how about I go first? I kissed Connor.'

Ruby's head snapped around, her shock visible.

'Connor? As in *Connor Mason*?'

A nervous chuckle escaped Nell's throat.

'The very same. It happened the other night when you were away and he stayed at our cottage.'

'A kiss?'

'A good kiss.' Nell couldn't help grinning at the memory.

Ruby's eyebrows shot up.

'Wow, Nell. It's been ages since you even liked anyone enough to go on a date. Over a year, in fact. I didn't realise you had those kinds of feelings for Connor Mason.'

'I didn't either, to be honest,' Nell admitted. 'It's just... there's been something between us since that first time we met on the road after Lester's accident, you remember? This insane attraction... I can't explain it.'

'You don't have to, trust me.' Ruby's voice was odd. Not her usual light tone.

Nell reached out a hand to her friend's arm.

'Rubes?'

'Ignore me.' Ruby forced out a laugh. 'Long shift. So, have you talked to Connor since the kiss?'

Nell hesitated. She and Ruby had been friends long enough, and been through so much as foster kids together, that they could reach each other better than anyone. But it was clear that something more was going on with Ruby than she was ready to talk about. Even now her friend's gaze wasn't entirely focused; she was still partially lost in her own thoughts. Part of Nell ached to ask, to press her, yet the last thing Nell wanted to do was push her before she was ready. All she could do was make sure Ruby knew she was there to listen when her friend was ready.

Squeezing Ruby's hand, Nell plastered a rueful expression on her face.

'No, I haven't really had the chance to speak with Connor.' Ruby wrinkled her nose thoughtfully.

'But you want to?'

'Yes. No. Maybe.' Nell shook her head with a strangled laugh, her eyes trained on some ducks across the old clay fields. 'I confess I haven't really had the courage. I think we sort of avoided each other for the rest of the time. But now I wish we hadn't. Sometimes I think there is a real connection there, but the reality is that we have nothing in common. I love Little Meadwood, he hates it. I worry that any connection we feel is actually just the shared experience of Vivian being ill.'

Ruby's gaze sharpened as she regarded her friend.

'I understand exactly what you mean,' she said, then trailed off. Once again as if there was something more she wanted to say, but couldn't.

Nell had to bite her own tongue to stop herself from prying. *When Ruby is ready*, she reminded herself.

'I don't want to make things awkward with him,' she made herself say instead. 'Especially with everything going on with Vivian.'

'Sometimes it's hard to know what to do with those kinds of feelings,' Ruby demurred. 'But I think you have to be honest with yourself about what you feel. And what you want.'

And there was something about her friend's tone that made Nell wonder which of them Ruby was really trying to convince. Maybe letting her friend come to her in her own time was a good idea, but then maybe Ruby needed a gentle nudge. Didn't everyone, sometimes?

'Sounds like it makes sense,' Nell pointed out softly. 'Do you think you'll take your own advice, Rubes?'

Turning her head, Ruby met her gaze. There was a vulnerability in her friend's eyes that Nell couldn't help but respond to. Ruby's voice was quiet as she spoke, almost hesitant.

'I don't know, Nell. It's all so complicated.'

Nell reached out and squeezed Ruby's hand comfortingly.

'Whenever you're ready, Rubes. I'm here for you no matter what.'

Ruby's lips quirked up in a small smile, but there was still a sadness in her eyes that tugged at Nell's heartstrings.

'Thanks, Nell. I appreciate it.'

The two of them sat there in silence for a moment, lost in their own thoughts.

'Rubes…'

But whatever else Nell might have been about to say was cut off as each of their phones shrieked alerts in quick succession. There was no need to read them to know what they would say.

'More emergencies.' The pair of them shared a look even as they turned and headed straight back to the hospital.

'One heck of a day.'

Connor's voice startled Nell as she snatched a couple of minutes to grab a coffee, after several hours of non-stop major emergencies.

She swung around, valiantly trying to stop her heart from galloping out of her chest.

'I haven't seen anything like it for about a year,' she agreed. 'Not at this time of year, anyway.'

'I enjoyed working with you again this morning,' he said unexpectedly, and there was no way she could keep her cheeks from heating up with the compliment. 'I confess that I was expecting things to be more awkward after the other night.'

'I was, too,' she admitted with a surprised laugh.

'You're a good doctor. Intuitive.'

Surely his approval shouldn't have made her fizz quite as much? Not that she was about to let him know. She lifted her shoulders in feigned casualness.

'And you're a good surgeon.'

They lapsed into silence for several long moments. He was

close enough for her to smell him—a fresh, clean scent that reminded her of fine summer rain falling on the freshly mown fields in Meadwood—and close enough for her to feel the heat of his body, seeping through her scrubs and into her.

'Listen, can we sit for a moment and just clear the air after... the other night?'

There was no accusation in his tone, only a quiet sincerity. Relief unexpectedly rushed through Nell. She'd thought avoiding any mention of what had happened or not happened between them would have been better. It hadn't occurred to her that it could actually make things more awkward.

Clearing the air sounded like a far more preferable solution.

'Sure.' Turning to lead the way across the atrium floor, she headed for an empty table at the unusually quiet coffee shop and sat down.

And it was strange, wasn't it, how both a chaos and a kind of stillness washed over her at the very same time? Even her very blood felt as though it had begun to effervesce thrillingly in her veins, every particle in her anatomy hurtling dizzyingly into the path of another—like nothing she'd ever, *ever*, experienced before.

'First of all, I should apologise for the other night.'

And still her heart raced.

Should apologise? Or *was* he apologising? Or was the difference only in her head? As though he was apologising because he felt he ought to, not because he regretted kissing her? And maybe it was semantics, but she couldn't seem to help it; there was no denying the chemistry between them.

Yet pursuing anything beyond a professional relationship with Connor would surely only lead to trouble.

'I understand that things might initially be a bit awkward between us,' Connor said, breaking the silence. 'But if nothing else then today proved we work together well—professionally speaking.'

'We do,' she concurred.

Working with him to help their patient, James, had felt seamless—as it had with the patients they'd worked on before that...*interlude* between them back at her cottage. If she could just keep her thoughts in the professional arena rather than straying as they seemed to have a tendency to do these days. Namely, right back to the way his hands had felt on her skin, back to that vaguely spicy taste of his lips, back to the wantonness of her soft body pressed against the sheer male hardness of his.

Her entire body was already heating up at the memory. With an outstanding effort, Nell snapped her attention back to Connor.

'Why don't we put what happened the other night down to a momentary lapse in judgement? I value you as a colleague and I usually make it my business not to blur those lines. I suspect you do the same.'

She tried not to wrinkle her nose. He was entirely correct in his assessment of her—she'd only ever dated Jonathon, she'd never worked alongside him—and she supposed she should have been gratified in Connor's opinion of her. But somehow it only made her feel all the more frustrated.

'I do,' she said instead, though she wasn't certain she'd succeeded in keeping her voice completely steady.

Then again, his words seemed so careful. So formulaic. Was it possible that he was struggling as much as she was with the idea that there was still something...*unfinished* between them? Or was she imagining that, too?

'So, that's agreed, then?' His eyes held hers intently. 'We'll keep things exclusively professional from now on? Patients, and the hospital.'

'Of course.'

It was definitely for the best. Colleagues, and nothing more. If only she didn't fear it might require more willpower than she had. But if there was a voice in him that whispered about maybe wanting more—just as it needled in her—then he gave no indication.

'Right.' He inclined his head but made no move to stand up. Neither, Nell noted, did she.

'And Vivian,' she heard herself add.

His forehead furrowed. Those two tiny lines right in the centre of his eyebrows that made her palms itch with the urge to trace them.

'Sorry?'

'Keeping things professional,' she reminded him. 'Patients, the hospital, and Vivian.'

He blinked. Slowly. Uncharacteristically.

'And Vivian,' he conceded after a moment. 'Yes, we need to work together for her, too.'

And that tension between them felt ramped as high as ever. Especially when neither of them seemed able to bring themselves to move even a muscle. Should she say something? Excuse herself back to work?

'I had intended to visit her after work.' Connor spoke just as she had willed herself to stand up. 'Or will you be going?'

She shook her head.

'I have to sort out the stall for the village's summer fete. Little Meadwood's Big Fete.'

'Ah, yes. Vintage clothing, wasn't it?'

'Right.' She was surprised he remembered.

'How is it going?'

'Well, I think I have most of the clothing together, though I ended up going in a bit of a steampunk direction in the end, but it's the actual build of stall that is proving a sticking point. I never was much of a DIY-er.'

'Would you like me to take a look?'

'You?' Her voice came out slightly higher pitched than she'd intended—hardly a surprise given that he was the last person she had expected to offer to help. Hastily, she sought to cover it up. 'What about keeping professional boundaries?'

'This is for Vivian.' He didn't shrug precisely, but there was some approximation of it. 'If she wants you to have a stall, then I can build it for you.'

'Right. Great. Still… I didn't know you were a builder.'

'I've been known to be handy with a drill or a saw. I've built cabinets, bookcases, and even constructed a new oak staircase once.'

She had to admit, the idea of having Connor's help appealed—though only for the *build* side of things, of course. Not because any part of her was that desperate to spend time with him.

'Are you trying to get brownie points from Vivian?' She sidestepped that line of thought immediately.

But there was no avoiding that delicious ripple that coursed through her when the corners of Connor's mouth turned up wryly.

'Naturally.'

Nell chuckled, shaking her head, glad that he retained his sense of humour despite the earlier awkwardness between them.

'Well, I certainly won't complain about the extra help.'

'Good.' Connor stood up, stunning her with a smile that was so different from the intensity of moments earlier. As if that had been the restrained Connor and this was now the real one. 'We'll make it the best stall at the fair.'

His grin was so infectious that Nell found herself smiling in response.

'Competitive much?'

'I make no apologies for it.' He laughed. The sound echoing thrillingly inside her as if mocking her earlier claims of just being friends. 'So, we'll start this weekend? Unless you're on duty.'

'I'm not,' she confirmed, urgently trying to slow her racing heart.

'Then this weekend it is.'

Before she could respond, he was walking away. Heading out of the opposite side of the atrium to where she needed to be, and yet the connection between them might as well have been a neon cord tying them together.

She really did need to get a grip. She couldn't help but be drawn to his confidence and competence, and, despite her earlier promise to herself, there was no ignoring the embers of attraction that still smouldered and crackled between them.

And unless she took major steps to control it, *that*, Nell decided firmly, threatened to derail the *professional relationship* they'd just agreed was paramount.

CHAPTER EIGHT

NELL WAS JUGGLING with the steampunk outfits, brass goggles and leather corsets that had spilled out of the stuffed bags and boxes and all over the boot of her car when she heard Connor's motorbike roaring down the lane towards her.

A tingle shot instantly down her spine. Not even a minute in and she was already failing at the 'keeping things strictly professional' part of the deal.

Great start, Nell.

Keeping her eyes focused on the goods, she set about shoving another purple corset and lace-up boot back into a bag as she pretended not to notice Connor pull up a few parking bays away and swing one motorbike-suited, muscular leg over his machine. Did he really have to be so attractive?

'Morning,' he called cheerily as he removed his sleek, aerodynamic crash helmet. 'Good day for it.'

'Great day,' she agreed, forcing a bright smile of her own. 'Forecast says it's going to be warm but not too hot, which is great if we're going to be working.'

'I heard. I even made a batch of Vivian's old summer mocktail recipe.'

'Really?' She straightened up as he headed over. 'That's amazing. So what's in the bag?'

'You said the theme was steampunk?' he checked, nodding as she waved her hand to the outfits in her car. 'Great, so I brought mechanical parts, cogs, tarnishing spray, all kinds of goodies.'

Nell peered into the bag he was opening up, caught off guard.

'That's a great idea. We can fix it around as decor.'

'Right.' Connor nodded. 'And I also thought the customers will need privacy to change into their steampunk costumes, so I could make some Shoji-like screens and tie them into the theme with cogs on the front.'

It took Nell a moment to regroup.

'That,' she told him sincerely, 'is a brilliant idea.'

'Seems like this is a bigger village fete than I ever remember it being,' Connor noted, heaving the bag onto his broad shoulders before leaning down to help her stuff the rest of the gear back into the boxes in her boot. 'I seem to remember it being quite a small community event.'

'It was,' she said with a sniff. 'It used to be quite a small, intimate affair, the kind where everyone knew everyone else. But with the new housing estates and the influx of new people to the area, it has become gradually bigger and flashier. In some ways that's good because it brings much-needed money into the village, but in another way it makes it more stressful because it's still up to the village committee to organise these events that now have to cater to hundreds. Even a thousand.'

'Looks like we have our work cut out for us, then.' Connor dipped his head, giving the impression that he wasn't the least bit fazed.

He probably wasn't. This was a man who looked as though he could handle anything.

Even, it seemed, being back in Little Meadwood after so many years of keeping his distance.

As they headed over to the old pavilion where the old stalls and timber were kept, Nell couldn't help but sneak glances at Connor out of the corner of her eye. He was carrying her boxes with complete ease, the muscles in his arms rippling as he expertly shifted them around. With his black leather motorcycle gear and aviator shades, he looked as though he had stepped straight out of being the stuntman for some action movie.

Of course he did.

Clucking her tongue in self-reproach, she tried to keep her mind on the task at hand. They needed to pick their stall, get it set up to see what needed repairing or replacing, and then start to add their decorations in a way that would make it bespoke for their theme. And woe betide them if they let Vivian down. It didn't help that there was already a considerable amount of activity by the pavilion; other villagers who clearly had the same idea to try to bag the better stall for themselves and avoid having to do complicated, time-consuming repairs.

'Plenty of people here.' He gritted his teeth, and she couldn't help but notice how Connor's eyes were roaming everywhere.

Was this just his natural tendency to observe his surroundings or something more deliberate? An overhang from his military days, possibly.

'Do you want to leave? You don't have to help me, you know.'

And whatever had been bugging Connor, he seemed to regroup quickly.

'It isn't a problem,' he answered smoothly, setting down their gear on a good, flat area of land. 'Let's get to work.'

'Okay, then.' And just like that Nell felt a shiver of excitement at the prospect of tackling this challenge together.

Quickly and efficiently, Connor began to delve through the remaining stalls to decide which one was in the best shape before setting out his toolkit to begin assembling the structure. Nell, meanwhile, felt completely on the back foot as she fumbled with various pieces of wood and struggled to get anything to stay in place.

'Here, let me help,' Connor said, coming over to her and

grasping her hand. A jolt of electricity shot up her arm at the contact, though she instructed herself to ignore it as he led her through the steps of assembling the stall. They worked in silence for a while, each lost in their own thoughts, until Connor spoke up.

'You know, Nell, I never would have taken you for a steampunk aficionado,' he said, glancing over at her.

She looked up at him, surprised. 'What do you mean?'

'I don't know, I guess I just never would have imagined you being into something so…alternative,' he said with a grin.

Nell feigned an indignant laugh. 'What's wrong with being different?'

'Not one thing,' he replied, returning to his task, though she hadn't missed the teasing glint in his eyes. 'Truth be told, I think it's hot.'

Heat suffused her cheeks at the compliment and she couldn't stop herself from stealing another glance at him before turning away to busy herself rearranging the tools.

'The rest of these screwheads are too chewed up to use.' He sighed. 'I think I might need to invest in some supplies. Is Jay's hardware shop still around?'

Nell shook her head sadly.

'No, he died and his son sold up and moved away. However, there's a big chain in the city who usually send us stuff each year. I think you'll find boxes of screws and nails, and maybe hinges, on the metal racks at the back of the pavilion. Plus, there are recycling bins for junk. Metal in one for scrapyard sales, and another one for wood that could go towards the Bonfire Night celebrations.'

'Wow, it's all go here at Little Meadwood, isn't it?'

'We've tried to move with the times,' she agreed, grateful they were back to less awkward conversation. The longer they worked together, the more she realised that Connor's easy banter and infectious laugh were the perfect antidote to the stress of building their stall. It should definitely make it easier to work around the hospital with him, without her mind constantly creeping back to that night together.

Nell felt a flutter in her stomach at his smile. She quickly shook her head, trying to push the thought away. She was here to work, not to get involved with Connor. But when his hand brushed against hers as they both reached for the same screwdriver, she couldn't help but feel that familiar spark of electricity between them. Especially when the summer day began to heat up and Connor stripped down to a simple black sleeveless tee, his lean muscles rippling in a way that made it almost impossible for her to concentrate on her own tasks.

All he needed was a can of pop, a rock-song soundtrack, and he could have been the next hot advert.

She shook her head as if to dislodge the X-rated image and forced herself to focus on her job. Easier said than done.

Bit by bit, they organised their stall, unloaded more from the boxes and bags in her car. With Connor's expertise and Nell's eye for detail, they soon had the steampunk-themed decor up and running like clockwork. They even managed to add a touch of Victorian class with an antique mirror and a few brass lamps. It was perfect.

Finally they stepped back to admire their handiwork.

'It looks amazing,' she breathed proudly.

'It does,' he agreed, lifting one dusty forearm to wipe a bead of sweat from above his eyebrow. 'I have to say that I think we make a pretty good team.'

Nell laughed. 'Not that I'm surprised, but I do have to admit it's been fun working with you. It's been a while since I've had such a good laugh.'

'Well, I'm glad to be here to remind you to have some fun.'

'And I'm glad to be reminded that you're more than capable of handling anything thrown your way,' she added, shooting him a sly smile.

Connor's eyes shone with amusement. 'I have my moments.'

Nell rolled her eyes. 'You're too modest. You're probably one of the most capable people I know.'

'Flattery will get you everywhere,' he replied with a chuckle.

Nell laughed and nudged his shoulder playfully. 'Don't get too full of yourself now.'

They stood there for a moment longer, admiring their hand-iwork, before Nell sighed and turned to him. 'Well, I guess that's it. We're all set up.'

'Looks like it, yeah,' he agreed, glancing around at the other stalls that were still being assembled. 'Photo for Vivian.'

'That's a great idea.'

Scurrying over to her bag, she retrieved her phone and then they both positioned themselves in front of the stall. She wasn't prepared for him to lean in closer to her and wrap his arm around her waist—hopefully he wouldn't notice that she slowed down a little to take the photo, indulging in the unex-pected moment.

Was it just her imagination that he also seemed to linger a little?

'I should probably get going,' she told him reluctantly when they finally moved back apart. 'I have a list of things to pick up from the shop, and I don't want to keep her waiting.'

Connor nodded. 'I'll help you pack up and get everything to your car.'

Nell nodded uncertainly and they set to work, carefully dismantling the stall and setting it in a bay where she chalked their names on the board. Any loose decor was packed back into the boxes and stacked in the same bay to make it easier on the set-up weekend. And then all that was left was to load the remaining supplies into Nell's car and say their goodbyes. But instead of each of them returning to their vehicles, she hov-ered by the open door of her car as he leaned his bottom on her bonnet, his impossibly long legs stretched out in front of him.

'Well, thanks for a more entertaining day than I was expecting.'

'You're…welcome?' she hazarded with another laugh and tipped her face upwards.

Despite the warmth of the summer sun on her face all she could feel was the cold regret that the day was over. Being with Connor had been fun: natural and effortless. She didn't want it to end.

He shifted on the bonnet, his eyes meeting hers, and she felt the energy between them once again.

'Seriously though, Nell, I had a really great time.'

'Me too,' she replied softly, her heart thudding in her chest. 'I'm almost sorry it's over.'

He offered a lopsided grin. 'Who says it has to be over?'

Nell's eyes widened in surprise, and she stared at him in confusion. 'What do you mean?'

Connor shrugged.

'Maybe we should end the successful day with a drink? Celebrate a job well done?'

Nell hesitated, the logical part of her brain telling her that this was a bad idea. But the rest of her was screaming *yes*. She hadn't been on a date in months, hadn't felt this kind of attraction to someone in even longer. And she was tired of letting her fears hold her back.

'Okay,' she said finally, trying to keep her voice calm and steady. 'I'd like that.'

Connor's smile widened, and he hopped off the bonnet, coming closer to her. 'Great. I'll see you later?'

Nell nodded, her heart beating faster with each passing moment. 'Sounds good but where? The Willow Tree pub?'

'No. Nothing local. How about heading back to town? There's a bar by the river I've heard is good.'

'Okay.' She glanced over at his bike, then down at her

clothes. 'I need a shower and change first. Should I meet you there?'

He flashed a smile.

'I wouldn't mind a shower, either. How about I pick you up in a couple of hours?'

'On your motorbike?' She looked dubious.

'It's a great bike.' Connor laughed. 'Plus, I have a spare crash helmet.'

Was he joking?

'I don't know what I'm supposed to wear to ride a motorbike,' she hedged. 'I guess I can just leave my hair in a ponytail?'

A grin tugged at his lips.

'Relax. I'm only teasing. Wear whatever you want. I'll ditch the bike back at the hospital and I'll pick you up in a taxi.'

'Oh, I should just meet you there. You don't have to go to that much trouble.'

'I want to.'

She tried not to look too thrilled. He'd clearly thought this through—it wasn't just an offhand invitation.

'Okay. Great.'

As Connor crossed over to his motorbike to head back to the city to clean up, Nell leaned against the door frame of her car, feeling the cool metal press against her overheated skin. The idea of having a drink with Connor felt ridiculously exciting. More than exciting, actually. It felt like something she had been missing out on for a long time.

How was it that she felt so changed from herself every time Connor Mason was near? As if she were caught up in a thrilling whirlwind every time he was in the vicinity.

As if he *were* the whirlwind.

And maybe that was what she needed right now—as long as she remembered not to get too deeply involved. It was just fun. After all, she was rooted in Little Meadwood; it was where her foster family were, where her friends were, where her career was. Connor, on the other hand, was just passing through. A proverbial rolling stone on the lookout for his next adventure. The very opposite of her.

Which, she conceded, might have been one of the reasons she felt so drawn to this transient soul. Connor's free spirit seemed to have ignited a restless fire in her that she hadn't ever realised was there before. A reminder that life was meant to be lived. And it had made her begin to question whether Jonathon might have been right all along when he'd accused her of hiding out in Little Meadwood.

She'd sunk into its relative safety the day she'd been brought here after her parents' deaths. It had been both her comfort and her safety net, and Vivian had always been there to catch her if she fell.

But now, as Nell stood there, contemplating the possibilities of a night out with Connor, she couldn't help but wonder if it was time to let go of that safety net and take a leap of faith.

Even if just this once.

'I've never been here before,' Nell admitted as they walked down the quayside where the taxi had dropped them off, to the trendy bar he'd chosen.

'Neither have I.' He grinned. 'I've just seen it a few times when out running in the evening, thought it looked good and heard a couple of positive reviews. The view is definitely worth seeing.'

'It is,' she agreed, standing with him for a moment to appreciate the lights shimmering across the water.

With only the low bass line of faraway music floating on the air, it was a peaceful and calming summer evening.

Or at least, it should have been peaceful and calming, if only Nell didn't faze him in that intrinsic way of hers. He didn't want to notice it, certainly not allow himself to get caught up by it. Yet nor could he seem to ignore it, and pretend it wasn't there, this pull that he felt towards her.

And right now, those stunning morpho-blue pools of hers sparkled in the marine light, holding an expression that he didn't care to examine but that made his chest ache all the same.

They moved off again, walked in silence towards the bar and Connor couldn't help but feel as if he was walking into dangerous territory. No matter how much he reminded himself that pursuing anything with Nell was a bad idea, he couldn't keep his eyes off her. Not least the way her dress hugged her curves in all the right places as she weaved her way through the crowd.

He would far, far rather have been somewhere else with her. Somewhere they could be alone. Private.

God, he was in trouble.

The bar was larger than he'd expected, the sounds of laughter and music filling the air as they boarded. Couples and groups of friends were scattered across the floor, drinks in hand, dancing to the beat of the music. And then Nell seemed to recognise one group, greeting them with a smile and a hug. Connor watched her, fascinated by the way she moved so gracefully and effortlessly—so unlike the guarded way he was around strangers. She was a breath of fresh air. Her laugh was infectious, her conversation was witty and intelligent, and her touch sent the most delicious shivers coursing through him. He couldn't remember the last time he had felt such a strong connection with someone, and it scared him.

Or it ought to have done.

But before he could consider that further someone jostled against Nell, propelling her forwards into his arms. And he ought to be more concerned that the urge to kiss her was almost dangerously overwhelming. One tiny tilt of his head and he could capture her mouth all too easily, tasting those deliciously plump lips that were too perfectly pink for their own good.

But he couldn't. He mustn't. It was too risky, too danger-ous, and everything that he'd warned himself about.

And yet he was the one who had invited her out for a drink.

Still, their bodies shifted and swayed together—the perfect fit. And before he realised it, they were dancing right there on the floor amongst the other couples, whilst this fire inside him burned hotter, brighter, consuming him as it made it im-possible for him to think of anything else.

'Are you okay?' Nell murmured, her warm breath teasing his neck as though she sensed his inner turmoil.

'Fine,' he managed, not trusting himself to say anything more than that.

He ought to stop this now. Step away from her.

Instead he stayed exactly where he was with his arms wrapped around her delectable body, and his mind pushing that warning voice further and further back until it was too muffled to hear. And perhaps they stayed like that for ten min-utes, perhaps ten lifetimes.

Connor had no idea how he finally managed to break apart.

'So, what can I get you to drink?'

And what did it say that he enveloped her hand in his as they made their way to the bar, and neither of them made any attempt to let go, even when the crowd was so thick that they'd had to crush together? By the time they reached the bar, Nell's body was still pressed up against his and he was wholly caught up in the magic of it.

In a daze that he wanted never to end.

Before he could stop himself, Connor leaned in closer, his lips brushing against her ear, and when Nell pulled her head back to look up at him, her blue eyes so dark that he thought they might almost be black, his fragile resolve crumbled com-pletely and he finally dipped his head to hers. Possibly the gentlest, most tender kiss he'd ever given any woman before—yet it held all the unspoken words between them. Nell's lips were so soft, so pliant as she kissed him back, so gloriously inviting that they made his heart race enough that he didn't think he could remember his own name.

Enough to make the rest of the bar—the rest of the world—disappear.

But then a loud cry abruptly shattered the peace. A woman's voice, high-pitched and panicked, screaming for a doctor.

Nell and Connor sprang apart abruptly, and Connor pushed through the already shifting crowd before exiting the bar and turning down the quayside in the direction of the cry. Instinct told him that Nell wasn't far behind. Sprinting together, they soon reached a small crowd gathering around and on the steps of a small houseboat and pushed their way through the gathering people until they finally saw her—a woman in her late fifties, perhaps, with a bloodied sundress and an ashen face, kneeling over a boy, maybe ten years old, who was lying motionless on the deck of the boat.

'Let us through, please,' Connor commanded, leading the way as he clambered aboard with Nell. 'We're doctors.'

'Are you the mother?' he ascertained even as he raced to the child to begin his initial assessment.

Behind him, Nell was lifting her voice to address the crowd.

'Has someone called for an ambulance? Okay, you, sir, with that phone…yes, you. Call emergency services and tell them that we have an unconscious child, and give them the location to get an ambulance en route. Then stay on the line to them and wait for us to feed you more information. Got it? Great.'

Dimly, Connor heard Nell's commands but he had concerns of his own. It was clear the boy had been stabbed—by the looks of it with a long, wide blade. Connor grabbed a nearby tea towel to staunch the bleeding even as his eyes darted around for a weapon. The last thing he wanted to do was to put Nell in any danger.

'What happened here?' he demanded sharply to the mother.

Connor was aware of Nell dealing with the growing crowd of onlookers.

'My h-h-husband was just making us a drink,' the woman hiccupped. 'I w-wanted lemon so he went to cut one. He was carrying the knife. He…fell down those steps just as…just as our son came out of his bedroom.'

Connor glanced around again. A couple of lemons were lodged against the baseboards of the kitchen area, as well as a long knife. The half-prepped drinks were still on the counter, and a cuddly toy was lying, dropped, by the dining table.

'Where's your husband now?'

'I…don't know…' The woman looked stunned. Clearly her priority had been her son. 'He fell.'

'He's here,' Nell exclaimed, hurrying across the deck to the floor on the other side of the counter, out of Connor's line of sight. 'Unconscious, with an open head injury.'

'Update the operator,' Connor instructed the man with the phone, watching as Nell began her ABCs.

'Did he fall, or did he trip, then fall?' Connor asked quickly.

If the man tripped, that was one thing. But if he tripped then fell, there could be an underlying issue. Heart attack, stroke—the list was long.

'He…tripped.'

The woman was beginning to cry again, and Connor took care to keep his voice calm and kind, but firm.

'Do you have a first-aid kit?'

The woman gave a jerky nod.

'Good. You need to get your first-aid kit. And some towels. Hurry.'

'Ambulance is on its way,' the man in the crowd called out.

'Make sure they send two.' Connor lifted his head as the man nodded in acknowledgement.

'Airway, breathing, circulation all okay here,' Nell called as quietly as she could. 'Looks like he slammed his head on the corner of the unit as he fell. I think he's starting to come around, but as soon as the wife comes back I'll get her to keep his head and shoulders slightly elevated.'

'The boy has just stopped breathing,' Connor muttered in a low voice, turning his attention back to their unexpected patient. 'We need to perform CPR.'

Nodding wordlessly, Nell carefully moved her patient into a safe position before hurrying across the floor to sit herself by the boy's head whilst Connor began chest compressions. He was counting under his breath as he went and she counted with him, thirty compressions followed by two rescue breaths.

Then again.

And again.

And again.

But the CPR wasn't working.

'First-aid kit.' The woman reappeared, thrusting it to them with shaking hands. 'It's a good one. My husband always insisted on good first-aid kits.'

'First ambulance is twenty minutes out,' the phone man called out at that moment.

'You need to do something.' Connor sensed, rather than saw, Nell's gaze on him. 'The kid doesn't have twenty minutes.'

He had already come to the same conclusion. There was only one option left to him.

'Get everyone out of here,' he murmured to Nell. 'Including the mother.'

Nell offered a silent nod. They both knew that cutting through the sternum would make a noise that no parent should ever have to hear. Though he suspected little could be worse than the absolute silence on the boat at this moment.

Connor worked quickly and methodically, prepping the boy for the emergency surgery and sterilising his hands, and whatever tools he could find to perform the operation. At least the kit contained a few pairs of surgical gloves. Behind him, he heard Nell command everyone off the vessel, returning sooner than he'd expected with two more strangers in tow.

'We've got two nurses from City,' Nell explained quickly. 'They were in a nearby restaurant when they heard the shouts.'

'Great,' Connor acknowledged with a quick nod. 'Thanks for heading over. Could one of you take over care of the male and the other keep the mother out of the way? Nell, you're here with me.'

Having both his and Nell's full attention on the boy was a much better scenario, and as the two nurses efficiently took up their roles he felt more comfortable focusing on his own patient.

'Okay, here we go.'

Working quickly and methodically, Connor began to cut open the boy's chest with Nell instinctively moving to help, holding the lungs clear as he took care to avoid the phrenic and intercostal nerves.

'Just move your left hand here,' he indicated after a moment. 'I can't afford to risk any injury to the pulmonary vessels right there. Yes, good.'

They worked seamlessly together until the young boy's heart was finally exposed and Connor could begin compressions directly onto the organ.

One...
Two...
Three...
Four...
Five...

And the boy was back with them, that welcome sight of the young heart pulsing back into life. Relief coursed through him, and from the emotion in Nell's expressive blue eyes when they snagged his, she was feeling just as charged.

'The paramedics are here.' One of the nurses suddenly appeared by their sides, and he realised that several more people were now on the deck, standing out of the way but ready to step in whenever he gave them the all-clear. 'The father has already gone with the first crew.'

'Right.' Connor nodded, his eyes not leaving his patient.

'They're going to need you to be with the boy in the ambulance,' Nell muttered in a low voice.

'Of course,' Connor agreed. 'But it won't be an easy journey either way. Okay, just put your hands exactly where mine are now. No, a little more…yes. There. Hold steady like that.'

He didn't need to voice the words to tell her that the chances of the boy surviving the ambulance ride to the hospital weren't all that good.

CHAPTER NINE

'I HOPE HE makes it.' Nell heaved a deep breath as she and Connor headed out of the hospital doors half an hour later. The paramedic driving had manoeuvred the ambulance through the mercifully quiet roads like some world-class driver, and they had miraculously got the boy to the hospital without further incident. The on-call trauma surgeon had swept the boy straight into surgery, and he was being operated on even at that moment.

'Time will tell,' Connor replied carefully.

His standard response, but she knew that in surgery it was often the only real truth. Her mind searched for something else to add, and it took her a moment to realise that Connor had stopped walking.

'I should have thought to book a taxi back to Little Meadwood whilst we were inside.'

'Good point.'

It hadn't even crossed her mind. The truth was she didn't even want to go. Too much energy ran through her veins; she was far too agitated and fidgety.

At least that was what she told herself.

'I'll go back in and call.'

It shouldn't have taken her so much effort to force her legs into action to walk away.

'Wait.' She'd stopped even before he'd finished the command. 'There's blood on your dress. And your jacket thing.'

'It's a bolero,' she answered as her hand flew instinctively to the fabric—more for something to say than anything else.

She glanced down at herself in dismay. She was very aware of what she had been through just moments before and, looking down, there was a stark reminder of it on her clothes.

'Ah, a taxi driver might not be too happy about me getting in like this.'

'Do you have spare clothes in your locker?'

'Usually.' Her smile was rueful. 'But I took them home yesterday to freshen them all up. I figured I'd take them back when I'm on shift on Monday.'

Connor didn't answer at first, his eyes scanning around them as if he was deciding on the best solution.

'You could come back to mine,' he offered at length, indicating the accommodation block just across the park. 'We can get the worst of the stain out and call a taxi.'

'That would be great.' She flashed him a bright smile, as though she were oblivious to the flutter of nerves in her stomach.

The night had been unexpectedly chaotic, but now she was coming down from the adrenalin of it, Nell found her thoughts were winding their way back to the kiss she and Connor had shared moments before they'd heard that first scream. As they began to walk through the prettily lit park, her heart was thumping harder and harder as if in anticipation.

Life was so damned short. Hadn't tonight been a stark reminder of that?

Nell couldn't keep denying the attraction between the two of them. More to the point, she didn't want to.

And then, they were there. And Connor was unlocking the door of his apartment and standing back to allow her to go in first.

The suite was like nothing she'd imagined. Surgeons' quarters or not, it was certainly unlike any of the hospital accommodation she'd stayed in during her training.

'This place is stunning,' she exclaimed.

Sharp, clean lines ran through the walls, ceilings, all converging on a large picture window that framed the park through which they'd just walked, with the hospital lights twinkling beyond. Like one of the most artistic urban pictures. Clearly not all the apartments would be like this one—this one was reserved for surgeons like Connor—but even so, the building was impressive.

'You've never been in here before?' Connor frowned.

'No. I saw it being built, of course, and I saw the architectural drawings.'

'Understood.' He nodded, striding through to the kitchen and reaching to a sleek, push-to-open cupboard. 'I'll get something to clean up those stains.'

A moment later he turned back carrying a damp cloth and a bottle of stain remover.

'You deal with your dress, and I'll take care of your…what did you call it…bolero thing?'

She nodded mutely, shrugging it off and handing it to him as surprise coursed through her. But even as she began dealing with the bloodstains on her dress it was impossible to stop her eyes from sliding to Connor as he worked. The muscles that rippled beneath his shirt made her cheeks flush with heat, reminding her of the sight of his bare chest that night in her cottage.

As if sensing her gaze, he lifted his head and, to her chagrin, caught her staring.

Too late, she snatched her gaze away, the heat in her cheeks growing hotter by the second.

'Sorry,' she mumbled, not even certain what she was apologising for.

She certainly wasn't prepared when he reached out and took her chin in his hand, turning her face back towards him.

'Don't be,' he said, his voice low, urgent. 'I like it when you look at me like that.'

And then, before she could register what was happening, Connor leaned in and kissed her. Warm, soft lips that sent jolts of electricity shooting through her body. For a moment, she was lost in the sensation, forgetting everything else.

But then, just as suddenly, he pulled back.

'I shouldn't have done that,' he said, his eyes troubled. 'I'm sorry.'

Nell felt a pang of disappointment.

'No,' she murmured firmly. 'Not again.'

'Not again, what?'

'You can't keep starting and stopping something over and over again,' she told him urgently. 'It's like a gravity ride, throwing me around everywhere until I'm dizzy and disorientated, not knowing which way is even up.'

'So, you wanted me to stop?' he gritted out, as if fighting himself more than her.

Sensations jostled in her chest.

'No,' she whispered. 'I want to know you *won't* stop. Not this time.'

Connor lifted his hand to her face, his thumb gently brushing over her cheekbone, his eyes practically black with desire.

'You're sure?'

'I'm sure.'

She'd barely even finished before he was lowering his head, his mouth claiming hers. Fierce, fiery, and full of passion. And all she could do was melt against the solid wall of his chest, melding her body to his, feeling herself grow weak yet powerful all at the same time. His mouth moved over hers, his tongue sliding expertly over her lips, teasing and coaxing as she parted them to let him inside. She clung to him, her fingers biting into the muscular lines of his shoulders as though if she let go, she might tumble into the fire within, even as she felt the flames lick at her and begin to consume her from the inside out.

Slowly, painstakingly, his hands started their exploration of her body, as if they had all the time in the world and he intended to use every millisecond of it getting every single inch of her in the most intimate detail. It was so gloriously indulgent that at one point she thought she forgot even to breathe. Connor's fingers trailed over her skin like a thousand tiny sparks sprinkled liberally over every line, every curve of her flesh. She found herself arching into his touch, an almost feverish anticipation making her body tremble. He traced whorls over her back, brushed patterns down each of her sides in turn, and slid his fingertips over the dip of her throat where his thumbpad made long, slow circles, making her feel like some exotic flower blooming for the first time in a century.

And when he buried his head to lay a wreath of kisses down the column of her neck from her ear to her shoulder, each one made her quiver that little bit more, sending her further and further to places she'd never been before.

Not like this.

There was something about him that was deeply intense, and he seemed to be leaving his mark upon her. Her thoughts, that the last thing she needed was another roller-coaster romance, seemed to be at odds with the way she felt.

But this connection between them was powerful and fierce, and it was impossible to deny it.

Nell wound her arms around his neck, pulling him closer. No matter how long they touched, tasted, explored, it didn't seem to be enough. The yawning ache in her just kept growing, wanting more. And more again. He was like a summer storm—thunder and lightning, rain and wind, all hurtling together, crashing and exploding around them until they found themselves in the very centre…in that perfect calmness as he lifted his mouth from hers, breaking contact.

Then he rested his forehead against hers, his eyes like bottomless depths, in which she could almost imagine she saw a future.

She shoved the errant thought away and struggled to catch a breath.

'Stay here tonight,' he managed, his voice raw.

'I thought you'd never ask,' she replied with a shaky laugh.

The primal growl in his throat seemed to pool right *there*… at the apex of her legs.

In one smooth motion he was scooping her up into his arms and carrying her through to his bedroom. The soft light filtering through the windows casting flickering shadows and leaving a warm glow over the room. Gently, he laid her on the bed before standing over her. Taking her in as if she were his own personal gift that he was admiring before he even began to start opening it.

But the waiting was killing her, and before Nell could register what she was doing, she had lifted her hands to wind them around Connor's neck and draw him down on top of her.

'I'm sure I warned you not to stop,' she managed to tease, before pulling his lower lip into her mouth with just the right amount of tenderness and demand that made him groan in response.

As if he was nowhere near as in control as she'd thought he was. The knowledge gave her an unexpected boost.

'Take this off,' she managed huskily against his mouth, her fingers toying with the hem of his black tee.

'Now you're giving orders?' he rasped.

It took all she had to respond.

'I'm trying. You're not obeying.'

The look he shot her was practically searing. Making her feel white-hot inside before shattering her. If this was all they would ever have together, then it would be a night she could cherish for ever.

'I approve of this side of you.' His tone was guttural.

'Still not obeying.'

He drew back from her at last, and she felt the loss acutely. But then his gaze snared hers, long and hard, as his eyes narrowed over her. That wickedly sensuous mouth of his far too far away from her pleasure.

'Then consider me yours to command,' he bit out after what felt like an age. 'For now.'

Was he really serious? Lying there, his body covering hers, he was really going to let her call the shots?

'Strip off,' she instructed, barely recognising her own voice.

She hadn't been entirely convinced he would simply comply, but Nell found herself propping herself up on her elbows in disbelief as he slid his body off hers, hard masculine lines grating deliciously over her as he stood up at the end of the bed and did precisely that. First hooking his tee over his head to reveal the most sinful set of abs that Nell had spent the past few weeks thinking she must have surely imagined being so damned perfect.

And then he moved his hand to his belt, unbuckling it with such a tantalising sound that it defied belief. Her mouth felt parched as he hooked his thumbs over the waistband and pushed his trousers and boxers down, discarding them to the side. Standing there, naked and unabashed in front of her—not that anything about Connor Mason had ever seemed the slightest bit *abashed*. His desire for her on show for them both to see.

'Satisfied?' he demanded, amusement unmistakable in his voice.

She swallowed once. Twice. Flicking her tongue out of her suddenly dry lips.

'I hope so,' she just about managed.

As if an aching heat weren't pooling between her legs where she needed him most.

'And what about you?' Connor drawled. 'Are you going to remain so…overdressed?'

It took her several moments to realise that it was she who was breathing so heavily.

'I think I'll leave that to you,' she uttered at last.

And it was apparently all the encouragement Connor needed. Smoothly drawing her dress up her legs, he reached around to cup each of her thighs in each of his hands, before sliding down the bed towards her. Then, without the slightest preamble, he sank to the floor, hooked aside the scrap of lace that barely even pretended to cover her modesty, and sank his face between her legs.

Fireworks went off all around Nell in an instant.

Nothing, *no one*, had ever made her feel so sexy. So wanton. So wanted.

He licked her, teased her, and ran those long, lean fingers of his up her inner thighs and round to hold her backside, lifting her closer up towards him as if to give himself better access. Her hips could do nothing but undulate appreciatively under his control, bucking and writhing as if they had a life of their own. No restraints, no inhibitions, she was all his—and he knew it. Over and over, he brought her to the edge, then made her back off. He trailed kisses up one leg then down the other, lazy licks wreaking havoc on her senses, until he flicked one devastatingly skilled tongue where she needed him most. Sensations unlike any she'd experienced before skittered up and down and all around her, pleasure warring with an almost unbearable ache for more.

So much more.

Raw need scraped at her as she speared her hands through his hair. And finally, when she didn't think she could take it any longer, he slid his finger inside her, his mouth still licking, and tasting and toying. The waves began to build higher than ever; Connor stoking them with every sublime sweep of his roguish tongue.

And then, finally, with one skilful twist of his wrist, Nell felt her muscles tighten around him and her nails dig into the skin of his back as he tossed her over the edge and into the fires below. Hot, intense, and all-consuming.

All she could hope was that he'd be there to pull her out of them before they incinerated her completely.

Connor felt the shudder of Nell's orgasm ripple through her entire body, and a possessive heat raced through his veins.

All mine.

He pulled back to gaze into her face, watching her eyes slowly flutter open as the pleasure subsided. Slowly. Perfectly.

Her cheeks were flushed, her lips soft and parted, and the look of sheer bliss on her face made his chest swell. Something so primitive coursed through his veins, making his pulse race so hard that he was shocked it didn't rock the entire room.

But he was just a man—and never a very good man, at that—and the longer he watched her, the more his body ached to be inside. To join with her on whatever journey she was on right now. To make her scream his name even louder than he suspected she hadn't realised she'd cried out just now. The need to bury himself inside her—inside this particular, maddening woman—was almost his undoing. As if there were some caged beast inside him, raging and roaring and fighting to break free.

He would never know how he managed to wait for her to come back to earth again.

'What…' she seemed to be having trouble articulating her thoughts '…was…that?'

'That,' he growled, taking in the way she was subconsciously arching her body towards him as if still subtly begging for more, 'was starters.'

'Starters?' she echoed, dazedly.

'Starters. But this is the main course.'

And then he dispensed with her dress and the rest of her ridiculously flimsy, lacy underwear with a haste that might have been unseemly had he even cared about such propriety. Then, his brain just about reminding him in time to slip on protection, he covered her now naked body with his own.

Flesh to flesh. Hot and flawless. Just like his Nell.

He kissed one breast, then the other, letting both his fingers and his tongue explore the valley that parted them. And all the while, he used his tip to tease at her core. He dipped in, then out again, revelling in the way her hips rose with him in a silent plea for more. And he would never reveal to her just what it took not to plunge deeper, right there, right then.

But then, if he did that, how could he keep enjoying the motion, the pleasure, the connection?

The connection.

It felt like some kind of sacrament. Sacred and pure. Something that would only ever be meant for the two of them. The way their bodies melded as though they were tailor-made for each other.

He moved his hips, dipping in that little bit deeper before withdrawing again, taking them both higher. Faster. Indulging in the sheer pleasure of her slickness around him, and the way she gripped him, as if trying to stop him from leaving her.

'If this is the main course…' the words juddered out of Nell as she sighed '…then I don't think I'll ever look at another meal the same way again.'

'I'm counting on it,' he growled.

And then he thrust into her. Deep, and hard, and true. Rewarded when Nell threw her legs around his torso and locked her heels, her nails grazing his back as she held on. A thing of wondrous beauty that made him think that he could do anything…

If only this woman would be in his arms like this.

Every night.

For ever.

But that made no sense. Connor pushed the thoughts aside as he threw himself fully into the moment. Moving faster, deeper, building that tempo as he grazed one hand over the soft swell of her silken abdomen, making her tremble with need.

There was nothing about her that didn't fascinate him. That didn't call to the basest parts of him. She was everything he'd never known he wanted. And more. She made his world tilt and spin, yet at the same time she somehow made it make more sense than it ever had in his life before. The way she made him feel so intoxicated, with lights and colours spilling out of her and breathing life into his whole world.

So, what was he supposed to do with that knowledge?

And then it didn't matter because she groaned his name and every last thought slid from his head as he gave himself up to the hold she had over him. Every touch, every kiss, every thrust, and he still couldn't get enough of her; of their synchronised rhythm, and the way her body was wracked with pulses of need that made him feel powerful and humble all at once.

Finally, *finally*, Connor gave in to every last wild pull, throwing them both off the edge and hoping that they'd never have to reach the bottom.

Or that, at least, they'd manage to find a safe landing once it was all over.

CHAPTER TEN

NELL WOKE SOMETIME in the early hours.

Beside her, the bed was cold. Empty. Yet the room didn't feel as though she was alone.

Sitting up straight, she peered into the darkness—allowing her eyes time to adjust. And then she saw him. Silhouetted against the window by the moon's soft glow, his back to the bed whilst his focus seemed trained outside, into the blackness of the space, as if that was where he wished he could go.

Far away from City Hospital. Even further away from Little Meadwood.

'Connor?' She spoke his name quietly. 'Are you okay?'

He startled fractionally, as if he hadn't realised she'd woken.

'Fine.' His voice was gritty. 'I didn't intend to wake you. Go back to sleep.'

'Come back to bed, then,' she urged gently.

She heard, rather than saw, him brace his hands on the window frame.

'I can't promise this...*thing* between us can lead to anything.'

'I know that.'

He said he couldn't promise...but did that mean he was considering it? Her heart leapt before she could rein it in.

'I can't even promise how long I can stay. Not indefinitely, anyway.'

'I didn't ask for more than that.' She tried to sound lighter, airier, than she felt, though she wasn't sure he even heard her. 'Why do you hate Little Meadwood so much?'

She wasn't sure she knew what had made her ask, but the question had just seemed to tumble out.

There was a beat before he answered.

'Who said I hate it?' His voice was even and controlled. Perhaps *too* controlled.

'So, I'm wrong?'

The silence swirled around them for a long moment. So long that Nell slid her legs slowly round and got out of bed, moving across the bedroom to stand behind him. She half expected him to move away but when he didn't, she summoned all her courage and rested her chin against Connor's back. As though she could somehow lend him support.

'Is it because Little Meadwood reminds you of your mother?'

'My mother?' He half turned, his voice sharp. Catching her off guard.

'You came to Vivian after your mother died, didn't you?' she pointed out carefully. 'When you were six?'

And she couldn't have explained what it was that caused a shift in the silence so that it felt suddenly fraught. Loaded.

She shifted her weight from one foot to the other uncertainly, not really expecting him to answer.

'I do understand, you know. My parents' passing was how I came to have Vivian as a foster mother.'

'Except that you love Little Meadwood.' His voice was so low that she almost had to strain to hear. 'You've made a life there. To you, it's a bucolic place filled with happy memories.'

'I know you don't see it that way.'

'No, I do not,' he rasped. 'To me…it was a prison. One to which I swore I would never, *ever* return.'

He paused, as if choosing his words, but Nell simply waited. Giving him time.

'If it wasn't for Vivian—the one woman who has been probably the closest I've ever had to a maternal figure—I never would have come back.'

He shook his head. Hard. But she still didn't answer—she didn't want to risk interrupting him and causing him to clam up again.

'It's a small village where people are on top of each other, and everyone knows everyone else's business—moreover, everyone sticks their noses into everyone else's business.' Even in the low light she could see him twist his face up into an expression of disdain, his breath heaving as if he'd been out on one of his ten-mile runs. 'And the sins of a parent cling to a child, no matter how innocent that child might be. Or how innocent any child *ought to* be.'

Nell reached out as though to squeeze his shoulder but then decided better of it. She still didn't answer. The truth was that she didn't know what to say. Everybody knowing everybody else's business was one of the things she had always loved most about Little Meadwood. It had made her feel as though the place were just one big, close-knit family.

But she knew many of the other foster children hadn't shared her sentimentality.

'That place taught me the harsh lesson that when you're the dirty, half-feral kid of a single, junkie mother then, no matter what goes wrong in the village, you'll always be the first one to feel the jabbing fingers of blame. For nine years, from the age of six right up until that very last day, almost a decade later, I was the *outsider*. Never to be trusted.'

'Oh, Connor,' she whispered. This time her hand did manage to reach out to cup his upper arm.

As if that could somehow help.

'Someone left a gate open and Tom Rickman's prize bull escaped…?' he gritted out. 'Blame the Mason kid.'

She squeezed his arm but didn't speak.

'Someone stole a bunch of chocolate from the local corner shop?' he continued bitterly. 'That Mason boy was definitely spotted in the vicinity.'

'It wasn't always like that, was it?' she whispered, an incredible wave of sadness washing over her.

It had been so different for her.

'Always.' He snorted bitterly. 'Someone smoked a cigarette behind the cricket pavilion that doubled as a youth centre on the green and inadvertently set fire to the dried-out, rotten timber decking...?' This time, he pulled a grim face, despite himself. 'Well, okay, so that time I had actually been one of the lads stupid enough to be smoking there. But it hadn't been my discarded cigarette end.'

'I'm so sorry,' she managed at last, her voice thick with emotion.

She wasn't even sure if Connor heard her.

'But recently, I've been wondering what came first.' His voice was little more than a rasp. 'The village folk being right about me being rebellious, and *trouble* even as a six-year-old? Or the idea that they were going to blame me whether I was guilty or not, so I might as well be hung for a sheep as a lamb, as that old proverb goes?'

Nell wasn't sure how to answer that, or even if he expected her to answer. Still, she found herself murmuring as soothingly as she could.

'I know Vivian would never have believed that. I'm sure there were plenty of others in the village who wouldn't have either—not the way they speak about you.'

'No, Vivian always supported me.' He balled up his fists tighter. 'She was the kind of foster mother that a kid like me could only have dreamed of having—well, you know that for yourself. If it hadn't been for her kindness, I've never cared to imagine where I might have ended up. Certainly not with the kind of lifestyle I have now. I know that for a fact. And how did I repay her? By never visiting? By resenting the fact that her illness meant I had no choice but to come back to this infernal place?'

'By all accounts,' Nell replied gently, 'you've flown Vivian all around the world—to any number of far-flung places, over the years.'

He turned sharply, his eyes boring into hers in the moonlight.

'You know about that?'

'Vivian is incredibly proud of the man you've become. She knows it was your way of thanking her—not that she ever needed thanks, I know—but she loved that you both got that time together to reconnect.'

'Perhaps, but I didn't do it often enough.' He pulled a face. 'I did it a handful of times over twenty years. I didn't really make the time for her that I could have made.'

'You made all the time Vivian needed.' Nell shook her head. 'Even if you'd wanted to do it more frequently, she couldn't have. You have to remember that she was still fostering other kids—*me*, for a start.'

'I suppose,' he began uncertainly. As if he hadn't actually considered it before.

'The first time you were able to fly her somewhere, Ruby and I were sixteen,' Nell pressed her point home. 'Vivian almost didn't accept because she was worried about us but we were so excited because the respite centre that would look after us was in the city. Two sixteen-year-olds spending a week in the big, exciting city—we convinced her that a mere seven days' holiday with you would be no time at all.'

'I hadn't even thought of that,' he acknowledged slowly.

'The second time you flew her somewhere—Mexico, I think, because she wanted to see the river where one of her favourite movie scenes had been filmed—Ruby and I were already at uni, and the two foster children she had were siblings who had just been able to return to their mother after her operation had been successful. There were similar circumstances for the other occasions she flew out to meet you, though I know she turned down quite a few over the years because you know how her foster kids always came first.'

'I do,' he admitted tightly. 'And I have to confess that I knew the fostering would prevent her from coming more often. I think I used it as an excuse not to keep regular contact.'

'You had your own reasons.' Nell shook her head, but Connor wasn't listening.

'I knew she hoped I would return to Little Meadwood to visit and I didn't want to keep letting her down so I was more than willing to accept the disconnect,' he bit out, clearly ashamed. 'It made it easier to put that less than palatable first half of my life firmly into my rear-view mirror. Ultimately, I drifted away—and Vivian cared about me enough to let me.'

He was so obviously beating himself up over it that it crushed Nell.

'She would hardly blame you if you had such unhappy memories of the place,' she reassured him.

'Except that I no longer even know if those memories are real, or if I just allowed a few individuals to taint my recollection of everyone else. Until you came along.'

'Me?' That part shocked her.

'You made me realise that I had some better memories buried inside. Deep down, perhaps—but there all the same. Flashes of images, or conversations, which make me wonder if not everyone had once been as hostile to me as I've always thought.'

'Memories like what?' she asked, going against every instinct she had not to push him too hard, or too fast.

She practically held her breath until Connor answered her.

'Such as the time the owner of the Willow Tree pub had given all the foster kids free jugs of orange cordial at the fairs, because he'd known they couldn't afford any of the home-made summer punch drinks on sale.'

'Yes, I remember that.'

'Well, I'd forgotten. I don't know how. Or one time when one of the older, kindlier farmers—not Lester Jones—had invited me to spend a few weeks on his farm learning how to be a cowhand one summer before he retired. I remember really enjoying it—the hard work, the learning—but until now I'd forgotten it all. Buried the good memories right along with the bad.'

'I suspect that's why Vivian pushed so hard for you to return here after all this time.'

Nell couldn't keep the smile from colouring her words, even as Connor shook his head.

'She couldn't have known.'

'Don't be fooled by Vivian's physical weakness.' Nell laughed affectionately. 'She's shrewder than you realise. It's why we love her. Why we've always loved her.'

And he just stared in silence for what might have been an entire age, before he finally conceded in a strangled voice.

'Perhaps that might be true, if only I knew what it actually means to *love* someone.'

And, in that moment, she finally understood what it was that had kept Connor constrained all this time.

'You think you aren't capable of love,' she realised aloud. 'Oh, Connor, of course you are. You love Vivian. You love life. You're more than capable of love.'

Connor was caught wholly off guard by Nell's declaration.

The certainty shone through her words like the brightest, hottest desert sun, filling him up and making him feel less hollow. Less empty.

She made him feel more whole than he thought he'd ever felt. More alive. Happy.

He wasn't entirely sure he deserved it. Yet he did nothing to stop her, just as he hadn't done anything to stop it these past weeks. He wanted so badly to believe her, and to be with her. Which was ridiculous because he didn't do that. He didn't do intimacy. He couldn't even bring himself to reveal his whole truth to her now.

'I'm not, Nell,' he bit out cautiously. 'Not real love, anyway. I want to, but I can't. I never have been capable.'

'Why would you say that?'

And the care in her words crept inside him like a velvet fist. It dug up the words he could never have found for himself.

'I guess I have no idea what it looks like. Aside from Vivian, no one has ever loved me—even Vivian came along when it was too late, when I was already broken. Damaged beyond repair.'

'That isn't true—' Nell began, but he cut her off.

If she was going to give her heart to him, as it had felt as if she was starting to do, and he wanted nothing more than to take it and cherish it for ever, then surely she deserved to know the real truth about him? To decide if he was worth it?

He suspected she would conclude that he wasn't.

He forced himself to continue.

'I was abandoned as a kid, Nell. My mother was a drug addict who would have happily sold me for a score—actually she *did* sell me for a score. Twice. And who knows who my father was? Probably the dealer she slept with in order to buy her drugs.'

'Connor…'

'I was left to fend for myself at the age of four. Probably younger.' He ignored her horrified interruption, too afraid that if she was too shocked he wouldn't be able to carry on. He had never told anyone the story about his past before. 'I don't even know how I survived as a baby—how she didn't just forget about me when she was on her benders. I think it was a neighbour who used to check on me until my mother accused her of meddling, and then we moved—if you can call it that.'

'What do you mean?' Nell gripped his arm tighter. He could almost have imagined she was trying to steal his pain away for him. And he loved…no, not *loved*…he was *grateful* to her for that.

Which only made him more of a liar.

'My mother schooled me to help her lie and steal from a young age,' he growled. 'I'd be the distraction while she took what she could: food, clothes, money. Then, when she went on one of her benders, I would fend for myself. I learned how to survive, and in that world there was no room for love. It was a weakness, something that could be used against you. So, I buried those feelings deep, convinced myself that I didn't need anyone, that I was better off alone.'

'You were just a kid,' she breathed, staring at him as if her heart were actually breaking for him. As if he were worthy of that kind of emotion.

'When I was six, my mother took us both to a motel where she was going to score. She locked me in the bathroom, and then she overdosed. That was when I ended up with Vivian.'

'I'm so, so sorry for all you've been through.' The feel of her delicate hand on his shoulder was pleasure and agony all at once.

'You don't have to feel sorry for me, Nell,' he ground out. 'I don't need your pity.'

He thought he was steeled against any reply she might make. He was wrong.

'It isn't pity, Connor,' she told him softly. 'It's admiration. You've been through and coped with so much.'

'You can't admire someone like me,' he choked out. Shocked. Disgusted. Touched. He couldn't decide which.

'Too late. I already do.' She reached out to take his hand. 'But you need to know that you don't have to be alone any more. I'm here for you, always. And we can work through this together.'

And even as he opened his mouth to tell her that he didn't need that either, he found he couldn't say the words.

There was something else flowing through him that took a moment to pinpoint. Another moment to realise it was uncertainty. And the first flickering of hope.

'I...don't know if I can, Nell. I don't know if I'll ever be capable of love.'

But maybe, just maybe, he might be capable of something close, so long as he had someone like Nell by his side.

No, not someone *like* Nell. Nell.

Only Nell.

'You are, and you have so much love to give,' Nell countered, her voice gentle as her thumb rubbed softly against the fleshy part of his hand. 'You've proven that time and time again. When Vivian was sick, you gave up everything to be here for her. When I needed help with the fete, you immediately volunteered your services. You've been there for so many people, Connor. Don't you think it's time to let someone be there for you?'

Connor stared at her, turmoil twisting him inside out.

'I don't want to hurt you,' he whispered. 'I have so many regrets.'

'You know, you aren't the only one who is scared,' she whispered suddenly, and he couldn't say how he knew she hadn't known she'd intended to say anything until the words had already left her mouth. 'You aren't the only one with regrets.'

He swivelled his head then, his eyes searching hers.

'You? I thought you had a good childhood? Loving parents?'

'I did.' She swallowed tightly. As if fighting to get past some knotted ball that had just wedged itself in her throat. 'My parents were everything to me. But I...forgot it for a moment. Just at the worst time.'

'What happened, Nell?'

And it tugged at him that the concern that filled him was for her. As though she was right, and he really was capable of caring for her that much.

'I was thirteen and I'd just got my first boyfriend. They hated him. With hindsight, I can see exactly why—he was a rebel for the sake of being one, not because he truly believed in anything. He encouraged me to skip class to hang out down in the local town centre and busk for money instead.'

'You sang?'

'I played the violin. I was pretty good and I loved playing contemporary pop songs. He was using me, of course, using the money to buy cider, which he drank at the local bus stop, but I couldn't see it. I was just flattered by his attention, and desperate to have a boyfriend like the popular girls.'

'He doesn't sound worth it,' Connor growled, an unexpected fury raging through him at the idea of anybody using Nell like that.

'He wasn't. He certainly wasn't worth falling out with my parents over,' she agreed sadly. 'And I'd like to think I would have seen it for myself given just a little bit longer. But my parents stopped me from seeing him and I was devastated. I imagined myself in love. Thwarted. Like we were Romeo and Juliet. I told my parents that I hated them, and would never forgive them. I told them that I wished they weren't my parents.'

'Nell, you can't…'

She put her hand up to stop him. As though she was afraid she would never get the next words out if she didn't say them there and then.

'Less than a week later they were in the car accident that killed them.'

'Nell, I'm so, so sorry.' His arms were around her, drawing her in before he realised what he was doing.

Wishing he could go back in time and change it all for her. Even if that meant he would never experience the wonder of meeting a woman like Nell Parker. As if, maybe, there *was* a part of him capable of such deep feelings, after all.

And if there was, then it could only be because of her. Because Nell was the light, glorious and dazzling, and she belonged in Little Meadwood, where she called home. Whilst before her, he had always been him—broken and damaged. And, in that place more than any other, he would always be that cold, unwanted Mason kid.

But he didn't know what else to say. Or how to explain it—even to himself. So, instead, he did the only thing he knew how to do—he kissed her.

Over and over.

Pouring everything he had into the moment. All the words he couldn't bring himself to think, let alone say. All these… *feelings* that he didn't know how to even begin to unravel.

As if Nell Parker was the only thing that could make this darkness inside him shift and skitter. As if he was running towards the light that this one, unique woman brought into his life. She flooded him with it, bright and brilliant as it illuminated all the better versions of himself that he wished he could be. For her.

And, for a while at least, he could pretend to himself that he really was that better man. Something he'd never wanted to believe in so much in his entire life.

CHAPTER ELEVEN

'APPARENTLY PEOPLE LOVE our steampunk stall,' Nell declared proudly as she bounced across the field, dodging the multitude of other fair-goers.

'Is that so?' Connor slid his arm around her shoulders as she pressed her side against his, falling into step together.

'Ruby swung by with Vivian, and she thinks they are the best stalls we've ever had. Plus, the mayor thinks we're going to have to make this a fixture every year.'

'Then I guess we have eleven months to work out how we're going to make it even better next year.'

She stopped, tilting her head to look up at him.

'So, you're sticking around Little Meadwood for a bit longer, then?'

Her lips parted, breathlessly, those morpho-blue eyes filled with such emotion.

Staying in Little Meadwood indefinitely had never really been part of the plan, yet right now he couldn't think of a single reason why he would refuse Nell. The past week with her had been incredible, whether they were working on the stall or at the hospital, or going on a date, or indulging in far more intimate pursuits. It felt as though this could be the start of something special—something he'd never before allowed himself to consider. And maybe they would have a long road ahead of them, but surely together they could make that journey?

'I'm considering it,' he hazarded, gently cupping Nell's chin with his hand as he lowered his head to kiss her.

A soft kiss but with so many unspoken promises. She tasted of goji berries and raspberries—that fruity fizz of her summer mocktail. She made him feel more alive, yet more grounded than any woman he'd ever known. The kiss deepened, but eventually he remembered where they were and reluctantly broke away.

'Later,' he managed, wondering how one word could be filled with such promise.

This was all so new and exhilarating to him.

'I might even move out of the hospital accommodation and rent an apartment of my own in the city. Between the army and locuming I've never actually had a place of my own before. And I might need some help decorating it. Though perhaps not steampunk.'

'Perhaps not.' Nell laughed, burying her head at his neck. A gentle rumble against his throat.

'I...' Connor opened his mouth to speak, only to realise that the words on the tip of his tongue were three words he had never, ever imagined wanting to tell anyone before.

He stopped abruptly, waiting for them to dissipate. Waiting for the sense of horror that he'd almost said something he could never mean. But it didn't come—even when she stood there, statue-still and staring at him with pupils so round that they were almost magical.

She was magical.

Perhaps it was those words still charging around in his mouth, hurtling themselves against his closed lips with such power that he almost couldn't hold them back any longer. Desperate to get out there into the world and be heard.

He loved her?

It seemed ridiculous. And impossible. And glorious.

'Connor...?' Nell breathed after what felt like a lifetime.

Perhaps it was.

'Connor?' she prompted again, her voice cracking. 'You… *what*?'

The silence swirled around them. Electric and exciting.

'I…' He faltered. But this wasn't the place to say it. Not here. Not at some summer fete in Little Meadwood. Ruthlessly shutting the errant thought out, he feigned a bright smile, which he suspected was a little too tight to look natural, and plucked her empty glass from her hands. 'I'll get us a refill.'

Without waiting for an answer, he turned his back and strode across the field to the drinks station. But the thoughts followed him. Prickling him. Making him feel *everything*.

'Another two Summer Suns, please,' he ordered, his head still lost.

He was still lost in his thoughts when he felt a sharp prod in his back. But when he turned, the smile on his face was wiped clean away.

'I don't know how you have the gall to come back here after what you did, my lad.' An unpleasantly familiar voice crackled through the air. 'You ought to be ashamed of yourself.'

He ought to have been shocked. It spoke volumes that he wasn't.

'Sylvie Calton.'

He fought to keep his voice level but even the old woman's name lodged unpleasantly in his throat. Sharp needles stabbing into the soft folds of his voice box like a prickly hawthorn into a soft thumb pad.

'It's Mrs Calton to you,' she hissed venomously, her gnarled features twisted in loathing. 'Or maybe *ma'am*. After all, you were supposed to be in the army, weren't you? I suppose Vivian knew it was either that or prison for the likes of you.'

'I don't know what you're talking about.' He refused to let this bitter individual transport him back to his sorry excuse for a childhood. He wasn't that kid any longer. 'But I can't say that I particularly care.'

If only there weren't that traitorous part of him that did indeed care. Arguably for the way it might affect Nell more than himself.

'You know damn well what I'm talking about,' Sylvie spat out viciously. 'Vivian took you in when nobody else would. Like a fool, she treated you like her own son and wouldn't hear a word against you, even though I wasn't the only one concerned about how a feral monster like you would taint our happy community. And how do you repay her? By costing her all her life savings and then, when she *still* gave you another chance, you hurt her by running off like a coward. But I know what kind of a person you really are. And I'll never let you forget it.'

Connor's grip on the plastic cups tightened until they threatened to crack, but he was determined to keep his composure. He wouldn't let this woman win.

'I know exactly who I am,' he managed evenly, though it cost him. 'And I'm proud of who that is. As is Vivian.'

'You're a disgrace to a good woman. And you'll be a disgrace to her memory when she is gone.'

In hindsight, Connor would decide *that* was the moment he let Sylvie get to him.

'Why am I such a disgrace, Sylvie?' he gritted out, his voice low and dangerous.

'Because you're a liar, and a thief. Does that Nell Parker girl know what you are?'

Connor steeled himself. Nell being drawn into anything in Little Meadwood was exactly what he'd feared.

'Nell knows,' he barked back. 'I told her all about the way I was dragged up, and how I used to survive. And do you want to know what Nell asked? She asked what was so startling about a six-year-old who was so desperate for his mother's love that he did exactly what she asked. Dragged up by a woman who hadn't even taught me the basics of right from wrong. I only learned that basic lesson when Vivian took me into her life.'

Sylvie's eyes glinted with pure malice.

'Oh, you might have pretended to learn that lesson, but we all know you were faking it. Just ask Vivian where her little nest egg went all those years ago.'

This time, he really didn't have any idea what she was talking about.

'Her nest egg?' He frowned, shocked, the cogs in his mind slipping as he tried to slot the accusation together.

Like a jigsaw puzzle with half the pieces missing.

Sylvie snorted in disgust.

'Don't pretend you don't know. Don't pretend you don't remember helping that wicked mother of yours steal hundreds of pounds from me.'

'That's a lie,' Connor scoffed instantly. 'I never saw that woman again after I arrived in this place to live with Vivian.'

'Yes. You did.' She prodded him in the chest, but he barely felt it.

'Ridiculous. She overdosed in a motel when I was six and that was the last time I ever saw her.'

Yet he couldn't explain the sudden heat that prickled through him.

'You can't really expect anyone to believe that you don't remember her coming here when you were about ten?' the old woman scorned. 'And you distracted me whilst she stole from me.'

'No.' He shook his head. 'I would remember.'

But things were still shifting hazily, and he didn't like the picture he thought they were making.

'Yes.' Sylvie sounded triumphant. 'You distracted me by paying for some toy with all pennies and tuppences. I ought to have realised then that was what was going on, but I'd foolishly bought into Vivian's version of you being a boy who had changed for the better.'

Connor felt winded. Waves of regret and remorse crashing over him. Threatening to wipe him out completely. He had been running from the pain for so long, but now it was catching up to him.

'I had no idea—' he began tersely, before Sylvie cut him off with a sneer.

'Of course you did. You distracted me whilst she stole. You knew. I saw you running after her afterwards, across the field to where some scrounger was waiting for her in some old car. Dusty red with a discoloured grey driver's door panel, I remember it like it was yesterday.'

And just like that, a memory dislodged itself from the darkest recesses of his brain. Buried so deep under guilt and shame that he'd forgotten it was there. He'd never wanted to see it again. His mother *had* tracked him down to Little Meadwood. How had he managed to stuff that memory down all these years? She'd given him the bag of copper pennies and told him to buy himself a toy like the ones she had never bought him. She'd claimed that she was clean and that it was her way of saying sorry for all she'd put him through as a child.

How desperately he'd wanted to believe her. Despite all the love and support Vivian had shown him, there had been that part of him that had still yearned for the love of the woman who was meant to be his mother. Who was meant to love him more than life itself. He'd seen other kids experience it—why not him?

So he'd taken the pennies from her and when she'd followed him into Sylvie's shop, he'd pretended that he hadn't known what she'd been planning. That he was still nothing more than her pawn. A part of him had known what she'd been about to do. And he'd let it happen because he'd felt this inexplicable sense of guilt. As though he had somehow left her all alone after her overdose. As if a social worker hadn't been the one to pack him in a car and take him to a home. Then to some foster family he could barely remember but who he knew hadn't been that kind. And finally to Vivian.

And when he'd got that toy—a bow and arrow set just like all the other boys in Meadwood had had, as if it had made him just like them—he'd chased the woman who had given birth to him but had never been any kind of mother across the green and begged her to take him with her.

And she'd laughed at him. Jeered. As if he was nothing.

'Who could love a runt like you?'

The words had echoed around his head for a lifetime. Worse, they had taken root. Because she hadn't been wrong, had she? He'd known what she was like yet he'd still allowed himself to be seduced by the idea that he was as worthy of love as any other kid. He'd allowed that desperate need to make him complicit in her crime against Sylvie, against Vivian, and against the trustworthy young man that Vivian had been trying to mould him into.

'I'm…sorry,' he managed. Simply. Sincerely.

He wasn't surprised when Sylvie merely sneered again.

'Excuses, excuses. You're a bad apple, Connor Mason. You were always a bad foster kid with a twisted, heartless soul. Always were, always will be, and the sooner you get out of here without causing damage for anybody else, the better. You even left it to Vivian to spend all of her savings paying me back.'

He ground out a curse.

'Well, someone had to pay me back, of course—but that someone should have been you. And then, a few years later, you ran off, abandoning her.'

Connor shook his head, guilt and shame knifing through him all over again. He had tried so hard to step away from his past, but he'd never thought he'd deliberately stuffed the truth out of his brain.

'I'm not the liar here, boy.' Sylvie couldn't have looked any happier with herself. 'You are. And you and I both know it.'

The accusation hung in the air, creating a heavy fog that threatened to engulf him whole. It was as if he were transported back to the days of his foster care. He could feel the hatefully familiar jagged edges of worthlessness and despair, feelings that had once consumed him. Only this time, he thoroughly deserved them.

He had spent twenty years fighting to escape Little Meadwood—fighting to be the best soldier, surgeon, man that he could be. He'd thought he'd finally escaped the feral kid he'd once been. He'd never wanted to feel like that scared, angry, worthless boy ever again. A boy who'd had nowhere to turn but inward—just as he felt as though he was doing now. He could turn himself inside out trying not to be that child, but he knew it wouldn't do any good. In the decade he'd endured living in Little Meadwood, the place had never allowed him to grow out of the feral six-year-old who had arrived, hissing and spitting like some wild animal, and he'd blamed the location and the people.

It turned out that the place wasn't the problem after all—he was. He always had been. And he'd been right in the first place in never returning here—it reminded him of the person he had never liked being.

A selfish, thoughtless individual who only cared about himself. Sylvie was right. He was a bad person and he didn't deserve love. He didn't deserve Nell or, more to the point, she deserved better than a man like him.

Emotions tumbled through Connor, too many and too fast to really identify any of them. Except for one.

Guilt.

Vivian had used up all her savings paying Sylvie back for his mother, so that she wouldn't go to the police. His mother had always been the one wrecking lives whilst he'd sworn he would never, *never* be like her.

Turned out, that was exactly who he was.

It was time for him to leave Little Meadwood before he caused any real harm. There was only one final loose end to tie up.

Nell.

A tight band pulled across his chest at the thought of her. Smart, compassionate, and full of integrity—all the qualities he'd once prided himself on possessing. Turned out he was just someone who was twisted and broken beyond repair. He had no love to give, no good qualities to offer, no one to keep him anchored. Not any more.

Nell deserved so much better—*someone* better. Not least someone who understood what it actually meant to love her back. This was his truth. He was a lost cause, and this was the only way to protect himself and those he cared about from the hurt and suffering he could cause.

The fact that he'd fallen for her—and he had—only made the thought of losing her that much more unbearable. It nicked at his heart.

Or what he had fooled himself into thinking was his heart. The truth was that he didn't have one. It had died long ago.

And it was time to make sure Nell understood that. For her own sake.

Nell reached Connor just as Sylvie was walking away. There was an odd gleam in the old woman's eyes.

'Connor.' She reached out to touch his arm, not entirely surprised when he pulled away. 'Whatever Sylvie said to you, forget it. You know she has always been spiteful.'

The woman had never been her favourite person here in Little Meadwood, although Nell could usually bring herself to feel a wave of sympathy for her.

'Doesn't make her wrong,' Connor bit out flatly, and it was the lack of emotion in his tone that sliced through Nell painfully.

'I know she lost her son when he was just a baby, and I can't imagine how much pain that must have caused her, but that doesn't give her the right to treat other people as she does. What did she say to you?'

Connor's step almost faltered for a moment.

'Sylvie lost a child? I never knew that.'

'I think about forty years ago. I don't know much about it; I just know he was her only child.'

'That explains a lot,' Connor muttered, though Nell had the impression it was more to himself than to her. 'But it doesn't change anything.'

'What does that mean?'

He hated that he didn't answer.

'This is goodbye, Nell,' he forced out instead, still marching across the green.

'No,' she cried, almost falling. Connor was so wrapped up in whatever turmoil was clearly going on in his head that he hadn't even noticed she was practically tripping over the tufts of grass trying to keep up with him. 'What did Sylvie say to you, Connor?' she pleaded.

'It doesn't matter.'

And the flatness in his tone buried itself like a scalpel in her chest.

'Clearly it does,' she pointed out, relieved when he finally stopped and turned to face her.

'She simply reminded me of the person I really am. That's all. And I'm not the man you think I am. I'm not even the man *I* thought I was. Frankly, I'm not a man worth knowing.'

'Too bad I've fallen for you, then, isn't it?'

And even as she uttered the words, she realised how true they were. Completely and utterly.

Connor stared at her for the longest time—a look that might have been dark and forbidding had it not been so very...compelling.

'Then you're a fool.' His voice grated.

'No...you love me too; you almost said it before. I know you did.'

He brushed her off and took a step away.

'I was wrong to think I was ever capable of love,' he dismissed, but it had the opposite effect to the one she suspected he intended.

It meant that he couldn't actually deny it. She was right, he *did* love her.

'Love is all that matters, Connor.'

She reached out to him, but he evaded her without even appearing to move. His teeth gritted so tightly that she almost expected his jaw to shatter under the pressure.

She almost expected *herself* to shatter under the pressure.

'That's a lie they sell you in movies, Nell. The truth is that love is not enough.'

'You're wrong.'

'Am I? Okay, then,' he challenged. 'If you love me so much, then come away with me.'

'Go away to where?' Her breath caught in her chest. 'You're leaving Little Meadwood?'

'Yes. And if you truly believe love is all that matters, then come with me. Leave this place, once and for all.'

The black look in his eyes almost reached down and suffocated her. He already knew she wouldn't be able to.

'You can't do it, can you?' He gave a brittle laugh after a few moments, and the sound seemed to echo coldly within her. 'Because no matter what you say, deep down you know that I'm not worth it.'

'No.'

That wasn't it at all, the problem was with her. She couldn't leave because this place was her safety net. Out there, in the real world, was where bad things happened. Like her parents dying. Jonathon had been right all along—she'd stayed in Little Meadwood for all the wrong reasons.

But she couldn't tell Connor any of that. She couldn't admit it out loud. She'd only just admitted it in the relative sanctity of her own head.

And so, he'd made up his own mind, and in *his* head, he was the villain. That was why he wouldn't stay.

'Don't go,' she pressed. 'You've got it all wrong. I may not know everything about your past, Connor, but I know you. I know the man you are today, and I love him. Whatever happened in your past, it doesn't define you. That isn't the man you are today.'

'You're wrong,' he gritted out. 'It moulds precisely the man I am today. The one standing right in front of you. And Sylvie reminded me how damaged, and how treacherous, that individual has always been.'

'Bruised,' Nell cut in desperately. 'Not *damaged* or *treacherous*. Just bereaved. Grieving for your parents. Like me.'

'Not like you,' he ground out. 'I was never like you.'

'Are you saying you never cared for me, Connor? That everything between us has been a lie?'

How she succeeded in keeping the quake out of her voice, she would never know. His expression was so black, so forbidding, that for a moment she feared he was going to say just that. But then something broke over his face. A glimpse of the tenderness that she recognised.

'That isn't what I'm saying.' There was a hint of anguish in his tone that gave her hope even as her heart broke for him. 'I cared for you... I still care for you. But that isn't enough.'

'It's enough for me,' she choked out.

'Then come away with me.'

It didn't even sound like an invitation. Just a test. One he knew she would fail again.

'This is ridiculous. We can't just leave Vivian,' she pointed out. 'Especially not now.'

'I'll visit,' he stated flatly. 'I'll commute just like I did in the beginning. You can, too.'

She shook her head, her voice too thick to speak. The look he shot her held no surprise at all.

'Ergo it isn't enough,' he said with finality. 'Not for you. And not for me. It's over—and I'm truly sorry about that, Nell. I never wanted to hurt you.'

And yet his expression was as implacable as his granite-like stance, making it abundantly clear to her that there was nothing she could say or do to help it thaw. He was lost to her.

If he'd ever really been hers in the first instance.

How could she have been so blind to the pain that he carried around inside him? Then again, how had she been so blind to her own self-imposed parameters? The boundaries she alone had created, which meant that even if Connor had been sincere about her leaving with him, she couldn't have done so. This valley was her crutch, and she couldn't face the idea of being without it.

Not even to be with Connor.

Which surely made her the one incapable of love—not him.

She'd told him she loved him but how could she really, when she couldn't even face her own demons? How could either of them help each other when they couldn't even help themselves?

And so, this time when he walked away from her—Nell simply let him.

CHAPTER TWELVE

CONNOR WORKED THROUGH the evening's patient notes in some kind of frenzy. The way that he had been doing for the better part of the past two weeks.

The past twelve days and twenty hours. He even knew it down to the minute—had anyone asked.

Though of course no one did. No one here knew him. He'd been fortunate that when he'd spoken with his chief of surgery at City, there had already been the option on the table of a month-long exchange with the general hospital on the other side of the city. It had meant being able to put some distance between him and Little Meadwood—and Nell—without anyone being left in the lurch. Not least his patients.

But even if he knew that staying away from Nell was the kindest thing he could do for her, it had to be the hardest thing he'd ever had to do in his life—including saving impossible lives in the most hellish warzones. How many times had he found himself on his motorbike in the middle of the night, screaming through the deserted country roads that led to the village? To her.

He'd always turned around before cresting that hill that overlooked the valley, though.

At least he had his work to get him through. It had always been his saviour.

Tonight alone, he'd already dealt with one patient who had

fallen down a long flight of steep, concrete steps in town, fracturing his forearm. Despite the original X-ray from a colleague showing nothing, Connor's suspicions had led him to insist on a more comprehensive chest CT, which had revealed the full extent of the patient's injuries, resulting in a trip to the operating theatre.

He had then treated another patient who had been drinking too much, got into a brawl with his girlfriend, and then picked a fight with the plate-glass window of a high-street fashion chain and lost. Another quick dash to the operating theatre had ensued the moment he'd come in, and now the same patient was in ICU, the worse for wear, but alive.

He'd even performed a splenectomy on one road traffic accident victim, and removed half the severed pancreas of another. But now Resus was oddly quiet and even the non-trauma cases weren't enough to stop his brain from creeping back to Nell.

She'd taken up residency in his head and he couldn't seem to evict her, no matter what he did. He'd found himself looking for her in the hospital hallways, imagining he could hear an echo of her lilting tone in the corridor, or catch the faintest hint of her citrusy shampoo scent. Missing her in a way that he had never allowed himself to miss anyone before.

And he didn't want to feel any of it now. It made him feel too... *exposed.*

But worse, he suspected there was a tiny part of him that actually did want it. That might even like it. It was like nothing he'd ever felt before, and somehow that felt like a good thing.

Even so... when the door to his consultation room opened before he could respond to the brief knock, Connor knew it was her before she walked in.

He couldn't allow this to happen.

'Nell,' he rasped, lifting his head.

But the warning simply melted from his mind.

Standing in the doorway, wearing a simple figure-hugging

tee, and a pair of inky-blue jeans, her hair pulled back into a loose ponytail, she was enough to snatch every last word from his head.

He didn't mean to sit up straighter in his chair, though Connor realised that was exactly what he was doing.

Somehow—he had no idea how—he managed to find his voice. A growl so dark that he barely recognised himself.

'You shouldn't be here.'

But rather than intimidating her into turning and fleeing as he wanted her to do—as he *needed* her to do—all Connor could see was a resolute glitter in her eyes. That inner strength of hers, which scraped at something inside him.

'Still self-flagellating, I see,' she offered dryly.

She seemed different…somehow. More sure of herself.

But he couldn't let that sway him.

'There's no punishment going on,' he growled again. 'I'm trying to spare you any hurt.'

'Only you're the one who is hurting the most,' she countered softly.

He shook his head, his words deserting him once again. And suddenly, there was no point still claiming that he didn't have a heart. Not when he could actually feel it right there, in his chest. Skipping a beat. The charged energy seeming to hum in the air around them.

But that still didn't mean he was capable of using it properly.

'I understand that you're scared,' she continued, stepping a little further into the room. 'But there's really no need to be.'

'I didn't walk away from you out of fear, Nell,' his voice rattled out oddly. 'I walked away because I'm not capable of love. I certainly don't love you enough to stay, just as you don't love me enough to leave.'

'You say that yet here we are.' She shrugged nonchalantly, her tone sending a wave of disquiet through him.

'Here we are?' he echoed, thrown.

It was a novel feeling.

'You claim you don't love me enough to stay, and I don't love you enough to leave, yet you haven't left, Connor. You've moved a couple of miles further away, I'll grant you, but I'd hardly call that leaving.'

'Nell—'

'You haven't left,' she repeated, not letting him cut her off. 'And yet, I *have* left.'

'Sorry?'

It didn't help that Nell was far too cool, too unruffled, too at odds with the knot of feelings currently tumbling inside him. She exerted the kind of calm, composed energy that he usually prided himself on exhibiting, no matter the circumstance. But it had all deserted him right now, leaving him nervous and tense instead.

'You heard me, Connor.'

Only that pyretic lustre in her gaze offered any indication that Nell, *his* Nell, was less than controlled. Dimly, he considered that he should be using that to his advantage…so why wasn't he?

There were so many conflicting emotions inside him right now, all vying for pole position. He felt flustered, and apprehensive, and yet…the way his heart was racing inside his chest was almost like the kind of adrenalin rush to which he'd long since become addicted.

Almost, but not quite.

Because *this* sensation felt more tangible, more real. Which somehow made it all the more dangerous.

'What is it that you want from me?' he heard himself asking instead.

And that pounding in his chest only sounded louder, and harder, as she stepped further into the room. Into his space— which ought to have felt like an encroachment but instead felt oddly like someone pulling up a warm blanket on the coldest of nights.

Nell took a deep breath.

'I want you, Connor.'

'You do not want me.'

He didn't realise he'd launched himself to his feet until he heard his chair clattering to the floor behind him. A fist gripping inside his chest.

And Nell, damn her, merely smiled gently. With such understanding. As though she were trying to teach phonetics to a toddler.

'You can fight it all you want, but I've wanted you from the moment we met on that road outside the village. And I know you want me too.'

'I want no such thing.'

It didn't surprise him that the words sounded flat. Wrong.

She took another step closer.

'The difference is, you've finally given me the courage I needed to do something about it.'

'To do something about it?'

He was echoing her again. But his brain seemed to have stopped working.

'I've left Little Meadwood.'

'That isn't what—'

'I've sold my cottage.' She cut him off again.

And this time the simple statement was like a fist in his chest, gripping so white-knuckle tight that it threatened to stop the blood in his very veins.

'You've sold your cottage?'

It sounded too unbelievable for words.

'I didn't want Little Meadwood to be my crutch any more—not when it was going to impede me chasing after you. And I understand why you're resisting—you had a hellish childhood, with only Vivian fighting for you. At least I knew loving parents and a warm family life before their accident. But you have more than one person now. You have me, too. I'm here, ready to fight for you. All you have to do is let me in. Let yourself feel.'

She made it sound so simple. So uncomplicated. But it wasn't that easy. It couldn't be. And the...*thing* that had festered inside him ever since he'd been that feral kid began to grow.

'I can't give you what you want,' he bit out. 'Even if I wanted to, I already warned you that I'm not capable of love. I never have been.'

'Yes, you are.' Her soft voice held such conviction that he ached to believe her. 'You've loved Vivian. You've shown love and care for your every patient. You've been part of a brotherhood in the military. That's love. It might take different forms but the trust, the loyalty, the promises are all there.'

He opened his mouth to argue but the words wouldn't come. Instead, a storm was beginning to howl through him, shaking his memories so that he couldn't even think straight.

Or maybe Nell was the storm.

Maybe she was the reason that the crashing in his ears only grew louder, as if a maelstrom were building up inside him with every comment this woman made, and it threatened to tear him apart, bit by bit.

'Even if that's true, it doesn't make me capable of...' he waved his hand between the two of them, as though to encompass all that he couldn't say '...this kind of love.'

Yet he barely recognised his own voice, it was so thick. So raw.

'It shows that you're capable of love after all.' Nell smiled softly.

He didn't answer. He couldn't.

His head was a mess of conflicting emotions, her words

were like a balm to his soul, a soothing salve to the deep-seated pain that had been festering inside him for years.

Never before had he allowed anyone in—not even Vivian. Not fully. Just as never before had he allowed himself to feel vulnerable and exposed. But Nell was different, she made him want to take a chance and open up to her.

But if he hurt her?

Something nicked painfully at his chest as he realised that he would never be able to live with himself. It was all he could do to draw his next breath and steel himself.

'You're asking for something I can't give you,' he growled fiercely. 'You need to leave, Nell. Now.'

She had him. She could tell.

He didn't want to believe her—clearly, he thought that was the only way to protect her—yet her words were getting through. She kept catching flashes of turmoil in his dark eyes even as he tried to shut her out, as he had in the past.

'Pity, since I'm choosing to stay.' Somehow—she didn't know how—Nell managed to crank up her smile, wander over to the sleek leather couch at the side of his office, and sink down with a nonchalance that she only wished she really felt. 'So you can glare and glower at me all you want. You can rail and storm. But it won't induce me to apologise for acknowledging my feelings.'

'Then you are only fooling yourself if you think it will induce *me* to share them.'

She noted how he deliberately echoed her words, trying to turn them back on her. And that, too, fuelled her.

'I think it's time we stopped going around in circles, Connor.'

And her stomach somersaulted again as she watched the way he curled his fists around the edges of his desk, fighting for his own self-control as much as anything else. She was clearly getting under his skin.

Good.

'I've come to fight for us,' she told him soberly. 'To show you that I love you. That you can trust me. That I will always have your back.'

And she would never know how her voice didn't shake with the intensity of emotions roiling around inside her at that moment.

'Then you're a fool. It isn't a battle worth having.' His jaw clenched and for a moment Nell thought that he was going to walk away.

But then he surprised her by stepping around the desk. Still on the other side of the room from her, but without that physical barrier, at least.

It was a start—even if he was simply staring her down with a fierce intensity that made her heart race. If time had stood still—the rest of the world grinding to a halt around them—then she wouldn't have been shocked.

The only thing that existed for her in that moment was her and Connor.

'You aren't defined by your past,' she managed, after what might have been an eternity. Maybe longer. 'You're defined by who you are now, and who you want to be. I'm not going to let you push me away this time, Connor.'

For a moment, there was silence between them, and Nell thought that she had said too much. But then he spoke, his voice hesitant, and rough.

"You have no idea what you're asking for.'

'I'm just asking for love, Connor,' she whispered. 'Nothing more complicated than that.'

'I don't know if I can be what you deserve.' But his voice cracked. Right there. Right then. 'I don't know if I'm capable of loving someone the way that you deserve to be loved.'

'You won't know unless you try,' Nell said, her voice gentle.

The air between them was electric, charged with the unspoken tension that had been building between them for weeks. Nell could feel the heat emanating off Connor's body, could see the way his pupils dilated as he watched her.

Desire.

Potent enough to make her insides begin to melt and flow through her. Thick, and warm, and thrilling.

And then, suddenly, he was crossing the room. Closing the space so quickly that she barely had time to react, much less think. He reached out his hand to take hers and pulled her to her feet and right up against his hard, lean body.

Like coming home.

'I've missed you,' he muttered, before lowering his head to claim her lips with a kiss that made her feel as though a dam had burst inside her.

As if someone had set off a thousand fireworks throughout her entire body.

A kiss that was hungry and desperate, as if trying to make up for lost time. Yet was also infused with every unspoken promise that she could ever have wanted. As if he was finally letting go of his fears and insecurities and allowing himself to fully embrace the passion and desire that he had been suppressing for so long. Pouring his soul into that kiss. Into *her.*

And Nell soaked up every bit of it.

Every seductive slick of his tongue was a silent avowal, every deepening angle an admission of need. When his hands roamed her body, Nell couldn't stop the soft moan from escaping her lips as her hands came up to tangle in his hair.

They stood there for what felt like an eternity, lost in the intensity of their passion, until finally they pulled away— Connor's forehead resting against hers as his ragged breathing mingled with hers.

'I can't promise that this will be easy; but I want to try.'

'That's all I ask,' she promised him, her fingers reaching up to stroke his cheek. 'Because I love you. And you don't have to say it back; I understand why you can't yet allow yourself to accept that you love me too. But I can wait. I can love you enough for the both of us. Until you're ready.'

'And if I never am?'

'You will be,' she told him confidently, his ragged breath spurring her on. 'You already feel it, you just have to recognise it.'

And as they stood there, wrapped up in each other's embrace, their gazes intertwined, Nell saw the exact moment Connor finally believed her. The moment his fractured shield finally shattered and fell away. His body told her the truth even if he hadn't yet found the courage to say the words. Every gaze, every touch, every kiss proved he loved her better than any promises could have done. Because anyone could say the words, but no one had ever made her feel the way that Connor did.

'From that first day we met, it was like you shone a light into my life when I'd never before known how dark it was,' he told her solemnly, his gaze full of wonder. 'And then, as I got to know you, I realised you weren't shining a light—you *are* the light. A blazing, dazzling sun that has breathed a life into me that I never imagined I could be. I *do* love you, Nell. I think I always have. I just didn't know what it meant.'

'Now you do,' she whispered, her heart swelling with emotion. So much that she thought it might burst out of her chest.

'I swear to you,' he continued, his voice cracking, 'that I will spend every day striving to be the man you deserve. Telling you how much I love you. And proving it to you.'

'I think we should start on all of that right now,' she agreed, lifting her hands to trail her fingertips down the sides of his face.

And then she half laughed, half cried as he scooped her into his arms, hauling her against his chest whilst his mouth came down to seal his promise.

'I love you, Nell,' he murmured, laying her almost reverently on the couch. 'You are my light, and my life, and you deserve to be worshipped. For ever.'

Then he bent his head and began to do precisely that, stripping her down one item of clothing at a time, and stoking the fire that burned so white-hot between them. And Nell knew they were like two pieces of a puzzle that finally fitted together, completing each other in the most perfect way.

The way they would for the rest of their lives.

* * * * *

If you enjoyed this story, check out these other great reads from Charlotte Hawkes

Neurosurgeon, Single Dad…Husband?
His Cinderella Houseguest
Shock Baby for the Doctor
Forbidden Nights with the Surgeon

All available now!

THEIR SIX-MONTH MARRIAGE RUSE

KRISTINE LYNN

MILLS & BOON

To my DU ladies.

Every good love story includes a friendship like ours.

Keep fighting the good fight.

CHAPTER ONE

DR. DEXTER SHAW hung his stethoscope around his neck and resisted the urge to slam the office door. The silence was suffocating. The cool air blanketing the sterile hallway did nothing to tamper the heat boiling beneath his skin. A tingling sensation crept up his arms and his feet itched.

He knew the signs. The onset of a panic attack if he couldn't breathe this one away.

One, two, three.

He inhaled through his nose and out his mouth and it worked, at least enough to keep the edge off. But it was getting harder to keep them in check.

They're getting more acute. More frequent, too.

Bing. Dexter's pager went off, the vibrations barely breaking through the blanket of worry. He clenched and unclenched his hands but the regular techniques—techniques he'd created to help patients deal with their anxieties—weren't working as well anymore. If Dexter was going to permanently outwit the attacks, something was going to have to change, and fast.

Starting with figuring out how he'd been able to keep them at bay for ten years and why they were back now.

Damn thing was his triggers kept changing. Forget the benign dreams-of-my-dad's-death-from-free-climbing-triggers-my-anxiety onslaughts of his youth. These adult versions were sneaky SOBs, ambushing him when he walked by day care and saw his ex, Kelsey, and her husband with their daughter,

Emma. Or pouncing on him when he walked through the antiseptic psych wing on the way to his office.

Fears scratched at the door he'd locked them behind after years of being on the patient end of therapy sessions. They whispered something unexpected, something he'd never considered, not after losing his dad so young, then growing up between foster homes without any stability, any consistency.

Maybe you chose wrong, they hissed when he laid in bed, alone. *Maybe your life is* too *sterile,* too *empty.*

Sterile was safe, and empty meant no surprises, but still...

He'd tried to stave the worries off with something new *and* cautious, first by attempting to play the doting dad to Emma when Kelsey adopted her. Maybe he'd been scared of fatherhood for nothing. Then the baby had gotten sick in day care, her temp skyrocketing for thirty-six hours until Kelsey had her hospitalized.

Turned out that kids were the most dangerous threat of all—at least for someone hoping to avoid as much risk as possible so he'd never feel again the way he felt when he lost his dad—like his world was spinning wildly out of control. So he'd tried again with something slightly safer and without the personal attachment he feared—a proposal for a trauma psych program at Mercy—but the hospital's board couldn't find a suitable team to staff it with, so it was on hold.

"Dammit," he swore. "I need to get my act together." A nurse in gray scrubs—one of his staff—gave Dexter a wide berth.

"Yeah, yeah. I'm supposed to be the one in charge, not the one having a breakdown, I get it," he grumbled under his breath.

He groaned into his hands, leaning against the wall of Mercy Hospital's clinically immaculate psych wing. It was his fault—all of it. The problem was he'd willingly cultivated the life that fed his feelings of obscurity, making way for something more serious.

From the moment he'd left the inner-city hospital—a building that had been torn down for a wellness spa since—after almost dying from exposure at eighteen, he'd been a man possessed. He'd sprinted through his twenty-year plan—one designed to leave his tumultuous childhood in the distant past once and for all—and made every single choice that led him to where he was today.

He'd broken up with Kelsey when he realized he couldn't be a dad—not without worrying every minute of every day for the rest of his life. Besides, what could he offer a child when he'd had such a crappy upbringing?

He'd taken the chief of psychiatry position at Mercy instead of the trauma psychologist gig at whatever remote horse ranch Kelsey found that helped first responders work through their PTSD. The chief job had provided the stability he not so secretly craved after a lifetime without it, whereas the horse ranch would have been temporary, in an unfamiliar environment, and—since the job had called for a committed couple to fill the two vacant positions—it had been too dependent on Kelsey.

It wasn't that he was completely immune to the desire for connection with another person, but a wife? No way. No spouse meant no encumbrances, no one to slip between him and his armor. It meant he could simply work and help patients—the one constant in his life.

Bottom line? He was no victim of his circumstances. *He'd* made every choice that haunted him.

The question was what was he going to do about it now that those choices no longer served him and, by proxy, his patients?

His phone rang, loud and obtrusive in the empty corridor, more difficult to ignore than his discreet pager. But his scowl dissipated when he saw the name on the caller ID. Some of the tightness in his chest loosened as he answered it, and he shoved through the double doors toward the employee parking lot.

"Well, look what the army dragged back. Sergeant Tyler, as I live and breathe."

"That's Staff Sergeant Tyler to you. Reporting for duty."

"Damn. Congrats. I didn't know if or when I'd hear from you. This is a nice surprise."

After talking to his best friend every week for fifteen years, he'd missed Tyler. This was the longest they'd gone without talking.

"Don't get all sentimental on me now, Shaw. Just wanted to let you know I'm back in town."

"I'm glad to hear your voice. It's been a minute."

"A year and a half. Got held up with the trauma center over there. Would you believe the government pulled their portion of the funding in January?"

"My surprise is overwhelming," he said, keeping his voice monotone and robotic. Sergeant Tyler laughed.

"We got it back, but it took forever to get the center up and running."

"I'm proud of you. Most medics would've quit. Anyway, welcome back. I know some folks that are gonna be happy to hear you're safe."

"Hold the welcome parade for now. Not sure how long I'm sticking around."

"Really? But you just got home. How long till the army yanks you back?"

The silence on the other end was punctuated by the crunch of Dexter's oxfords on the gravel parking lot.

When the hell is this renovation gonna be done so I can stop wrecking my shoes on this shit?

"I'm not going back."

Dexter stopped, the dust he'd kicked up settling on the brown leather of his shoes.

"What do you mean, you're not going back? You're a career army medic."

"I was." Dexter could picture Tyler's furrowed brows on the other end. "Now I'll be some kind of other career doctor."

"What happened?"

"Nothing out of the ordinary. Job's getting stale." Dex smiled at that one. Tyler was impossible to pin down. The opposite of him, in almost every way possible.

"What else?" Dexter knew his best friend better than anyone. Tyler wasn't being honest.

"I'm lonely," Tyler whispered. If Dex hadn't been standing parade-still, he'd have missed it.

"Oh." Of all the responses, he hadn't expected that. "I thought you'd finally found a solid group of friends."

"I did. They were like family, but they're…they're moving on with their own actual families, starting to put down roots."

"And you want to do the same?" Hope barricaded the fears from earlier. If he could convince Tyler to come back to where it was safe, maybe he'd sleep better at night.

"Not exactly." Dexter recalled the time Tyler had come home with a swollen eye and sliced arm from shrapnel. Dexter had begged Tyler to leave then, before the injuries were more severe. Or worse still, Dex, as Tyler's emergency contact, was delivered the remains of his best friend in a plastic bag. "But I'll fill you in later."

He understood. Tyler might crave the adventure Dex avoided at all costs, but they both wanted the same thing deep down—something that was theirs, something no one could take from them.

Maybe his best friend could find that a little closer to home. "Well, I'm sorry it went down like that. I know how much you liked the people, the travel and hell—even the danger." He raked a hand over his chin, stubble pricking his palm. He'd keep his mouth shut about how relieved he was that Tyler was getting out of a life of risky trauma work, no matter the reason.

"You're the only one who understands that. Thanks for

listening. Anyway, I didn't call just to complain. I wanted to know if our Freedom Fridays still stood. I could use a drink."

"Hell yes. But I'm buying."

"Of course you are. Same place, same time?"

Dexter smiled. He and Tyler did these "Freedom Fridays"— the freedom to say anything without judgment—every week Tyler was in the States. The tradition had been going on since Dexter had hit a telephone pole one night after a long shift and without Tyler's lightning quick army medic reflexes, he would have died. A grisly burned-in-his-car death.

Dex offered to take Tyler out for a drink to say thanks when he was out of the hospital—that and to say he owed Tyler one. One drink had turned into them closing the bar followed by a decade and a half–long friendship.

Suffice it to say, Dexter needed that drink, too—and the friendship that had gotten him through some shit.

Death. Deployments…

Panic attacks for mundane nonsense?

"Yep. Maniac MacGee's at six?"

"You done with work by then?"

Dexter's laugh was more a humorless bark. "Whether or not I am, I'm outta there."

His admission was met with a dry laugh. "Wow. I've never known you to leave before the cleaning staff forcibly removes you so they can empty your trash."

Dexter kicked at a small pebble in the shape of a heart.

"Things are changing for us both, sounds like."

"Sounds like we need to tell Mac to keep 'em coming. You have anything tomorrow you need to be sober for?"

Dexter cringed.

Just figuring out what to do about my life and these panic attacks that have been cropping up the past year.

He had a sneaking suspicion it might include leaving a decade-long career at a hospital that had shaped his time as a psychiatric trauma specialist.

"Nah. I'm good." Tomorrow was a lot of drinks away and he wasn't on call. Hopefully the liquid clarity would help him make some tough decisions. Because as he thought of Mercy, of its austere white walls and tranquility, of Kelsey and Liam, her husband and new Mercy trauma doctor, walking through the halls and pointing out his own failures as a boyfriend and father, the painful truth settled in his chest.

He needed to leave. And sooner rather than later.

"Okay, then. Fair warning, I'm gonna talk your ear off once I have one drink. My tolerance is shit these days."

"Noted and acknowledged. All I hear is you're cheap, so that works for me."

The laugh from the other end was laced with a gravity Dexter wasn't used to. A shiver ran down his spine, tickling senses he'd honed in his profession.

Sergeant Tyler was in trouble, which made Dexter's problems seem like dodging mosquito bites during a firefight. His anxiety—and the panic seizing his chest every third day—would have to wait.

Millie smiled, letting the cool air wash over her. There wasn't a lot in her life worth smiling about, but the spring breeze was a welcome change. She'd lived in surface-of-the-sun heat the past year.

Her smile deepened when she caught the orange neon glow missing the "Gee's" so the sign read "Maniac Mac." That tracked. Mac—her friend from boot camp—hadn't made it past his first deployment when he decided the medical field, especially one in which bombs were being hurled at him while he triaged patients, wasn't for him. He'd quit after his first enlistment and opened Maniac MacGee's, a bar frequented by service members and first responders.

Good thing, too. If it weren't for this watering hole, Millie wouldn't have gotten through the past decade. Her hands trembled as she opened the door, but the shrill twang of a steel guitar worked on her like no therapy could.

She smiled and tossed her unruly curls over her shoulders.

"Well, *holy shit*. I didn't think I'd see your militant ass in here again."

"Mac, you wouldn't know militant if it shot you in the ass."

"Listen, I'll have you know my commanding officer said I had the best IV placement out of any medical recruit if I just—"

"Didn't get that damned case of sciatica," Millie finished.

Mac scowled. "Will you quit bein' mean and come give me a hug? I missed you but making fun of my *medically documented realities*," Mac whined as Millie mouthed the same words along with him, "is no way to treat the man who's gonna be feeding you drinks all night."

"Good point." Millie walked over to the serving window and reached through, embracing Mac. It felt good, holding something solid when her insides felt like they were flapping in the wind. "It's good to see you, Mac."

He squeezed her tight enough to pull the breath from her. "You, too, kid."

"You're three months older than me, Mac."

"Yep. And as your elder, I demand you take a shot to gain entrance into this fine establishment."

"Fine. Whiskey. And not your cheap shit. As the outranking officer here, I'm also gonna demand you join me."

"If you insist."

Mac made a poor attempt at a salute, then poured them each a shot.

"Yikes. That had some teeth," Millie hissed when hers was down, the slow burn of the liquor waking her up like a shot of espresso. "I'll take another, but with a dram of water this time. No need to rush this buzz, it'll come all on its own tonight."

"That bad, huh?"

Millie shrugged as Mac placed three fingers of whiskey in

a rocks glass in front of her. Only one person would understand the loss she felt at willingly saying goodbye to a family
she'd built, anyway.

"Yep. Hey, uh, not that I'm not glad to see you, but is he
here?"

"You know, if you were at all my type, I'd be pissed you're
abandoning me for another guy."

She shrugged again, a crooked smile on her lips.

"Sorry, Mac."

Mac nodded to the back, to the booth that had kicked off
the friendship all those years ago. "Back there. Here, bring
him this," he said, putting another whiskey on the mahogany
bar. "I'm not a cocktail waitress."

Millie climbed atop the barstool, leaned over and placed a
kiss on Mac's cheek.

"You're the best. I owe you one, Mac."

"I'd settle for an introduction to that man you were in a picture with on Facebook. The hottie in camo. Not everyone can
pull off that look, you know."

"Sure thing." Millie laughed as she walked toward the back
of the bar, which was shrouded in shadow. Mac had the same
taste she did—tortured men with their own abandonment issues.

When she rounded the post at the edge of the dance floor,
she halted in her steps. A smile spread across her cheeks at
the same time heat built behind her eyes.

"Dex," she whispered. He couldn't hear her—she was still
too far away—but he rose and strode over to her, holding a
bouquet of purple daisies that were crushed when he wrapped
her in his arms and cradled her head against his chest. The dam
holding back a torrent of hot salt water broke and her tears fell.

"Damn, Tyler, you're gonna give a guy a complex if he hugs
you and you start sobbing."

She choked out a laugh on the edge of a sob and he chuckled, his thick barrel chest vibrating beneath her cheek.

"Okay, okay. No more teasing." He stroked her hair. When his lips pressed against the wild curls, her breathing slowed along with her tears.

Millie pulled back, wiping her damp cheeks with the back of her hand.

"It's good to see you, Dex. You look…*strong*." She didn't let her eyes wander down his frame, which had filled out with hard-earned muscle since she'd last seen him. But her expertly trained touch—a lifesaver when she performed surgery—came in handy. "Been working out?"

He nodded, his shoulder muscles taut. No more runner's body for this guy. He was a brunette Thor now. Like she needed another reason to ignore his pull on her heart.

"Got some stuff to work through and running doesn't do the job by itself anymore. I need to throw a little weight around."

She appraised him through wary eyes.

"Will you settle for sixteen-ounce curls? Because we've got work to do tonight," she said.

His smile broke through. "Hell yes, we do." Dex nodded to the second drink in her hand. "That for me?"

She gave it to him, sipping her own as she sat in the booth. "Mac sends his love."

"Good man. Hey, cheers to you being back in the States. It's really freaking good to see you, Millie." She bristled under the use of her first name. It didn't rub her the wrong way, just made her skin tingle. He'd called her "Tyler" as long as she'd known him. It kept a distance that felt…safer with Dex.

Until… The way his gaze dipped to the deep vee of her light blue blouse added stomach flipping to the mix. *Great.*

He just hasn't seen you in a while and you're different, too.

Millie had always been on the curvier side of the army's regulations, but she'd been doing runs of her own to exorcise the demons that had followed her since childhood. She was still tall and full figured, but with some tone now.

"So, what's been going on with you? Because you look—"

"Like hell?" he finished for her.

"Maybe. A little. Just tired, I guess." That was only partially true. While he did look exhausted, the circles under his eyes textbook markers of sleeplessness, he also looked pretty damn fine. The auburn scruff dappling his cheeks and jaw didn't hurt, nor did the gentle Clark Kent wave in his espresso-colored hair that had grown out since she'd last seen him.

When had he gotten so handsome?

Please. You've always thought he was hot. Do not shove your neuroses on your best friend, her subconscious warned.

It wasn't wrong—she did have a propensity for falling for the wrong guy. Usually that was purposeful; scratching an itch didn't mean the guys had to buy her dinner or anything. It just meant she got what she wanted and could count on not being disappointed when they turned out to be something other than they advertised.

Dex was different. She'd turned him down once—a long time ago, when she was a different younger woman who somehow knew the man whose life she'd saved would mean more to her than just a casual hookup. What that might mean had scared her to death.

Unfortunately, what it had actually meant was she'd guaranteed he only thought of her as a friend since.

So, she'd gone back to casual relationships with emotionally unavailable guys instead of crushing on the one man she couldn't have. Thank goodness, since she'd gotten a best friend out of the deal.

She didn't regret the route she'd forced them down but from time to time, especially as she healed from her childhood baggage, she wondered...

What would it have been like to say *yes* to Dexter Shaw?

Either way, he was off-limits now.

"It's nice being here. Feels familiar," he said. "Remember the first time?"

"Like I could forget. You still had bandages on your head like you escaped a psych ward."

He chuckled.

"This place has heard some shit, that's for sure."

"No joke," she said.

She might have saved his life the day he'd slammed into her life via the pole on Hollywood Boulevard, but he'd been her white knight ever since. Who else could have brought her back to herself after her stepmom—a textbook narcissist—had turned Millie's dad's death into a reason to stop parenting the stepchild she'd never wanted in the first place?

Millie had raised herself from age twelve until Dex came along, the night he got in an accident.

Yeah, he's great, but don't forget he's high maintenance, too, her heart chimed in.

That's an understatement.

While she'd be fine with a toothbrush and running shoes for a week, Dex wasn't his best self unless there was a full-service spa within a hundred-meter radius. That was part of the reason they'd promised, after he asked her out that first week of knowing each other and she shot him down, not to ruin their friendship with a hookup.

They were night-and-day different and what they had was so much more important.

So, yeah. Ignoring the way his looks affected her decision-making was the new standard operating procedure.

"Well, anyway, you're not wrong. I feel like hell. They're back, Millie."

"The panic attacks?"

"Yeah. And worse. They're happening at work now, too."

"Crap. You can't have that." She reached out and took his hand in hers. The familiar warmth that settled between them was punctuated by small bursts of something...*warmer*. With more energy.

"Nope. Not when I'm the literal expert at that place for kicking anxiety and depression."

"What're you doing about it?"

Another shrug. "The usual. Breathing, counting, working out."

"You considered treatment?"

"Long term?"

She nodded.

"I dunno. I've been there and it helped, but… I've been thinking about some other ideas."

"Like?"

Dex shrugged and she tilted her head. "Did you get the trauma team going? That idea sounded right up your alley."

"No, and that's part of it."

"What else?" she asked.

Millie leaned back against the bar and gestured that he continue.

"It seems ridiculous with everything you're dealing with."

"Nope," Millie said, shaking her head. "If I were your patient spouting the same nonsense, you'd tell me not to compare traumas. It's hard for you right now. Period."

"That's fair. Well," he said, running his hands through his hair, "I'm thinking about quitting."

"Your job?" Millie sat up straighter. Damn. That threw a wrench in her plans for the evening.

"Yeah. It might not be the source of the anxiety, but being there isn't helping; I'm sure about that much."

"Can't you step down as chief and just practice?" She bit the corner of her lip. Everything she knew about her best friend said the job was perfect for him—it was safe, consistent and as reliable as a Swiss train.

Selfishly, she needed that to still be true.

Dexter shook his head and only then did she notice the dappled gray hair above his ears, the depth of the lines around his eyes. He looked more than tired. He looked *done*.

"It's not that simple."

"What's Kels have to say about all this?" She'd called out her big guns with that one. Millie knew Kelsey wanted kids, marriage and the whole shebang. She also knew Dexter didn't.

"We're through."

"I've heard that before," Millie said, snorting.

"No, this time it's for good. She adopted a baby and then the dad came looking for the kid and, well, they fell in love. It was a whole thing."

Millie felt the warm bar air settle in her gaping mouth.

"A *baby*? She fell in love with someone else? What the—"

"You missed a little bit while you were gone."

"Apparently."

He filled her in on a story that sounded like a made-for-TV movie. When he was done, they sipped in silence for a while, the weight of Dex's story heavy on Millie's mind. A tiny voice broke through the fog.

He's single.

She silenced it with an admonition. *It doesn't matter. Only helping him through this does.*

"How about you, Tyler?" Dexter asked when their glasses were more ice than liquid. The return to her last name was jarring. She kind of liked the way "Millie" rolled off his tongue. "I've been patient and unloaded all my trauma at your feet. Your turn."

It was always that easy with them.

She took the last sip of her whiskey, relishing the chilled liquid that still managed to warm her from the inside.

"Well, I'm guessing now isn't a good time to ask you for a job."

CHAPTER TWO

"A—A *JOB*?" Dexter sputtered.

He spit out a half-melted piece of ice. In the background, the lead singer of the band Mac had hired belted a country tune that sounded as heartbreaking as the mood at Dex and Millie's table. A few battle-worn regulars sat at the bar, heads bent over whatever medicinal cocktails Mac had drummed up to cure them of their woes that evening. It was an odd juxta-position against the three couples slow dancing in the middle of the worn hardwood floor, love—or at least alcohol-induced desire—wafting off them like cheap cologne.

Then there was the woman in front of him, who'd shocked him silent. Just when he thought the stuff out of Millie's mouth wasn't ever going to surprise him again.

"A job? Why do you need a job?"

"You didn't hear me when I said I'm not going back?" She leaned back in the booth, her long brown curls tucked over one shoulder, leaving the other one exposed. He licked his lips in spite of himself. In spite of their fifteen-year-old friendship.

The carnal side of him had to admit—Millie Tyler had grown up. And only gotten more gorgeous in the past year and a half.

But that didn't change the fact that she was abso-freaking-lutely off-limits. Or that what she was asking for was off the table, too.

"If I'm being honest, I didn't think you were serious. You've said it before, Tyler."

"Yeah, when I thought that a job could stand in for my screwed-up family. This—the realization that I've been kidding myself—is different."

Her *voice* was different. Softer. Filled with more than badassery and wit.

"Wow. I didn't know you'd been struggling with them again, Tyler. I mean, your family."

"It's not just that. I was getting restless, anyway. Besides, you're all I need." She blew him a kiss, but the frown lines gave her true emotions away. He stopped short of telling her that putting her happiness in any one person—even her best friend—wasn't healthy. She knew. Besides, he wasn't exactly the paragon of health himself at the moment.

God, he wished he could offer something—anything—that might help them both.

"And if I'm not able to get you a job?"

"Why wouldn't you be able to?"

"Just humor me. What then?"

"Well, if I don't find something here, I'll pick up a DWB contract. They're hiring for the round that will head out in six months. If I hurry, I can get my application in."

Dex's fingertips tingled. Doctors Without Borders was a good gig—one most docs coveted—but it wasn't much less dangerous than a field army medic's job.

"There's really nothing else?" he tried. "Nothing…calmer?" He couldn't lose her to another risky career. Not when he had a chance to keep her here, with him. But at what cost? He wasn't staying—*couldn't* stay—at Mercy. At least not without a leave of absence to make sure he was in the right headspace to treat his patients.

But you have the chance to save her. Like you couldn't save your dad.

"I could go back home to Missouri. At least my stepmom's in a home now."

"Yikes," Dex offered, scoffing at the idea. "That's a non-starter, isn't it? I mean, she still resents you for leaving in the first place."

"Yup. She still thinks my duty is to her instead of my patients or sanity, despite kicking me out when I was sixteen. Which is why I came to my dear friend Dex with connections at a hospital."

She sipped at her drink and he willed himself to not stare at the way she licked her lips after putting down her glass. Sexy but *dangerous*. Two words he'd always secretly used to describe his best friend when he needed reminders of why they'd stayed just friends all these years.

"Yeah, connections." His voice sounded far away, like it was being funneled from the other side of town.

"So you'll do it? Reach out to your chief medical officer and get me a job? Maybe with me there, it'll save two lives with one set of AED paddles, or however the saying goes. I can help you."

"I dunno—"

"C'mon, Dex. I'm double California Board–certified in psych and trauma emergency medicine, used to long hours and I have great bedside manner. You can vouch for me."

Dexter sighed, the desperation in her voice palpable like the layer of vape smoke hovering over the smoking area on the patio behind them. "It isn't that simple. I know all that and yeah, I can get you the job—hell, I can probably get you *my* job. And if you could find three more trauma docs that are double board-certified, you can take over the program I proposed. But I meant it when I said I was done. I've got no love left for LA, Millie. I need a change as much as you do. This is crappy timing, is all."

She pulled her bottom lip between her teeth. Usually that was a sign she was happy, but tonight it came with weight that knocked him on his ass. He had to adjust his jeans to accommodate the way his body was reacting to her.

Knock it off. She's the same person who slapped you when you tried to hold her hand the night you started Freedom Fridays at Mac's. The same woman who can drink you under the table and still shoot your balls off from fifty yards if you annoy her. But in a sexier package than ever before.

He shook his head, dissolving the battle between his head and…another, less trustworthy, organ.

"Please," she whispered. "I never ask you for anything, Dex. Don't make me beg. Not now." Dexter groaned and put his head in his hands. He'd never had the power to deny his best friend anything, but this was an impossible ask. It was her mental health or his.

"I won't. If you want the job, it's yours. I just won't be there by the time the ink on your contract dries."

"You know that's the important part to me, right? That I'd love you there while I figure my crap out?"

"I do."

"And you aren't gonna make me bring up the fact that you're all I have, are you? You're my family, Dex. You're literally it."

Dexter waved his empty glass in the air in Mac's direction. Their friend nodded and grabbed the bottle and two fresh glasses.

"Oh, thank God," he grumbled when Mac left the bottle and glasses on the table. "Reinforcements."

"Be nice to each other, guys," Mac warned.

"What're you looking at me for?" Dexter asked Mac's back as he walked away. Dex poured them each a full glass of whiskey and slumped back against the hard wood seat. To Millie, he simply said, "I'm sorry. I don't know what to tell you."

"If I'm working with you, I can help you manage the stress," she pleaded. "We make a good team. I'm sure that'll apply to work, too." He tried not to notice the way her bottom lip quivered. An urge to kiss it almost overwhelmed him.

Quit lusting after your best friend. Be there for her.

"Mercy isn't an option for me, Millie. It just…isn't. For a lot of reasons. What good would I be to you if I stayed and fell apart when you need me to be strong for you?"

Millie sat up straighter, her chest out and shoulders back. God, she could have been a general, the way she commanded attention. "Okay, I didn't want to do this, but I'm calling in my favor."

Dexter stared at her, his pulse quickening while his brain slowed. "You wouldn't. Not now, Millie."

The stare she shot back intonated all the seriousness of a three-alarm trauma. "Why not? It's not a favor if you don't have to give something up for the other person. I know what I'm asking is impossible, but you told me I could use it for anything. I saved your life and you owe me." She sat back and downed the rest of the liquid in her glass, hissing after slamming the glass on the wood table. "So, I'm using it for this."

"Whether or not you saved my life remains to be seen," he muttered. "You should've left me in the Porsche that night. Would have done us both a favor."

"Uh-uh. Nope. We're way too far down the line to start up that pity party. Dex, if you can't help me, I'm gone. I'll take the DWB job, but it's not what I really want."

Dex groaned. She was handing him what he'd wanted for so long—his best friend close by, safe and in a stable, permanent job. But taking that gift would be to shut out all the change he knew he needed to get his own life on track.

But then an idea hit him. She just needed a job. Frankly, so did he. But they didn't need to be at Mercy… Did they?

Part of his current anxiety stemmed from overcorrecting when it came to creating a life of safety. *So, what if…* What if he did something totally out of character and tried something *new*? They could apply somewhere as a team—a small clinic somewhere, or even a rural hospital. If it didn't work, he could always leave after the usual six-month probationary contracts most places offered.

And he could take a leave of absence at Mercy so he didn't cut that tie completely. It wasn't like he didn't have the PTO after a decade of slight workaholic tendencies.

Hope surged in his chest, pushing back the fear that had taken up residence as of late. He leaned across the table, regretting it immediately when the dim bar lighting illuminated gold flecks in Millie's green eyes. He could get lost there, no doubt. But she'd shut that down a million years ago, which meant he'd best honor her choice.

Not that they were similar enough to make a go of it, anyway. And he'd never treat her like a one-night stand. Never. She was too important.

"What if I could get you a job with me, but not at Mercy?" He studied her reaction, the way her eyes focused, growing wider even as her lips twisted in scrutiny.

"Like where? I'm not working at a drive-through, Dex. Not that there's anything wrong with that, but I still want to help people. I'm a doctor and I don't want to give that up."

"Me, too, Millie."

"So, why would you leave the job you're in? You're established at Mercy. And I know damn well you aren't going to follow me to a gig where there's less than top-notch amenities available."

He tilted his head in thought. Because what she said was true. He'd love to travel with Millie, seek out a new adventure, but he'd done enough adventuring and restarting for a lifetime. He could use a change, but she'd called him on a fundamental truth of his—he needed a sure thing in a safe place. The opposite of what Millie wanted.

He swallowed a groan.

"I dunno. Maybe we can take a road trip and check out places we're interested in."

She snorted. "We travel well together, I agree, but *you*? In a car for who knows how long? Yeah, no thanks."

Dexter tried to keep his face passive, but after three shots of hundred-proof liquor, that was getting more difficult. "Excuse me. What's that supposed to mean?"

"You're a diva."

"Am not."

"Are, too. Remember Italy?"

He sighed. "Are you always going to throw that in my face? It was *Europe*. You're supposed to be fashionable."

"Were we supposed to wear different clothes to each meal?"

Dexter drained his glass. "See if I ever buy you a welcome-home trip again."

"All's I'm saying is I don't think that's the answer. I'm not against looking for a new place to land together, but it'd be better if you could use the connections you've made over the years if we're going to find something outside LA. Then we're not shooting in the dark."

"I wish I had any. That was Kelsey's MO, not mine." He looked down at his drink, wishing it had the answers.

"Hmm. Well, calling her is off the table, huh?"

"Uh, yeah." Dexter didn't like the sarcastic snort that escaped his throat. "Besides, the only connection she had that would have related to us and not obstetrics was at a ranch for wounded vets. It was some trauma psych job that used horses and other ranch-related stuff to treat PTSD in veterans and first responders."

"Equine therapy."

"Yeah, I think that's what she called it."

Millie sat up straight. The twinkle in her eyes was all too familiar to Dexter. It was the same glimmer that had led to the two of them at the top of the tallest peak in Arizona one autumn night. The same one she'd had right before she convinced Dexter to try skydiving in Temecula.

It was mischief and resolve and the signal that he'd already lost whatever argument she was going to make.

"Let's do it. That's *perfect*, Dex. I mean, working with horses? It'll do us both good and think of who we'll be working with—the same patients we always wished we could focus on. Weren't you trying to start a trauma psych program at Mercy?"

"Yeah, that part's true, but the rest?"

Safety. Security. Consistency.

None of those things existed at the equine ranch.

"I don't ride horses, I don't like to be dirty and I don't own a set of cowboy boots. You said it yourself—I'm a diva. It won't work. Besides, it was for a married couple."

Checkmate. Gin. Yahtzee.

He let the smug grin spread across his face.

"And?"

He took a long sip of whiskey, feeling fidgety again. He shifted on the bench. "And we're not married, Millie."

"Neither were you and Kelsey."

"True. Kelsey and I were gonna fib a little for the sake of the job, but we were at least *dating.*"

Millie leaned forward, the look in her eyes steely and determined. His smile fell.

"Tell me she knew you half as well as I know you."

"She didn't. Obviously. And in the end, I realized I didn't really know her, either."

"Exactly."

"So, what does that have to do with us?"

"I can pretend to be your wife."

Dexter choked for the second time that evening, this time on the alcohol. It burned along the length of his throat.

"You can do *what*?"

Millie smiled in a crooked half grin that said he wasn't going to like what came next. She stood up and motioned that he scoot over to let her in his side of the booth. He did and regret followed swiftly. Forget the gold in her eyes... Her scent—something floral and feminine—snaked around his throat, suffocating him.

He...*liked it*. Liked it on *her*, even though anything floral or feminine was diametrically opposed to the fierce army trauma medic he knew.

"I'll be your wife. Do you need my credentials for that, too?"

"Oh, no, Millie. I—"

"As long as you do the cooking, I can take care of the rest," she continued. "I work all day so I won't nag when you have to, I don't mind keeping the place clean and—" she paused and sent him a little wink "—I'm a freaking maniac in the bedroom."

Dexter swallowed hard. He did *not* need to know that.

She licked her lips. "And outside the bedroom if that's more your taste."

Dexter shook his tingling hands and damn if his jeans weren't a little too tight around the waist.

"Even if I agreed to this asinine plan—which I'm not," he added when her eyes got as big as her smile, "it'd be a fake marriage. Sex wouldn't... It wouldn't be part of it."

His whole body sagged under the pathetic statement.

"Why not?"

"Because you're my best friend." His tongue was suddenly too thick in his mouth.

"I didn't mean the sex, silly, though I'll add that's your loss. I meant why won't you consider the plan?"

"Besides the fact that it's not a plan?"

"It is, too. Are they still hiring?"

"As far as I know." He'd overheard Kelsey saying the couple that had taken it when she passed it over was done with their contract and she wished her and Liam could take the job, if only they could bring their daughter.

"Great. Call them up, tell them you'll take the gig, and send our credentials."

"Fine. Let's say we did that. There's a million other reasons this still wouldn't work," he added so the topic could move away from things that were sounding more appealing with Millie by the minute. Like how the body he'd known most of his adult life might feel pressed against his.

"Oh, yeah? Like what? Your lack of horse awareness? So what? You'll pick that up."

"Maybe," he hedged. Though the thought of being around the smelly animals day in and out wasn't exactly appealing. That was part of why he'd turned down the offer the first time. "But there's also the fact that no one will believe *we're* married."

She scowled, the look somehow endearing.

Just friends. You're just friends.

"Excuse me, Dexter Shaw, but why not?" He cringed at the hurt in her voice. "Are you saying I outkicked my coverage with you?"

"Not at all." He rubbed his eyes with the heels of his palms. Where was Mac when he needed the guy? The idea that Millie wasn't good enough for him was laughable. If anything, it was the other way around. What did he have to offer a woman of the world—a stunning one at that—with his stale, safe life? "I'm saying you want to travel and have an adventurous spirit and I...don't."

"And?" Why did he get the sense she was winning this whole argument with that one word?

"And our lifestyles don't fit. You belong with some mountain man who chops his own Christmas trees and hunts everything he eats. Someone who'll bring you wildflowers from his expeditions."

"I'm more of a beach gal," she teased, picking up a pretzel from the bowl on the table and popping it in her mouth. "Especially after Trevor."

"Yeah, he was a tool. But at least he lived within a hundred miles of you. And I agree—you belong with some long-haired hippy who plays the acoustic guitar by a bonfire and can sweep you off your bare sand-covered feet."

"That sounds like heaven. Just so you know, I'm picturing Jason Momoa with a ukulele, though." A small twinge of jealousy pricked Dex's skin. He shook it off. "But I get what you mean. You'd fit more with some charity do-gooder with coiffed blond hair and a closet full of suits. Like Kelsey, or that other girl you dated who wore makeup to the gym."

"Bev." He'd made it a whole month with the aerobics instructor before he was bored stiff. And that was saying something.

"Ha! Yeah, her."

Millie was right—that was more his taste. Someone safe, planned. Not someone who flitted through adventures like she was in a Bond film.

Not someone like Millie.

"Okay, but this would only be a six-month gig. What happens after that?"

"I apply to DWB," she said, shrugging in her usual nonchalant way. "And you're off the hook."

Why didn't *off the hook* sound as appealing as it should? Especially when she would be off doing God knew what with Doctors Without Borders. An urge to take care of her, protect her, almost choked him.

"Do you have to do work that's so dangerous?" he asked.

"It's not like I have a choice. You took LA off the table, so what's left? Besides, someone has to." Millie pulled her hair back off her face and tied it up with a band from her wrist. Though he'd always appreciated the wild curls that framed her face, he couldn't keep his gaze from the curve where her slender neck met her shoulder.

"Still."

"You know," she continued, "one might argue that living without the trappings of a life of luxury makes me free."

"I'm sure someone might. You, on the other hand, know

better because you know why I'm like that, Millie. I'll tackle my issues, too. I'm just asking—as a friend, and your best one at that—that you consider not always throwing yourself into such threatening situations."

"We'll talk about that later. Unless you want me to apply to DWB right now, I'd say we have other things that need our attention. Like this equine doctor job."

She clapped her hands and the smile she wore resembled a kid who got a pony for Christmas. He chuckled, realizing that if they took this job, she would actually get a whole barn of horses for the holiday.

"But what if the job actually isn't available? What then?" It was his last attempt to stave off the inevitable.

Millie dug around in her purse and Dexter took the moment her back was to him to appreciate the sculpting of her shoulders, the curve of her waist. She turned around as he was mid lip-lick and he cringed. Great. It only took fifteen years for her to catch him looking like a creep.

"If you like what you see, we can always put sex back on the table. Literally." She winked and handed him her phone while he tried to find his voice. That had to be the whiskey talking, right? Because they'd already crossed that bridge and decided to stay in the neutral zone where only friendship was allowed. "Here. Call them."

"Seriously?"

"Serious as an effing aneurysm. We both need the job, and really, what other options are there? I'm also willing to bet that whatever trauma recovery program we'll be running will do us both some good."

Dexter couldn't disagree with that. In fact, the only thing he could disagree with was pretending to be Millie's husband. Not because he didn't know more about her than anyone on Earth, or because it wasn't plausible that the two could be together, but because...*it could.*

He'd watched her walk into the bar, slide up to Mac and

own the place with her confidence and, if he were being totally honest, her knockout looks. She'd always been pretty,
but she'd become captivating since the last time he saw her.

His head hurt trying to come up with a way to convince
her this was by far her worst idea yet. Hopefully the headache
and sobriety that greeted her in the morning would do what
he didn't have the guts to do.

"If we do this, I'll need to take some time off to get my
head right. I can't dive right into something else until I know
I'm good to take on new patients."

"That would be good for me, too, to be honest."

"And if they don't want to wait, then I can't entertain it,
Millie."

She nodded and put her drink up to her lips, draining it.
"Nope. I understand."

She licked her lips, and between that and the mischievous
gleam in her eye, Dex didn't have a chance.

"Okay," he blurted out. "Let's give it the ol' college try."

Millie squealed and leaned over, planting a kiss at the corner
of his lips. "Thank you! You won't regret this, Dex. I promise."

She wrapped one arm around him and used the other to
fill their drinks.

Oh, I think I just might.

CHAPTER THREE

Two months later

MILLIE HAD NURSED her hangover for two days after that night at Mac's. Her head had pounded from the multiple tumblers of whiskey she'd thought was a good idea at the time, but that was nothing compared to the way her pulse raced every time she thought about the lie facing her down. It was almost two full months later and she still couldn't calm her racing heart when she thought about it.

Christ, she thought for the thousandth time since she'd received the one-line text.

We're in.

What have I gotten myself into?

In less than a week, she'd be Dexter's *wife*. Not really, obviously, but for the six-month provisional contract, that'd be her secondary role after trauma physician and psychologist. Which meant she and Dex would have to sell the lie every damn day, since the contract had them living on site in a small one-bedroom cabin.

Millie paced in the small hotel room she'd rented now that she was back in LA.

Two months.

Two months had passed and she'd barely spoken to the guy

since Mac's. He'd been serious about taking a leave of absence, checking himself into some fancy wellness spa where every sip of water was probably flavored and the thread count on the sheets didn't dip below four digits.

She'd crossed her fingers and wished on every damn yellow light that he found the clarity he needed in his wellness sessions to stay at Mercy, where they could work side by side but stay just friends.

No dice. He'd sent another one-liner the day prior.

Out. Looking forward to catching up, cowgirl. See you soon.

Ugh.

Soon sounded like another four-letter word.

At least she'd had two months to get in some of her own therapy sessions, which were honestly something she should have done years earlier.

Except they hadn't prepared her for having a *husband.*

Millie grabbed her running shoes. She'd call Dex that afternoon to make a plan, but not until she ran out her feelings—feelings a therapist couldn't touch. Tying her shoes and throwing on a running hat over un-showered curls, Millie replayed their last non-text conversation from the morning after Mac's.

"You sure this is what you want? That working on this ranch for half a year and pretending to be married to me is gonna help you fill the hole in your life? Because I can get you a spot at my retreat and we can look at other options," he'd said the next morning. She'd seen the "get out of jail free" card for what it was, but some mix of pride and negative thought indicators had prevented her from speaking up.

"Yup," was all she managed to squeak out, to almost immediate regret.

Dex.

As my fake husband.

Dex, who'd tried to hold her hand out of pity after a few too many drinks that first night he took her out to thank her for saving his life.

As my fake husband.

Dex, who she turned down because he was too good a guy to lure in with her "charms."

As my fake husband.

Not exactly living the life she expected of her patients, was she?

Someone knocked on her door just as she got to it, water bottle in hand. A glance around her sparsely decorated hotel room said room service couldn't have come at a better time.

Take-out containers from every region and ethnicity littered the surface of the desk-slash-table. Scattered tissues left evidence of a *Bridget Jones* level of self-pity, dotting the paper and plastic containers. Then there was *her*.

A glance in the mirror confirmed it—she'd seen better days. Her hair looked capable of housing a small family of sparrows, hat or not. Her cheeks could land planes with the moisture dappling her pale skin, and her eyes... Well, racoons would be jealous of the circles she'd developed. She'd never been as ritualistically clean as Dex—only a select few people were—but this was bad, even for her.

"Ugh," she said, slapping her cheeks to give them some color. "Get a grip."

She whipped open the door and blanched.

"Dex," she croaked. "What are you doing here?"

He glanced over her shoulder at the self-loathing bomb that had exploded behind her.

"I could ask you the same thing."

She attempted to tuck the nest on top of her head farther under her running cap, but only an exorcism and prescription-strength moisturizing conditioner were fixing that mess.

"I'm...um... I'm relaxing a little before we start." Didn't she deserve a couple days of bingeing Netflix and eating takeout after leaving her old career behind?

Dexter pushed his way into her room, and as if her mortification knew no limits, he sniffed the air and his amused smile twisted like he'd inhaled antiseptic-masked defecation in a patient's room.

"A few days to relax is a jaunt to Telluride or a weekend getaway to Catalina Island. This is a cry for help."

She sniffled, another round of "my life, a dry comedy of errors" pushing at the back of her sinuses.

"I know."

The admission seemed to buy her an ounce of empathy. Dexter pulled her into a hug and kissed the top of her head.

"I'm sorry, Millie. You've been through hell and I all but left you the past two months."

"You texted," she said, her voice muffled by his strong chest against her cheek.

"Well, I'm not going anywhere again. Being present is what good husbands are supposed to do, at least according to the blog I read this morning."

She pulled back and looked up at him.

Big mistake.

His blue-gray eyes were the only things on earth capable of cracking through her carefully constructed armor.

"You read a blog?"

"Turns out a thirty-eight-year-old man who's never been married isn't exactly an expert in the field of faking what marriage should look like. So yeah, I may have opened a tab or two in the name of research."

She smiled, the chink in her nerves letting in a thin swathe of light. Maybe this wouldn't be so bad, after all.

"Did you forget the part about me knowing you better than anyone? I'm pretty sure your apartment looks like my hotel room if you swapped the fast food with clinical psych books on healthy relationships."

He smiled, too, and the light grew brighter.

"Elliot Aronson and his theories on cognitive dissonance send their best."

"Are you saying this thing we're doing doesn't mean we're certifiable?"

"He'd argue that, so sure. Let's go with it. Anyway," he said. "We can't do a thing while you look like that."

He gestured to the whole of her and the heat of mortification flashed up her neck.

While she appreciated the solid strength of his chest propping her up, she was also painfully aware what that strength mixed with his scent was doing to her. Whatever pine tree wrapped in coffee grounds he'd rubbed up against made her want to simultaneously climb him limb by limb and run her tongue over his body in the same way.

Not a good way to start a *fake* marriage.

"I was going running."

"Sure you were." He walked her toward the bathroom instead of the hotel room door. "Okay, here we are," Dexter declared, depositing her in front of the shower. "You can be lonely, but you can't be lonely *and* smelly while you're out with me."

"Out with you where?" Fear dappled her skin. "I'm not ready for public consumption yet."

Dexter clicked his tongue and winked. "I know, which is why we're shopping. To get ready."

Maybe it was the wink or the sodium in her veins from too much takeout, but her knees buckled. He caught her under the arms. If Dex wasn't…*Dex*, it would have been romantic, being held in the arms of the man she cared most about.

"Why do we have to shop? I have plenty of clothes." He steadied her again, but the weakness in her body remained. She really could use that run to get her head and heart rate right.

"You're making me take a job on a *ranch*. In case you weren't aware, there are animals the size of trucks there, and they don't care if my loafers are genuine Italian leather. We're shopping so we can survive in Cambria."

He turned on the water and went to lift her arms, but that shame she wouldn't recover from.

"I've got it from here, Dex."

He rested a hand under her elbow, and though he'd seen her in all stages of undress and vulnerability over the course of their friendship, this felt the most intimate. His gaze bore into hers and a chill raced over her exposed skin.

"Hey. I'm just worried about you." That was Dex, through and through. He always worried about her choices, her adventures, her one-night stands, even though they were just friends.

Not anymore. Now she was his friend-slash-wife.

"I'm fine. My therapist might have been off a dark alley with a threadbare couch instead of in Malibu with cucumber water, but she was good. I've got this."

"We can joke all day long and it won't change the fact that your family left you high and dry—both families. You're allowed to feel things, Millie."

He'd dropped the *Tyler* altogether. With a job that required them to manifest a five-year-long marriage starting in just days, that was probably a good thing. But she could use a little distance right now.

"Thanks," she finally said. "I'm glad you're here."

"Me, too." He opened the cheap plastic shower curtain and all but shoved her in. "Okay. No more stalling. Get in before the stench of three-day-old Thai food sends me into my own ward of the hospital."

Millie obeyed, grateful for the stinging heat of the water that pulsed over her skin. She felt better under the hot spray. Under Dex's care, too.

Half an hour later, a brush easily slipped through her hair and, more importantly, Millie didn't feel the thick heat at the back of her throat anymore. Wrapping a towel around her chest, she poked her head out to see what Dex was up to.

"What did you do?" she asked. The whole place was...clean. Not even the corner of a soy sauce packet was left behind.

"I made this place livable," he said, coming around the corner of the suite's small kitchen with a dish towel draped over his shoulder. Despite his efforts not to, he looked domestic. It suited him, despite his persistent disagreement about the merits of domesticity. "You're welcome."

"Thanks, Dex. You didn't have to." She gestured around the room.

He shrugged. "Gets me what I want, too, so it's no big deal."

"What's that?"

"Seeing that smile on your face."

Heat crawled over her cheeks, settling on her neck, as she pulled her bottom lip between her teeth.

"Oh, yeah?"

"Yep. Which is why I have full intentions of spoiling my wife with the best wrangler gear Boot, Barn, and Barrel has to offer. Hell, we'll probably get you a lady Stetson, too."

"I'm pretty sure they just call them Stetsons, *dear.*" She gave that last word the sarcasm it deserved. "And thanks, but I'm fine with my old jeans and a ball cap."

"Nope." He tucked a wet curl behind her ear and planted a kiss on her cheek. "You wanted marriage, you got it."

Oh, boy.

Standing there in front of Dexter, clad only in a towel that barely hid her rapidly beating heart, she wasn't sure what she wanted anymore. Only that if she looked too deeply into that question, she wasn't sure she'd like the answer.

CHAPTER FOUR

DEXTER SWALLOWED A Millie-in-tight-jeans-induced lump back into his stomach where it belonged. You'd think after two months of prepping to come to Cambria—including deciding how best to sell their fake marriage—he'd feel more prepared, but that wasn't the case. Besides the lie, neither of them had worked with horses, or even been on a ranch, so there sure as heck wasn't anything he should find alluring, except...

"This is hideous."

Not the word he'd choose to describe her, but like hell he was gonna say what was really on his mind.

"You look—"

Sexy? Gorgeous?

"Dexter Shaw, if you know what's good for you, you won't finish that sentence. I'm an expert marksman in three combat rifles and two handguns."

"Duly noted." He tipped his Stetson in her direction, trying to loosen the tightening in his chest. "But fitting in will be half the battle in getting the patients to trust us as their doctors."

She scratched under her hat, her pink lips twisted into a tight scowl. It wasn't so much that the light green flannel he'd purchased—along with the matching boots and hat that yeah, were a bit much—brought out her eyes. It was also the way the jeans hugged curves he'd never let himself check out.

"Whatever you say, *honey*," Millie grumbled. She twisted

the gold band on her left hand until he grabbed both her hands and squeezed.

"It's going to be okay."

"I know," she shot back. She wriggled out of his grasp and opened the door to the cab. "Seriously? You don't have a ladder to go with this thing?"

"The salesperson said—"

"It was the best they had to offer, right? Jesus, Dex. You're nothing if not consistent." They'd bought a truck—or rather, *he* had, with the substantial savings he'd accumulated before taking this leave of absence from Mercy—and he had to admit, cowgirl outfit notwithstanding, she looked good riding next to him.

If only she wasn't ready to tan his hide, or whatever cowboys called it. Millie was pissed.

Pissed is better than lonely and sad.

Besides, as adorable as she looked angry with him? Yeah, not a good reason to stop teasing her.

"Wait there, wifey."

Dexter hopped out of the truck, sprinted over to Millie and carried her out of the truck.

"What are you doing?" she hissed.

"What I didn't get to do since we eloped," he said, alluding to their cover story. "Carrying you over a threshold."

She glared at him from under the wide brim of her hat.

"Dexter Shaw, you are skating on thin ice."

"You wanted this life, and you've got it. Let's try and make the most of it."

"That's pretty uncharacteristically optimistic of you, Dex." Her gaze raked over him and it got a few degrees hotter under his flannel.

She's right, his subconscious demanded. *You're happier.*

Maybe it was being around Millie, the one person he didn't have to hide from, or the way the country air in Cambria moved freely in and out of his lungs. Or even the eight-week stint working on himself before they left the city. But he felt…lighter. No hints of the inky black tendrils pulling at his thoughts, closing his throat with fear.

"Okey dokey. And if I forget to thank you later, I really am grateful that you're doing this," she said. "This outfit is ridiculous, but I'm actually…excited about something for the first time since I enlisted out of high school."

He took her hand and walked down the long dirt driveway to the barn where they'd been told to meet. Risking one of the weapons Millie was so proficient in being trained on him, he bent down and kissed her cheek.

He appreciated the bloom of pink that spread across her cheeks.

"Me, too. All right, it's go time. Ready to be Mrs. Shaw for the next six months?"

She nodded right away, but he saw the way her throat struggled to swallow. He understood. This was a big lie to keep up. If it were anyone other than his best friend on the other end of it, he'd have canceled the whole thing.

Dexter pushed open the heavy oak door, the creak in the hinges exactly what he'd imagined when he thought of this moment. In fact, every inch of what they walked in on was par for his expectations.

Dust they kicked up lingered a few inches off the ground, clinging to every surface in the barn—the doors, the walls, even the ceiling was coated in it. The only two exceptions were the riding equipment hanging on the stall doors—*tack*, if he remembered right—and the horses themselves. They were both shiny and clean. Interesting.

"Wow," Millie whispered. "This is just what I imagined."

Dexter smiled at the synchronicity. "Me, too." It was always that easy with her.

Just like that, his smile fell, though. He couldn't let himself slip into an alternate reality where he and Millie were *actually* together.

Why not?

Dexter lifted the hat from his head, desperate to let what little breeze there was in. No time for that line of thinking. He might have worked out his recent anxiety issues, but Millie's penchant for danger would ramp them back up if he were her actual spouse.

And risking their friendship when their differences inevitably clashed? A nonstarter.

"Well, howdy," a deep, booming voice called out behind them. Dexter spun around and was hit with a wave of embarrassment. The man walking toward them was every inch the cowboy. Tall, strong like he'd been lifting the horses out of their stalls, and wearing a Stetson that didn't look like it was bought yesterday.

The only thing not "cowboy" about the guy was his simple black T-shirt and worn pair of loose-fitting jeans. No flannel chambray, no butt-huggers as Millie called them. Dex glanced down at his own outfit and realized Boot, Barn, and Barrel had duped them.

"I'm Gale Brooks, the owner of this outfit. You must be the Shaws."

He extended a hand to each of them, a steely gaze to go with it.

"That's Tyler-Shaw for me. I'm a hyphenate." She smiled up at Gale, whose crooked smile said he liked her spunk. Or was it just that he liked *her*?

She's married, buddy. Eyes off.

Hmm. Where'd that jealousy spring from?

"I'm Dr. Dexter Shaw, and this is my wife, Millie."

The words rolled off his tongue easy enough, but the ripple back into the cavity of his chest was severe. *My wife.*

"Dexter Shaw… You shoulda been born into ranching with a name like that."

Millie grinned like she'd won a prize. "He doesn't like horses."

Dex shot her a scowl. "I like them fine. I just haven't seen the need to be on the back of one in the city."

"We'll take care of that. Riding isn't required, but it'll help you bond with your patients to get them out on the trails between individual and group therapy sessions."

"I can't wait," Millie added. To Dex, she whispered, "That'll teach you to dress me in flannel."

His jaw set. "You forget, married couples get divorced all the time, dear," he whispered back.

Gale clapped and gestured to the fields and main ranch house visible in the distance. "Well, okay, then, Tyler-Shaws. Welcome to Hearts and Horses Ranch. We're not your typical roping-and-cattle-riding ranch, though we are fully operational."

"I read on the website you hire vets and first responders who've gone through the treatment program to work the ranch," Millie said. She did? Research was usually *his* forte and she just showed up ready to go along for the ride.

"That's true. Every person here is either a United States veteran, like myself, or a retired first responder, like my partner." Gale tipped his hat to Millie. "Corporal Brooks, ma'am."

"Staff Sergeant Tyler—" she started, then glanced at Dex "—Tyler-*Shaw* reporting for duty."

Dex exhaled. They needed to corroborate and practice their backstories more seriously if they were going to pull this off. Slipups like that were gonna get them found out.

"And lemme just ask. Your paperwork didn't mention you served in the military, fire department, or police force, Mr. Shaw. That correct?"

"It is." Why did he feel like that was a shortcoming all of a sudden?

"No worries. It's not required for the physicians on contract. I just want to know how to introduce you to the patients."

"Dr. Shaw is fine."

"All right, then. I'll show you to your bunk, then you can

meet the clients at dinner. Just so you know, we all pitch in around here, outside our general duties. Since y'all are just settling in, I won't hold you to dinner duty, but come breakfast, it's all hands on deck."

"Sounds good," Millie said. "We're excited to start."

Speak for yourself, Dex thought. They walked back to the truck, Gale insistent that part of the welcome package included his assistance with their bags.

"After that," he said, "you're on your own."

Gale hefted the first of Dex's oversized suitcases out of the bed of the truck like it was filled with goose feathers. "You're lucky you drove. I don't think a plane could take off with this bag," he said, smiling at Millie in a way that made Dexter uncomfortable. There was friendly and then more than friendly. This was the latter.

"That's my bag," she deadpanned, pointing to the carry-on sitting on the tailgate.

The cowboy laughed. "Well, I'll be. Don't know I've ever met a wife who packed less than her husband."

Millie gestured back to Dexter, who had to repress an urge to defend his masculinity. "This guy plans for all possible scenarios. I just brought jeans and a few tops. Hope that's okay."

"You've got the right idea. All's you need out here is a comfortable pair of boots for work and a cleaner pair of the same thing for hitting the town on your nights off."

Gale took both heavy bags over his shoulders. Millie carried her own, leaving Dex empty-handed.

"I can get those," Dex said.

"No problem, son. I'm used to carrying more than this, though you're testing that limit," he teased.

"I've got medical supplies packed in there, too."

"So do I." Millie grinned, clearly not helping his case for overpacking.

"You know, for all the teasing you do, you're forgetting the time you had to use one of my button-downs as a dress when your luggage was lost on that Vegas trip," Dexter whispered to Millie. "My overpacking has saved your ass once or twice."

"Maybe. But that was only 'cause I didn't have *anything*. You, on the other hand, could have opened up a Brooks Brothers."

"You two sound like you've been married longer than five years," Gale laughed.

"We've been together fifteen," they said in unison.

"Feels like more than that," Dexter grumbled under his breath.

It was clear, then. Of all the jobs he'd had in life—therapist, chief of psychiatry, even being a medical transcriptionist in college—being Millie Tyler's husband was gonna be the toughest gig of all.

Millie whistled while she changed. It was quiet out here— no gunfire, no shouting. But also no laughter from her army medic bunkmates, no teasing from her nurse, Sarah, about her crummy card-playing skills, no one to read her like a book when she got quiet imagining the ghosts of her past.

Just the distant sounds of cowboys doing whatever cowboys did. She didn't hate it; fake-marrying Dex notwithstanding, this seemed like a good move. But after being alone most of her teen years, then filling the void with chatter from work the next decade and a half, the quiet would take some getting used to, for sure.

One thing was certain—she hadn't breathed this easy since, well, maybe ever.

Dex jumped in the shower after unpacking, citing "dust in every damn crevice" so she had the room to herself for a moment. It'd been obvious why the ranching doc job called for a married couple when they saw the bunkhouse. Theirs was the only "suite" and even then, it consisted only of a full-sized bed, a shower with a clear curtain and a toilet that—*thank the gods*—was tucked away behind a door that closed and locked.

No kitchen, no office. *No privacy.*

Dex hummed a country song from her high school years. George Strait, if she remembered right. At one point, he launched into the lyrics and she froze, listening intently.

The man can sing.

Of course he could. Aside from his penchant for the finer things, he was perfect. Not exactly *fake* husband material.

The shower turned off and Millie sprinted through putting lotion on her legs. It might be dusty, but it was also dry as the desert she'd left mere weeks ago.

"Hey, have you seen my—" Dex said, coming around the corner from the tub. He stopped at the corner of the bed and before he caught himself, she saw his gaze travel across her stomach and bare legs before landing at her feet. It gave her the split second she needed to give him a once-over without letting him in on just how gorgeous she found him.

Clad only in a towel—and a small one at that—water dappled his skin and wet hair hung across his eyes. But his chest and shoulders... The strength complemented the emotional, sensitive man she knew. Which she very much appreciated.

"What are you doing?" she asked, grabbing an off-white T-shirt and throwing it over her nude lace bra. Dex had the good sense not to say anything, but the heat that flashed on his cheeks said it all. She'd embarrassed him on day one. *Great.*

"Showering. What are *you* doing?"

"Changing. There's no damn way I'm showing up to meet a group of rugged patients in creased jeans and a green flannel. I don't know why I let you talk me into getting that shirt in the first place."

Dex smiled and her guard lowered just enough to let the grin past her defenses.

"C'mon. You looked adorable."

"Yeah, just the professional impression I was hoping to make."

Millie watched, horrified, as Dex combed his hair, dug

through his queen-bed-sized suitcase and brushed his teeth—all in a towel small enough to make a Victoria's Secret model blush.

She fought to look away, but she was only so strong and Dex was…tempting enough to test that strength.

"Okay," he said ten minutes later when—thankfully—he came out of the bathroom in jeans and a loose-fitting shirt. "So we can both agree those outfits I bought were a fail. Luckily, I overpacked," he said, shooting her a pointed look, "or I wouldn't have any replacements."

"Yeah, real lucky you brought—" she lifted a white button-down shirt off the top of his garment bag "—a *white* shirt you have to iron after you wash it. To a *ranch*. We don't have an iron or bleach strong enough to get the country out of this if you stain it."

She grinned until his gaze dipped to the bigger of his two suitcases.

"You didn't," she laughed.

"It's just in case. I wasn't planning on using it."

"Sure. You brought an iron *just in case.* Dex, you're always good for a laugh, that's for sure. We should head out, though, unless you need to shine your oxfords or something."

"Knock it off. Hey, before we leave, you wanna talk about the sleeping arrangements?"

"What arrangements? There's one bed."

"Yeah, but we're not—" he lowered his voice as if he didn't want the cows mooing off in the distance to hear him "—actually married."

"I know," she whispered back, conspiratorially. "I was there when we agreed to it."

His glare was adorably overdone, like the rest of the man. Good grief, she was gonna have to hold his hand through this thing, wasn't she?

"Well," she continued in normal volume, "you packed pj's in that clothes coffin, didn't you? We'll be fine."

"Pj's? What are you, ten? I'll have you know the only things I wear to bed are a plan for tomorrow and a smile."

Her body froze cell by cell despite the heat. "You're kidding."

"I'm not. How didn't you know that about me? Remember Vegas when you got in my bed by mistake?"

She didn't. The amount of vodka sodas she'd consumed that night could have floated the Titanic back to the surface. She wasn't sure whether it was a bad thing she didn't recall a naked Dex or a miracle she'd give thanks for later. As it was, she had the image of his Greek god physique in a tea towel seared into her retinas.

"Whatever. I'm an adult, you're an adult, and we'll just manage. It's only six months." Her brain did the math without prompting.

One hundred and eighty-some days. Good luck, sister.

"I'm good if you're good."

"I'm good." This trip, this job, this place—none of it was so that she could jump her best friend and satisfy fifteen years of curiosity and longing. It was to help patients like her start their own healing process.

Her heart beat to the tune Dex had sung in the shower.

Shut up, she told it.

Maybe his wouldn't be the only hand she'd have to hold as they navigated their new circumstances.

"Okay. Now that the sleeping stuff is handled, should we get to work?" she asked.

"Yep. Let me just get my cell."

"Why bother? We won't have service out here, anyway."

Dex's twisted lips and furrowed brows said this was going to be a long six months for him, too.

"No cell. No nice clothes. No iron. You have no idea how much you owe me for this, Tyler. And a night of drinks ain't gonna cut it."

She smiled, but the *Tyler* dug at her heart. They could fake being in love to the outside world as much as they wanted, but behind closed doors, they were still Shaw and Tyler, best buds who kept their hands to themselves.

For a split second, she played the what-if game with the day she met Dex—something she did when things were tough, or the wanting of him threatened to override her promise to stay friends.

In a different life, the man who'd slammed into Hollywood Boulevard right in front of her bistro table where she'd been on a shitty first date would have been strong, capable and, yeah, a little bit of a diva. The same as the man she knew and cared for today. But if she could choose? She would have been open to more, to the possibility that, regardless of the crappy short hookups she'd had in the past, *they* could be more. However, thanks to the wreckage from her past *situationships*, all she pictured back then was the morning after when she'd have said goodbye to Dex like all the rest and then where would she be? Without a helluva good man that she was lucky to count as her only family.

Maybe in a different life.

When they shut the door behind them, Millie waited for Dex to fix his boots. She inhaled deeply, the scent of pine laced with a hint of salty sea air.

"I keep forgetting Cambria is close to the water. Maybe we'll get a day off and can head to the beach sometime."

"Sure," Dex mumbled. "Who doesn't love sand in all their skin folds?"

Along the tree line, something moved. Millie trained her gaze and saw a deer and her baby emerge. They weren't hesitant here—they must feel safe from predators on the ranch. She inhaled deep and let that resonate.

"Is there anything you actually like about this place?" she asked when Dex stood up.

"The shower's got good water pressure."

"Wow. High praise," Millie said, snorting.

"It's just not my cup of tea. It'll be fine, though. We're here to practice medicine. I don't need to fall in love with it or anything."

"Maybe. But all this fresh air, the songs and sounds of the wildlife—this place will grow on us and I'll bet my salary you won't even want to go back to LA when this is done."

She went to toss him a wink and smile and instead found herself wrapped in his arms, his gaze hot and pinned to hers. His lips were only half a breath from hers until…they weren't.

When his mouth crashed into hers, heat flashed across her skin along with confusion.

What the—? her brain tried, but her heart silenced it.

Shut up. We're kissing Dexter Shaw.

Millie let his tongue tease open her lips just enough that she tasted the mint from his toothpaste. She moaned as her body relaxed into his. His arms tightened around her, his strength the only thing keeping her knees from buckling.

This. This is what we've been missing just being this guy's friend.

When his hand tunneled into the base of her curls, her stomach flipped in response.

And then, with the same unexpectedness of being kissed in the first place, it was over and Millie was standing there—*where*, she couldn't be sure of anymore—alone and wanting.

"I'm happy to be here with you, hun."

Hun? She was still dizzy from the kiss. Maybe she misheard him?

"Uh…me, too, Dex." Her fingers traced where his lips had just been. That simple five-second time lapse had shifted everything she thought she knew. All she comprehended was wanting more. Like, *now.* "That was nice. I mean, do you want to talk about—"

"Okay. We're clear. Whew. That was close."

"Clear? Close?" Millie's head spun to catch up to her racing heart.

"Gale was watching us from the barn, and I just wanted to show him how in love with each other we are so he doesn't get suspicious. I think that did the trick."

"Yeah. I'll bet it did." Disappointment settled in the crack that had opened up in her chest during the kiss. *Of course* it was fake. Their whole relationship, aside from being best friends, was fake, so why would that earth-shattering kiss be any different?

Maybe she'd gotten it all wrong; maybe Dex would find faking it with her easy because he didn't have any real feelings for her. Maybe she was the one in trouble because she couldn't separate the physical longing for him from the show they were putting on.

"Anyway, what were you saying? Oh, yeah, how this place would grow on me?" His smile was so clueless, so genuine, it hurt to see. "I think you might be right, Tyler. I already feel better."

He strode off toward the barn and she sighed. This gig might do wonders for her medical career, for finally putting her crummy childhood behind her, but her heart was going to end up an unforeseen casualty.

CHAPTER FIVE

D<small>EX SAT ACROSS</small> from Millie on the wooden bench, careful not to let their feet touch under the table. Not that it mattered. His whole body had been buzzing with electricity since he'd kissed her.

What the hell were you thinking?

As bright ideas went, that wasn't his smartest. The thing was it'd made sense to him to dip in and kiss her since Gale's face was scrunched up like he'd stepped in something. Dex had reasoned that getting found out would be worse than playing a game of lip-lock with Millie, who he'd explain himself to after.

But…*whoa!*

The aftereffects of the kiss weren't something he anticipated, nor could he shrug them off. He swallowed and pulled at the neck of his soft cotton T-shirt that seemed too tight all of a sudden.

Everything came into sharp focus for a second.

The refurbished barn looked chic enough to host a wedding, with string lights, pale blue tablecloths and mountains of food. The massive pine table was filled with good home cooking—thick palm-sized biscuits sat in a basket in front of him, their warm buttery scent tickling his nose; monstrous slabs of pot roast smothered in onions and a brown gravy vied for attention next to the basket. There was even a salad and what looked like a berry cobbler farther down the table.

But he didn't have a damn bit of appetite. For food, at least.

He glanced at Millie, her head tipped back mid-laugh, the bare skin of her neck glistening under the barn lights.

Could she distinguish what they'd have to do to keep from getting caught from the truth—that they were just friends? Or was he the only one who all of a sudden couldn't figure out what was real and what wasn't?

"You're the doc from LA, right?" a voice on his left asked.

Reluctantly, Dex pulled his gaze from Millie, a near-impossible feat since her bottom lip was pulled between her teeth as she listened intently to a police captain tell his story of finding Hearts and Horses.

"Um…yeah. Dexter Shaw, nice to meet you."

"Ray Warren. Nice to meet you," the man said. "You just get here?"

"Yep. Arrived this afternoon. It's a nice place."

"Sure is. It's my fourth year and I still don't get sick of the fresh air, the morning rides."

"Wow," Dex said, sneaking a sideways glance at Millie. Were her eyes always so bright when she talked? "Four years, huh? You must find it pretty therapeutic."

"You could say that. I'm actually one of the staff now. I did two summers here as a patient and now it's my second as a stable manager."

"I'll have to pick your brain about how to get on the good side of those half-ton beasts we saw in there earlier. I know my way around a trauma bay or hospital, but this is like Mars."

"You bet. We'll start tomorrow. You mind handing me that bowl of potatoes?"

Ray's smile was wide, his hair long. But when Dex's gaze dipped for a fraction of a second, he saw limp fabric where a right arm should be and metal protruding from beneath his shorts on the same side. "I'd grab 'em myself, but…"

"Of course." Dex handed Ray the potatoes and tried not to look at his injuries.

"It's okay to ask. I'm used to it by now and that's why we're all here, to heal from what ails us, right?"

Did that include missing limbs? Dex had worked with critically wounded patients before, but few inside the walls of Mercy.

"A bomb?" Dex asked.

"Gas explosion after a fire in an office warehouse we responded to." Ray pointed to his shirt, which read I Had a Blast Working for Redondo Beach Fire Department in black letters against a red-and-yellow explosion.

Dex couldn't help but chuckle at Ray's sense of humor, but the weight of what he and Millie were going to face sat heavy on his chest. Would she be able to work with these folks after her own traumatic experiences as a child and in the military?

He risked another glance at her, but she was smiling, the small gap between her front teeth showing. It looked good on her—damn good—but more than that, she was smiling despite talking to a young man with a burn scar running the whole length of the right side of his face. Her chest rose and fell evenly and a glance at her hands showed them steady and calm.

She was okay, it seemed. *Good.* But the last thing he wanted was to be the weakest link with her on a personal *and* professional front. He needed to get his head right, put aside the feelings from the kiss—likely just a hormonal reaction after too long without physical affection.

"Damn. I'm sorry," Dex said, focusing back on Ray. "You still ride?"

"Why not? I'm not gonna let a couple measly limbs keep me from doing what I love. Besides, that handsome man over there wouldn't let me live it down if I gave in to these injuries and stopped living." Ray nodded to Gale at the end of the table.

"Is he your...?" Dex trailed off.

"Boyfriend? He doesn't put titles on things, but we've been living together for two years now, so he'd better start."

Ray laughed and scooped a heaping serving of potatoes

on his plate before sliding the bowl back to Dex, who added some to his plate as well.

They ate in silence while Dex considered all he'd been wrong about in the past few weeks.

Gale, for one. Turns out he hadn't been flirting with Millie earlier that day, and if the smiling patients up and down the table were any indication, he ran a pretty stellar operation.

Which meant Dex might just be wrong about this place, about the possibilities that awaited them.

Then there was the infinitesimal nudge his heart gave his chest when it thought of Kelsey. He didn't want *her* anymore—maybe never had, not fully—but perhaps he wanted what she had in Liam and Emma? A…a *family*?

A couple months ago, the idea would have been unconscionable, but now?

That might still be a stretch, but his reaction to another glance at the group of people swapping stories and dinner plates said more human connection might not be a bad thing.

Look at Millie, the most consistent part of his life and what he'd gotten most upside down. He'd worried about caring for someone else most of his life, thanks to a mom who hit the road before he was old enough to drink from a cup and a dad who'd been solid and wonderful to Dex, except for his penchant for adventures that had ultimately gotten him killed. The aunt who had watched Dex for the short times his dad had been away hadn't been keen on adopting him, so he'd been forced into the rough end of a foster system that wasn't kind to six-year-old boys. All these years later, he straddled two lives—one of solitary existence that posed no risk to his heart but was lonely as hell, and one where he craved what he'd lost when he lost his dad.

Millie was the bridge, the first person he'd trusted since his dad died. She'd shown him that caring for another person wasn't a death sentence, even though she, like his dad, often chose risk and danger over calm and safe.

"Hey, Dex." He looked up and saw at least four pairs of eyes on him, including Ray's and Millie's. "They wanted to know how you proposed."

At her words, the entire room fell silent as if they'd been waiting for this moment all night. Dex's jaw tightened. They'd rehearsed the story, but he hadn't thought he'd have to deliver his first performance in front of the twenty or so patients and at least a dozen staff.

"I figured since you're the one who popped the question, you'd want to share it." Her grin was wide and her eyes sparkled with mischief.

"That's so sweet of you, *honey*," he said.

"Y'all might not believe it, but this man here is as romantic as they come." She blew him a kiss and Dex swallowed back a snort. Not even *he* believed that. No way they would, especially as the six months wore on and he couldn't act on that lie.

That was one problem he'd always had with wanting a spouse or family—aside from the juxtaposition they created. They demanded to be put first, and with the exception of doing this for Millie, he didn't operate that way. None of his foster families ever taught him how, nor did his time living on the streets when he'd run from the system. He was good at taking care of others when he could follow a clinical procedure, but predicting the needs of someone not under his medical purview?

Impossible.

"Well, where do I start?"

"Start with the flowers you brought."

"Flowers?" he asked. They hadn't discussed flowers.

"Yeah, to the pier." She winked. What game was she playing at, trying to trip him up? Didn't she know what they risked if they were caught? Fraudulently misleading an employer at best.

"Oh, yeah, the pier. Well, I brought pale purple daisies, which are her favorite, but damn hard to find in winter." That much he knew from fifteen years of friendship. Her smile said he'd done okay. But her eyes narrowed in surprise. Did she not expect him to remember? "Luckily Pietro's keeps them in stock year-round."

"They do?" Millie asked. Dex tried not to gloat at the matching incredulity in her voice.

"How else do you think I got them for your homecomings?" Another truth sprinkled amongst the lies. He brought her a bouquet of the rare flowers every time she came home.

"Hmm," she said, her gaze focused and cheeks painted a light pink. "Anyway, go on."

"Yes, please," Ray said, leaning his chin on his hand in rapt attention.

"Well, I brought the flowers and her favorite maple-glazed donut from Donut King since it was the morning of the anniversary of our first official date," Dex continued.

"From when you hit the telephone pole?" Thomas asked. She'd already told them that?

"Uh, no, the drinks I took her to after I got out of the ICU. We walked along the beach, talking and eating. Then, when we came up to a small crowd at the water's edge, she wanted to see what was going on."

"Tell me there was a ring, maybe a band playing her favorite song," Ray said, his eyes closed and a wide grin on his face.

"Oh, please, Ray," a woman from the other end of the table chimed in. The scar on her cheek was visible from where Dex sat. Maybe he'd call his closest work colleague, Owen, out to consult. He was a genius when it came to reconstructive trauma surgery. "He's the incurable romantic here. Unrealistic, too."

"It's not that unrealistic, actually. There wasn't a band, but Dex did ask a guy from his hospital, Remy, to play his acoustic," Millie said.

Remy was just the kind of guy Dex was always teasing Millie about since he was more her type—long hair, played the guitar, believed in romance... *Him* with Millie the patients would have no problem believing. Too bad that wasn't the story they were selling.

Dex swallowed his insecurities with a sip of tea.

"Am I telling this story, or are you, hun?" He winked, taking a play from Millie's book. Her lip tucked back between her teeth and her cheeks flushed the same color as the vibrant pink sunset that evening. His heart fluttered in his chest and he rubbed the spot absently.

"Go for it," she said.

"Well, between my buddy playing 'Unchained Melody' and the message I'd had a local artist draw in the sand, it didn't take much convincing once I got down on one knee."

The crowd of patients and staff erupted into cheers and questions, which Millie fielded like the expert she was. Even Gale came over for a moment, putting his hand on Ray's shoulder and squeezing it. He kissed the top of Ray's head before heading back to the kitchen, a soft smile on his face.

That was nothing compared to the one on Millie's. Dex had watched her face transform as he shared their fake engagement tale. What began as a teasing smile had turned serious yet warm. She wanted those things—the romance, the wooing. She wanted a great love, even if she wouldn't admit it since every adult in her life since she was a kid had shown her how silly a notion that was. But it wasn't, and he was only keeping it at arm's length from her by pretending to be something he wasn't.

But that kiss...

He shook his head. The kiss was an anomaly, a reaction to someone he cared about deeply, but it wasn't portentous of anything more. They'd promised to stay friends, and even if they hadn't, their differences were far greater than their similarities; they'd drive each other up the wall.

"Ten minutes till the evening group sessions," Gale called out from behind the pony wall separating the kitchen from the open dining space. "Drs. Tyler-Shaw, you're welcome to sit in on this one until tomorrow when you pick up your own sessions."

Thank God.

Dex had never been so happy to go to work.

"Well, that's it, I guess," Millie said, shrugging.

"You guess? It's all incredibly romantic, but don't forget to keep it up now that you're working together. You know that—?"

"Fifty-eight percent of couples who work together end up divorced," Ray said to a patient with an emergency medical technician T-shirt on. "We know, Thomas. Please stop reminding us of dire circumstances and let them be happy. Clearly, they're in love and doing fine. See the way they look at each other."

Dex glanced at Millie, whose chin was lowered. Her eyes met his, though, and the promise they'd made didn't loom as large as before. How *did* they look at each other? He wouldn't know love if it slapped him upside the heart, but he knew he couldn't live without Millie in his life. That wasn't the same thing, though.

You sure about that?

Confusion swirled with the food in his stomach, and he grew queasy.

The last thing he wanted was to send Millie mixed signals, but she knew the gig. This was a part they were playing so neither of them had to go back to jobs that were killing them. That, and so they could help people like them—damaged and slow to trust. If they blew it, more than healing would be broken in the process. Besides, it was six months, then she could chase a real happily-ever-after and he could, well, figure out what he wanted next.

You're sure that's not her? his heart asked.

A whisper of doubt crawled along his skin. His fingers traced the place her lips had been just an hour ago, recalling the very real, very *intense* feelings the kiss had drudged up. The question that sat on his mind, weighing it down, was what it all meant.

Was it the result of a lonely body finally given a chance at affection? Or was it Millie's effect on him? Dex sighed as he got up from the table and gathered a pile of plates to clear. He wasn't sure of anything anymore, it seemed.

Millie nodded, listening intently as Ray shared his story for the trauma group he was leading. The group of firefighters, EMTs, veterans and police officers who shared afterward were from varied walks of life, but all injured in the line of duty. The stories might have been drastically different, but their circumstances weren't—each struggled to regain physical and emotional well-being.

As group therapy went, the setup was pretty standard. They sat in a circle, all of them equal in rank and experience. No one's previous positions were mentioned—just their diagnoses of acute PTSD. Not all of the patients had physical injuries, either. Some of them shared stories of watching everyone around them bleeding out or blown to bits only to walk away with nothing more than survivor's guilt.

But the collective weight of loss in the room was palpable. She and Dex had their work cut out for them if they only had six months with these patients.

"Would you like to share?" Ray asked after everyone had taken a turn. He'd been kind and patient with each of them, explaining what wasn't their fault and thanking them for being brave enough to share with the group. But Millie wasn't ready.

Her skin itched as she plastered on a fake smile and shook her head.

"No, thanks. I'd love to soon, though."

"Of course." Ray closed out the session and the vets broke out of the circle to mingle. The fact that they liked each other enough to bare their souls, then hang around and chat pulled at Millie's chest. She desperately missed the community of her fellow service members.

Would she ever find that sense of family again?

"Hi, Dr. Tyler-Shaw." Millie smiled. She'd been Sergeant, then Staff Sergeant Tyler, but this was the first Dr. Tyler of her civilian career. It sounded good. "I'm Sergeant Banks—third battalion, first squad army ranger. I just wanted to introduce myself since I'll be your first patient on Monday."

"Nice to meet you, Banks." Banks's eyes shifted toward the door, then the window. Millie's heart ached for the man. On the outside, he looked fine—tall, muscular, every bit the soldier. But she recognized the invisible injuries—darting eyes looking for exits, assessing the unforeseen risks around the room, cataloging the escapes… It was classic PTSD. "I'm glad you're here."

"Me, too. I'm looking forward to talking more to you and your husband. It'll be nice to have his perspective as a civilian."

Her husband.

Dex.

A shiver raced across her skin, which she attributed to the cool mountain air closing in around her. But she couldn't mistake what it meant when her fingers absently traced her lips, recalling the kiss that had seared them.

"I'm looking forward to it, too, Banks. Have a good night." He walked away and Millie caught a slight hitch in his right knee.

"Are you settling in okay?" Ray asked.

"We are, thanks," Millie said. *We?* Why had she roped Dex into it?

"Good to hear. You know, this is a safe space for you to share, too. I know you're the doc, but it'll do them a world of good to know you have your own story."

Millie gulped a grenade-sized lump back into the pit of her stomach.

"I know," she whispered. "And I want to. It's just… I'm not sure how to…"

"How to say it and keep it all together?"

Millie nodded. That was exactly it. Of course, Ray would get it.

"Well, give it time. The sessions will help; even leading them puts my mind right most days. The horses won't hurt, either. There's something about being outside, the ocean air swirling around you, sweeping your problems away while you work with your animal."

"That sounds nice. I'm looking forward to riding, actually. Practicing medicine again, too."

"And then, you can't beat curling up with your sexy man at the end of the day, nothing but the sounds of the hills between you."

Ray winked. Hopefully he didn't notice the heat that traveled up her neck. Of course, she'd pulled her hair back so her skin could showcase every emotion she felt as she felt it. Darn her half-Irish heritage for making it impossible to hide her feelings.

Curling up with Dex.

She licked her lips. In fact, that one thought had plagued her since he let drop the fact that he slept in the buff. Then, of course, he'd gone and kissed her, sending her spiraling and unable to think of much else. Even the delicious-smelling dinner had been an exercise in mechanics only. She couldn't recall a bite—a travesty since that berry cobbler had looked delicious.

"Anyway, I'll leave you to it, but Dr. Tyler-Shaw?"

Millie glanced back at Ray. "Mmm-hmm?"

"I'm mighty glad you're here. Gale did a good thing bringing you two to Hearts and Horses."

All Millie could do was nod, a meaningless gesture she lamented as she walked back to the bunkhouse suite. The attached building housed the rest of the staff and the sounds of a guitar and laughter drifted from the open doorway. Millie ached to head that way, if for no other reason than to avoid going "home" to her fake husband.

Until she glanced at her door.

Dex leaned against the wooden frame, his feet bare and his undershirt untucked. He'd discarded his dress shirt and his hair was tousled. His arms crossed languidly across his chest and he held two bottles of beer by the neck in one hand. When he held one out to her, she took it, appraising him after they clinked bottles and silently pulled at the beverages. The cold liquid should have been unwelcome, given the way the night had sucked the heat from the desert air, but the warmth wafting off Dex was enough to counter the chill.

"You look relaxed," she commented.

"I feel relaxed. I know I gave you grief earlier, but this is growing on me."

"Me, too."

They sipped in silence, and when he lifted an arm, she took the unspoken invitation and leaned against him. His solid frame held her upright like it had dozens of times over the course of their friendship. But this was the first time she felt like she could open up about what she wanted in the darkest hours of her nights. Things like her desire for a family and life that looked relatively boring on the outside.

Planting gardens instead of traipsing through vast desert wastelands.

A good man to love and cherish instead of sleeping with the worst of them to sate a physical ache without the guilt of using someone.

A career spent near her life at home.

At one point, Gale and Ray walked by them toward their cabin, Ray's arm draped around his boyfriend's. The couples nodded at each other and Millie's heart clenched. On the outside, she and Dex looked every bit the married couple in love. They knew everything about each other, joked and were tender in equal measure, and even physically showed affection like an actual couple.

But one problem stuck out to her as she filled Dex in on her group therapy session instead of the hidden treasure trove of secrets she held close to her chest.

She was crushing on the wrong man. Optics aside, Dexter Shaw would never want a real marriage and family. The sooner she remembered that, the less painful being his wife would be.

CHAPTER SIX

MILLIE CHANGED HER mind immediately after their teeth were brushed and *her* pajamas were on. This little arrangement they had would never get easier, not when Dex stepped out of his jeans, draped them on the side of the bed, then did the same with his boxer briefs. He stood there in all his fine masculine glory a full three and a half seconds, plugging in his phone, before pulling back the covers and slipping under them.

"Ready for bed, wifey?" he asked, a sly grin on his face.

She nodded, feeling more naked than he was in her baggy T-shirt and pale blue lace underwear. Trying not to stare at how he somehow kept the ridges of his abs when he was sitting, Millie followed and got into bed.

"You're really not going to wear boxers?"

His brows quirked. "I can, if you'd prefer it."

"Um, maybe." She swallowed hard. "I mean, yeah. Would you mind?"

"Of course not." He slid them back on, but it didn't make a damn bit of difference now that she knew what hid beneath the thin fabric. "Good God, this thing is comfortable," he said.

"You say that like you're surprised."

"I dunno. I kinda figured Gale wouldn't spring for the good stuff when the point is that we're supposed to be roughing it."

"I don't think that's the point, but yeah. I'd never have thought it by looking at this place," she said, gesturing to the sparse room acting as the entirety of their home for the next six months, "but between the food, company and this bed, I'm already happy we left LA."

Dex's crooked smile snuck under the thin defense she'd mustered to avoid staring at him naked. Shoot. The fact that she could still see his smile meant they'd forgotten to turn off the lights.

"Dex, the lights," she said.

"Yep, they're on. My wife—you know, the last one in bed—forgot to turn them off."

She shook her head. "Nope. You promised to love and take care of me for life. That means shutting off the lights before bed so I don't, I dunno, break a toe or something."

"Is that right?"

"That's right."

Dex sighed. "I'd kill for a remote-operated light right about now."

Millie grinned, her hands pressed together in silent pleading. That is, until he threw back the covers and, wouldn't you know it, he hadn't somehow in the past few minutes put more than his boxers back on. Why hadn't they moved to Siberia or Alaska where Dex would be forced into wearing more clothing?

"You know what?" she proclaimed, hopping out of bed in one swift move. "I just happen to love you enough to take this one for the team," she said, more to her heart than to Dex. Because the less she had to watch her desires strut across the room in godlike form, the better.

"Wow. I'll take it."

Millie sent up a tiny prayer of thanks that he pulled the covers back over his body just as she turned out the light. She fumbled back in the pitch-black, feeling in front of her for obstacles. The biggest one, unfortunately, was in bed with her.

"See? No broken toes," Dex teased.

"Um…nope. All good here."

A total lie.

Her heart raced loud and fast enough she worried it could be heard over the whirring of the overhead fan.

"Another thing I miss about LA?"

She couldn't see Dex between the new moon and lack of anything resembling a streetlight, but she felt him inch closer to where she lay still as a body in the morgue.

"What's that?" she whispered. There weren't many, but another bed sounded good right about now.

"Ambient light so I could see you while we talk." She inhaled a sharp breath when his calf settled against hers. It wasn't unexpected, especially with how tall the guy was, but it sure felt like it right then. He might as well have picked her up, pinned her against the wall and made love to her, the way her leg tingled with awareness.

"I'm actually pretty tired," she said, garnering a yawn that sounded as fake as their marriage. "Maybe we can chat over breakfast?" She turned her back to him, curling up into as tight and small a ball as she could.

"Sure. Good night, Millie," he said. She flinched. Why did it have to sound so intimate when he used her first name? The flinch turned to a full body freeze when his hand rested against the small of her back. Jesus. He was going to make this as difficult as possible, wasn't he?

He was a *good* guy—and her best friend, at that. But giving into this...*thing* she felt brewing would ruin both. She stared at the place where the blinds met the edge of the window and willed herself to fall asleep.

Despite the inauspicious start to their night, Millie awoke to her alarm, surprised at the time. She must've drifted off immediately, but her body felt heavy, weighed down as if she'd tossed and turned all night.

She stretched—or tried to at least.

Something heavy was literally pinning her down. A glance to her right showed the culprit. Dex's arm was wrapped fully around her, and only then did she notice his body curved against hers.

Oh, God. They were *spooning.*

She gave in for a moment, letting his solid warmth hold her, knowing the moment she moved, he'd shift and the dream would burst open like a summer coastal storm, leaving her shattered against the rocks of reality. When he nuzzled closer, his hips tucked close to her backside and he let a small moan escape as his length—clearly in full morning salute—pressed against her.

Oh. My. God.

If what she felt was any indication, he'd be more than enough to fill and satisfy her. Hell, she already knew they had the chemistry to back it up—their kiss still reverberated hot on her lonely lips.

Dex rocked into her, his breathing still deep. He might be asleep and unaware, but she was wide-awake.

She bolted up, throwing his arm off her in the process. His eyes fluttered awake but he didn't look aware of their previously compromising position.

"Good morning, Millie. Damn, I slept like a dead guy."

"Good morning. Uh…me, too."

"You been up long? I didn't hear you get out of bed."

"No, just a few minutes. But I'm going to head out for a run before we have to start the day. Feel free to go back to bed if you want and I'll wake you up when I'm back."

The run wasn't part of her plan—yoga was, actually—but the cramped space in the room would feel too much like she was posed on display for him. She needed distance.

"Actually, a run sounds good. Mind if I join you?"

She swallowed back the retort sitting at the base of her throat. *No. You can't. You're too much of a distraction.* Calling attention to that would be giving the thought power, and she needed to nip it where and when she could.

"Sure. We leave in five."

She dressed quickly, desperate for the desert-meets-ocean air that Cambria was famous for. Anything to take her mind off her naked best-friend-slash-fake-husband.

Dex's hand brushed against the small of her back.

"I'm ready. Shall we?"

"Yeah, follow me. Ray gave me some ideas of which trails to take."

Irritation gathered where his hand once was. She wanted his hand on her back. And on her stomach, cupping her jaw while he kissed her, sliding down the waist of her tights… But she couldn't have it—not all of it, anyway. Not the emotion that came with the caresses.

So she needed to avoid anything that would lead to those emotions.

Millie took off toward the hills behind the ranch, faster than was probably smart, but literally running away from her feelings seemed the only option.

Dex's heavy breaths behind her drove her around the edge of the property and up the steep embankment at its border. The terrain meandered between cactus and tall yellow grass interspersed with thick sea green bushes. It was typical central coast landscape, especially on a ranch, but she wanted what came next. Ray had told her there were ocean and wine country views at the top, but she couldn't look up to see how far that was or she'd stop. She needed to take this step by step.

Think about something else.

Her breathing became labored. A flash of sprinting away from her childhood home with all its broken skin and promises, breathing much as she did now, seared her retinas.

Millie pushed harder.

Who are you most excited to work with?

From a staff perspective, she was excited to work alongside Ray. His expertise may not be in practicing medicine, but it was earned in personal experience. When he completed his master's in psychology, he'd be an asset to the whole field.

Dex's footsteps stumbled, but she didn't glance back. They fell back into step, just a few paces behind her now.

The young woman, Reese. I want to work with her most, I think.

The first responder had a severe limp in her left leg, and from what Millie saw on her way out of the dining hall the night before, scarring around her knee that said she'd barely kept her leg at all.

"Can you hold up a sec?" Dex asked. His question came on the wheezing end of an exhale. "I need to tie these shoes."

She shook her head. She couldn't keep waiting for him.

"I'll see you at the top. I've got to keep moving."

Millie felt his absence behind her as she took short quick steps up the steep rocky trail. It was freeing, but also empty. So much of her life was like that, wasn't it? She made her choices, left behind the toxicity of her family, which was liberating but lonely.

When the terrain evened out, her breathing slowed and she finally allowed herself to look up. Half a breath lodged in her throat and she coughed.

"Damn," she whispered. "Thanks, Ray. This was worth it."

In front of her, the pale yellow light of the early sun painted the edge of the horizon and reflected in fragmented shards across the expanse of deep blue Pacific water. The breeze hummed with salt and life and everything she'd missed about LA's beaches. Behind her, rolling hills draped delicately with dry gold grasses were dotted with bright swathes of green where vines had taken root and found life beneath soil too sparse to keep anything else alive.

She, Dex, the patients at Hearts and Horses—all of them were kind of like a pinot grape vine, resilient and tough enough to make it through the hard times.

Her hands rested on her hips and a tenuous peace settled over her. She'd given up so much—her job as a trauma doc in the army, her military family, her childhood—but she had this, her future. And that was something.

"Good God, woman. You can run, I'll give you that."

Dex stumbled up the edge of the path, out of breath and flushed. He'd shed his cotton T-shirt along the way, tucking it into the back of his shorts like a tail. Millie averted her eyes from the gleaming bare skin of his strong chest, keeping her gaze pinned to the sparkling water below instead.

"Damn," he said, echoing her assessment of the three-hundred-and-sixty-degree views. "This is ridiculous."

Millie nodded. "It's beautiful."

"Worth spending the next six months here?" he asked. He rubbed her shoulder, something he would have done any other time in their friendship. But today, it landed differently. She read meaning into it where there wasn't any. The kiss had been a decoy, the morning cuddling a sleep-induced mistake.

Dex might be able to separate the physicality of their relationship from their emotional one—and maybe at one point, before the fake-wife thing, she could have, too—but she couldn't any longer.

"Yeah," she said, maneuvering out of reach of him. "I'm glad we'll be able to make a difference here."

"Me, too."

They gazed out over the water, the distant sound of gulls the only noise aside from the brisk breeze whipping around them. Millie's skin had begun to cool now that her heart rate had slowed, and she shivered. Dex reached for her as if he meant to rub her arms to keep her warm, but she shook her head.

"Don't," she whispered.

"What's going on, Tyler? What did I do?"

She scoffed at the use of her last name.

"Seriously? Tyler? *That's* what's going on."

"What do you mean? I've always called you—"

"I know. Let's just leave it. We've got breakfast in forty-five minutes and our first round of patient sessions just after that."

"I'm sorry if I offended you somehow, but I'm just trying to find my way through this thing. This thing *you* asked for, need I remind you."

Millie's arms prickled, not with the chill, but the truth in his words. She gazed over at him, a mistake since the gentle morning light reflected in his eyes along with hurt. Hurt she'd caused.

See? This is what happens when I let my misguided feelings get tangled with a man like Dex. I take his heart of gold and dull it with my own nonsense.

"I'm sorry. It's just—" She shook her head, weighing her options. The truth? Or her friendship? "I didn't sleep well," she offered, going with the latter. No reason to involve him in her inappropriate feelings after all this time.

"No worries. I'm sorry if I kept you awake."

She shrugged off his constant attentiveness, his pervasive need to see her happy and safe when the one thing that might actually work was the one thing he couldn't give her.

"I think I know what might help," she said, trying on a grin.

"What's that?"

She gave one last longing look at the ocean spread in front of her like a bounty. "I'll be back soon," she whispered only loud enough for herself. To Dex, she said, "Race you to the bottom," and took off down the hill without waiting to see if he'd keep up. When it came to him, she'd always be three steps ahead but still finishing last.

Dex listened to Sergeant Dominic's story with rapt interest. The man had been a police detective for eighteen years, lost six friends in the line of duty and was the father of two boys, one of whom needed special care for his autism.

What the hell do I have to complain about? Dex wondered. *My life's been a Lifetime movie compared to this guy's.*

He knew enough to know he shouldn't compare traumas, but still, George Dominic was showing him a perspective he'd not had in a while. Sure, he'd worked with a couple firefighters and EMTs who'd seen or experienced something horrific, but for the most part, his practice dealt with the Hollywood elite and their specific brand of nuanced trauma, most of which was caused by too much money and not enough boundaries.

This was a tough new gig, but far more rewarding.

"Anyway, I don't really know how I found Hearts and Horses, but I'm glad I did. They're already helping me get back to being the kind of man I need to be for my sons. I damn near gave the force everything and now it's time to save what's left for my family."

"That's a great outlook," Dex said, putting his legal pad down and leaning on his knees. "But what're you saving for yourself?"

Dominic's lips twisted in confusion. "What do you mean?"

"I mean, what are you doing in all this caring for other people to fill your own cup?"

"I'm here, aren't I?"

Dex smiled kindly. "You are, and that's going to be a huge step in your recovery. But so is working on something that's just yours, something that your career or your family can't touch."

"Hmm. I never thought about it that way. But my wife has been through so much supporting me in this career that only chipped away at both of us."

"She sounds amazing," Dex said, reverence in his words. "Worth doing right by."

"She is," Dominic agreed. "Can we talk about how to do that next session?"

"You bet," Dex said, walking Dominic out. He thanked the man for his public service and honesty in the session and closed the door behind him.

As Dex poured himself a cup of coffee, his thoughts drifted to Millie, to all she'd been through with no one to support her, no one to help her relax after her own military service and frenetic childhood.

Was he doing right by *her*? Fake husband or not, he was still her best friend, which meant it was his job to keep her safe and look out for her when she rode too close to the edge. God, this push and pull of his heart when it came to her made his chest ache.

She'd pull him in with her charm, her humor, her easy way of looking at life, and each time he'd swear maybe she'd be the one who could convince him to love another person enough to start—and build—a life with them. After all, they had the foundation of a solid relationship.

Then she'd push him right back out again when she did something stupid like take jobs where people were trying to kill her—and one of these days would succeed. How could he ever love someone like that? Loss was the only outcome.

You're too damn reckless, he'd told her once, about a decade prior.

To you, maybe, but that's not saying much when you won't even jay walk across the side street of your apartment.

No one had ever accused him of being a risk-taker, that was for sure, but when *everyone* in his life had turned out to be one, who was supposed to hold level ground, keep everyone healthy and safe?

It's what his dad *should* have done; he didn't begrudge the man too much—it was his only fault, and a fatal one at that. He also couldn't blame Millie for how he grew up. However, he didn't have to court that side of her, either.

Easier said than done...

His heart pushed against his chest as it had every time he'd thought of her the past week since their kiss. He'd crossed a line with her and there really wasn't any going back now that he knew what she tasted like, felt like, and what that did to his heart. Forget push and pull—it was a damn rodeo beneath his ribs now.

Made worse by the way she avoided him like *he* was the dangerous one.

Millie sprinted off before the sun rose each morning to get in a run before their days got away from them. Then, after dinner and some light chatter in the barn with everyone but him, she'd head to the bunkhouse before him, softly breathing by the time he got in from his evening group therapy. Since she was hired on both as a therapist and trauma doctor, she was only scheduled for two evening sessions a week.

Dex sighed. The thing was, if he ignored the inherent risk Millie posed to his heart, he *missed* her—missed their banter, how her lip pulled between her teeth when she was truly pleased with something, the feel of her against him while he slept...

That last part was a state secret he'd take with him to the grave. The first morning they'd woken up together, he'd been awake long enough to feel her breathing change, to feel her close the millimeters between them. His body reacted almost immediately; he was hard and turned on like he'd never been before, the memory of the passion in their supposedly fake kiss still hot on his lips.

But she'd shifted away and that had been it. Since then, she tucked herself in the farthest corner of the bed, a compact ball of his longing. He'd be a complete jerk if he tried to touch her when it was obvious she wanted to keep her distance.

His phone buzzed on the small table beside his chair. Shoot. It was his alarm for their first trail ride of the season, something he wasn't exactly thrilled about.

He finished his coffee and closed up the office Hearts and Horses had set up for him; even with a fraction of the comfort of his LA office, it had more than enough to do the job. Which said more than a little about how he wanted to live going forward.

Down at the stables, a small crowd formed around the entrance.

"What's going on here?" Dex asked Ray, who stood toward the back, his hand tucked into his jeans pocket and a half smile on his face.

"Take a look." He nodded toward the first stall, and Dex smiled as well.

Millie.

In a fitted black tank top and snug jeans, her hair tied back in a long braid, she looked the part of a cowgirl. A cowgirl who made his own jeans fit a little snugger around the waist.

Damn. She might have been his best friend and off-limits to anything more, but hell if he didn't want to give a roll in the hay with her a try.

That's not true. You want more than that with her.

He swallowed hard. That was impossible, wasn't it? Because as her friend, he could pretend what she did wasn't his concern; as her boyfriend, that would be impossible. Look at Kelsey. He'd cared for her and Emma, had tried to go against his biology and give being a dad a whirl, but in the end, he'd hurt them both with his pervasive fear of something going wrong.

He couldn't do that to Millie, the most important person in his life.

"What's she doing?"

"Taming the untamable," Ray said, tossing Dex a wink. Dex shifted on his feet uncomfortably.

Yeah, she's been doing that a lot lately.

"A new horse?" Dex asked.

"Nah. We've had the mare a while now, but no one can get through to her. Millie's been down here half an hour and already has Elsa breathing normal. She even took a slice of apple from Millie's hand."

Dex relaxed, too, until Elsa flinched and her nostrils flared. His senses went on full alert. Millie didn't know horses any more than he did, but of course, if there was danger or risk, she was front and center.

Millie remained calm and eventually Elsa matched her energy, stilling.

"Wow. I had no idea Millie was so good with horses," Dex said. Awe filled the empty space in his chest, and it overflowed when Millie nodded to Reese Laramy, one of their patients. But the nerves didn't settle. Millie was still in the lion's den.

"Come on in here, Reese," Millie said.

"You've got an amazing woman there, Doc. There's a line out the door for her one-on-ones and she beat Gale at pickleball, so I'm eternally grateful to her for that. He's been insufferable with no one to challenge him here."

Dex considered that. He'd seen Millie army-tough, laying down the law when she needed to. He'd seen her slaphappy and giving him grief for one of his idiosyncrasies. But he'd never seen her so patient, so calm.

He found himself leaning in like the rest of the patients and staff.

"It's okay, she's just got to smell you and get to know your scent from the rest of these guys'," Millie told Reese.

"She won't hurt me?"

"She doesn't want to. She wants to get to know you. But she can see you're gentle, like her. Just a little wild along the edges."

Reese smiled and so did Dex.

"Put your hand out slowly, and leave it palm up so she can take the carrot from you," Millie instructed, demonstrating with her own carrot. "That's it. You're a natural."

Reese smiled under the compliment. She looked...*happy*. All because of Millie.

When Reese got Elsa eating out of her hand, the crowd erupted into hushed cheers and laughter. Reese bowed, which earned a more raucous round of applause.

"Okay, show's over, folks. Time to hit the trails before the only light we have is from the moon."

Everyone nodded and followed Ray into the stables. Dex

slid next to Millie, nervous all of a sudden. He'd never been uncomfortable around her, not like this. Part of their friendship was their easy way of falling into step with one another. But faking a marriage while harboring real feelings was getting more and more difficult.

"You were amazing back there."

"Thanks," she said. She didn't glance over at him as she placed the tack on her mare, Tillamook. But the familiar hint of pink traveled up her neck.

"Mind showing me what you're doing so I don't look like an idiot out there?"

"I thought Gale was gonna teach you how to saddle up yesterday."

"He was. But I've worked the past three nights, which you know since you're asleep already when I get home."

"That sounded a little judgmental." She stopped working on the buckle in her hand and gazed at him. Gone was the fire, the spark that had always flitted between them. Replacing it was a nonchalance that hit him like a punch. "Which, frankly, I don't need from you."

What had he done?

"It wasn't. I just miss you, that's all." He rubbed her arm with the back of his hand but she pulled back immediately.

"What's there to miss, Dex?" she asked, turning her attention back to the horse. "This isn't real, so there's no use pretending otherwise when no one's looking. We can just be friends. People who call each other by their last names and steal food off each other's plates. Isn't that enough?"

Dex glanced over her shoulder and sure enough, everyone was busy with their own horses and gear.

"There's more than just a fake relationship here and you know it."

"Yep. We're friends and have been for fifteen years. Don't worry. That hasn't changed."

"Millie—"

"I've got to run. I'm supposed to be working with the patients on being present in every part of this ride, from the gearing up through brushing a horse down after a ride."

"Can we talk later?"

Millie shook her head. "I'm heading out with Ray after dinner for a drink in town since I have tomorrow morning off."

"Seriously? Millie—"

"Have a good ride, Dex."

She led her horse to the other side of the barn, leaving Dex confused for the umpteenth time since they'd arrived in Cambria.

It was time to figure out what was wrong with his wife and just what kind of penance he had to do to fix it. If that meant risking more than he was comfortable with? Well, too bad.

Surely *nothing* could be worse than the feeling in the pit of his stomach, knowing he was disappointing the one person he loved most.

CHAPTER SEVEN

MILLIE ENCOURAGED HER horse into a trot alongside Reese, who continued to wear the smile she'd first shown back at the stables. There'd been a lot Millie wasn't sure about when they took this job—being around patients with similar trauma to her, sharing a bunkhouse and a bed with Dex—but moments like this made it all worth it.

She sighed, thinking back to earlier that morning, to Dex's pained expression when she left on another run and didn't invite him. Yes, even with him, with his constant tempting presence, being here was worth it.

"How're you feeling?" she asked Reese.

"Good. Better. I wasn't sure about this at first. You know, with my leg and all. But it's actually pretty great. My knee doesn't hurt up here."

"That's fantastic. Do me a favor and straighten your bad leg."

Reese shot her a nervous glance, but did as Millie instructed.

"Okay, nice. Your mobility looks good."

From reading Reese's medical chart, Millie knew that was the spot that had absorbed the full impact from the police car chase. Since then, Reese had been reticent to take on new challenges, fearful of the unknown and detached from her physical and mental health.

Right now? Millie didn't see any of that. She knew the benefits of equine therapy for children and folks recovering from alcohol and substance abuse, but to see it working in real time to assist a police officer in overcoming her injuries was pretty incredible.

"Why don't you schedule a consultation with me tomorrow? I'd like to work with you on some exercises that could loosen it up more over time, give you even more range of motion."

"You don't mind? I know you're here to fix our heads and stuff…"

"I don't mind at all. I'm actually double-board certified in trauma medicine and recovery as well as psychiatry."

"Wow. That's cool." Reese whistled, and her horse's ears perked up as she whinnied and shook her head. Reese tensed before Millie could say anything. But it was too late; fear was clear in Reese's eyes, showed in the way her hands gripped the reins.

"It's okay. Buttercup's just nervous. Relax your legs, Reese, and loosen the reins."

Reese shook her head vehemently. "I—I can't."

"You can. You've done much harder things than this, Reese. Remember, Buttercup can feel everything you're feeling, so let's give her a chance to calm down, okay?"

"O-okay."

"Do me a favor and take a deep breath in and then tell me your favorite kind of ice cream."

Millie kept her gaze pinned to Reese's, but didn't miss the way Reese's hands loosened on the reins.

"I don't like ice cream."

"What?" Millie asked, grinning, but pretending to be out-raged with her hands on her hips. She was careful to keep her voice even so Buttercup didn't spook again. "You're kidding me."

Reese shook her head, her hands resting on her thighs again like she'd been taught.

"I think we may have to talk about that."

Reese smiled, her shoulders and legs relaxed. Buttercup

was back to normal, ambling down the trail like nothing was amiss. Millie breathed in deeply, following her own advice after the near miss. They were almost back to the stables, at least. She glanced ahead and saw an empty stall where Dex's horse, Prince Reginald, was supposed to be.

So he'd made it out, huh?

Curiosity gripped her and after making sure Reese was safely off her horse and promised to see Millie the next day about her leg, Millie took off back down the trail they'd come from. A couple hundred yards in, she caught a glimpse of the dark eyes that haunted her dreams each night she lay less than ten inches from Dex.

Dex chatted with Charlie, a veteran from the coast guard who'd lost 80 percent of his sight during a training exercise gone wrong. He couldn't fly anymore for obvious reasons, but each time Millie had seen him on a horse, he looked content, at least.

"That's interesting," Dex said. He met Millie's gaze and shook his head. He needed to be alone with this patient. She nodded and turned Tillamook back to the stables, listening as she rode. "Tell me more," Dex urged Charlie.

Millie smiled. It was such a simple therapy move, to ask the patient to tell them more, but god was it effective.

Eventually they all made it back to the stables and as everyone else followed Ray to the barn to set up for dinner, Millie and Dex were left alone to hang tack and shut everything off until their next long ride. With only eight weeks until the families came out to visit, they needed all the riding time they could get.

There was one family visit per session where the patients could invite their loved ones to participate in their therapy sessions, meals, even rides through the rolling hills. From what Millie understood, this one would be special since it included a beach ride at White Rock State Marine Conversation Area.

The patients would love the combination of salty sea air—

therapeutic in its own right—and the connection to the animals they loved. As long as their regular rides were like today's.

"How's Charlie doing?" Millie asked. She cleaned off a dusty saddle and placed it on the shelf next to the others.

"He's good. Thinks he might try to teach at Embry-Riddle so he's still around pilots and all that."

"That's a great idea. You come up with it?"

"Don't sound so surprised," he said, frowning.

"I'm not." She let out a puff of air. That was the way of things lately—she was constantly holding back when it came to Dex. "I'm sorry, I just… I've been having a rough week," she finally admitted.

His brows furrowed. "Yeah, I know."

"Sorry if that's a problem for you, Dex, but I could do without your anger right now. I know we picked this place for me, that I called in my audible, but I need some time to acclimate."

To living with you as my fake husband while I care about you for real.

"I'm not mad at you for taking some time, Millie." There it was again—the use of her first name, an ounce of tenderness attached. The oscillation gave her whiplash.

"Then why *are* you?" she hissed, lowering her voice when a stable hand walked by. "Because I can read you like a book and you're pissed. At me."

"I am. But only because you're my best friend. And you're treating me like a stranger. You won't talk to me, look at me and you're sure as hell not sharing anything with me anymore. So why am I risking *everything* being here for you when you're treating me like a communicable disease? You don't get to be distant from me after calling in *the* favor, okay?"

She sighed. "I'm sorry." He looked down at her, shock on his open lips. "It's only because I care about you," she said. She couldn't meet his gaze, though. Not without risking everything—specifically, her heart.

"I care about you, too. That's why this whole silent treatment is making me nuts."

"Not—not in *that* way," she whispered. Her voice was almost swallowed up by the evening air that no longer seemed laced with possibility. Now it felt heavy, repressive.

"What do you mean?" he asked. He'd put down the piece of brass he was polishing and walked over to her. Averting her gaze was impossible with him this close, and she felt the heat of his undivided attention. "Millie, talk to me."

He tilted her chin up, and it quivered at his touch. Her eyes watered and his gaze softened.

"Please tell me what you mean by that. Not in *what* way? As friends?"

Millie nodded and then twisted her chin out of his grasp. He caught her cheek with a gentle palm and slowly guided it back to center.

Dex opened and shut his mouth as if he wanted to say something, then he finally shook his head.

Of course he wouldn't feel the same. How could he? He'd said a hundred times over that her life wasn't anything he envied or wanted to be a part of. And he was right—their wants might have been similar, but their needs were polar opposite to one another.

Tears stung the corners of her eyes, blurring her vision. That was the only reason she didn't see Dex inching closer to her until his lips touched hers and heat spread from there across her cheeks, her neck, her chest.

She pulled back, surprise etched in her gaze, her lips tingling where they already missed the feel of his.

"Dex, please don't do this if you're not—"

"Shh…" he said, brushing her lips softly with his again. "Just shut up and kiss me, wife."

Dex spent the next few minutes in absolute bliss. Kissing Millie before had been a chore, something he'd done to protect them—and it had still been the hottest thing he'd ever experienced. But now? When it was his choice? *Her* choice? Damn if he didn't erupt into flames right there in the stables.

His hands finally knew the exquisite pleasure of tangling in her messy curls. His lips and tongue found ways to explore her mouth that hadn't ever occurred to him before. And now he wondered how he'd gone fifteen years—*fifteen years!*—without kissing Millie Tyler every damn day.

She moaned into his mouth, pressing closer to his chest so that only molecules of air separated them. He straddled her legs and cradled her against him.

"Dex," she whispered into the space their mouths shared.

"Millie," he replied.

The dinner bell rang then, loud and unwelcome. The spell was broken and Millie pulled back, breathless and her skin showing all the places the heat flashed against it. God, how he wanted to touch each bloom of heat, kiss each burst of warmth, cherish all of her. Had he been hungry for anything other than more of Millie's kisses before this? He didn't think there'd ever been a time he'd have chosen food over her mouth, her hands.

He released her shoulders and stepped back. Only then did his conscience step in and interrupt his thoughts about how to get his fake wife naked sooner rather than later.

What are you doing? it asked. *She's your best friend and the only person in the world who knows everything about you.*

Wasn't that a reason to keep doing what they were doing?

Why? So you can disappoint her, too? What do you think is going to happen if she wants more than a quickie in the bunkhouse? What if she loves *you, huh? Wants you to give more than you're able to? Have you thought about* that?

Shit. He hadn't considered what would happen *after* kissing her, but now that was the only thing on his mind. Would his moral compass allow him to pursue her, knowing the risk it posed to their tenuous new start? More importantly, would their friendship survive?

His heart lurched as she smiled up at him. God, he wanted this, even if it was short-lived. They could say it was to keep up appearances, couldn't they? And enjoy the fruits of the lie that had gotten them into this in the first place?

He and Millie were doing more good at the ranch than the construct they'd built would hurt. But if they rode the line between truth and fantasy, what would it do to *Millie*? She'd been burned before; could she separate the lie from reality so soon after losing the only other family she'd ever known when she separated from the army?

She traced her bottom lip with the tip of her finger. He wanted to suck both into his mouth until she cried out with pleasure.

"That was..." she started.

Incredible. Mind-blowing.

"Yeah, it was," he said instead. "We should go."

"Oh, okay." She frowned and he cursed under his breath. *Christ.* With a medical degree from Stanford, he couldn't come up with anything more articulate than that?

"I just mean—"

"Mmm-hmm. It's fine."

"Can we please spend time together after dinner?" he asked.

"You have group therapy and I'm going out."

He sighed. If they really were husband and wife, this schedule would be the quickest route to divorce. "I miss you, Millie."

"You can't miss what you never had." Her voice was so quiet, so filled with anguish, so...not Millie. Was the kiss too much? Was he delusional in thinking she'd kissed him back with the same passion he'd given her?

She strode out of the stables toward the bunkhouse, jogging once she was out of view. Dex watched her until she got to the door, his heart yanking at his chest as she ran.

He started for the barn, tucking his desire away until they got a chance to talk. The facts were simple: they were best friends, she was his only family and he was half of all she had left. Losing her would do him in. Even when she wasn't around, she lit up his thoughts, knowing her sass and sarcasm and brilliance was out there making the world a better place.

Was sex even a pale comparison to all that?

"Hey there, Doc. Mind if I run something by you?" Gale asked the moment Dex walked into the dining space. His gaze scoured the room, looking for the familiar wild curls. He flexed his hands, recalling what those curls had felt like laced between his fingers just moments ago.

"Sure," he said.

Where is she?

"What can I do you for, boss?"

"It's actually a private matter. Can we talk outside real quick?"

"Of course." Dex glanced over his shoulder, but still didn't see Millie. He followed Gale onto the porch, where the waning sun had cooled the coastal ranch temperatures enough that he wished he'd brought a sweater this evening. "Go ahead," he urged Gale.

"It's about Ray."

"Is he okay?" Dex asked. He'd come to respect and like the guy in the short weeks he'd been at Hearts and Horses.

"He's fine, but he's getting antsy. You know, about…" Gale gestured to his left ring finger that was, of course, empty.

"Ray wants a commitment?" Dex asked.

"He does. And he deserves it, but I'm not sure I'm ready."

"For him or for what loving him fully would mean?"

"Hmm. That's a good question. I can't imagine life without the pain in the ass always nagging me to do things better. He's the reason I wake up smiling."

"But?" Dex asked. His thoughts conjured Millie, but he shoved the wispy image of her away until he could focus on it, bring it to life. It didn't sate the ache in his chest, though.

Gale shook his head. "When I say that out loud, the *but* doesn't seem as powerful."

"That's a good sign, but it's still there, I'm guessing, and not talking about it will only give it power."

"Fair enough. Okay, well, here it is." Gale shoved his hands in his pockets and glanced around him as if to make sure they were alone. When Dex followed his gaze, he caught sight of Millie leaving the bunkhouse, and even in the dim light, he could see the puffiness under her eyes, the damp red on her cheeks. She'd been crying.

Dex shook his head. He couldn't be in two places at once. He'd connect with her after Gale was done.

"I love Ray, I do. But once we sign, seal and make this rodeo official, well…" He trailed off, his pained gaze set on the dining hall. Dex could relate.

"You're responsible for someone else's happiness?"

"Exactly. And I've been running this place for too long to know that's not how it goes, not really, anyway. No one can make you happy but yourself, but I've got a long way to go with my own mental and physical rehab. What if we take this on too soon and I wrap him in my mess?"

Dex widened his stance, looked at Gale through appraising eyes. "Have you yet?"

"No, or at least, I don't think so. If anything, he's calmed me down, made me better."

Again, Dex found himself nodding, not because Gale's admission was revelatory with what he'd assumed of his and Ray's relationship, but because it shined a light on how Dex felt for Millie. It was as if Gale held up a mirror for Dex to gaze into the whole time he spoke.

"Then, you have your answer, don't you?"

However, the question remained: would Dex take his own advice?

"Thanks, Doc. This is what I needed."

"No sweat. Hey, speaking of, I might beg you for an evening off one day next week so Millie and I can connect about our days before she's too exhausted to do much but snore me into submission," Dex said, only half joking about the second part. Millie was gorgeous, brilliant, funny and the kindest person he knew...but she could put grown men to shame with the way she sawed logs.

"Consider it done. Both things. I'll make sure you share a few evenings off, and now that you've met with all the patients we have here, we'd like to have you on a more consistent five-day workweek."

"Thanks, Gale. That'll be nice." The men walked into the barn, where the delectable scent of fried chicken and corn bread filled the space. So did the sounds of laughter and pleasant conversation. Dex inhaled it all as he watched his and Millie's patients all chatting and talking about their days.

This. This was what Dex had been missing at Mercy Hospital. The connection, the camaraderie, the community of healing. Maybe he'd have stayed if they would have followed through on funding a program like this there. One that would help trauma victims from the area in a safe, all-inclusive space that paid attention to the whole patient, not just their injuries.

Even Millie was animatedly discussing something with Reese. The remnants of whatever had upset her were almost invisible, but Dex knew what to look for and found it in the way her smile didn't meet her eyes, in the way she picked at the corner of her lip.

Still, she was stronger than she'd been three months ago.

No matter what happened between them, this was a good move, for that reason alone. But that didn't mean he should give in to his desire. He cared for Millie a whole hell of a lot, but Gale's words rang loud in his ears. What if he let her in and took her down with the parts of himself that were barely healed?

He sighed. Longing washed through him, but it wasn't worth the risk. Millie was off-limits not only because of their different lifestyles but because he couldn't imagine what it would be like to have everything in his arms and lose it because he turned out to be too damn broken to really love anyone.

Millie wouldn't be collateral damage in his war against demons that weren't quite out of his rearview.

CHAPTER EIGHT

DEX'S EVENING THERAPY sessions had gone pretty well, considering he was mildly distracted by thoughts of Millie. All throughout dinner, she'd ignored him, laughing with Reese and Ray as if nothing were wrong.

As if he hadn't caught her drying her eyes coming out of the bunkhouse.

"Dr. Shaw, you're an incredible asset to these guys," Ray said, walking up beside Dex. For a man with a severe injury, he didn't let it slow him down. He kept pace with everyone on the ranch and had even had a horse saddle made to accommodate his prosthetics.

"Thanks, Ray. They're pretty great. Making good progress, too. Which I actually wanted to talk to you about."

"Shoot."

Dex glanced up at the moon. It was still only a sliver, but without lights from a city, it cast a pale glow over the camp, bathing it in blue. He had to admit, though the city had always held his dreams and aspirations, the resources he'd thought he needed, this life gave him a peace of mind he hadn't found elsewhere. Maybe Millie was on to something.

"Everett and Tom aren't where I want them to be."

"Mmm. How so?"

"Well, neither has accepted where they've been or what they need to do in order to form healthy relationships in the future. Having their families here in a couple weeks without much change is gonna be tough. Maybe a setback."

"I agree. Let's talk about that at our staff meeting Monday."

Dex nodded his agreement. "I'd actually like to get them working the stables and managing the schedule down there. They've both got the experience, and are excited about the animals, which means they'll be motivated to do right by them."

"I'll run it up the Gale pole, but I think that sounds like a great idea. Thanks for thinking of it. See what I mean? You and Millie are good for these folks."

"I appreciate it." Dex spared a glance toward the bunkhouse. He was glad for the way the thin moon and starless night sucked the color from the landscape because he was sure his cheeks were flashing red. If only he could be good for Millie.

"Everything okay on the home front?" Ray asked.

Dex fidgeted with a coin in his pocket.

"Yeah, we're just figuring out how to work together and keep the romance alive, too," Dex lied. What was one more in the pile they'd amassed? "But Gale's scheduled a shared day off for the latter."

Ray considered him a moment, his gaze steely, even in the waning light.

"I get that," he finally said. "I'll make sure you get time without patients to touch base about work, too. Striking this balance will be key to all of us staying sane and keeping our significant others happy."

"I appreciate it. I'm sure Millie will, too."

Would she, though? More time with him might set her off like their kiss had earlier that day. Maybe if he could keep his libido in check…

Dex waved and headed back to the bunkhouse, his heart heavy. Heavy and split in two. On one hand, he was happier than he'd been in a while, more fulfilled professionally, too. Here were patients who *needed* them and the work he and Millie were doing.

On the other hand, he was wading in dangerous territory, going against what he knew was good for him. His growing—and surprising—feelings for Millie were going to burn them both. He wasn't equipped to show and give love, especially to someone whose life of danger and risk drudged up all too familiar fears stemming from his tumultuous childhood.

Faking it for the sake of their jobs was only adding to the pile of guilt.

He leaned his forehead against the door, his shoulders sagging with indecision.

"I wish I could love you the way you deserve," he whispered against the sturdy oak door.

He opened it, careful with his footsteps so he didn't wake Millie, whose back was to him. Her smooth bare skin exposed by the tank top she wore to bed appeared to glow under the moonlight streaming in through the windows.

His fists clenched, a feeble attempt to quelch his desire to run his fingers along the curve of her.

Good grief, what was he thinking, agreeing to be her fake husband? The unmet desire alone would run him ragged over the next few months. Because somewhere in the stolen glances and touches, the longing had become very freaking real.

"Oh, Millie," he whispered soft enough for the early night breeze to take the words away, "I love you, but I'm not sure it's enough."

She stirred, but didn't roll over. He slipped out of his shoes and clothes, then brushed his teeth and got into bed beside Millie.

Her eyes fluttered open, then. "How was the therapy session?" she asked.

"Good." He resisted the urge to lean over and kiss her, the pull on him so real and so damn tempting. "I'll fill you in when we wake up, or maybe when we have the time off together to consult on patient progress."

He gave in to his desire, halfway at least, tucking one of Millie's curls behind her ear.

"Mmm... That'll be nice. I'm exhausted."

"I know. Go back to sleep, hun."

His lips twisted into a scowl. He hadn't meant to let that last word slip.

She caught the error and her eyes grew wide, her lips softened into an *O*.

"Sorry," he whispered.

"Don't be," she replied, her voice as faint as the ambient light from outside. "I like the sound of the word on your lips."

Millie shifted under the covers and her leg rested against Dex's.

Damn. He was hard as the ground outside just seeing her pale skin bathed in moonlight. The caress of her smooth skin under the covers was enough to eradicate any self-control he had left.

"What are you doing?" he asked. His heart pounded in the silence.

"Do you not want me to?"

Her foot ran up his calf, finally hooking around his thigh and Dex emitted a low growl.

"What I want and what we need aren't the same thing, Mil."

Even in the fractured dark, he could see her draw her bottom lip between her teeth. Her palm rested on his bicep and then trailed along his shoulder. Her words from the stables echoed in the liminal space between them.

I care about you. More than a friend.

"Haven't you wondered what this might be like?"

Dex gulped nothing but dry air, the moisture drained from his throat. He had. Often. But it always ended in the same conclusion—they'd probably have run their course by now, her bored of his control freak tendencies, and he'd be without her amazingness. Amazingness he was attracted to. What a damn double-edged sword.

"I have, but that doesn't mean we should act on it."

"Why not?"

A thousand reasons.

Not the least of which was the fact that she wanted more from him than he could give.

"You're my best friend," he settled on. But the way her fingers brushed his jawline, then tangled in his hair said she was capable of more than that.

Good God, he wanted to know more—what she tasted like, felt like pressed against him…

How could he act on his basest desires with a woman he cherished for so many other reasons? He loved her, sure, but loving Millie in the way she deserved meant taking on risk he couldn't stomach.

On the other hand, how was he supposed to resist making love to her, especially when she was offering herself up to him on a silvery blue-tinted platter?

"What we need might be to get this out of our systems," she whispered. "Maybe if we give in to whatever this is building between us, we can go back to being just friends."

A one-night stand? With his best friend? The idea had merit.

Millie pulled him closer so their hips were aligned. No way now she couldn't tell how badly he did, indeed, want this since his erection pressed against her.

"You make a good point."

She rocked into him.

"So do you, it seems," she said, her smile mischievous but her eyes focused with desire.

It was all he needed to give in. The consequences couldn't be greater than living in purgatory with her the next five months.

"Come here, wife," he said, pulling her the rest of the way on top of him. "I think it's high time we consummate this marriage."

She giggled until he kissed her, and then it was as if a match had been lit in a room filled with fumes of longing. They exploded, their kisses and hands hungry for more. When he teased her mouth open, she moaned into him, flicking his lips with her tongue.

She tasted like mint but the scent of plumeria from her shampoo was what almost undid him. He breathed her in and committed that scent to memory, as if he'd ever be able to forget a moment of this.

Dex's hands wrapped along the curve of her jaw, his fingers clasping around the base of her head as he let his tongue explore her mouth. Her own hands traced down his chest, then stopped as she reached the part of him so filled with wanting it was about to burst. She took him in her hands, firm and strong, moving over him until he groaned.

"Please," he begged. "I want you so damn bad, Millie."

"Show me how much," she whispered against his ear before tracing it with her tongue.

He flipped her on her back, eliciting a squeal of delight. "Careful what you wish for, Millie Tyler." Starting at her neck, he kissed along her collarbone, sucking the curve of her shoulder while she rocked underneath him.

"Yes," she uttered.

Taking that as a sign of encouragement, he peppered her chest with kisses, too, stopping to pull each of her nipples into his mouth so he could tease them with his tongue. She cried out, but he wasn't close to done. He wanted to taste each curve, each swathe of her bare skin. He wanted to make her feel what he felt every time he looked at her.

Had he wondered what loving her would be like? Only every minute of the past few months.

He traced her belly button with his finger as his mouth closed over one of her breasts. She screamed out his name and he couldn't hold back a grin.

"Shh…" he teased her. "You'll wake the neighbors." He took the other breast into his mouth, giving it the same attention.

"Eff the neighbors. I want you inside me," she moaned.

Goddamn, had he ever wanted anything so badly? But not yet. Not until he'd left her satisfied and sated.

His tongue moved down her body, drawing shapes on her hips. When he moved to the small swathe of hair covering her sex, her breath halted. Dex waited for the exhale as he ran his tongue up her center, and when it came, so did she. Her body shook with the aftereffects, but she opened her eyes and met his gaze.

"Take me," she whispered, her lips quivering.

He reached into the stand beside his bed and procured a condom, sheathing himself and then thrusting into her in one movement. She screamed, her hands gripping the pillow behind her head.

"Goddamn, Dex," she cried out. His name on her lips while he rocked in and out of her warmth almost made him come right there. "I want you to come."

He dipped down and kissed her, softer and deeper this time.

"I'm close." His breath was tight, his whole body on edge as he moved against the beautiful woman beneath him.

"Come for me, Dex," she urged. When he did, she tightened around him, her own body shaking against his. He held tight to her, kissing her gently between shuddering breaths. She curled against him and he rolled to his back so he could tuck her in the nook of his shoulder and chest.

His lips lightly grazed the top of her head and he brushed the damp curls from her face.

She relaxed against him, her arm draped over his chest, her legs tangled in his, and they lay that way for minutes. Not talking, just…being. He sighed. The eventual soft purr of her breathing said she'd fallen asleep, but it wouldn't be that easy for him.

He squeezed her tighter to his body, desperate to shake the feeling that had come over him after making love to his best friend.

She'd claimed it would be just the thing to get rid of whatever sexual tension was building between them, and she'd been right—the tension was gone. But what replaced it was far worse. Because it hadn't done a damn thing to quench his desire for her.

No, if anything, it made him want more of her—*all* of her—and the problem with that was simple. There was no way their friendship was going to remain unscathed.

Millie lay awake, staring at the wall. Or, the part of the wall she could see over the arc of Dex's sculpted chest. God, she should be exhausted, given her day and the night that followed, but a frenetic energy buzzed through her veins. She'd been awake when Dex came in and his whispers still haunted her.

He loved her. Just not enough. *Enough for what*, she wanted to ask.

In the end, it hadn't mattered. She'd made her case—internally arguing that sating a physical desire had worked in the past to keep unwanted feelings at bay—and they'd given in to each other. Millie finally knew the divine pleasure of his lips, his hands, his... Well, *all* of him.

But damn. Her tried and true one-night stand approach hadn't worked. Not one little bit.

Her fingers traced the definition in his muscles, awe at the perfection of them hitting her on multiple levels. Speaking as a physician, he was an Adonis sculpture like those she'd studied in medical school. Perfect, symmetrical, ideal in all the right ways.

But as a woman, all she saw and felt beneath her was a work of art.

I just made love to Dexter Shaw.

Her best friend, her only family, her fake husband.

Those lines were blurred to hell now.

Heat crept along her skin as she recalled what loving him had been like. His hands caressing every inch of her, his mouth on places she'd only dreamed he'd kiss one day, the rest of him filling her like he was the missing piece to her anatomy.

I just made love to Dexter Shaw, she repeated.

Unfortunately, it came with an addendum this time.

For the first and only time.

After all, that was the agreement they'd made. Once, to get it out of their systems. Who knew it would be like that cheesy potato chip advertisement from the '80s and once wouldn't be near enough to satisfy her.

Because—*whoa!* The man was the best sex of her *life*. She swallowed a scream of injustice that she'd discovered this about her best friend, the only man she knew who was off-limits.

Dex shifted beneath her, stretching. He groaned and then turned his gaze to hers, which she was wholly unprepared for. She'd expected sweet, maybe reticent, but the heat wafting off him was palpable and she was suddenly grateful for the windows they kept open at night.

"Good morning, gorgeous," he said, his voice still thick with sleep. He pulled her tighter to him and kissed the top of her head before tilting her chin up so he could do the same to her lips. Her greedy lips that craved more.

What is he doing? It was only supposed to be the once.

Shut up, she told her brain. As Dex's hands slid around her waist, cupping her butt and drawing her on top of him, it wasn't the time to listen to that particular organ.

Millie deepened the kiss, drawing Dex's tongue out to tangle with hers. When he reached for the nightstand drawer again, she whispered, "I'm covered that way."

"And I'm clean."

"Then leave it. I want to feel you."

Dex wasted no time releasing her onto him, filling her again. She moaned with pleasure, lifting herself just enough so the tip of him remained buried in her, then she sank back, taking him back in. He peppered her chest, her shoulder, the nape of her neck with kisses until she felt wholly, fully cherished.

"You're perfect," he whispered against her hair.

I want this forever, she wanted to say.

"I'm close," she answered instead.

"Come, babe. I want you to come."

He thrust harder, faster, until she squeezed around him, coming to orgasm. She gasped, digging her nails into his back. He rocked his hips deeper, moaning with pleasure as he joined her.

Afterward, they lay on top of one another, sweaty despite the almost frigid air blowing in. Millie's head rested on his chest while he ran his fingers through her tangled curls.

"We sorta broke our rule," she whispered.

"I don't count this. We're in the same bed we went to sleep in, so it's technically not a second time."

She giggled, but sobered when his hand tightened around her. Her eyes squeezed shut. All she wanted was this, forever. But that was impossible. Her best friend could be her lover, but that was it. He didn't want more, or at least he hadn't three or four orgasms ago. It wasn't like she didn't know why—he'd lost every important person in his life and the fear shaped every choice he made.

She had her own demons, too. When her mom had passed at the same age as Dex had been when he lost his father, she'd thought her father's marriage to a new woman would fix the hurt; instead it made her life a living hell—a hell she'd been in until she met Dex on her first pre-deployment leave. So, how could she risk their friendship for sex?

It's more than that, all her organs agreed.

Ugh. All she knew with certainty was that she didn't want this to end.

"We should get up and get ready. You've got a full day and I'm using my morning off to run some errands if you need anything in town."

Millie tried to slide off Dex's torso, but he kept her pinned in place.

"What if," he said, shifting so they could see each other. His bottom lip was tucked between his teeth. Was Dexter Shaw *nervous*? "What if we made a pact?"

Millie sat up and draped her arms over her bare breasts. Somehow, in the light of day, the pillow talk seemed more intimate than what they'd done the night before. And that morning.

"What kind of pact?"

Dex sat up as well, leaning against the headboard, his arms languidly crossed behind his head. He looked like a damn model for underwear or something. Only the way he bit the corner of his lip and the subtle way he couldn't hold her gaze said he was anything other than at peace.

"Well, I was thinking about it. What kind of married couple are we, not kissing and holding hands and stuff in public?"

"We're not in public. We're at work."

Her heart screamed something that made her stomach flip over itself a couple times. She ignored it.

"Agreed, but why don't we lean into the thing we're selling? You know, go for it while we're here."

"You mean, be a real couple?"

He stiffened, but then relaxed just as quickly. "Sure, yeah. While we're here, anyway. We know we work as friends and colleagues. We found out last night that it extends to the bedroom, so why sell ourselves short? Let's just enjoy what we have for the next five-plus months and then we can reevaluate when the contract's up. Think of it as *leveling up* our friendship, even if it would be a disaster in the real world."

She didn't mention that this *was* the real world, that the lie didn't change anything but others' perspectives of their relationship.

On the surface, his level-up idea made sense. Hell, she wanted it as much as she'd ever wanted anything. But just below the surface, the tepid truth lay waiting. Now she understood the tremble in his lips. If they did this and messed it up…

"If I don't find something permanent, I'm headed to Doctors Without Borders after this."

He frowned. "I know."

"And you've got no interest in traveling for work. You want your stability."

"I know that, too, Millie. Do you not want to do this, because—"

"No," she shot back. She placed a hand on his chest. "I do. I just want to make sure if we do this, we do it with our eyes open to reality."

"Sure. Of course. I know we're different, Millie, that we have different goals in life. It's why we haven't done this sooner, right?"

The breath was knocked out of her chest with the admission.

"Is that why?" she asked. "It's not because you can't have someone rely on you? Or because you just saw me as a friend?"

Dex drew her in close to him. "Millie, I've always been curious about us. And friend or not, you've always been hot." He grinned, though it didn't assuage the unease in her chest. "But you're right; I worried about my own limitations and what I had to offer you. I still do. This little pact could give us time to explore more, though."

Explore more.

That was the problem. She didn't want more; when it came to Dex, she wanted *everything*.

"And if one of us wants more after this?" Not just from one another, but from life? Because one thing was still unequivocally true about her best friend—he'd never want any risks in his professional life, either.

"Then we talk about it like adults. Listen to one another like we have since we met."

"You didn't exactly listen to everything. I gave you a treatment plan to follow and you all but told me to go to hell."

"I didn't know what a brilliant doctor you were back then."
He smiled and kissed her lightly on the lips.

God. This was all she wanted—the ease and perfection of loving her best friend and having him love her in return.

"And now?" she asked, gazing up at him.

"Well, we've established your brilliance, obviously. But I don't know that I ever thanked you for that day."

"The day we met? You did. Multiple times. And I called in the favor, so we're good."

"No, Millie, I mean for how you upended my life that day. You know I'm crap when it comes to relationships, but not just the romantic ones. You coming into my life showed me I'm capable of so much more than I give myself credit for. I can care for someone and take the risk that comes with it." Millie pressed her forehead against Dex's chest, letting the warmth of his words and skin take away the chill his "pact" gave her. "And it looks like you're not done doing that, either."

He bent down and kissed her. His hands were tender where they'd been hungry, his mouth passionate where it had been desperate. On paper, this was exactly what Millie craved from him—the desire bleeding into their fifteen years of friendship. They'd earned this, hadn't they?

That doesn't mean it's any more real now than it was last night. Your relationship is still built on a sham.

Millie ignored her pesky, obtrusive subconscious.

Her relationship *status* might be a fraud, but that didn't mean her relationship was. There was a reason she and Dex had decided to do this at all—besides the favor she called in. They shared a genuine friendship that spanned far longer than most folks' actual marriages.

As Dex deepened the kiss and she let his hands explore the places he knew would drive her to distraction, faces flashed behind her eyelids.

Reese. Charlie. Dominic. *Ray and Gale.*

If she was wrong and this backfired, what she risked was

so much greater than just her heart. Somehow, unexpectedly, she'd stumbled into another family, and losing this one would do real damage.

CHAPTER NINE

DEX WENT THROUGH the next five weeks of work in a daze. A sex-induced daze, but still. Twelve-hour shifts—including the promised time to share notes with Millie on their patients' progress—were bookended by lovemaking sessions with his fake-wife-but-real-girlfriend. It was like trying to sate an unquenchable thirst.

Dex simply couldn't get enough of her.

And yeah, he was well aware of how problematic that was. Because it wasn't just sex—*damn good sex*—to him. *Feelings* were involved. Big messy ones that looked a lot like the ones on the end of Cupid's arrow and started with a capital *L*.

Shit.

On one hand, that was a good thing. He cared enough about another person—a person whose needs and safety he wanted to put in front of his own—to feel something other than abject horror at the idea of spending a life with them.

Dex Shaw was capable of a relationship.

On the other hand, boy, had he picked wrong. Millie Tyler was all sorts of bad for him when it came to making him feel safe. Twice that week she'd gone on a solo run and come back with stories of a cool snake she saw. Three times, she'd burned herself at the campfire, and once on the hot plate where she made them tea at night. Then there were the constant conversations at work; he'd caught snippets of what she'd encountered overseas and it wasn't pretty. Bombs, tribal wars and insurgents were the norm.

The black tendrils of his anxiety hadn't come back, but he knew they were close by.

How was he supposed to *ever* sit back and watch this woman he lov—*cared for* get hurt? And to make matters worse, he'd found a pamphlet for DWB in her dresser drawer that morning when he'd gone looking for the underwear she sent him to find. It was next to the front page of their contract, with the end date in bold.

Three months, three weeks and six days left.

It was a countdown for him, too. But he wasn't sure to what anymore.

"Shoot," she muttered, looking down at her finger before sucking on the tip of it.

"What'd you do?" he asked. His pulse raced.

"Just snagged it on this clip. I'm fine."

He exhaled. *He* wasn't fine. Sexually satisfied? *Yes. Absolutely.* Happy? *Mostly.* But calm and fine? *Nope.*

"I'm glad Tom and Everett get some time with their families this weekend," she said, closing the door on his worry about her for the time being. It never stayed shut long, though. She consistently pushed against one of his self-made barriers—this time it was his peace of mind. One of these days, she wouldn't be fine—she'd be really hurt, and he'd be irrevocably devastated.

He sighed, earning him a kiss. *That*, he didn't mind. "Yeah. Me, too."

They'd changed the therapy and treatment protocols for Tom and Everett and both men were looking forward to a truncated weekend with family in a few days. They weren't ready to share beyond an afternoon, but even that was headway.

They just had to get through the moonlit ride along the beach first.

Millie's excitement about the trip was palpable. According

to her, this was the most romantic idea anyone had ever had. Not to Dex. Taking a half-ton animal along a dark poorly lit beach with unpredictable tides and keeping track of twenty trauma patients with various mental health triggers wasn't Dex's idea of romance.

It was the kind of thing that kept a trauma doc like her in business.

"I love the ocean at night. There's something therapeutic about the dark skies and the sound of the water crashing against the shore."

He gave a half-hearted laugh. He might not agree, but he'd buy stock in anything that made Millie smile like she was.

"See, when you say the word *crashing*, it loses some of its appeal. And here I thought *therapy* was therapeutic."

She nudged him playfully with her shoulder while they gathered tack in the waning daylight. The staff would join them after dinner to prep the horses, but until then, it was nice to be alone with Millie. That didn't happen often during work hours.

"Ha ha, mister. You know what I mean. To be alone with your thoughts and nature—it's calming." She ran a hand along the leather saddle she carried. He leaned over the pile of brass and kissed her.

"Yeah, if nature behaves. She's a fickle beast, though."

"Maybe, but she's still beautiful. You know, I'd love to sleep under the stars with you one night. It's romantic—I don't care what you say."

He tried for a smile, even a half-hearted one, but shuddered as he recalled the nights he'd slept under the overpass the first month after he ran away from the system, and later for almost a year when he'd been an eighteen-year-old without a plan.

It was the only story Millie didn't know about him, the only one he'd never shared with anyone. No one quite understood how quickly it could all be taken away. Not even Millie, or she'd also understand why he worried every time she got so much as a papercut.

LA was supposed to have mild winters, but that first year of homelessness he'd almost lost a toe and some fingers to frostbite thanks to an unexpected—and unwelcome—cold front. The ER doc on call who had helped bring his limbs back to life had offered him a glimpse at another world, one where nice things and creature comforts were an everyday occurrence. The doc had been caring and kind, answering all Dex's questions about what his job entailed, even laying out a ten-year plan on the back of a blank chart, which Dex still had back in LA, in case Dex wanted to pursue medicine.

In case? Dex was baited, hooked and reeled in.

With four words—*you've got promise, kid*—the doc had covered Dex's bill under a pro bono case, then left in a Porsche with one of the nurses in the passenger seat.

That was all Dex needed to change course. That, and the list of shelters the doctor gave him so he'd have a safe warm place to stay while he put his plan into action.

He'd gotten his GED, applied to a community college and never spent a night outside after that, not even to camp. The rest was history.

If Millie knew the secret shame he kept from her—he had been homeless and a runaway, not some tormented kid with daddy issues like she believed—would she want anything to do with him?

But at the same time, he had a hard time denying her anything.

"We'll see." He kissed her forehead. "For now, let's get ready to lead half a dozen traumatized first responders through the dark on uneven ground with beasts that could spook at the sound of their own tails swishing."

"Look at my boyfriend, the incurable romantic."

Millie dipped lower and kissed Dex on the cheek, then

the lips, eliciting a smile from him even as he looked over their shoulders.

"We're alone. Don't worry."

"You want to know what I think is romantic?" he asked.

"What's that?"

He slipped a finger beneath the thin strap of her tank top and slid it down along the fabric until his hand reached the curve of her breast peeking out from the top of the shirt. She inhaled a sharp breath but didn't answer.

"You," he said, tugging on the strap, pulling her close enough that he could kiss her shoulder. His lips traced the edge of the shirt, until he got to the rise of her breast. Pulling the cotton down, he peppered her exposed flesh with kisses until he reached her nipple. He sucked it into his mouth and teased it with his tongue until she groaned with pleasure.

"Dex," she whispered on an exhale. "We can't. We're in public."

Dex flicked her bud with his teeth and she gasped, arching her back, giving him better access to her. He didn't respond to her worry—or his. Instead, he moved to her other breast and gave it equal attention, the allure of the outdoors Millie had been preaching suddenly making sense.

This *was* kind of therapeutic, being in the semi-covered space, the wind tickling his skin. Taking Millie in his mouth, pleasuring her while the thought of keeping their tryst quiet consumed them both.

It was a risk he was comfortable taking.

When he unbuttoned her jeans and slid his hand along her sex, she gasped.

"We can't," she said, her words broken by each ragged breath she drew in. Yet, when he lifted her shirt, she arched her back to allow him access to her. In times like these, lost in lust, he could almost pretend no outside danger waited in the wings. He could picture being happy with Millie…forever.

"Let me," he whispered, kissing down her stomach while

he tugged her jeans and underwear over her hips and knees. She nodded and her approval stoked the fire of desire in him. His thumbs pressed into the hollows of her hips and he lifted her so her back lay against the soft give of the barn blankets they'd just laundered.

Dex trailed his tongue along her hip bone and Millie moaned softly.

"Shhh, darling. I'm going to make you come with my tongue but you can't make a sound, okay?"

She nodded and sucked her bottom lip between her teeth. Dex wasted no time kissing her chill-dimpled skin until he came to her center. He ran a finger along her opening, teasing her wide for him. She tensed, but didn't make a sound.

His tongue ran the length of her before sucking and pulling at her bud. Millie's back arched and her fingers tangled in his hair as he spread her legs wide. His hands caressed her until they came to her full exposed breasts. He cupped them, teasing her tight nipples with his thumb and finger. His tongue darted inside her warm fleshy folds and his thumb strummed at her core until she bucked beneath him. Her breaths became shallow and quick as he sped up his kisses. Suddenly, her hands froze and her body rocked with breathless release.

He didn't stop, just kept kissing her as wave after wave of pleasure rolled through her.

I could get used to this.

When her body calmed and her breaths evened, he pulled her down onto his lap and held her.

"That was nice," she said, her voice as soft as the new barn kittens' fur. He liked all versions of Millie—the ass-kicking side, the part of her that always knew just what to say to make him laugh the moment he took a drink of something. Hell, he even loved the side of her that craved adventure and danger—even though it was diametrically opposed to what made him feel safe. But he had to admit, he *really* liked the sexually satisfied, soft and reticent Millie, too.

"Nice, huh? Looks like I'll have to work a little harder, then," he teased, bending down to her stomach and kissing it until she squealed.

"Please, no. I can barely stand as it is."

That's more like it.

Her skin was flushed and small beads of moisture traced her cheekbones as he helped her stand.

Goddamn, she's gorgeous.

"You know, we have a little time," she said, unbuckling his jeans, her eyes wide and her lips shining with moisture as she gazed up at him. "Let me return the favor."

Dex's breath caught in his chest as her hand cupped his hard length over his pants, caressing it. When it slipped between his skin and boxer briefs, he groaned. The woman knew what she was doing.

"Jesus, Millie."

Her hand wrapped around his girth and stroked him up and down with a firm grip.

His head rolled back and heat flushed his veins.

The distant sounds of the dining hall screen door and voices floating back to the bunkhouse broke the spell almost instantly. The patients would be headed down to the stables shortly. Dex pulled back, forcing Millie to release him.

"Shit," he grumbled, fumbling with his zipper.

"We're fine," she said, reaching for him again.

"No. We should get going. We wouldn't want Ray to ask us why we're behind with the gear. He might not like the answer." Disappointment settled in his chest, even though he tried to keep his voice light. Not at needing to stop Millie from what she'd been doing, but at the idea that twenty patients were about to descend into their quiet private space. He *liked* being alone with her, her humor, her sass... More and more each day.

But the outside world would eat them alive.

He pulled her underwear and pants up and kissed her stomach as he straightened her shirt.

"Yeah, that would be bad," she said, helping him up. "But if anyone understood, it would be Ray. What do you want to bet he and Gale have done the same thing?"

"Oh, I'm not taking a losing bet. I *know* they have."

They laughed.

"Rain check, then?" she asked.

"Abso-freaking-lutely."

Millie wrapped her arms around Dex, squeezing him tight. The sudden seriousness threw him.

"What was that for?" he asked.

She gazed up at him and the thrilling heat from earlier was replaced with a tenderness that almost put him on his ass.

"I just…" She dropped her gaze. "I like this. Whatever this thing is between us. I was worried if we gave us a shot, I'd lose my best friend, but all I did was gain someone to kiss and do dirty stuff with."

The levity at the end of her small speech was so *Millie*. She always found a way to make light of a serious topic. It didn't shroud the heaviness of what she'd been alluding to, though.

"I like it, too," he lied. Because he didn't just *like* it. He'd come to depend on her arms around him at the end of the day. On her kisses to wake him up each morning. On her words to soothe his ragged thoughts.

But one small nagging thought took root and grew in his head as he held her tight to his chest. The greatest risk he'd ever taken was about to blow up in his face, because he had no idea what would happen in just under four months when she walked away from him, toward the one iteration of her future he couldn't follow.

Millie inhaled deeply. The moonlight reflected off the water in shimmery fragments, making it appear that the ocean surface was dappled with small tea lights for miles. It was breathtaking.

Breathtaking in a different way than her experience earlier in the stables, of course. But now that the memory had weaseled its way to the front of her thoughts... Just thinking about it left her feeling warm despite the cool ocean breeze rippling over her skin.

Dex had gone down on her in the middle of the stables, a scene that would keep her giggling when she was old and senile in a nursing home somewhere. But it wasn't that part of the night that lingered on her tongue like the last of a favorite dessert.

It was holding him, feeling the strength of his physicality matched by their shared vulnerability. Maybe it was just her, but she felt like something had shifted tonight, like a lock clicking into place.

But...for what door? And what did it unlock? If it was a lifetime of trust and joy with this man, then she'd gladly open it. Though there were a hundred other possibilities. Like a door that led right to a repeat of her lonely past if things went wrong. Or one that opened to the worry that falling for Dex would tie her down. Fear knocked around in her chest.

"I'd know that smile anywhere," a familiar voice said. Ray rode up beside her and she grinned, happy to see him even if the rest of her life was a confusing mess at the moment.

"Well, hey there, stranger. And what was that about my smile?"

"It's just nice to see the smile of a woman still in love after five years of marriage. That's usually when folks give up and head for the hills."

"Oh, I, uh—" she started, before cutting herself off. She couldn't really refute that, or Ray might read into it. But what he said wasn't true, was it? Was she...*in love*?

She swallowed a groan. That would be so damned inconvenient, especially with so many unanswered questions. Her pulse sped up and she recognized the physical signs of elevated blood pressure.

"Yeah, you know Dex and me," she hedged. "Anyway, I was hoping you'd make it out with us. What was the holdup?"

"Oh, just a quick chat with Tom to get him comfortable with a new horse. No biggie," Ray said, taking the bait she'd laid for switching the topic off her and Dex.

"I hope you don't mind me saying, but Ray, you're glowing."

Ray let out a wistful sigh.

"Yes, I guess you're right." If Millie was seeing things right in the dim blue light, Ray actually blushed. "It's Gale. He's been communicative, observant and even—" he lowered his voice, a conspiracy building "—*romantic*." Ray and Millie both laughed.

She glanced up the beach at Dex, who rode next to George Dominic. The two were laughing under the moonlight and she didn't need the romantic atmosphere to feel a tug at her heart watching him at work. Ray's words came back to her like she'd been shocked with an AED.

Was what she was feeling *love*? How would she even know? It's not like she'd ever experienced anything like it.

Before she could delve too deeply into that particular trauma of hers, Gale rode up beside Millie.

"Mind if I steal my beloved?" he asked.

Ray shot her a look and mouthed, *See?*

She just smiled and shrugged. She was happy the two of them had found their stride.

She and Dex had, too, but that was what worried her. They were fully living in the present, but the future—and their separate goals—would smack them upside the heart sooner than either would realize. Maybe it was time they talked. Like about the half-ton horse-sized topic neither of them wanted to broach.

Wouldn't he have said something already if he wanted more with her—professionally and personally—after this six-month contract? The clock was ticking…

The unknowns with him were scarier than heading into combat, more terrifying than saying goodbye at her father's funeral.

She nudged Tillamook to trot up toward Dex, who was actually heading back to her. "What's up?" she asked. "You okay?"

"Yep, but keep a low profile. I'm on a secret mission." Dex held up his cell phone, which was set to video mode. He was confident and relaxed on his horse, another shift of late.

Millie glanced to where Dex's gaze landed. Gale and Ray were falling behind.

"Wait, is Gale—"

"Yep," Dex said, a wide smile on his face. "He sure is. And he asked me to film it. Keep an eye on things up here?"

She nodded. "Sure. Of course."

Her stomach flipped and the nerve endings along her skin felt too sensitive all of a sudden. The cool air blowing across her arms made her itchy and uncomfortable.

She glanced back, after checking on the riders, to see Gale—or the hazy silhouette of him swathed in moonlight— down on one knee. Swallowing hard, she turned Tillamook around, pulling on the reins tight until she stood on the outside of the proposal. Millie arrived just in time to hear Ray shout, "Hell, yes. It's about damn time, my love."

Dex, Gale and Ray all laughed as Gale swept up his husband-to-be and twirled him in the sand before planting him firmly on safe ground, his arm wrapped tight around Ray's waist until he was settled. When they kissed, Millie wiped at a tear she hadn't felt fall.

She clapped enthusiastically, whooping with congratulations.

"Hey, hun. Wasn't that romantic?" Dex asked her, riding up next to her. He leaned over and she met him halfway across the distance between their horses and their lips grazed.

"It was. Terribly." But that wasn't why her stomach still hadn't settled. Dex actually seemed to mean what he said, and not because they were within earshot of the happy couple.

"C'mon," Dex said, tossing her a smile that made her knees as squishy as her stomach. "Let's give them some time alone."

"Hold up," Gale called out. He ran up to them, his breathless smile and bright eyes visible even in the pale moonlight. "We just want to thank you both."

"For what?" Millie asked.

"You gave me the courage to live my truth with Ray. Loving him has been an adventure, but until I talked to you both, saw how you work alongside each other with such ease and still keep the romance alive, I didn't think that would be possible for us."

Millie shot Dex a look, but he was just smiling at Gale, nodding along to the little speech.

"I'm glad you two are taking this leap. It's worth it, trust me," Dex said. Millie had to work against gravity and abject shock to keep her jaw from hitting the sand.

"Dex, I know we talked about it earlier, but are you still okay with me riding back with Ray and taking the rest of the night off?"

"To quote your fiancé, *hell yes*!" They both laughed while Millie kept a smile plastered to her face. It might have been a demonic clown smile, but it was all she was capable of as she watched Dex flippantly talk about marriage and romance. As far as she'd been aware, he considered both to be illnesses with only fatal outcomes. It's not like she'd disagreed with him, either. Until lately, anyway. But then…why hadn't he said anything to her about their future?

"Great. You two have fun and thanks for taking the patients back to the barn. You've got this weekend off to show our appreciation."

"Normally, I'd refuse politely, but I've got plans for this little lady, so we'll take it."

Gale jogged back to his fiancé and helped him back on his horse.

"We've got plans?" Millie asked, her brows raised in question.

"We do. Secret plans."

"So secret I can't know?"

"Yep. What good is making a surprise date for my wife, only to tell her about it?"

Millie glanced around as they meandered back toward the trail of patients. "You know it's just us, right? Everyone else is too far away to hear anything."

He cocked his head. "Yeah. So?"

So we're not actually married. You don't need to pretend.

"Nothing. Never mind."

He shrugged like this was all normal. It was *not*. Dex Shaw talking about proposals and love and other sappy stuff he usually avoided like it all came from the infectious disease wing? Yeah, she'd have bet on cigarettes making a comeback to cure asthma before Dex's sappy streak.

And yet, he'd still kept his feelings about her tight-lipped. She wasn't sure anymore what was the truth and what was fabricated for their positions.

"You don't feel the least bit guilty for what he said back there?"

Dex's brows furrowed and his trademark shrug looked almost comical in the blue tint of the evening.

"No, why?"

"For them giving us praise for showing them how a relationship can be. I don't want to be the one to shine a light on this, especially tonight, but—" she lowered her voice so it was nothing more than a whispered hiss "—*we're not actually married.* We're just best friends who have good sex."

She held out her hands as if to say, *See?*

Was she imagining it, or when Dex pulled back on his reins, did she see hurt etched on his handsome, rugged features?

"That's all this is to you?"

"I didn't mean that. I just meant—"

"I know what you meant, but I disagree. I care about you and I like what we're doing. I thought we were more."

"More?" she asked, her voice sounding wounded and almost unrecognizable. She'd hoped to have "the talk" at some point with Dex, but here? Under these circumstances? It was less than ideal. "Dex, wait." He slowed, then paused before turning back to her. "I like you, too. A lot. In case you forgot, I'm the one who admitted that first. I'm just trying to navigate what's real and what's…fiction," she said.

He sighed and nodded as if he understood.

"I get it. And believe me, it's just as hard for me to tell you the way I feel—I found the DWB pamphlet, Millie."

"Oh."

"Yeah. It threw me. I want…something *bigger* with you but it's clear you're marching ahead, ever the good soldier."

"That's not fair. You haven't said anything about what you're doing after this contract and it's not like we've looked for something together. I was pretty clear what I'd need to do if I didn't find anything permanent here. It wasn't a state secret."

Not like the rest of her feelings. Or the entirety of their relationship.

"I know, and you're right. I just don't…" His jaw was set, worried. "I just don't know what to do." His voice was barely above a whisper.

She hedged her next words carefully. "Then why not—?" The rest of the words stuck in her throat. *Why not marry me for real? Let's give this a try!*

Yeah, that would be rich.

Their marriage would likely be as short as Dex's towel in the bunkhouse. Because even if she let DWB go, her life was filled with more adventure—more risk—than he would want. And she didn't see a life of being tied down. More things they'd both known when they started this affair. It hadn't stopped them from leaving their good sense at the door, anyway.

Good soldier, indeed.

Her heart thumped out a rhythm of longing for the man beside her. Was it loud enough for him to hear this time?

"What do you want?" she asked instead.

Another Dexter Shaw shrug greeted her by way of an answer. *Typical*.

"I'm not sure," he said, finally.

"Me, neither," she replied.

"Would you be up for doing what we're doing and seeing where it goes the next couple months?"

Why? So this cut can slice deeper when we say goodbye later?

"Yes," she whispered instead. Then, "Sure. I like what we're doing."

The lie sat heavy on her heart, making the pale blue seem darker, more ominous than romantic.

She *didn't* like what she and Dex were doing. Not one bit. If it were up to her, he'd hitch a ride on her train and they'd travel the world together as a couple, building memories and a life together.

But she'd chosen the wrong man for that. Especially because the infinitesimal flutter in her chest had turned to a gentle roar that couldn't be quieted anymore. How she felt about Dex couldn't be clearer—or louder.

She *loved* him.

She loved him, and yet…she couldn't imagine changing her life and her dreams to be with him. So there she was, stuck in the middle of a tar field, unable to move in either direction. Though it was far too difficult to imagine walking away from him while they still had some time left to enjoy each other, the next months would pass in the blink of an eye.

Her heart swelled against her rib cage.

And it would be damn near impossible to leave him then.

CHAPTER TEN

A WEEK HAD passed since the romantic beach ride. When they got back to the bunkhouse after work, Millie collapsed on the bed. She kicked off her boots and unbuckled her belt, but that's where her energy petered out. She was three seconds from catatonic. When she yawned, her eyelids fought against gravity to open again. She could sleep in her jeans and flannel, right?

Yeah, if you want your sheets to smell like wet horse all week.

She pouted, her bottom lip stuck in a three-year-old-who-wants-ice-cream position. Her eyes caught a photo on the nightstand that hadn't been there earlier that day. It was a framed image of her laughing at something Dex had said—was it when he'd wondered aloud if Cambria had a dry cleaner?—and him gazing down at her with a warmth in his eyes, his arm around her shoulder.

Gale had taken it before she and Dex were actually to-gether. She smiled.

"When did you print that?" she asked, gesturing to the frame.

He shrugged, classic Dex. "When I ran into town to get stuff from the pharmacy. I like that smile on your face, so I figured why not put it out so I can see it every day."

It was so simple a statement, but it had the force of a hur-ricane, spinning Millie's world around. They probably should print some photos of the past fifteen years and put them up, since they didn't have wedding photos or other mementos a real marriage would have.

"Well, I like it, too. Thanks."

"You bet. Wanna clean off with me?" he asked.

"I don't wanna shower. I'm exhausted, babe."

She cringed as the word *babe* came out of her mouth. They weren't lying anymore by saying how much they cared for each other, but she'd been lying to herself and Dex for a good week about her true feelings. She loved him. And not in a sham best-friend-posing-as-a-husband way. Somehow, the "faking it" had turned into something genuine and irreplaceable.

Too real.

He didn't seem to notice her slipup, though. He bent over her, planting a kiss on her forehead.

"You're gorgeous either way."

"I'm not worried about my looks, but thank you." Heat fanned her cheeks at his compliment. "I smell like the floor of a barn."

As much as she tried to hold his liquid gaze, the way his triceps flexed as he balanced above her pulled her focus. The heat on her skin spread south—way south, pooling in her stomach.

His pull on her was magnetic. Feral. Nothing phony about it.

He kissed her again, this time on the lips, his tongue teasing her open.

"Well," he whispered, his breath hot on her skin, "good thing I made arrangements so you don't have to shower."

"Are you bringing the wash stall hose in here?"

He shook his head, his eyes gleaming. "Nope. I'm bringing you to the wash stall."

Confusion spread from her furrowed brows to her pursed lips.

"If you hope to make it till tomorrow, you'd better be kidding."

He gave his quintessential Dexter shrug, but the smile tugging at the corners of his mouth said he was up to something.

"Come on. I'll show you."

"Dex," she whined, curling into a ball on top of the comforter. "I'm tired."

"I know." He held out his hand for her to take.

When had he ever steered her wrong? He might be a little intense when it came to her safety, but he always had her best interests at heart. She grabbed his hand and squealed as, in one swift movement, he hoisted her into his arms, cradling her like the toddler she was behaving as.

On the way out the door, he grabbed a bag she hadn't noticed perched at the base of their entryway.

"Where are we going?" she asked.

"Shh… Relax and trust me," he whispered. Her head rested against his chest, the *thump-thump* of his heartbeat matching pace with his steps, nudging her further toward sleep.

Trusting Dex was as easy as breathing. They worked well together as medical professionals and partners, each complementing the other's strengths with their own.

The harder thing to do was relax into him. Physically, sure. That was a pleasure she took advantage of all too often. But emotionally? Their fairy tale still had an expiration date and no matter how much she loved him, she couldn't fully relax knowing that.

"What're you doing?" she asked when they showed up at the front door of Ray and Gale's cabin. Dex kept her in his arms, but procured a key from his pocket, using it to unlock the front door. "Dex, what are we doing here?" she hissed. "This is Ray and Gale's place."

"Yep." He smiled and shut the door behind them.

"Put me down, Dex. This is crazy. We can't be here."

"I kinda like carrying you over thresholds, wifey. And don't worry. They offered the place to us."

"Why would they do that? We have a cabin."

Her eyes darted around the room. Even though she was on edge, she couldn't help but notice their surroundings. This cabin was bathed in rustic chic, a Chip and Joanna–looking masterpiece. Whitewashed frames housed photos of the couple and other family members, fresh flowers graced the large oak dining table and a floating natural edge pine shelf above the fireplace made the place feel…like a *home*.

It triggered a vague memory of her stepmother—before the death of her father—putting roses from her garden in a pale green vase every Sunday night. The news came from the naval chaplains on a Sunday, and flowers never graced their table again. In a sense, Millie had lost both parents when her dad was killed in Kuwait. What filled the gaping hole her father's absence made was a deep desire to be like him. She was a preteen when he passed, but she recalled him as kind and loving, if a little quiet. Her stepmom, on the other hand, became a shell of the woman she'd been when Millie was a child, leaving Millie to raise herself on good days. On bad? The woman was abusive and cruel, blaming Millie for her misery. That is, until her stepmother became sick and all but demanded Millie stay to care for her.

Any semblance of a family or childhood was stripped from her, carving out a need that seemed impossible to fill most days. Lacking any other guidance, she'd followed in her dad's footsteps and joined the military, which covered her bachelor's degree. In his death, her father's service to his country had then paid for her medical school. The army medical corps gave her back a family, even if it was short-lived.

It was a good life by some accounts; a desperately lonely one by others.

An ache opened up in Millie's chest, releasing a longing that she'd kept locked away tight. This place—this *home*— made her crave more.

A home of her own. Love to fill it. A family that would come home to her…

Her breathing relaxed, but her pulse raced. She'd been able to curb those desires by meeting others, but now, sexually satisfied with a man she actually cared for—the rest came crashing back into her.

"Because of this," he replied, setting her down. The rose-tinted bubble of her overactive imagination popped, leaving her stranded alone, back in reality. A reality where she was in love with her best friend, who abhorred the lifestyle that had fulfilled and sustained her when nothing and no one else had.

Grabbing her hand, he led her down a hallway to a large oak door. When he pushed it open, she gasped, forgetting all about what she didn't have. What she *did* have was a deep clawfoot tub filled with bubbles and lined with candles. More fresh-cut flowers from around the property lined the marble shelves around the tub. It was breathtaking.

"Is this for me?"

"Of course. I'm here if you need me for anything, but there's a bottle of wine in the chiller by the tub and you don't have to leave until the water gets cold."

"What if something happens to one of the patients?"

"I've got the pager and my cell. I'm on call. You rest."

"But how—*when*…?"

Dex chuckled. "I had a little help. From Ray and Gale for letting me borrow this, of course. And Opie for setting it up while we were on the ride."

Opie, the property manager, did have a soft spot for Millie and Dex.

Millie's hand rested on her chest. "Why?" she whispered.

"Because you deserve it. Do I need another reason?"

She shook her head and Dex wrapped his arms around her, drawing her into him. She breathed him in, marveling at how he didn't smell like he'd been riding horseback all day, but like sweat and pine instead. It was earthy, magnetic and wholly seductive. So was his uncharacteristic romantic gesture—he'd told her he wasn't capable of it, but this scene begged to differ.

Okay, she admitted. *Maybe his penchant for nice things isn't always a bad thing.*

"I'm not sure I want to get in…" she said, turning to face him.

"Oh…uh… That's fine. You don't have to. I just thought with as hard as you've been working, you haven't had time to—"

"Without you. Join me?"

The tub was more than big enough to wrap them both in its warmth.

A smile spread across Dex's face. Good grief, he was handsome. And for the time being, that smile was turned on her. What more could she want?

She ignored the injured voice putting up an argument for a love that went beyond the physical. There was too much risk in opening that door tonight, while her body was tired and her heart sore.

Right now was time for her to get something else she wanted.

Her husband.

Her brain didn't correct her with the "fake" part of that agreement, finally going along with whatever fantasy Millie needed tonight.

She held Dex's gaze as she undid each button on her flannel. She wasn't taking her time, but she wasn't in a rush, either. All she wanted was to enjoy this moment with Dex. She let her shirt fall to her feet, revealing a white lace halter bra. Choosing to keep that on for now, she undid her belt and jeans and slid them off.

Dex licked his lips when she sat on the edge of the tub in nothing but matching lace undergarments and pointed to him.

"Your turn," she said.

He followed her lead, unbuttoning his own flannel, revealing a glistening chest and torso that also just happened to look like a diagram of the perfect male specimen from medical school.

Dex added his shirt to the pile and went to unbutton his jeans, but Millie frowned and shook her head.

"No. That's my job." She crooked a finger to call him over.

He obliged and she pulled his pants down just far enough to spring his length free from his boxers. Both of them gasped at the same time.

She stroked him, marveling at the pleasure personified in front of her. Teasing the tip of him with her thumb, she tucked the moan he made in the back of her heart for later. Whatever came of their relationship, she made him happy *now*. Desire flashed through her, hot and instant.

Moving her hand to cup his base, she took the rest of him in her mouth, sucking and flicking the tip of him with her tongue. He tasted of brine and salt, and her heart welcomed the reminder of the sea on her tongue.

His hands fisted in her hair, pulling her closer to him as he groaned with rapture. She worked her mouth and hand over him until he stiffened and released inside her. When he'd calmed, she pulled his pants off each leg one at a time.

"I think we should clean up together," she said, her voice thick with lust for the naked man in front of her. She lifted her arms, wordlessly instructing him to remove the last two articles of clothing she wore. He made quick work of the lace, adding them to the denim and cotton detritus behind them.

"Goddamn, Millie, you're going to be the death of me." The smile on his face said he wouldn't mind leaving the world that way, though. She smiled and slid into the water, gesturing that he join her.

This man—in all his glory, with more than enough to satisfy her—may not actually be her husband, but he was hers for right now and she was going to make damn sure she enjoyed it while it lasted.

Dex felt Millie's breathing slow and deepen before a gentle buzz of a soft snore confirmed she'd fallen asleep in his arms. He inhaled her damp hair, which now smelled like flowers and vanilla thanks to Gale and Ray's assortment of lathers.

The tub water was still warm enough that he could justify not disturbing her yet.

His arms pulled her tighter to him, the feeling that he couldn't get close enough to her constricting his chest. The problem with Millie—her only flaw, and his fatal one—was that he could only ever get so close.

But now, with her safe in his arms, warm water blanketing them under quiet, understated light, he could rest easy. Except for the small tickle of an idea bothering his calm thoughts.

What if I ask her to stay? it wondered. *What if I asked her to actually be my wife?*

He pressed his lips to her hair and closed his eyes tight against the fear that answered the question for him. If she said yes, and ever got hurt, it would destroy him. Sure, that was the risk when you loved someone—a glaring reason he hadn't let anyone in until Millie—but when he knew her as he did, it was almost a certainty.

He sighed. The only thing worse than watching her get hurt would be seeing her attempt to mold herself into a life that didn't fit her shape. Watching her shrink and change just so he could selfishly cling tight to his own desires would ruin them both. His heart seized.

There has to be a way you can love each other where both of you get what you want out of life, it pressed.

It was all he wanted—he was pretty damn sure of that now. But if there was a way, he hadn't found it yet. Not only wasn't time on his side, but if he tried and failed? He'd lose the only thing that had ever mattered to him.

Millie wasn't just his best friend, nor simply his lover. She represented what he wanted—a partner he could trust and love, and not bear to lose.

That's impossible, his brain argued. *Loss is a part of life.*

But the response was purely academic. Dex knew that; he just didn't care.

She shifted, slipping into the nook between his chest and

shoulder. He moved a string of damp hair off her forehead and gazed down at her smooth skin. This woman had never worn makeup, never hid behind anything other than who she was. Her authenticity made his attempts at it possible. The lie, the one that claimed they were married, was the steepest untruth she'd ever lived and it was only possible because of the degree of truth behind it. They loved and cared about each other and had for a decade and a half.

How was he supposed to ask her to live a bigger lie—one where he pretended she was happy staying in one danger-free place, and she pretended she didn't want to sprint from a life of sameness, routine and safety?

That kind of loss—watching her die slowly from boredom—would be worse than seeing her get hurt.

A shrill whine accompanied a steady buzz of something hard and plastic on wood, invading the tranquility and pensiveness of the moment. Every muscle in Dex's body tensed and flexed.

"Dammit," he muttered as the shift woke her.

"Wow. I must've dozed off," she said, stretching against him. "What is that?"

"The pager and cell are going off at the same time. Sorry it woke you. I was supposed to be back at the cabin if they went off."

She twisted so their faces were only an inch apart. Her lips pressed against his and his groin ached to love her again.

"I'm glad you stayed. This is exactly what I needed." She kissed him once more, this time teasing his mouth open so he could explore her. Maybe they could ignore the persistent beep and howl of the outside world encroaching on their moment. Only a few seconds later, though, she pulled away. "Let me get dressed and meet you outside."

"Just stay here. I'll be back as soon as I'm done."

"I'd like to help."

"Let me see what's going on first. I'd prefer you rest and let me handle whatever's up."

She smiled and sat up so Dex could stand and exit the tub.

"It's too lonely in here without you."

Dex checked the pager. It was a panic attack in Reese's room. He could treat her alone so Millie could stay warm and relaxed. When he answered the call, though, that idea flew out the window.

"This is Dex."

"Hey, this is Opie. Sorry to bug you, but we've got a situation."

"What's going on?" Dex asked, skipping pleasantries. Opie never called unless he had to. Millie stood up and leaned in, listening. Dex traced her dripping, naked silhouette with his eyes, his hands itching to join.

"Kelly Price sliced her leg on the edge of the bunkhouse coffee table and her roommate saw the blood. She's not doing so hot, Doc."

"Kelly or Reese?"

"Kelly's fine, but the gash is pretty deep—probably needs to be sewn up. I already fixed the chipped part of the table so it won't happen again."

"Good thinking, Opie. And Reese?" he asked. He was already using his free hand to towel off and his heart sank when Millie followed suit. When she held up her lace underwear, he nodded. He'd need her help, like it or not.

"She's curled up in a ball, shivering even though the heat's turned up in that bunkhouse hot enough to bake cookies on the windowsill. I ain't never seen anything like it, even here."

"It's an acute panic attack," Dex said, shimmying on his jeans. "She'll be okay, but we need to get there fast. Do me a favor, Opie."

"You bet."

"Move all the residents to the male cabin for now and help

them set up the cots we have out for family weekend. I'd like to not move Reese if I don't have to."

They hung up, each with tasks to check off. Dex's were simple. Get dressed, kiss Millie and apologize for ruining the calm he'd promised, then sprint to the female bunkhouse. He packed a clonazepam in case Reese was still in active panic but hoped he wouldn't have to use it. Millie had told him Reese was trying to manage her symptoms medication-free since her biological father was an addict.

"I'll grab my suture kit and meet you there," Millie said, already dressed with her hair tied back in a braid. She kissed him before he got the chance. "And before you even think about apologizing, don't. This is the kind of stuff I took the job for. I'm happy to help."

He only nodded, a thread of his feelings for her from earlier tugging at his heart. The woman always seemed to surprise him, but that shouldn't have been much of a shock anymore. She was amazing. End of story.

He'd just have to wait until all their crises were behind them to decide what he'd do about that.

When they were both dressed and the cabin was locked back up, they jogged over to the women's bunkhouse behind the small apartment they shared. Dex knocked just in case, and Opie opened the door.

"Glad you're here, Doc. It's gettin' worse."

"Thanks, Opie. We've got it from here, but you did good tonight."

The man blushed a warm pink that made him look younger than his mid-seventies.

"I've got Reese if you can suture Kelly's leg," Dex told Millie quietly.

"Sure, but then I'd like to join you with Reese. I've seen a lot of the same things she has and we've built a strong relationship."

"Sounds good."

Dex slowed his pace so he didn't frighten Reese or trigger her panic attack. He put his hands in his pockets, tracing the edge of the pill packet as he approached Reese.

His heart lurched at the sight of her crumpled body, pressed as tight against the corner of the cabin as she could be. Her personality was one of the more infectious of the patients at Hearts and Horses; she could always be counted on to crack a joke just when it was needed. The way she hummed when she walked places had earned the nickname Happy Feet for her.

But like this? Compact and shivering on the cold wood floor? It was soul-crushing.

Take a deep breath and be there for her.

Confidence filled the space in his chest carved out by seeing his patient in pain. He'd done good work and made time to heal himself in the process. Even the hints of darkness each time Millie had gotten hurt had stayed put.

Sure. It has nothing to do with that same woman screwing you into fake wedded bliss.

Ignoring the less than helpful snark his subconscious drummed up, Dex kneeled next to Reese. He brushed the skin on the inside of her wrist and though her eyes darted toward him, they went back to the invisible spot she focused on in the distance almost immediately. Since she didn't flinch, he rested two fingers on her pulse and took note of the elevated heart rate.

"Reese, it's me, Dr. Shaw. Can you look at me?"

She did, briefly, then her bottom lip quivered, her eyes watered and she looked away again.

"Your pulse is a little too high for my comfort. I'd like to give you a small dose of clonazepam to settle your blood pressure and make it a little easier to come down from this. What do you say?"

It was his ace in the hole, telling her his plan. Hopefully it would rouse her enough for him to talk her off the knife's edge of panic she rested on.

"No," she said. Her voice was rough but quiet. "I—I don't want medication."

"Okay. That's fair." He breathed out a sigh of relief. He didn't want to have to medicate her, especially when it was against her own vision of her long-term treatment. But if she'd remained unresponsive, he wouldn't have had a choice. "Do you mind telling me what happened?"

Reese's eyes focused, leaving only a faint hint at the trauma brewing beneath her exterior. This was a hardened police officer meeting his gaze, a woman used to walking up to her breaking point, staring it in the face and standing tall against the pressure to cave in.

"I lost it. It's not like it's even a bad gash," she said. But the subtle shiver that rolled through her told Dex she didn't fully believe that. "And it's not like I haven't seen worse. I was in downtown LA, for eff's sake."

Dex chuckled and the corner of Reese's lips twitched up. She was going to be okay. This was a scare, but one she'd recover from.

"Yeah, but you know darn well healing isn't linear."

"Your wife said the same thing," Reese said. "I wish I was strong like her, that blood didn't bother me."

"She's a smart, strong woman to be sure. You are, too, though."

"I—I don't feel like it right now. I couldn't get myself to stop imagining Urie—my partner—on the ground. He was shot saving me."

"I'm so sorry to hear that. But you did talk yourself down. You refused medication, and that's a huge step, Reese."

A blush of red splashed her cheeks. "It is?"

"Very much so. So what would you like to do? You're the expert of your own life, Reese. I'm just here to help."

Her shoulders rolled back, her jaw set with confidence.

"Can you help me get to bed? I'm cold and exhausted."

Dex helped her into her cot and glanced at the partition

where Millie worked on her patient while he made sure Reese was comfortable.

Your wife.

The words no longer sent a ripple of fear through him when he heard them. Instead, a warm flush of something else spread from his chest outward.

Pride.

He liked the sound of Millie as his wife. More than that, he liked the *feel* of it.

From their vantage point, he couldn't see Kelly, but Millie was in view, her gaze pinned to where Kelly's face must be. Her voice was calm—a healing cadence and tone he recognized as her "doctor's voice."

She's so good at this.

Her laughter at something Kelly said rippled through the air, hitting him square across the chest. He loved this woman, and always had.

Fine. But could you let her loose into the world to pursue the dangerous career choices she craves? Because if not, you're setting yourself up for disappointment. Her, too.

He knew that. And he could. Because it wasn't so bad, the worrying-about-her thing. As it turned out, there was something worse than that—imagining her doing all that and never knowing how it went, or what amazing feats she accomplished.

Well, hell.

Was he really thinking about committing to someone and risking the chance that, one way or another, he might lose her?

I am.

The only remaining question was when to tell her how he felt. Because if he told her and they really did this, he couldn't walk away.

Dex was inclined to be careful, but for the first time in his life, being cautious was the last thing he wanted. It was time to be bold and brave like the woman he loved.

CHAPTER ELEVEN

ON THE FRIDAY of Family Weekend, the ranch was abuzz. The twenty-two patients were outside, cleaning the grounds in lieu of a late morning group session, and all the talk Millie passed expressed excitement over who was coming to visit and what the patient couldn't wait to share about their camp experience.

"I think my son's favorite will be Lightning, same as mine," Charlie said.

"Yeah, no way my wife is going near the stables, but she'll like the wine tasting we have on the last night."

Millie smiled. That was a nice little perk Millie had proposed to Gale.

When she walked behind Reese, Millie caught a snippet of her conversation, too.

"My mom loves horses, but I really can't wait to introduce her to Dr. Tyler-Shaw. That woman is one of the only reasons I'm ready to see my folks again."

"Same here," Peters, a former airman, said.

Millie beamed. She was doing good work. Work that mattered.

Doctors Without Borders does good work, too.

Without another full-time option to follow this contract, it was the only one in front of her.

We could always ask to stay here.

Yeah, if you tell Ray and Gale the truth about who you are.

That was more difficult than imagining sticking around and working here with Dex indefinitely. The lie had spun out of control... The thing was, it was closer to the truth now, though; she and Dex were together, and lately, she couldn't recall the impetus of her drive to travel, to ship herself off to foreign countries, some of which didn't approve of a female physician.

She hoped it was because her dreams had shifted, not because of Dex. She *couldn't* be the kind of woman who sacrificed her dreams for a guy.

Not even a man she'd cared for her entire adult life.

Not even a man who knew just how to use his lips to make her toes curl with desire.

Except...

When that man walked by her, deep in conversation with Gale, he winked at her and her body flat out didn't get the memo. As always happened when he flirted with her, her knees went weak and her heart thumped against her chest, wildly trying to get her attention.

Let him do that thing with his tongue and you'll forget all about DWB.

She frowned until he circled back around and kissed her cheek. She flushed, heat spreading out and down from the spot his lips touched.

I get it, she told her heart. *We work when it comes to* that. *But what about the rest?*

"How's your day going, beautiful?"

The flush deepened and she fanned her cheeks. At least he couldn't read the not-so-innocent thoughts racing through her head.

"Good." She busied herself picking weeds around the entrance sign so she wouldn't be tempted to shuck this whole cleanup and take Dex behind the barn for a literal roll in the hay. "I'm excited to meet the families and for them to see the progress their loved ones are making."

"It'll be a good weekend for sure. I'm a little worried about new riders on the horses, if I'm being honest, though."

"I hear you, but it's pretty cute that you're calling other

people new riders now," she teased, dumping her handful of weeds in the compost. He chuckled and his eyes danced with a spirit she hadn't seen in them in all the years she'd known him.

"Well, I'm three and a half months into my new professional riding career, so I can hardly call myself a novice anymore. I mean, I'm surprised they're not calling me up to stunt ride for *Yellowstone.*"

Millie laughed, sobering only when his arms wrapped around her waist. She still wasn't used to the whole PDA thing with a man she'd loved from afar for so long. Somewhere along the line, they'd taken their fake-marriage-but-real-dating thing out of their cabin, and no one seemed the wiser. What did it say that their now real romance was believable enough to think the two were newlyweds?

Would it be so different outside the ranch?

It will if I try something outside his comfort zone and he flips out. What will I do then? I won't shrink for any man, not even Dex.

"Your time's coming, I'm sure. Anyway, Ray is a rockstar and won't let anything happen to any of the guests."

"You're right, as usual," Dex said, planting a soft kiss on her lips.

"I could get used to that," Millie said, meeting his gaze.

"Well, then come here and let me do it again," he said, pulling her in.

She backed away and smiled. "I meant you telling me I'm right."

Dex laughed, his head tossed back. With his hair grown out long and his beard filled in, he was starting to look the part of a cowboy. His shirt was wrinkled along the sleeves and he didn't seem to care. He'd tucked away his clothing iron under the bed and even stopped using hair gel a couple weeks ago. Someone else might think he'd all but given up, but Millie saw it as a sign of growth. He was letting go of his need to control every situation.

She was growing, too. Letting Dex into her bed was one thing, but she'd opened up and told him more about her stepmother, too.

Only a small worry nagged at her when she remembered what their arrangement was. He still hadn't asked her to stay, or looked for jobs with her. If she asked Ray and Gale to stay, it would be just for herself unless she and Dex had a talk and ironed things out.

Nerves tickled her skin.

If they talked, and it didn't go the way she hoped, she'd lose Dex as both her fake husband and her best friend. Things were fine as they were—why mess with them?

"Oh, honey, we've got a lifetime of you being right and me just hanging on for the ride."

He grabbed her hand and any unease about their future slipped away through their palms like sand. His words washed over her like a balm.

We've got a lifetime...

Were they just words spoken for the benefit of the staff and patients walking around them? Or was Dex hinting at something more? The back and forth of wondering what to do with her growing feelings was bugging her.

"Hey, you two lovebirds. When you get a sec, I'd love to steal Millie for a debrief."

Millie pulled out of Dex's hand, the space Dex had just occupied empty and cold.

"But of course, Ray. I'm just saying goodbye to this guy since he's on second shift."

She and Dex were trading off the first day so there was someone always on call in case the patients needed it when their families arrived.

"Bye, babe," she said, reaching up on her toes to kiss him perfunctorily.

He nuzzled her neck, then whispered, "Bye, love," before winking and walking away.

Love? He'd never called her that before. *Tyler*, yes. *Millie*, more often of late. But *love*?

Dizziness swirled around her. So many clues were stacking against her heart, but if she was misreading the signs, if Dex was just playing the game, they'd topple and her heart might break. Why couldn't things have just stayed as they were—best friends sleeping together and faking a marriage?

A real relationship was much trickier and even though she enjoyed the perks, she wasn't sure she appreciated the discomfort.

"You two are almost too adorable for words," Ray said as they walked toward the main barn.

Millie forced a smile as she shoved her overactive thoughts to the back of her mind.

"Coming from you, that's a compliment."

"We're happy, Mil."

She gazed over at her friend and colleague and grinned at Ray's sudden change in tone.

"I can tell. But you're worried?" she guessed.

He nodded. "What if this isn't what he wants in the end? I mean, I come with a lot of baggage," he said, gesturing to his leg and arm.

"No," Millie disagreed. "You don't. Not physically, anyway—your injuries are part of your story, but they aren't baggage. Now, your penchant for reality TV?" she teased. "That's some hefty emotional baggage, but," she said, growing serious again, "it's up to our partners to decide what they're willing to carry. And Gale made his choice."

Millie let that settle on her shoulders as they entered the barn. Ray had just given a name to the slinking, pervasive fear lingering just below each kiss, each embrace from Dex. When would it get to be too much for him? When would she do something that triggered his past memories of being abandoned?

"All we can control is what we do and how we show up. You know darn well we can't pin our hopes on what-ifs so we shouldn't let them hold up our fears, either," she said, as much to herself as to Ray.

"And that's why you're my favorite therapist-slash-friend."

"Don't you forget it," she joked back. They joined the rest of the first crew on deck for the arrival of the families in a couple hours.

"Okay, now that we're all here, let's talk about a game plan for emergencies as well as who will be where for the arrival." Gale had a clipboard out, a pen in his other hand and a whistle around his neck. He looked like a cross between a camp counselor and a serious cowboy.

"Look at my man, all serious and organized. God, he's never been hotter," Ray whispered. He winked and Millie snorted back a laugh.

Gale's brows rose a good two inches.

"You're gonna get me in so much trouble," she hissed.

"Not as much trouble as my fiancé is gonna be in. I have big plans for that whistle later. The clipboard, too."

Millie barely masked the laugh that rose in her chest as a cough. When the fit of giggles subsided, what replaced it almost knocked Millie on her backside. It was guilt, hot and acidic. But...*why*?

A glance at Ray confirmed her worries.

You feel guilty about lying to them.

Sure, she always had, but it was worse now that they considered each other friends and not just colleagues. All she wanted was to dump her woes at Ray's feet the same way he'd trusted her, but if she did, he'd know the truth—that the thin veil of authenticity about her and Dex was a result of their employment as physicians at Hearts and Horses, not the precursor.

And then what? Would Ray and Gale—and the patients— ever forgive them?

Just get through the next few months. Then you'll be off on another adventure and Dex will be...wherever he is. It's the bright side of this short contract.

But that didn't sit well, either.

Because she didn't want a short contract; she wanted to stick around at a place closer to home that needed dedicated trauma doctors and psychologists like her and Dex. A place like Hearts and Horses.

"Hey, Ray," she whispered while Gale walked around to give everyone their assignments, "can I talk to you later?"

"Sure." He turned to face her. "Is everything okay?"

She nodded, regretting speaking up at all. It wasn't fair to spill her guts to him without running it by Dex first, since it was his job and friendships on the line, too.

She made her lips twist into a smile. "Yeah. Perfect. Hey, I'm gonna run and check on Reese before we gear up. You good here?"

He nodded and Millie left the barn, the half lie about where she was headed adding to the pile of mistruths at her feet. She wanted to come clean, to tell Ray and Gale and beg for forgiveness if need be, but first she had to clear a few things up.

First on the list was arguably the hardest. She had to ask Dex what all his dropped clues meant, the risks of it going awry be damned. Regardless of his answer, she needed to tell him how she felt about him, the *L* word thick on her heart and tongue. If he didn't want more from her, the lies piling up around them were the least of her concerns.

Picking up the shattered pieces of her heart would most certainly top the list then.

But that could only happen after she met with her patient, meaning she had to push back the talk she'd asked Dex for, too.

Great, she thought as she wound through the camp to where Dex was helping with the last of the cleanup. *So much for looking forward to a relaxing weekend.*

Dex whistled along the dirt road leading up to the entrance of Hearts and Horses. Just a few short months ago, he and Millie had arrived through those gates with a fabricated story and hidden traumas.

God, had it really only been a few months? It felt more like a lifetime with all that had changed. Not just his feelings for Millie, though having those out in the open and reciprocated—most of them, anyway—was enough to make a man believe in the kind of healing he practiced on others.

No. *He* was different, down to his core. Calm, the kind he'd worked to get his patients to experience, rolled through him. His panic attacks were almost a thing of the past. And darn if he wasn't getting accustomed to loving Millie's little quirks, including the edge she rode between danger and fun. That was *her*, and loving her meant loving *all* of her, or at least he thought so.

Only a shred of doubt remained regarding their future, but that was normal, right?

Okay, so maybe their future—where they'd live, where they'd work, did they want a formal marriage, and perhaps kids?—was bigger than it seemed, but they'd made such amazing progress so far. What lay ahead had to be easier than the path it'd taken them to get here, right?

All that was left was to tell the woman. And he had a plan for that, one that would give him a chance to show off his romantic streak of late. It was also, hopefully, foolproof so it minimized the risks of her turning him down and taking with her the best thing that had ever happened to him.

"Speaking of the she-devil," he called out when she strode around the corner. Her curls blew behind her in the breeze and she tilted her head, smiling the bright toothy smile that had first wormed its way into his heart fifteen years ago.

"Not sure I love that nickname, but I'm glad to know you were talking about me." She glanced around and her smile fell. "But…to whom?"

He laughed. "Myself. I had some minor convincing to do before you and I connected tonight."

"Uh-oh. Do I like the sound of that?"

"I hope you do." The lunch bell chimed at the barn and Dex cursed it under his breath. Doubts or not, he was going to tell Millie he loved her. The magnitude of that one little statement, the three shortest words he'd ever said, both weighed on him and lifted him up. Hell, they'd been bubbling around in his chest for fifteen years, even if they sounded different to him back then. "But…duty calls right now."

"Actually, I was hoping we could move our talk?"

"Now *I'm* worried. What's up?"

She smiled, which curbed the bottoming out of his stomach. With her hands shoved deep in her pockets, she tilted up on her toes and planted a kiss on his cheek. She smelled sweet and salty at the same time. Like the Pacific Ocean breeze had kissed a caramel candy before settling on the nape of her neck.

They held hands on the short walk to lunch. Could she feel the heat building between their skin every time they touched? She had to—it was too intense to ignore. He didn't take for granted how new this ability was, to love her so openly in front of everyone they knew.

"I promised I'd take Reese's family to the local beach that Gale showed us that first week so they can see the stars out here, and you've got that night shift. Can I get a rain check for after the ride tomorrow? I think we both have an hour off before lunch."

"Sure. Yeah, sounds great." The idea of waiting any longer to put his plan into action was excruciating, but what choice did he have? He kissed the edge of her lips and Millie's cheeks turned the shade of pink that made her look caught in a windstorm. With her wild curls and moisture-lined eyes that belied a storm beneath her calm exterior, she painted a pretty picture of what getting lost in her tempest would be like.

"Thanks. See you, cowboy," she said. She jogged ahead to a waving Reese without looking back and the doubt pulsed in his chest. It was a huge risk, telling her he loved her. More than not having a home to go back to at night. If he gave her his heart, it could be left out in the cold or hanging over a cliff and he couldn't very well ask for it back, could he?

Cheese and rice.

This is why he'd never let his feelings see the light of day until now. They didn't know how to behave.

After lunch, he headed to finish cleaning up the common areas. The barn was next, a chore he definitely didn't mind anymore. Horses were, as it turned out, kinda cool. And it didn't hurt that the rides with patients helped his job immensely.

Sure, that was the point of equine therapy, but in LA, even in a progressive hospital like Mercy, there wasn't a lot of stock given to alternative treatments for mental health. Physical, sure—every juice bar, Pilates or yoga studio, and gym cluttering up downtown said as much. But for mental health? It was exercise, meditate and make weekly pilgrimages to a therapist, or medicate.

Horses—all animals, actually—were a new treatment protocol for Dex and it suited him. The danger of putting a patient challenged with PTSD on the back of a half-ton animal even seemed normal by now.

If only that—the horses, the excitement on the patients' faces as they took their family on a tour of the facilities they'd called home the past few months, even the knowledge that he was doing damn good work that was making a difference in people's lives—could hold his focus.

All he could think about was Millie as he mucked stalls, shined equipment and introduced himself to the loved ones of his patients. Every second he couldn't tell her how he felt was another moment the shred of doubt grew. Especially as he watched her jump on the back of a moving four-wheeler, then come back riding the new horse bareback as she prepped for the big ride coming up.

The doubt swirled with fear.

He'd thought he nipped both, but there they were, ugly and pervasive.

"A penny for your thoughts?" Gale asked, and Dex tried on a relaxed smile. Like the rest of his mannerisms that afternoon, though, it fell flat. He closed out of the check-in email with the family members' names he was still attempting to commit to memory. "Oh, I see. A dollar, then? Looks like you've got the weight of the world on your shoulders this morning."

"Just the North American continent," Dex joked.

"Wanna talk about it?"

Dex froze. He did. And Gale had become a close enough confidant that he was just the sort of person he'd like to unpack his feelings with. No, that wasn't true. Gale wasn't just a confidant... He was a *friend*.

And Dex couldn't tell his friend what sat heavy on his heart because he'd been straight up lying to the guy since the start. He couldn't really just come out and say, "Well, actually, I'm in love with the woman posing as my wife and I'd like to ask her to be in a real committed relationship, but I'm afraid of what that'll do to my insecurities about being abandoned. I'm also afraid of loving a woman so bent on living on the edge when that kind of life makes me feel unsafe. More than any of that, I kinda want to stay. Here. So, what do you think I should do?"

"I'm just wondering what to do next. I think Millie would like to head off on some adventure in a place where she can help patients who don't have access to good care..." Dex drifted off, the truth of his admission buoying the weight of his guilt ever so slightly.

"And you don't want that kind of danger, that kind of risk?" Gale asked. He handed Dex a diet soda.

"Thanks," Dex said. Gale had nailed his feelings, even working with a limited scope of knowledge. "And yeah, that pretty much sums it up. How'd you know?"

Gale laughed heartily. "Because you're the mirror image of Ray and me."

"Really?" It shouldn't make him feel better to know he wasn't alone in his feelings, but it did.

"Yep. Every month or so, Ray gets a wild hair up his ass and wants to upend the life we've built here. I don't blame him. It's who he is. But it doesn't sit well with me. I'm a creature of comfort."

"Yeah." Dex gave Gale a half smile. "Me, too."

"And there isn't anything wrong with that."

"No, there isn't." Dex thought of his time living under the bridge. As if he had another choice other than seeking creature comforts after that.

"But there's also nothing wrong with the loves of our lives—bless their hearts—being a bit on the wilder side."

Dex's smile turned sour.

"I agree, but it isn't the easiest to live with."

"That's no joke." Gale looked off toward the entrance, where Ray was laughing with a patient's mother, his head tilted back. "But maybe there's another perspective."

"What's that?" At this point, Dex would take anything. Because he loved Millie. Loved her as much as he'd ever loved anything, really. But he still wasn't sure how to live with her, at least not in the long term.

"Millie and Ray are special. They see the world on their terms, not through the lens the world made for them. And that kind of special—the kind that shows up with a bouquet of wildflowers, a horse and a prepacked picnic at the bluffs? It grows you into the person you're meant to be." He inhaled, closed his eyes, and smiled. "And damn if that isn't the most frustrating part of it all."

"What's that?" Dex asked. He was following Gale up to that point.

"That they were right all along. Life's better with a little risk."

Dex sighed like he'd been waiting for that line to let him

release what'd been stuck in his chest for months. Years, actually. He opened his mouth to offer a rebuttal—risk was inherently unsafe, though. And with his childhood, he needed safety, caution, security. But not more than he needed Millie; that much he'd decided. Even if he didn't know fully how to rectify the two.

There was a truth in Gale's words that hammered against his chest. Going to medical school, his residency at Stanford, then working at a premier hospital like Mercy—none of it had let him settle into his life, relax. If anything, it led to a different kind of anxiety. The kind that pressed against his back, shoving him forward, forward, forward at all costs.

Until Millie.

She'd not only awoken him to the possibilities he'd previously considered off the table, but Gale was right; they came with a serenity that he'd never felt, not one day in his life until now.

He…he wanted to be here, in Cambria. With Millie.

"Thanks, Gale."

Something else hung on Dex's neck, heavy and hot. *I have something to tell you*, it pulsed. But Dex couldn't get the words out.

"Don't mention it. I'm gonna go check in with our paramours, but you take your time."

He nodded, even though he didn't agree. He'd *been* taking his time. The wasted hours, days, months and years were at his back now, insistent that he not squander another damned minute.

But there was something else there, too. *Guilt*. For lying to Gale and Ray, and for what that meant—not just for him, but for Millie, too. She was the most honest person he knew so this must be eating her alive.

Sure, in the beginning, it'd seemed necessary, but now that they'd befriended their bosses? It stunk of duplicitousness. His skin itched and his chest burned when he couldn't take in deep enough breaths. The edges of anxiety slunk in amongst the fear and doubt.

One, two, three, he tried.

He breathed through it, but the fact that he hadn't gotten over near-attacks like that bothered him.

How was he supposed to be there for Millie if he couldn't handle his own messes?

But Millie wouldn't rely on him. Hell, that's why he loved her—she could handle her own stuff and they'd just be good partners. Still, no matter how they felt about each other—and he hoped they felt the same—they couldn't move forward like this. They had to tell Ray and Gale the truth and risk the consequences.

If they didn't come clean, the future he saw ahead of them wasn't ever going to happen. But if they were honest, it might not, either.

Damn, he thought. That was the problem with caring for someone—if it went wrong, it sure hung you out to dry, didn't it?

CHAPTER TWELVE

THE FAMILIES' EXCITEMENT down at the stables was palpable. Delight over the horses was matched only by George's preteen boys' joy over finding a pair of barn kittens. The boys pet the kittens, their voices a full octave higher than when they'd strode into the barn attempting to look tough enough to rival Ray and Gale's stoic cowboy stares.

Millie smiled. There was hope for the future generation, no matter what the pundits said. In her previous line of work, she'd almost lost sight of that, but here, optimism shone from some pretty dark places.

"I wonder if Dad will let us get some cats when he comes home," the taller of the two, Ben, said. He was the one challenged with autism, Millie knew, but out here, among the horses and miles of fresh air, even she had a hard time picking up on the stimming. Only his excessive blinking gave him away. Another win for equine therapy.

"No way. You know how he feels about animals in the house."

Millie pretended to watch a young girl pet Tillamook as George Dominic strode over to his sons.

"I heard you talking about those kittens. They're a lot of work, you know."

Ben nodded, a hesitant smile on his face. Millie stifled a laugh when his brother, Lance, rolled his eyes.

"Told you so," Lance muttered.

"But if you're willing to take it on, I reckon you're ready for the responsibility."

Millie couldn't keep the smile from her face. George had come a long way to accept that level of change, risk and uncertainty into his life. Pets didn't always follow the rules of a human who craved control, like George had been when he'd arrived at Hearts and Horses. Cats especially.

Who needed to travel to exotic locales to work when she could help people who needed it here—first responders like George, who did their jobs bravely, only to lose part of themselves in the process? Her help had a direct effect on more than just the patients. It saved families.

Millie glanced at Dex, who was showing Charlie's teen son how to saddle his horse. Would he ever accept the quandary that came with loving Millie, a woman filled to the brim with risk and uncertainty? Only time would tell. And time wasn't necessarily on their side. Not just because their contract was more than half over, but because of a single sheet of paper Ray had given her that morning sitting heavy in her back pocket—and on her heart.

She'd read it with interest, but how could she respond when she wasn't an "I" anymore? Being part of a "we" meant talking to Dex was necessary, especially since the paper had his name on it as well.

Needless to say, their long overdue conversation after the ride was even more necessary.

Millie focused on readying Tillamook while Gale issued instructions for what was coming up that morning. The ride would have the families paired with a staff member from the stables, Millie and Dex acting as roaming medical sentries, keeping an eye on the health of their patients. Gale didn't say as much out loud, but at the slightest nod from Millie or Dex, he would find an excuse—the weather, lame horse or something similar—and shut the event down.

The horses were part of the medical practice at Hearts and

Horses, but they could be a liability when new variables were introduced. A tickle of nerves flitted through Millie's chest, but she tampered it. They were professionals.

"Hey there, beautiful," a velvety deep voice said from behind her. The worry turned to lust, hot and quick against her skin. She'd never get sick of hearing Dex's voice directed at her. Especially when he called her *beautiful*.

"Hi," she said. "How's your morning been?"

"Great, since I woke up in the middle of the night to a gorgeous woman curled up against my chest. Did you have fun last night?"

"I did. Reese cracks me up. We had a good talk, checked her levels of cortisone, then watched some reality TV."

Dex pretended to gag. "Better you than me."

"There's nothing I could do to convince you to watch baking shows with me?" she asked, trailing a finger along his chest, until it hooked his chin and brought his mouth to hers for a fiery kiss.

When she pulled away, he looked stunned. And happy.

"Okay, fine. Maybe a season or two if you keep that up."

Millie laughed, but it came out half-full.

His brows fell into a deep vee. "Is everything okay?"

Millie nodded, taking his hand in hers. "It is," she assured him. "With us, anyway."

"Okay," Dex conceded, though his eyes were still hard under furrowed brows. "We're still talking after the ride?"

"Yep."

"Then I'm looking forward to it."

His words didn't match his demeanor, though. He kissed her cheek, then walked toward the barn entrance, but not before glancing back at her twice. She sighed. If they weren't surrounded by people they cared for and needed to care for, she'd come right out and tell him. She didn't want to lie to Gale and Ray anymore.

And—this was the big one—she wasn't sure she wanted to travel for work anymore.

Not because of Dex, or at least not just because of him. The offer Ray made her that morning—an official contract folded in her jeans—fluttered in her rib cage like a bird in flight.

Stay on, he'd urged her. *Stay on and run a trauma program. If you do, and you can convince your husband to work on building a clinical therapy program, we can expand two-fold, at least.*

The salary he'd offered on behalf of Hearts and Horses was absolutely competitive, but that wasn't the real reason she was considering it. Damn if she didn't feel like she had a family for the first time in a long time. What she'd found—trust, companionship, honesty…*love*? It was more than she deserved but was quickly becoming impossible to live without.

Maybe—this was the part Ray had offered that meant more than the offer—she'd always run from job to job, looking for what she lacked from her family. That information sat square on her chest until her heart had cried uncle.

Ray was right.

If she wanted the love and support Ray and Gale gave her, she had to earn that in return.

But then…what would Dex think of that development? Would he be okay with coming clean, even if it meant they lost the deal on the table?

Her biggest fear, though, was that he'd feel an immense pressure on himself if she stayed in the US, whether or not she was doing it for him. This relationship worked because of who they were to each other. If she asked more of him than he was ready to give…

She gulped back a wave of nausea.

"You ready, Dr. Tyler-Shaw?" Gale called back from the front of the stables. The riders were all on horses and she was taking the first stint at the back of the pack.

"Sure am," she shouted, mustering a smile wide enough to let in a horse fly.

"All right, riders. Stay between Dr. Tyler-Shaw and myself and let's go have some fun."

As the riders left the barn one by one, Millie watched Dex at the middle of the pack. He was strong on top of his horse, confident and able in a way he hadn't been when he'd arrived. It looked good on him.

But good enough that he'd want a life of practicing this kind of medicine every day? With no cities, no nice restaurants, no clothes tailor-made to fit his impressive frame? To him, it was a life of adventure and wholly outside the comfort zone he resided safely within.

He did this for me, for the favor I called in.

And Dex made the most of everything, no matter what. Maybe this worked because it was temporary.

The air—cool with a hint of fall on its breath—was an intoxicating blend of woodfire and briny sea breeze. The scent tickled Millie's nostrils and reminded her to stay present in the moment. The future wasn't guaranteed one way or another, but this ride, this time in nature with patients she'd come to care about as much as for was.

"Good job, Tilly," she praised her horse as the gentle giant carried them up a steep embankment. It was the toughest part of the trail, especially for new riders, but everyone did great.

Okay. They'd made it through the hard stuff. Time to relax. The patients and their families laughed and talked and pet their horses, seeming to enjoy this part of their weekend.

Good. Horses were integral to their therapy now, but this weekend signified a shift of responsibility to the patients' families to take over some of that, while the rest of the onus fell to the patients themselves.

"This is pretty great, isn't it?" Dex asked, sliding up next to her. They were stopped at the top of the ridge for one of George's boys to use nature's facilities.

"It is. I'm glad it's going well. For everyone's sake."

"How about you? You looked like you had something on your mind back there."

"Not here," she whispered.

"Why not?"

Oh, Dex.

If there was one thing Dex liked to see coming, it was anything that might throw his world off its axis. They had a rare moment together while Gale explained the history of the property and how Hearts and Horses came to be.

She exhaled, then took a deep slow breath. "I want to come clean about our...relationship."

He smiled and relief washed through her. "I agree. I wanted to ask for the same thing this afternoon. I can't stand lying to our friends."

"Exactly." She breathed a sigh of relief as large as the ocean looming in front of them. "And you're okay if they fire us on the spot? Because..." She pulled the sheet of paper from her pocket. "They offered us a full-time place here."

"Whoa. Then I guess we have to tell them. We can't keep this up forever."

Forever.

Warmth washed over her. This was going better than she thought it would. Dex had an aversion to risk, and their jobs on the line would definitely qualify. Would that translate to the other thing she had to tell him?

"I think we need to talk about the offer, but I agree about the other part. We need to tell them," he said.

"Okay, then, so it's settled."

"If we weren't on thousand-pound beasts right now, I'd hug you."

Millie's heart slammed against her chest. "You're happy about the contract?"

"I am. Holy hell, I hate worrying about you when you go to places that want to kill you. Are you thinking you'll take it?"

"Um, yeah." *You.* Not *we.* Her heart missed a beat.

"Awesome. You'll be safe, and I'll be happy." George called back to Dex something about his son's horse. Dex needed to concentrate—they had patients who needed them. "Anyway, let's talk more after the ride, okay, Tyler?"

Millie nodded, but Dex didn't see it since he rode off in service of his patient. Any delight she'd felt when Dex seemed pleased about her consideration of the full-time job was lost in the response he'd given her.

I'll be safe, so he'll be happy.

And he'd called her Tyler again. Like they were back to being good buds and nothing more.

Nothing about how they could be together now, or how he'd love to work alongside her. Just…*safety.* Benign concern for her well-being that he'd had throughout their whole friendship.

Are you thinking you'll *take it?* Just her. Alone. Again.

Anxiety rippled through her, followed by a wave of grief. It really was too much to hope that he'd want to settle down in the way she wanted to. His past all but guaranteed he couldn't love someone else fully, and she couldn't fault him for that.

Could she? Not entirely, but she *could* blame herself for letting her heart get so invested. He'd been honest from the start—this was temporary. But…but it didn't feel that way to her.

He made love to her more evenings than he didn't, and every night she fell asleep with his arms clasped tight around her bare waist.

He kissed her, his hands tangled in her hair.

He'd whispered that he loved her when he thought she was asleep.

Heat built behind her eyes. Had she made this whole thing up in her head?

No. She'd done everything right, from being vulnerable to doing good work.

Had he only been playing a part for the sake of the watchful eyes around the camp, the nights a way to scratch an itch and fill the time?

No... He'd never lead her on like that, would he?

Except she'd conveniently forgotten the second half of his admission of love from the night they'd first slept together—that it wasn't enough.

A commotion up ahead brought her back from her spiraling thoughts.

"Millie, have you seen Ben?" Ray asked, suddenly appearing beside her. His voice was a hushed whisper, but even if the crowd didn't know what was going on, they seemed to sense something was amiss. They were muttering to themselves and tension sat like a cloud above their heads.

"George's oldest? No, why?"

"He and his horse are missing."

Millie's veins turned to ice.

"I'm sure he's just wandered off to feed on the wild grass."

"Opie already checked. Can you run a perimeter check and see if he's gone back to the stables? Prince Philip would know to go back," Ray said, mentioning the horse they'd picked for the boy.

"Of course."

Millie used the reins to steer Tillamook toward the way they'd come when a shrill cry from behind her tore through her heart. *Ben*. Where was he? They'd been watching him, hadn't they?

Yes, until she'd been distracted by Dex's dismissal of her.

"Help!" Ben shouted. The plea had come from the cliffside that overlooked the ravine they'd just climbed out of.

Oh, no.

If Ben's horse got too close, they could both lose their footing on the scree field that lined the edge of the path.

Without giving it another thought, Millie kicked her heels into Tilly's sides, whooping the horse to a gallop. Fear nipped at their heels as she raced toward the edge of the cliff, praying they weren't too late. Memories of the other patients she'd lost gnashed their teeth at her, urging her on. This life had to be different; otherwise what was the point of it all?

Dex's heart rate was damn near tachycardic. The pressure building on his chest prevented his lungs from drawing in a full breath, but he couldn't stop. Not when Millie was in danger.

Everything happened so fast, but at the same time like he'd been viewing the scene from afar in slow motion. First, he and Millie had agreed to tell Gale and Ray about their relationship. That was almost as good of news as the full-time contract. He hadn't wanted to dive into how he'd like nothing more than to take it and live with her for the rest of their lives, because he had the plan set up for after the ride; she'd see then just how he felt.

So he'd played it cool.

But then...

Gale had whispered something to Ray, who'd approached Millie at the back of the group of riders. He'd seen the worried twist of her mouth turn to an *O* of shock and fear he recognized. It was the same look she'd had on her face that night at Mac's bar.

Gale whispered what his concern was to Dex—the missing child and horse—just as Millie had turned back to the stables. Only a few feet into her turn, a distant cry came from the ravine they'd just meandered up. Millie broke her horse into a run, headed directly for the perilous edge of the cliffside overlooking the ranch.

That's all it had taken for Dex to whip his horse, Ouray, into action. He had to catch Millie before it was too late.

"Please," he urged Ouray and whatever deities were listening in. "I need her to be safe." Fear trembled through him like an earthquake.

A few months ago, Dex would've worried about his own

safety atop a horse, especially as he reined around the bushes and rocks blocking his direct path to Millie. But now he maneuvered like a professional rider—which he sort of was after all this time.

Not that he could enjoy the realization of how far he'd come. If he didn't get to Millie in time, he wouldn't be able to enjoy anything ever again.

Another cry tore through the erratic, quick beat of Dex's heart and the thump, thump of Ouray's hooves on the dry ground. As Dex rounded the corner, what he saw stopped his heart momentarily, but forced him to kick Ouray until the horse was racing at breakneck speed toward the rocky scree.

Millie was riding alongside Ben's horse, one arm linked around Ben's body as it dangled from the side of the saddle. Prince Philip wouldn't stop at the boy's urging, though he was going slow enough for Millie to unhook where the boy was tangled in the reins and move him over to her horse. She was still heading right for the loose rock that would send them all tumbling over the precipice until at the last minute, Ben safe in her arms, she veered into safety.

Dex caught them just as Millie slid to a stop on Tillamook and slipped off the saddle, Ben in her arms.

"He…he got spooked by somethin'," Ben sputtered through sobs. The boy protected his left arm against his chest as Dex breathed a sigh of relief. The boy and Millie were okay. His heart didn't get the message, though, rapidly slamming against his chest for several seconds until his breathing regulated. He kept the panic at bay, but barely.

He dismounted and fell to his knees next to Millie, who was inspecting Ben's arm and shoulder.

"It looks broken, and at the least, it's out of the socket."

Dex nodded.

"What's that mean?" Ben asked. "Will I need a cast?" Millie smiled softly as she felt around the boy's joint.

Dex resisted the primal urge to take her into his arms and never let her out of his sight again.

"Probably, but before that, I'm going to move your shoulder so it doesn't hurt anymore, okay? But it'll sting a little, Ben."

"That—that's okay. I'm brave and old enough to get a kitten. I can take it."

"I know you can." Millie counted to three and twisted Ben's arm into place. To his credit, the boy hissed in a sharp breath but didn't cry. "You did amazing, Ben. I need your flannel, Dex."

Dex handed it over, rubbing Millie's back in the process, but she didn't seem to notice his presence. She fashioned a sling for Ben out of the shirt.

The rest of the group materialized over the hill and George ran to his son's side.

"Oh, God. He's okay?" he asked Millie. His jaw trembled but he was keeping his cool. Dex was proud of the man's progress. A month ago, this would have undone everything he'd worked for.

"He's going to be fine. He's actually one of the bravest patients I've ever had. Takes after his dad, I'm guessing."

Father and son beamed under Millie's praise and Gale helped them back onto George's horse for the ride back to the stables. George held tight to his son, but his muscles had otherwise relaxed.

"I'll follow in a sec to check in on them, but his arm needs to be x-rayed."

"You bet. I'll call ahead for an ambulance. I'm so sorry, George," Gale said, the set of his jaw more pronounced than ever. It wasn't his fault, though. Just a freak accident when Prince Philip spooked.

"Nah. Could've happened to anyone."

"Yeah! And it happened to *me*! I might get a cast for my friends to sign, Dad. Did you hear that?" Ben's glee made Gale chuckle as the pair moved away.

"That was pretty reckless, taking off like that," Dex said to Millie when the group, animated and tittering about the rogue horse and rescue, left the two of them behind to get Ben situated. Millie had promised to be right behind them but, of course, was trying to wrangle the horse that was now grazing at the edge of the grassy field as if nothing was amiss. "Are you okay?"

"I'm fine," she said, looking away from him. "And it wasn't reckless, it was my job. But you've never understood that, have you?"

"I'm sorry, but what's that supposed to mean?" He was the one who was supposed to be mad. She'd put herself in unnecessary danger. Again. She always would, wouldn't she?

His plan to tell her how he loved her, wanted to start a life with her, got fuzzy around the edges as the black tendrils of his anxiety snaked in.

Her gaze shot back to him. "It means you've never liked my choice in career, the places I choose to work, or hell, *me* for that matter."

Dex felt like the air had been stomped from his chest.

"Whoa, Millie. That's not true—"

"You're telling me you're fine with my time in the army, that DWB didn't scare the crap out of you?"

"It did, but only because of how much I care about you. And you're not doing DWB anyway, so what's this about?"

"It's about you refusing to acknowledge that my decisions aren't supposed to make *you* feel good. They're for *me*. *My* career, *my* life."

The finger she punched against her own chest might as well have been a fist thumped against his, the way her statement knocked the wind out of him. He loved this woman and she was blowing him off like the past three and a half months— hell, the past fifteen years—hadn't mattered at all.

"Doesn't it matter that I care that you have a life to come home to?"

And that I wish that home was with me, that I'd told you how I felt sooner?

"That doesn't give you the right to question my choices."

He sat back on his heels. "You're right."

Millie's face twisted into a scowl. She probably wasn't expecting him to agree, but there wasn't an ounce of her proclamation that didn't ring true. No matter how he felt about her, this was her life, not his.

"I've only ever cared about your well-being, but I can't control that any more than I can control the weather."

"No. You can't."

"So will you tell Ray you're taking the job?" It was an honest attempt at reconciling with her but she glared at him.

"Here we are again. What am *I* doing?" She spat the sentiment out like poison.

Wait…*what*?

"How did I screw this up? Please explain that, Millie."

Resignation seemed to sink her shoulders. "I…" She paused and looked back toward the camp. "I'm staying here, yes. The offer is amazing and I think I can do a lot of good. But I understand why it's too much for you."

"Too much *what*?" he asked. *Intimacy? Commitment?* The damned thing of it was he wanted that with her. All of it, and to hell with what it meant.

"Dirt. Animals. Country living. You name it. We're not exactly swimming in metropolitan bliss here, Dex."

He smiled. He hadn't thought about all the trappings of the city in a while now. Not since waking up to Millie every morning became his new dream, the true thing that filled his heart. Fancy dining and shopping would never compare to the peace it brought him.

"Nah. But I can handle it." A gentle truce lifted the tension that had fallen since the accident and the ensuing argument between them.

Only when she wiped her hair from her forehead, did Dex

see the smear of blood on her cheek and neck that had been hidden before. He traced it down and saw a deep gash on her shoulder, another along her arm.

What he could and couldn't handle blew away on the breeze that had picked up.

"You're bleeding," he whispered. A chill raced across his skin as she shrugged him off.

"I'm fine." The gentle armistice between them shattered and her wall shot back up, locking him out. Her gaze darted to the gnarled bushes she'd raced through without thinking, and his chest clenched again, reminding him that, with Millie in his life, a panic attack was never fully off the table. Traveling around the world or not, she would always court danger, wouldn't she?

And he'd always have to reckon with what that meant for him. He knew what he wanted, but was he strong enough to keep it?

"Jesus, Mil. You could've been seriously hurt. Can you at least acknowledge that? For me?"

"For *you*?" she hissed. "I'm sorry, but I didn't think of *you* when Ben's horse took off. I thought of my job as a trauma physician and a patient in distress. And it's a good thing I did. That horse wasn't stopping and that cliffside wasn't getting any farther away."

Her breaths came in shallow gulps and her eyes watered. But that didn't stop her from shooting him a withering stare.

"Are you mad at me?" he asked. "Because I care?"

"It's not that you care, it's that you only seem concerned about whether or not my physical self is okay. Not if my heart hurts or what I'm thinking about, or what my concerns for the future are."

"I listened while you told me what your plans are."

"Exactly. *My* plans. What *I'm* doing next. You didn't even say if it was something you'd consider, only that you can handle the dirt. But what about me, Dex? Can you handle *me*?"

That was the million-dollar question. His grand plan to share his feelings said yes, but that it was easy enough to put off when his anxiety flared up said maybe not.

God, did he want to, though.

"I'm here right now, aren't I?"

He cringed at his answer. *Way to be defensive, big guy.*

"Yep. Well said. You've always been a here-and-now guy."

"Oh, come on. I've been by your side for fifteen years, Millie. Doesn't that count for something?"

"It did until you told me I didn't matter to your future."

"When did I say that?" Dex stood up and paced before he was tempted to give in to the compulsion to clean and dress Millie's wounds. To wrap her up and care for her and about her until his last breath.

"When I told you about the contract with *both* our names on it and you asked what *my* plans were. There's never been a *we* or *us*, has there?"

Dex sighed, tossing his head back and swallowing a scream. He'd kept quiet on the ride to buy time till he could talk to her under the perfect conditions he'd drummed up with wine, an ocean view and his declaration speech carefully rehearsed.

But...maybe it was a good thing this was happening now, more organically. He'd always courted control, so maybe if he could let go a little...

"I'm trying, Millie. I've been talking to you, opening up to you in a way I never have with anyone else." He exhaled and let it all go. "I... I love you, Millie."

Her eyes grew wide, but she didn't relax her arms.

"Love means loving who I am, Dex. Not who you want me to be."

"I agree, and I do. I know I can't change you, and it might take a second to adjust how I think about our future, but the love I feel for you matters more than anything else."

Her face, her smile, her eyes lit up for the briefest of moments before they fell.

"It does, but as you so delicately pointed out before, it only matters if I choose jobs and situations you think are safe, that you agree with. Otherwise, you won't be okay, will you?"

"That's not fair, Millie. You know what I've been through in my life. You know what those kinds of risks—the kinds you take every day—do to trigger my past."

"I do. And I know you've been spouting that party line for a decade and a half without doing the work to get past your history. A couple months in a health spa won't fix you if you won't confront your fears. Look at those men and women down there. They've braved what I have and worse and they're ponying up and digging deep. You don't think they'd love to use their trauma as an excuse to never get close to anyone again?"

She finished her speech, breathless and heaving. Ten or more feet separated them now, but it might as well have been the breadth of the ravine below for as distant as he felt to Millie in that moment.

"You don't get it, Mil. What I've been through, who I've lost along the way—it's not fixed overnight. But I'm doing it, I'm making things better in the only way I can. Then you go and race toward a cliff and I—"

"You what? Because you aren't my therapist or my father. You can't tell me not to take risks when it's for my *job*, Dex."

The thing about it was…she wasn't wrong. He'd been hiding behind his wounds for too long. Maybe it was time for him to pull out the ace he'd been holding up his sleeve—literally. His way to show he'd changed, that he'd thought of their future. No point in saving it for that afternoon…

It was now or never.

His heart pumped wildly as he slipped the bracelet he'd fashioned out of twine from one of the riding blankets off his wrist. He undid the knot, slipped off a ring and bent on one knee.

"Millie, will you marry me?"

"*Wha…? What?*"

"I do love you and I want to be better for you. Please accept this ring as proof I want the best for you."

His hopes were dashed completely when she shook her head, her eyes brimming with moisture. She hadn't even glanced at the one-and-a-half-carat diamond surrounded by a rose gold braid that reminded him of the braid she kept in Tilly's mane.

"Get up, Dex."

"Does that mean—?"

"Are you serious? It means no, Dex. I won't. And not because I don't love you. Because I do. More than almost anything. But I've been *not enough* or *too much* my whole life, and I can't go into the best thing that's ever happened to me worrying if being myself will trigger who *you* are. Because I love the person you are as well as who you're becoming, and I wouldn't want you to be anyone different. Even for me. I'll take the job and you're free to go back to whatever safe career you want. We can tell Ray and Gale we've split up."

A figure rose up on the horizon behind Millie, who winced as she inspected the gashes on her shoulder and arm.

"Millie—" Dex tried.

"Stop. It doesn't matter, Dex." She shook her head and wouldn't meet his gaze as he tried to stop her from continuing. Ray was right behind her, but she hadn't noticed him. "Let's just get through this stint and then we can get back to where we were three months ago—"

"*Millie*—" he tried again, shaking his head more insistently, but she ignored him.

"Leave it alone. We can stop pretending to be anything more than just friends who needed a job. This relationship, though fun while it lasted, was fake from the start. It's time I realized that and let you go."

"Oh, Millie."

Ray gasped and Millie whipped around, scarlet covering her skin like a sheer red blanket.

"Ray," she whispered, and finally the tears that had been

building along her bottom lid fell, staining her shirt. Their marriage might be fake, but all Dex wanted was to hold her. Even though it was too late. The damage was done in more than one way.

"Ray, that's not what I meant," she said, crying. Ray turned around and rode back to the stables and Millie broke down in sobs.

Dex inhaled, then sighed out a breath of instant shame and regret as he gazed up at Ray's back, praying that their friend—and boss—hadn't understood Millie's admission for what it was. But the set of his jaw, the steeliness of his gaze before he'd left said Ray had heard every single word.

And he wasn't happy about it.

CHAPTER THIRTEEN

MILLIE SWALLOWED THE regret as deep into her throat as she could shove it, but it didn't matter. It filled all the empty spaces in her and showed no signs of relenting. Nor should it. She'd messed up so badly and in so many ways.

On top of how horrible she felt? She'd made Ray feel that way, too. And that was worse. Way worse.

He'd actually gasped with surprise, but then a cold stare had captured his expression, holding it hostage until they all got down to the camp. Things had calmed down but all Millie wanted to do was drop Prince Philip off at the barn to be checked out, then peek in on Ben to see how the boy was faring.

What she had to do instead, as a result of blowing up her future with her callous carelessness, was pass Prince Philip off to Opie and follow Ray to where Gale was finishing up a report with the EMTs.

It felt like she was fourteen again and waiting for the principal to issue her sentencing for throwing food in the lunchroom.

While they waited for Gale to wrap up, Millie had plenty of time to consider her crummy life choices up to that point. The army had been a good job for a while, but she'd stuck with it until she came out the other side changed, unrecognizable and damaged all thanks to chasing a ghost of a family that would always disappear on her. Then there was the lie that she'd married her best friend, a poor decision that had too many ramifications, including the real relationship that had sprouted as a result of the fake one. Of course, it meant she'd had to maintain the lie to keep up appearances and in doing so, irrevocably hurt people she deeply cared about.

Yeah, she wasn't batting a thousand. Not even close.

Dex squirmed next to her.

"What?" she asked. "What is it now?"

"I do love who you are, Millie. It's just that if you get hurt again—"

"Dex, I could get hurt walking down the street in LA. It's a risk of being alive, that I could be injured, or worse. I can't hide from it."

"But you don't have to run toward it, either."

"No, I don't. That's my choice. But in making a different one, you run other risks, like not truly loving anyone." She closed her eyes against new tears that built, warm and hot behind her lids. "I don't think I can take this job anymore," she whispered. "If it's even still on the table. I'll give my notice now and beg DWB to take my late application."

"Why would you do that?"

"Because I can't keep living with you like this. It isn't real and it's only going to break my heart when we part ways at the end of this."

"Please just finish the six-month contract with me, Millie. What harm would it do?"

"You have the gall to ask me what *harm* it would do? When you have absolutely no plans to stick it out with me aside from a proposal that seemed more like a desperate attempt to get me to stop chasing kids on horseback?"

"It wasn't desperate. I had a plan—"

"Of course you did. And plans change, Dex. That's part of life. Holding onto control never works."

"I know. And yet… I *want* to make plans with you."

"Well, I hate to be the one to point it out to you, Dex, but if we stick it out, I'm going to do everything in my power to help my patients, even if it makes you uncomfortable."

"I know that, believe me. And I'll be there for you if you'll let me. But you know how hard it is for me to accept change in my life. It was all I had when I was—"

"A kid. I do know that. But you're not a kid anymore, Dex. You're not risk-averse, you're stuck."

Dex's gaze dropped to his feet. "I didn't tell you about being homeless."

"Wait, what?"

"There was a year of my life I almost didn't survive. I was on the streets—twice, actually—because no one would take a teen boy with my foster-care track record into their home."

She gasped again, then shook her head.

"When?" she asked. She moved to hold his hand, but he kept it just out of reach.

"When I was a teen. I lived under a bridge for most of it, a park for the rest. The first winter I almost lost body parts to frostbite." Tears welled up in her eyes but he made no move to comfort her. "It's why I won't camp, why I like nice things—because I never had them before. But you—you make me want to forget my past entirely. I'm better with you."

"You never told me," she whispered.

"How could I? Even with your past, you had it all together."

"No, I didn't. But I didn't hide behind my past, either. You never trusted me enough to tell me the worst part of your life, even when you know what I've been through."

"I'm sorry, Millie. I just—"

"You just what?" Her gaze turned steely. "We only worked when you could control the variables. But that isn't love. You waited fifteen years to tell me something that would let me in. What else are you hiding from me, Dex?"

He snorted a laugh that surprised her. None of this was funny.

"Nothing."

"What?" she insisted. Her heart hurt, not just because this was ending, but because the man she loved had been through so much he'd kept to himself. No wonder he hadn't healed.

"Did you mean what you said back there?"

"Which part?" she asked. Millie's eyes were set on the cabin door in front of them, her heart somewhere near her stomach, in pieces.

"You know what part. You love me."

"I do. And?"

Don't look at him. You can't if you want to make it out of this with any shred of dignity.

But Dex's finger hooked her chin and turned her to face him.

"And I love you, too. Dammit, Millie, I have for my whole adult life if I'm being honest with myself. We can make this work. If you can just be patient—"

Heat built behind Millie's eyes but she'd cried all the tears she had on the ride back to camp.

"I've *been* patient. And nothing's changed."

"How can you honestly say that? *Everything* has changed."

And then she did it. She made the mistake of raising her gaze to meet his. She was met with searing liquid gray-blue pools that reflected the depth of her feelings back to her. In the middle of the pools was just what she'd feared—*love*.

It had been all she'd hoped for from Dex since they'd met, but when he gave a voice to his own trauma and how she re-opened those wounds just by being herself, well... How could she let him love her when it would kill him with a thousand tiny papercuts every time she did something risky or danger-ous in the scope of her work as a physician?

Wasn't that gross negligence in the extreme?

"Who you are, fundamentally at your core, hasn't." She touched his chest as she said this, regretting it immediately. It'd been her pillow, her rock and her passion for months now and touching it only reminded her of what she was walking away from.

"Haven't I been growing from that person every day since we came here? I don't need the ritz or glam I've cultivated. Heck, I've even given up hair gel and shaving, for crying out loud." He smiled, but she wasn't in the mood. "Millie, I've been working on getting over my triggers every damn day."

"And I'm so happy you are, as a friend and a physician. But when I got hurt today, you reverted right back to a man who only seems to care about my physical well-being."

"Again, not true. I proposed to you, for eff's sake." The pain in his eyes shot through her armor to her heart.

Her chin fell, and she winced at the pain that shot from her shoulder down her arm.

"No, you tried to give me a ring, Dex. There's a difference."

He took her hand in his, and the heat that passed between their palms couldn't be ignored. "I want to let you in. I have, Millie, already. But I want to learn how to love you better, too. You mean so much to me."

And you mean everything to me.

Her heart screamed what her mouth couldn't say.

They loved each other fiercely, and that was the greatest tragedy of all. Because love wasn't enough this time. She couldn't love him into letting her be who she was and wanted to be. Her love couldn't teach him how to let go when he thought it meant he should cling tighter.

Just then, the door to the cabin opened and Ray came out. His jaw had loosened, but his gaze was still as steely as his fiancé's.

"Millie, can we speak with you?" he asked.

"Not Dex?"

Ray shook his head. "We'd like to talk to him separately."

Millie gulped but nodded. "Okay." She shot Dex a longing glance filled with all the things she couldn't say.

That she loved him and always would.

That no other person would ever mean as much to her.

And a final pronouncement that succeeded in shattering her heart: that walking away from him was the biggest act of love she could give him—because it would save him, but ruin her.

Dex's foot tapped out a tattoo of regret that was only matched by his rapidly beating pulse. As a physician, he'd agree he was in distress. As a man in love, he knew it was more than that. He was heartbroken and filled with shame.

He'd let Millie go without telling her what his heart had been mumbling to him for months now.

I'm safe with you, *Millie.*

It wasn't that he couldn't love anyone without worrying he'd lose them, or didn't let them in because his dad died when he was a child. It's because no one in his life had ever allowed him to feel safe enough to open his heart fully. Until her. Until Millie.

But parsing through that realization—and that it came too late—would have to wait until he'd finished talking to Ray and Gale. Millie had left half an hour prior, out the back door of the guys' cabin. She'd walked, head down, toward their bunkhouse without glancing back at him before shutting the door behind her.

No word about what was said behind the closed doors, no clue as to her emotional state. All he'd wanted to do was run to her—a pull as strong and natural as the coastal tides—but that wasn't in the cards. He needed to be where he was and make amends with his friends and bosses before he could make things right with Millie. At least he had a view of their bunkhouse from the window to his left.

He hadn't seen her leave, so that was something, an infinitesimal thread of hope that he still had time to fix this.

"Ben's okay, though?" he asked Gale.

"He is. Dr. Tyler-Sh—I mean, Dr. Tyler—is consulting with the pediatric doc at the local clinic and will keep us updated, but it looks like a bad sprain and not a break. We're really lucky."

"We are." Dex exhaled the half a breath he'd kept in since the boy had gone missing.

"Obviously, Ben's lucky, too, but I meant that Dr. Tyler was there when she was. If she hadn't gone after him…" Gale paused and looked to Ray, who gave his partner a look of pure love. Dex only recognized it because he'd been staring at Millie that way since he'd met the woman. "If she hadn't gotten there when she did, this would have been infinitely worse."

Dex nodded, then let his gaze fall to the floor. "She's amazing."

Maybe if he hadn't been so obtuse, so wrapped up in what he *thought* was the biggest problem—her getting hurt—he'd have realized the truth. Her risks helped people who couldn't help themselves. Without her, so many people's lives would have been worse, if not cut short. His included. And he'd effed up the best thing that had happened to him because it took him too damned long to realize that.

Well, that and because he still didn't know what to do with that information.

"I'm glad you're finally figuring this out," Ray said.

Dex lifted his head, surprised by the comment. What shocked him more was the hesitant smile on Ray's face. Dex looked at Gale, who was smiling, too.

"Wait, *what*?" was all Dex could get out.

"I mean, we hoped when you two finally started hooking up that it wouldn't take you long to realize you really were meant for each other, but what could we do except stand by and hope you didn't bungle things," Gale said.

"Which you did," Ray chimed in, complete with an eye roll that would make Millie proud.

"You—you *knew*?"

"Oh, Doc. We may be simple cowboys, but we're not stupid."

"But—but *how*?"

"First of all, there wasn't any record of a Dr. Tyler-Shaw. If you look at our contracts, they're written out to your actual names. Then there's the way you looked at each other."

"How was that?" Dex couldn't recall a time he hadn't looked at Millie like he did when they spooned, locked in an embrace after making love.

"Like you wanted to bone but couldn't."

Dex laughed then, deep and long.

"Damn. Who knew we were that transparent?"

"You have no idea," Ray said.

Dex ran a hand through his hair. "Does she know you were aware this whole time?"

"She does."

Gale narrowed his gaze at his fiancé, then shook his head. What weren't they saying?

"Then why'd you let us take the gig?"

Gale shrugged. "If you wanted to saddle yourselves to a small bunk in the middle of nowhere together, that was your business. When you got here, we actually bet you wouldn't last a week," he said. "We had another couple on standby."

"Yeah, we almost didn't," Dex admitted, recalling their fight about the horse-riding part of the job. Now he couldn't imagine life without the gentle beasts. Or Millie. Or Ray and Gale, for that matter.

"I meant *you*."

Dex chuckled. "That was probably a safe bet."

"But when we saw you two together, we realized that no piece of paper could define what you two had. You're best friends," Gale said. Dex just nodded.

"Soulmates," Ray challenged.

"Not anymore. I seriously effed things up and she said she was giving her notice."

Ray and Gale shared a look that said Dex was missing something.

"Well, we may have convinced her to stick around a little

while so you have time to fix whatever mess you made. But she does need some time alone, without you around, to process things, so I—"

"We," Ray interjected.

"*We* think you should use that time wisely. Get help—real help—healing from your past and being a hundred percent ready if you want to win her back. We'll help with the former, but you have to put in the work."

The surprise that flashed hot on Dex's skin felt a lot like embarrassment. It came after the sting of hearing she needed time away from him, but he didn't blame her a bit for that.

"Of course. But...why would you help me when we lied to you?"

"Well, we were more concerned that you were lying to yourselves than to us. We got two expert physicians and good friends whose troubled love story helped us see the happy-ever-after of our own."

Hmm. Dex gave that some thought. If he was that transparent from the beginning—enough that his bosses were less pissed about the lie than they were about him screwing this all up—maybe there was more hope than he thought. For more than just him and Millie, but their professional futures as well.

"Where do I start?"

"We'd love it if you agreed to keep working with us for starters," Gale said.

Millie had shared the details of the contract—it was as sweet a deal as he could ask for. "Of course. I'm just glad that offer's still on the table."

"Then, you start Operation: Get Her Back," Ray quipped. "With our help, of course. Because we saw how you flubbed it up when left to your own devices."

"*Only*," Gale said, "after we know you're serious about her. About why you want to pursue this. And that you're ready for what loving her would mean. And after you meet us each night to dive into how to keep that work up."

Dex just smiled, locks clicking into place in his head and heart, syncing them for the first time in, well, forever.

Working on himself was the most radical act of love he could give to Millie. And she was worth coming out of the shadows for.

"Okay. I'm in. I love this woman something fierce and she's worth the work."

"Good. But if you screw this up and we lose two friends *and* colleagues, I'll put a hex on you for the rest of your life."

Dex laughed as he got up and strode toward the door. He had work to do and not a lot of time to pull it together. The plans had been starting to come together in his head for two months, since he and Millie had first woken up together and he'd—slowly—come to the realization he wanted to be able to do that every morning for the rest of his life. He'd just needed time to get out of his own way and recognize the reason behind his need for control. It wasn't the lack of love from his childhood or even needing to control Millie's safety.

It was finding a place *he* felt safe.

And wouldn't you know it, the "place" wasn't a place at all—it was a person. A tall, curvy, brilliant, quick-witted woman with long curly auburn hair. It wasn't that she made him a better person—that would be too selfish a reason to love and pursue her. It was that he became the person he was capable of being when they worked together. When he made her laugh. When he listened to her dreams and they fueled his own. When he explored her body and gave his up to her in return.

Now that he knew all that—and Ray and Gale were going to help him learn how to keep his fears at bay—he could be the man Millie needed.

"Ray, if I don't get this right and I lose Millie, there's no spell on earth that'll be as devastating as how I'll make myself feel. But once we're at a place you're comfortable with me pursuing her again, I could actually use your help with one phase of my plan."

Ray clapped and bounced on the balls of his feet.

"I'd better be invited to the actual wedding," he cooed.

"Hell. You'll be my best man if you'll take the gig."

"Excuse me," Gale said, shooting Dex a withering stare from under his bushy cowboy brows.

"Gale, I know I speak for Millie, but if she accepts my proposal, we'd actually love for you to officiate."

Gale, the perpetually unemotional one of the group, wiped at his eyes and sniffed.

"Um, I could do that. Sure." He wrapped Dex in a bear hug and squeezed. Ray joined in and a calming warmth washed away most of the guilt sitting at the base of Dex's throat.

Dex pulled away; his smile evaporated like the morning fog off the Cambria coast.

"But seriously, guys. I'm deeply sorry for lying to you both. It isn't excusable no matter what you were aware of or not. Friends don't lie, and I can promise that won't happen again."

"We know why you did it. I'm just glad it brought you to us. Hearts and Horses is better for having you both. Now, let's get our girl back."

That was all Dex needed to hear to put the final touches on a lifelong plan to show Millie not only how much she meant to him, but how he'd be able to care for her heart, if she'd only give him another chance. It might take some time to pull off, but when forever was stretched out in front of him, what did a few days matter?

CHAPTER FOURTEEN

DEX STRUMMED THE GUITAR, glancing over at Millie through the dancing fire. Each time a spark floated up with the breeze, she'd track it, the ember reflecting off her emerald irises. Occasionally, she'd meet his gaze and heat not from the bonfire would glow on her cheeks.

He longed to brush the space where the red bloomed on her skin, feeling the warmth for himself. But it wasn't time for that yet. His fingers itched, but he steadied them with even breaths, born of patience.

There was only one more chance to get this right.

They'd come to a gentle impasse the past few weeks, one that required very little of either of them. Neither one had said anything, since words were what got them in trouble in the first place. But work and their friends and patients had consumed them, easing the hurt. If he was watching from the outside and had to put a label on it, he'd say they were tentative friends, with an echo of love pulsing between them. Probably much the way they'd looked when Gale and Ray had sussed them out all those months ago.

She'd moved into the spare room at Gale and Ray's and their therapy sessions had been split so he rarely saw her anymore. Of course, she stopped wearing the gold band he'd given her all those months ago and he couldn't say he liked that development, either, not when he'd gotten so used to seeing it as their tether to one another.

But he wouldn't be giving it back anytime soon, either—he'd save his grandmother's band for the actual wedding. The one burning a hole in his jeans—the Tilly braid, he called it—would make a damn fine replacement until then.

All he wanted was to see his commitment to her worn out loud for all to see.

Which was why it had been damn near impossible for Dex to keep his true feelings to himself as they wrapped up Family Weekend and got into their new routines, including his agreed upon nights of therapy with Gale and Ray.

They'd done wonders to give him techniques he'd never considered to work through his anxiety, but more importantly, because he trusted them, he was able to dig below the wounds of his youth and excavate them once and for all. Including his time without a home when he'd lived on the streets.

To be honest, he'd be keeping those sessions up regardless of how things went tonight.

"You doing okay?" Gale asked, scooting closer to Ray on their log bench.

Dex nodded. He was better than okay.

"He's nervous," Ray whispered.

That was only partly true.

In all honesty, his heart was simply impatient to start the rest of his life with a woman he loved as completely as he loved medicine, as he loved his job, as he loved his own growth. She was a part of him.

"Okay, guys. We ready?"

Ray's smile and vivacious nod spoke for his answer.

"Hell yes," Gale added.

With that, Dex got up and the crowd of first responders quieted. He strummed a chord on his guitar and they began a gentle humming that matched pitch. They harmonized beautifully, the gentle lap of the water on the sand as background vocals.

He'd been taking secret guitar lessons since Millie—only half joking—mentioned wanting a long-haired man who'd play her songs on his guitar. He'd give that woman anything she wanted, even if it meant learning their unofficial proposal song from their fake relationship over the past month.

From the corner of his eyes, he saw the shock on Gale and Ray's face. They didn't know this was part of the plan—him singing, yes, but the patients who'd been a part of his and Millie's journeys? He'd kept that quiet. In the beginning, he hadn't been sure what sharing the truth about him and Millie would do to the trust he'd built with them, but he'd underestimated his patients for what would be the last time. They were forgiving and supportive—more than he had a right to expect. Involving them in the proposal had been Reese's idea, one he'd agreed to right away.

Even though it made him happy to see the love and joy on his friends' faces, it only half registered with him. His gaze and hopes for the future were pinned to the soft glow on Millie's face, to the curious expression drawn on her lips as she tried to figure out what was happening.

Her eyes darted from Dex to the others, then back again, but when Dex broke out in the lyrics to "Unchained Melody," a smile erupted, scrunching her cheeks and eyes in the way he found wholly adorable and altogether sexy.

He and the crowd circled Millie, then walked out of the fire circle. He kept her in his periphery, watching to see what she'd do, and thankfully, she got up with Ray and Gale and followed them. Dex led the group around the rocky outcrop blocking a hidden bay Ray had shown him a couple weeks prior on the moonlit ride on this same beach.

Dex handed off his guitar to Gale, who kept the melody playing as Dex turned to face the entrance to the bay. When Millie came around the corner, he walked over to her, delighting in the look in her eyes.

The dozens of solar-powered candles he'd set up with the help of Gale and some of the other staff sparkled and shimmered off the water and her deep green eyes. Her hair was wild and free and the gentle breeze moved her curls in a sway that hypnotized him. But the most arresting part of her features was the way she'd drawn her bottom lip between her teeth— her I'm-deliriously-happy look.

Seeing that settled the frenetic beat of his heart against his chest. His one goal was to make her nibble on that bottom lip every day of the rest of her life, and he was already batting a thousand.

"Hey there, pretty lady," he said, and she laughed, her head thrown back in joy. Hopped up on painkillers, he'd said the same thing to her when she'd checked in on him in the ICU all those years ago, just hours after his accident.

"Hey there, killer," she replied, harkening back to her own reply fifteen years ago.

"Can I talk to you a moment?" he asked. She nodded, and he continued, "You're right, Millie. Your life is too danger-ous, too outside my comfort zone."

"What—" she started, but he shook his head.

"But the thing is, *love* means being constantly outside one's comfort zone, no matter what else is safe. And make no mis-take, Millicent Rebekah Tyler. I love the hell out of you."

She smiled, but it didn't reach her eyes. She was still con-cerned, and had a good right to be.

"Loving you is my heart walking around outside this body and to be honest, I don't mind you holding onto it for the rest of your life. You'll protect it. I know that much now, thanks to Gale and Ray." He smiled back at them and Ray sighed like he did whenever anything romantic happened.

"I gave my heart to you a long time ago and even knowing it's a sunk cost if you turn me down isn't enough to make me want it back. I only want *you*. And not just because you make me better—which you do. But because you make everyone around you better, because you're the light in so many dark places. I love your energy and want to orbit around you for a while just so I can watch you glow. But you need to know one thing before any of that can happen."

"What's that?" she asked. The edges of her eyes were etched with laugh lines. All he wanted was to deepen them.

"I've done the work. And I'll keep on doing it so you never have to worry about being your beautiful, amazing, brave self ever again."

"Okay," she whispered.

"Millie, will you trust me with your heart and know I'll only ever help it chase down its deepest desires? Will you let me chase you around while you save and change lives?"

"What about all the risks loving me poses?"

"They aren't risks, Millie. They're bonds and connections I'd never trade for all the safety without them. As long as you want me to be, I'll be there beside you, even if it's hard at times."

"But I don't want you changing for me, either."

"Too late. I've been changing cell by cell since you pulled me out of the car and kept saving my life every day since. And that's not a bad thing. Nor should it be any kind of pressure on you," he added when her smile fell just enough for him to notice. "It'd happen with or without you in my life simply because you being you inspires me to reach for all my potential."

"Me, too," chimed Ray.

"Same here," Gale added.

The whole chorus of veterans and first responders all added similar sentiments, making Millie laugh.

"See? That's the effect you have on others, Mil. And I want to give that back to you every amazing day of our lives if you'll have me."

"If I'll have you?"

He knelt in the sand.

"At the risk of being rejected again, I want to know if you'll marry me and let me make you bite your lip like that every day for the rest of our lives."

He gestured behind him and the crowd of their friends and patients parted, showing off a towering sandcastle that was crafted to resemble their bunkhouse on the ranch set on a hill of sand and shells, two sand characters depicted in the window, holding hands.

Along the base of the cabin castle, he had written *Marry me, Millie Tyler* in shells and seaweed. Her eyes twinkled and gleamed in a way that had nothing to do with the candles outlining the sculpture.

"You used both my names," she said. He nodded. "It's just like the story we told a few months ago." Her voice was distant, like she was a thousand miles away. "It's perfect."

"It's what you deserve."

She walked through the shell-and sand-sculptures, then reached down and touched the top of the castle, a soft smile playing on her lips while the patients hummed the song and Gale strummed the chords along with them. Peace settled on her features and when she turned to face him, he was knocked across the chest with emotion.

Good grief, she was beautiful, wasn't she? His opposite, yet equal partner.

"So, what do you say, Millie? Will you do me the honor of becoming the second Dr. Shaw?"

She shook her head.

"I don't think so," she said. Dex's smile fell along with his heart.

Well, damn. He honestly hadn't expected that. Not a second time in a row.

"Oh, okay." He started to get up, but she joined him kneeling in the cool, damp sand.

"I'd rather be the first Dr. Tyler-Shaw."

He looked up and met her gaze. It took a second for his brain to catch up to his heart and process the warmth spreading from his chest outward.

"So, you'll marry me, Tyler?"

"I will, Shaw, if you're sure."

"Sure? Hell, I should have married you fifteen years ago when you pulled me out of that vehicle. Well," he said, grinning at the look of shock on her face, "after you cleaned and dressed my injuries, of course."

"Oh, Dex. We might not have been ready then, but I'm more than ready now."

"As am I. I can't wait to make all your dreams come true."

"Don't you know?" Millie asked, her eyebrows frowning even though her smile stayed glued in place. "You already have."

He dove into her, all but knocking her on her backside, and wrapped her as tightly as he could in his arms. Gale, Ray and the others whooped and hollered, but he was only vaguely aware of them leaving the beach to give them the privacy they needed to celebrate this momentous occasion.

"I love you, Millie Tyler, and I'm going to make you the happiest woman on the planet."

"I love you, Dexter Shaw, and I think I just might let you."

When he kissed her this time, it was with a promise fifteen years in the making. And it was a promise he couldn't wait to keep every day of the rest of his life.

EPILOGUE

A year later

MILLIE GAZED OUT the window, over the ranch that had become home to her and Dex over the past year and a half. Two days a week, they commuted into Mercy to use their services in a new partnership with their trauma and psych wings, but the rest of the time they lived and worked and played in South Central California. Hearts and Horses took them on full-time and with the influx of physicians and new programs, they'd more than doubled their outreach. Owen Rhys, the plastic surgeon from Mercy, even did consults for the injured first responders out at the ranch.

It was a beautiful time, but not near as beautiful as what lay in front of Millie, actually and metaphorically. The gazebo, flower-lined aisle and horses with flowers in their manes were physical manifestations of her excitement over her future, as were the tulle dresses hanging in her old bunkhouse suite.

Since they were staying on and partnering with Gale and Ray now that the couple were back from their honeymoon in Turks and Caicos, she and Dex had had a small cabin built on the back of the property. So, for now, the bunkhouse was an elaborate bridal suite in which she, Ray and Reese used to prep for the big day.

She'd wanted a few minutes alone in the bunkhouse, a reminder of where she and Dex had first fallen in love, first decided to test the stability of their friendship. Could it hold a big love?

Oh, how it could. And when things had grown heavy—like when her stepmother had died suddenly of a heart attack—their love had just expanded to carry them.

They really had grown so much over the course of the past year. Dex had learned that he was worthy of love and that control and safety weren't to be found in places, but in himself and those he cared for.

And Millie? Well, she'd learned how much adventure could be found in the love of another, in the exploration of the ordinary, in the depth of a heart. She didn't need to travel to get it. Not all the time, anyway. She *was* rather looking forward to her and Dex's honeymoon, though.

A month driving up the Pacific Coast Highway, through Canada, and into Alaska, where they'd spend the remaining time in a small cabin on a remote island off the coast of Kenai? Yeah, that would be nice.

Someone knocked and she smiled. "Come on in," she said, expecting Ray and Reese, her two best friends and both of whom were standing up for her in the small intimate wedding in less than an hour. She'd finagled Ray over to her side by promising he could wear a kilt and Dex had agreed that was far more appropriate than the stiff outfits on the groom's side of the aisle. For all Dex had changed, she kind of liked that he'd kept his penchant for the finer things, especially since he dragged her along for shopping trips and lavish weekend trips around the southwest that filled her heart with joy.

She turned around, putting a final layer of gloss on her lips.

"Oh, my goodness, Dex. You shouldn't be here," she said, though her heart argued otherwise. She'd been counting down the seconds until she got to marry her best friend.

His eyes were on the ground, intentionally not looking at her in her off-the-shoulder white lace dress. Even with his chin tipped, though, she caught the smile that damn near arrested her heart every time he flashed it on her.

"I can go…" he said, his voice laced with mischief.

She laughed. "No. I want you here."

"Can I look at you, or is that bad luck?"

Millie made her way over to him and tilted his chin so he could meet her gaze. He smiled, his eyes watering as he took her in, from peep-toe heel to the long waves she'd somehow miraculously tamed with a half updo.

"You're stunning," he whispered. "Tell me I'm really lucky enough to be marrying my best friend who's also sexy as hell."

"I'll just say that if you meet me by the altar in an hour, you might just *get* lucky. Every night until you tell me otherwise." She winked, her bottom lip drawn between her teeth, and he laughed.

"I'll *never* tell you otherwise." Dex's face grew serious. She noticed the telltale way he nibbled on the inside of his cheek, something he did when he was thinking about something. "Millie, I don't know if I ever thanked you properly."

"For what?"

"Saving my life."

"You did. Hundreds of times, love."

He pulled her into a deep kiss, his palms cupping her cheeks.

"Not on the day of the accident, though I'll never stop being grateful for that, either."

"What do you mean, then?"

He brushed his lips lightly over hers and tingles spread like fire through her veins. God, she hoped he would always have that effect on her.

"The day you agreed to try this," he said, gesturing to the infinitesimal space between their bodies. This time she reached up and pulled him down into her, their lips meeting in the space their hearts already shared. "The day you helped me realize what I needed to do to keep saving myself so I could be there for you."

"Then, in that case, thank *you*."

His brows quirked with curiosity.

"For saving my life, too. I never thought I'd know happiness like this, Dex. Not after all I've been through. I'll never stop being grateful for the life of love and family you've given me."

"And I'll never stop trying to make you happier than you are today."

The door slammed open and Ray burst inside.

"Excuse me!" he shouted, though his mustache couldn't hide the smile he wore. "You all might not stand on decorum, but I most certainly do."

"I'm just kissing my bride," Dex said, his eyes gleaming with joy and something saucier.

"Well, do it in front of God and everyone who showed up to see you two get hitched. Not before the wedding, for crying out loud. Now, shoo." He all but shoved Dex toward the door.

When he got to the doorframe, Millie called out to him, laughing, "I love you, Shaw. I'll see you at the altar."

"I'll be the one in the tux, Tyler. Time to put those long runs to use and hurry down the aisle to me. I can't wait to make you mine."

"Me, neither." She smiled as Ray shut Dex out of the suite. It was the last time in her life a door would be closed for her and the love of her life, her best friend.

She stood up an hour later, Ray and Reese on either side of her.

"Okay, you two, take me to get married. I have a groom waiting on me."

With that, she opened the door to her future, and it was as bright as anything she could have hoped for.

* * * * *

COMING SOON!

We really hope you enjoyed reading this book.
If you're looking for more romance
be sure to head to the shops when
new books are available on

Thursday 26th September

To see which titles are coming soon, please visit
millsandboon.co.uk/nextmonth

MILLS & BOON

MILLS & BOON®

Coming next month

FALLING FOR HER FORBIDDEN FLATMATE
Alison Roberts

'Grace?'

'My new housemate. The midwife who was at that last emergency C-section we did together.'

'Ah, yes...I remember her. Blonde. Cute. Seems quite shy.'

"Cute" wasn't quite the word Jock would have chosen to describe a woman who was not only gorgeous but intelligent and clever and...caring. "Shy" wasn't exactly appropriate, either. Grace was wary. And she had reason to be.

'Blonde and cute is way more your type than mine,' Dan said dryly. 'And, come to think of it, I did notice the way she was smiling at you when you were holding that baby. And you're living with her?' He gave Jock an incredulous glance. So how's *that* working out so far...?'

Oh, good grief...did Dan think he was incapable of keeping his hands off a gorgeous woman?

'She's my sister's best friend,' he said firmly. 'Which puts her completely off limits as far as I'm concerned.'

'Why?'

'It just does. It could end up messing with their friendship and my sister might never speak to me again.

It was Jenni who told her about the job going here and she made it clear that nothing was allowed to happen between us. So that's that.'

Continue reading

FALLING FOR HER FORBIDDEN FLATMATE
Alison Roberts

Available next month
millsandboon.co.uk

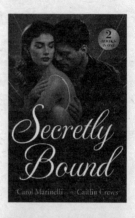

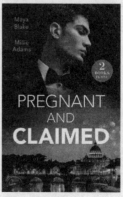

afterglow BOOKS

Afterglow Books is a trend-led, trope-filled list of books with diverse, authentic and relatable characters, a wide array of voices and representations, plus real world trials and tribulations. Featuring all the tropes you could possibly want (think small-town settings, fake relationships, grumpy vs sunshine, enemies to lovers) and all with a generous dose of spice in every story.

♪ @millsandboonuk
⊙ @millsandboonuk
afterglowbooks.co.uk
#AfterglowBooks

For all the latest book news, exclusive content and giveaways scan the QR code below to sign up to the Afterglow newsletter:

SCAN ME

afterglow BOOKS

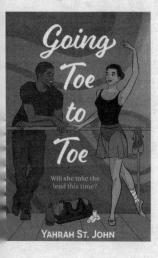

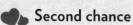
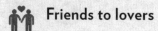
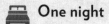

LET'S TALK

Romance

For exclusive extracts, competitions and special offers, find us online:

- **f** MillsandBoon
- **X** @MillsandBoon
- **⊙** @MillsandBoonUK
- **♪** @MillsandBoonUK

Get in touch on 01413 063 232

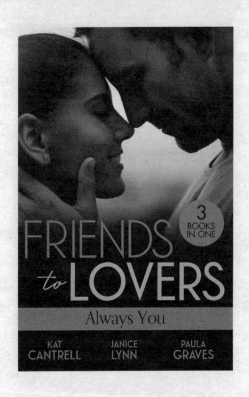

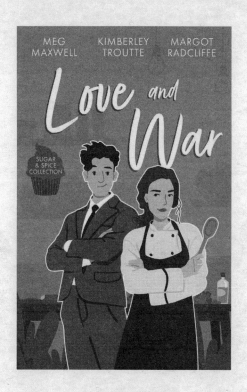